RICHARD MATHESON

Collected Stories

Volume Three

RICHARD MATHESON

Collected Stories
Volume Three

EDITED BY STANLEY WIATER

EDGE BOOKS
■ 2005 ■

RICHARD MATHESON: COLLECTED STORIES
VOLUME THREE

Cover Illustration by Harry O. Morris
Layout and Design by Dara Hoffman

FIRST EDITION
Trade Paperback Edition

EDGE BOOKS
An Imprint of Gauntlet Press
Gauntlet Publications
5307 Arroyo Street
Colorado Springs, CO 80922
(719) 591-5566
Email: info@gauntletpress.com
Website: www.gauntletpress.com

With many thanks to Stanley Wiater for his help and dedication on the three volumes of my collected stories.

—RM

TABLE OF CONTENTS

EDITOR'S PREFACE

By Stanley Wiater

THE BOOK YOU are presently reading is in fact the last of three volumes, which have been published annually by Gauntlet Press. It was originally entitled *Richard Matheson: Collected Stories*. It was first published in the fall of 1989 as a deluxe limited hardcover collection, with a total print run of only 1250 copies. Believe it or not, a trade edition never followed until now.

There is little the present editor can add to the reasons for the original collection ever coming into existence—those reasons are most eloquently handled by Matheson himself in his lengthy and deeply revealing Introduction.

What the present editor has sought to bring to the present collection was simply a bit of desired history. Or a dollop of frosting to the cake, as we so drolly described it in our previous collection with the author entitled *Richard Matheson's "The Twilight Zone" Scripts*. (Still available from this very same publisher in paperback, and originally published in hardcover back in 1998 by Cemetery Dance.)

Simply stated, we asked Richard to tell us a little something about each and every story, as it seemed only appropriate to at last be allowed "behind the curtain" after the international success of so many of the stories collected herein. (Not to mention their often classic status as stories in their original form, or as television movies or as episodes of *The Twilight Zone*.)

This was undeniably done out of personal curiosity—and at the request of Matheson's many long time readers.

For the Richard Matheson bibliophiles, after each story (collected roughly in chronological order of original publication by the author himself) we have indicated its first American magazine or book publication. We have also briefly noted, where appropriate, any television or motion picture adaptations later produced from any story. (The vast majority being by the author himself.)

For further and much more in-depth background on the classic stories which later became episodes of *The Twilight Zone* (1959-1964), the reader is respectfully directed to the previously mentioned, two-volume collection of *Richard Matheson's The Twilight Zone Scripts*.

All of the commentary quoted herein with the author originated from a series of interviews conducted in the spring of 2002 by the editor.

The reader will also find several tributes to Richard Matheson in various sections of each volume. These first appeared in the original Dream/Press Edition then titled *Richard Matheson: Collected Stories*. In some small way, the personal "After-Words" of interview-commentary which appear after each story can perhaps be considered our own tributes to the timeless fiction of this master fantasist.

Stanley Wiater
December 10, 2002
Deerfield, Massachusetts

DREAM/PRESS INTRODUCTION 1989

By Richard Matheson

I DO NOT INTEND for this introduction to my collected short stories to be either a soul-baring confession or an in-depth psychological analysis of my personality. In the first place, I do not believe that the contents of this volume are comprehensive enough to provide the raw material for a baring of my soul. In the second place, I am not skilled enough at psychological analysis to do justice to an in-depth study of my personality as revealed by these stories.

What I plan to do is present a few observations which I hope will cast some illumination on the genesis of these stories and the general theme which runs through most of them.

It has been my contention that a reasonably careful examination of a fiction writer's body of work can reveal a workable profile of the writer's mental state in too as well as during most if not every step along the creative way.

I am sure that this contention is neither innovative nor profound. But, since I have never applied it to my own work—and, since your acquisition of this book indicates interest, on your part, in my writing—it might prove thought-provoking for you to examine the stories in this collection from the standpoint of their psychological source. I have, with this in mind, stipulated that the stories be printed in chronological order. In this way, I can comment on my mental state along the aforementioned creative way which took place between the years 1950 and 1970.

A twenty-year period of creativity reduced to the psychological background of my output of fantasy and science-fiction stories. If this were a thesis, that would be my premise.

I hope it proves to be a moderately diverting one.

It has been well over a decade since my last short story was published. The writing of such stories seems to have represented a circumscribed phase in my creative life. Said phase may have existed for other than psychological reasons, of course.

1. I was just beginning to write and the short story form was more accessible to my ability. I had taken short story writing courses at college and felt more comfortable in that form than in any other. (Not that I believe, in any way, that I "conquered" the form in a couple of decades, then moved on to "greater" things; the form is far more demanding than that. Simply that I wrote science-fantasy stories for twenty years, then stopped.)

2. I graduated from college at the time of a flourishing of fantasy and science-fiction magazines. Accordingly, there was a ready market for this type of story. And, since I had been a devout reader of fantasy stories since childhood, the conjunction of taste and desire to publish proved compelling.

What I am saying is that my writing science-fiction and fantasy stories for publication had a number of causes other than those of a strictly psychological nature. I do not want to pretend that I thought of nothing but satisfying inner compulsions to produce this type of story.

The fact is, however, that there was more than an adequate amount of inner compulsions at work to make me produce this type of story. I just didn't know it at the time. And didn't realize that this particular form of story provided fertile ground for the seeds of these compulsions. This book is, you might say, the harvest of that agricultural period, circa 1950-1970.

Since approximately 1970, I have never had the least desire to write another short story. I am not sure why—except to speculate that, considering the underlying motivation for the creation of these stories, I "got it out of my system." In that form, I mean. I have little doubt the motivation still exists though in a modified and, I hope, matured form. Still appearing moreover, in other creative places, other creative ways. More on that later.

If a fiction writer's work is openly autobiographical (Thomas Wolfe, for instance) there is, of course, less effort involved in locating the roots of his (or her) theme or themes.

When, however, a writer functions in a field of fiction which is apparently as removed from direct autobiographical manifestation as science-fiction and fantasy, the roots are more hidden. I believe, however, that these roots are just as discoverable. It simply takes a bit more probing to locate them.

I could—with the necessary assistance of a skilled psychiatrist—go through every story in this collection and glean from each the underlying reason I wrote it and what the story content reveals about my personality at the time I worked on it. I will do this to a limited extent but a story-by-story analysis would prove laborious; certainly repetitious since the same points would be examined again and again, and, in the long run, undeniably self defeating. So I will, in general, look to the overall picture with an occasional foray into specific examples, seeking to examine the forest rather than the individual trees.

In psychiatric terms, *paranoia* is a mental disorder characterized by systematized delusions and the projection of personal conflicts which are ascribed to the supposed hostility of others.

An accurate thumbnail description of the bulk of my work in these stories.

I could have with justification (if not much commercial insight) entitled this volume *Systematized Delusions*. For that is, by and large, what they are.

The projection of personal conflicts? Absolutely.

Ascription to the supposed hostility of others? Without a doubt.

To which, I might add, the supposed hostility of things as well. With that the picture becomes complete.

Paranoia—again according to psychiatry—often exists for years without any disturbance of consciousness. As it did in my case. At what point in my life it began to surface in my consciousness, manifesting itself in creative terms, I can't be sure. Relatively young, however, I believe.

Let me take a moment to observe that I am not saying that, clinically speaking, I belong in a padded cell. When my children called me *Mr. Paranoia* it was not with dread and trembling but tolerant amusement. Excess caution was my bag rather than fear that my life might, at any moment, undergo a state of siege.

Still, paranoia (albeit non-incapacitating) it was most definitely and it showed up in my stories time and again.

The French writer-anthologist Daniel Riche expressed it this way in 1980, in the opening sentence of an introduction he wrote to an anthology of my work which he assembled. *Le maître mot est angoisse.* And Riche's title for his introduction is *Itinerairies Of Anxiety* (*Itinéraires De L'Angoisse*). Rather a good description of literary paranoia, I think. And one which depressed me for weeks after I read it—or, rather, had it read to me. Because, at that time, I had not, as yet, come to terms with the concept. Loosely, yes. Specifically, no.

Now I think I have. Thus this introduction.

I come from an immigrant family. My father and mother came (separately) to this country from Norway, immigrating here in the early years of this century.

What better background for the breeding of a paranoiac point of view.

Consider my mother. In her early teens. Landing in a country where she knew nothing of the language, nothing of the ways of this new, strange land. An orphan before she was ten, raised by an older brother. Insecure and frightened, thrust into an alien environment. Is it any wonder that she turned inward for refuge? Saw all threats to security as existing outwardly? Any wonder that she carefully maintained a tight, nuclear family unit as protection against this outside menace? Unconsciously fostered lack of knowledge of that outside world thereby creating mounting distrust and suspicion of it, increasing uneasiness regarding it? Married a fellow immigrant thus compounding the closed-in family structure? Finally—the ultimate nuclear refuge—turned to religion?

This was on my mother's side. On my father's, refuge from this alien world was sought in alcohol which served to blunt the nerve ends and numb away the fears and anxieties. The same escape was sought by other men in my family; an escape which could result only in eventual death.

Such was my natal environment. A tightly knit family with no outside friends. Protection from exterior threat by a process of closing in, shutting off, avoidance and denial. I have not, like so many men in my family, turned to alcohol although I might have. Neither have I turned to religion—although some would contest that for, in fact, I do subscribe to very strong—if not organizationally oriented—metaphysical convictions.

The point I make is this. Existing in this cloistered family world, the outside world representing a threat to me, I found personal escape in writing. Instead of imbibing drink, I imbibed stories: became addicted to fiction. Instead of turning to religion I turned to fantasy. In the Freudian sense, the manifestation of my escape was fantasy itself; a re-structuring of the world into more acceptable form. The creating of a new world of imagination in which I could work out any and all troubles. A therapeutic battlefield on which I could confront my enemies (my anxieties) and—in relative safety—deal with them in socially acceptable ways.

In this manner, was I able to prevent this paranoia from damaging my personal life by releasing it, in safe bursts, through my stories. Writing into existence a many-layered realm of fantasies—most of them fear-oriented—then sealing it off from my private world. To use a simile: the vessel contained excess steam—I discovered an outlet by which to release that steam—the vessel did not rupture but prevailed.

The leitmotif of all my work—and certainly this collection of short stories is as follows: *The individual isolated in a threatening world, attempting to survive.*

Strange to reduce hundreds of thousands of words to this one statement. Yet, with obvious exceptions, it is accurate.

How revealing that the very first story I sold—the first story printed under my name—was a veritable (if tiny) explosion of paranoia; the epitome of my leitmotif: "Born of Man and Woman". The fact that its presentation is in childlike, almost primitive terms further emphasizes the exposed root of the theme: an individual isolated in a threatening world, attempting to survive.

I trust it is a good sign that, from the very beginning of my work in short stories, an attempt to survive is part and parcel of the recurring theme. However the main character—usually (predictably) a male of whatever age—is afflicted, however he fails to "fit in" or is harassed by outside forces, he attempts to survive. The protagonist in "Third From The Sun" (my second published story) tries to survive and help his family survive. The protagonist in "When The Sleeper Wakes" (my third published story) tries to survive if more involuntarily and with the aid of a larger survival mechanism, society itself.

These survival attempts rarely succeed, of course; my initial cynicism on display. Outside menace most often overcame the isolated individual despite any attempt to survive ("Dress of White Silk", "Blood Son", "Through Channels", "Lover When You're Near Me"). The apogee of these early paranoiac flights was surely reached in the story "Legion of Plotters". Can any title better express the paranoiac point of view? Still, there was always that thread of attempted survival—for which I am gratified. Nice to note that Mr. Paranoia did have his positive side from the start of his creative appearance.

How does this leitmotif manifest itself in my stories? What is the immediately apparent reflection from my personal life?

Not difficult to assess.

Some of my early stories, for instance, ("Mad House", "Disappearing Act", "To Fit The Crime") displayed a noticeable bias toward the married state. This was, of course, because I had not yet crossed the border of that state and, with my paranoiac grounding (separated parents added to the rest), I saw the outside institution as a threatening one.

My views on marriage in those early stories is obvious. I felt uncertain and fearful about it. In the stories published here—as well as others unpublished from the same period—I revealed myself as highly apprehensive that marriage would entrap me and destroy my creative freedom. I saw, in marriage, little but acrimony and bitterness which, in the case of two of the stories, leads, in one ("Disappearing Act") to literal extinction of people from the protagonist's existence; in the other ("Mad House") to psycho-kinetic self-destruction motivated by married frustration with resulting fury and resentment.

As far as my views on children were concerned at that time, I knew very little if anything about them. In the case of "Born of Man and Woman", this ignorance was a blessing since it resulted in a story which has been called a classic and one which introduced me noticeably to the field of science-fiction and fantasy. Today, as a parent of grown children, if such an idea were even to occur to me, I would never, for a moment, attempt to write it because I would never, for a moment, believe it logical in any way. At the age of twenty-three, however, unhampered by parental knowledge, I plunged right in Hurrah—at times—for naïve immaturity.

Parental love I could conceive of reasonably well in those days ("The Last Day", "The Test"), for I had seen it in my own mother. But the concept of selfless married and parental love from myself was far beyond me at that point. I was a queasy bachelor and little more.

Later on, after I discovered that marriage was not the total threat I had assumed it to be, my attitude toward it eased somewhat ("Return", "Trespass", "Dying Room Only", "Being"). The circumstances in which these now more successful marriages existed remained, as ever, paranoiac. But, at least, within the confines of the terrifying situations, husbands and wives got along.

(I might add momentarily that, after leaving my nuclear family in the New York area and moving to California in 1951, I quickly went about establishing a new nuclear family in which I could find refuge from "that awful world" out there as my family before me had.)

During this period, my stories were deeply imbued with a sense of anxiety, of fear of the unknown, of a world too complicated which expected too much of individual males, sometimes humorously ("Clothes Make The Man", "SRL Ad", "The Wedding"), more often grimly ("Mad House", "Trespass", "Shipshape Home", "The Last Day"). "We are beset by a host of dangers" says my male protagonist in "The Wedding". I believe it.

Add to this another aspect of my paranoiac leitmotif: the inability of others to understand the male protagonist, to give him proper recognition. Their inclination (virtually insistence) on victimizing him with ignorance, stupidity, cliché thinking and unwitting power

("Return", "Mad House", "Legion of Plotters", "The Test"). That I, sometimes, gave alternate emphasis to the possibility that the male protagonist might be partially responsible for his own problems— that his real adversary was his own mind—does not alter the fact that he is, in the end, threatened by actual outside forces. Or, to paraphrase the old joke, just because he's paranoid doesn't mean that someone isn't out to get him.

So I dealt with my personal anxieties, my own fear of the unknown, relieving my angst by exteriorizing it in the form of characters in my short stories. Even objects could be used to represent outside menace—clothes in "Clothes Make The Man", household items in "Mad House", a television set in "Through Channels", a bed in "Wet Straw". The world is a scary place, I was saying in my stories. If I'd said it aloud as myself, I would have gotten uncomfortable looks. Saying it in the form of "fantasy" stories not only was acceptable, it was *recompensed*. That menacing world out there actually began to pat my little paranoiac head and say "Well done. Here's some money for your trouble."

How remarkable a psychological event. The very world which was the "cause" of my paranoia received my disguised accusations of its menace, accepted them, validated them, then, incredibly, permitted me to support my wife and four children by this very process of expunging my anxieties. That world did not demand that I re-evaluate and regard it with more circumspection. It asked me only to entertain it by converting my dreads into stories of science-fiction and fantasy. My paranoia had become legitimized and, wonder of wonders, commercially valuable.

I did not consider, at the time this happened, that I was not only exteriorizing my own dreads but those of my readers as well. That these presented dreads existed at the "neighborhood" level only made them more accessible—and readers rewarded me for helping them, in some obverse way, to deal with their own fears.

Marriage, parenthood and increased maturity did not, in any way, eliminate my leitmotif as years went by. My paranoia rolled on, taking other forms but remaining essentially unchanged.

Interestingly enough (to me at any rate), after marrying I never wrote another story in which a writer's creativity is imperiled by marriage; or about a married man who, feeling smothered by the demands of marriage, reacts negatively. (With, perhaps, a slight backslide in "A Visit To Santa Claus", although that really was inspired by a news story more than a home situation.) Clearly, even Mr. Paranoia saw that marriage—at least to the woman I wed—was not as ominous as previously envisioned. After 1952 (my wedding year) the paranoiac visions (as previously noted) consist of outside menaces being visited upon otherwise adjusted married couples ("Being", "The Test", "Descent", "One For the Books", "The Edge", "Deadline", "Crickets", "A Drink of Water"). No longer is the individual isolated in a menacing world. The individual and his wife—later his children—are.

Occasional variations appeared, addenda to my leitmotif. Addenda which may, in fact, not have been pure paranoia at all—or, if it was, was a form of it shared by most people the majority of whom would not qualify as paranoiacs—although the apprehension spoken of partakes of both inner *and* outer threats.

This is, in brief, fear that one is not experiencing life to the fullest in the present because of responsibilities and lack of genuine effort to do otherwise. That one's life is passing one by, engendering regrets and sorrow and desires to recapture something lost. While this appeared most vividly and at greatest length in my novel "Bid Time Return", it is certainly evident in such stories as "Old Haunts", "Mantage" and "Button, Button".

Generally speaking, however, despite the fact that my leitmotif mellowed, it remained evident in most of my stories. In some, the outside threat is clearly evident, the survival attempt obviously necessary ("The Test", "When Day is Dun", "Dance of the Dead", "Descent", "Pattern for Survival"—another "right on the money" title—"Steel", "The Creeping Terror", "Crickets", "Mute", "'Tis The Season to be Jelly", "Full Circle"—many of these obviously prompted by a fear of nuclear holocaust). In others, the outside threat is tinged with "inner" causation, the motivation for the survival attempt less clear-cut ("Long Distance Call", "Death Ship", "Wet Straw", "A Flourish of Strumpets", "The Holiday Man", "Mantage", "The Likeness of Julie", "Shock Wave", "Nightmare at Twenty-Thousand Feet", "Prey", "Button, Button").

None-the-less the fundamental leitmotif remained intact—

some one or some thing out "to get" the protagonist either individually or in company with others, most likely his immediate family ("Slaughter House", "The Disinheritors", "The Curious Child", "The Funeral", "One For the Books", "Miss Stardust", "The Children of Noah", "First Anniversary", "Deus Ex Machina").

The very last story in the collection—my last major printed story, "Duel", is certainly as intimately paranoiac as one can imagine—a truck driver, never seen, out "to get" the male protagonist no matter what.

Where am I now, as I write this? Have I changed? Improved? Broadened? Lightened up? Is it possible I discontinued writing this type of short story because, in writing them, I overcame enough of my anxiety so that I no longer felt the need to write more of them? That my world of fear became ameliorated during that twenty-year period? That I—the "new kid" in the neighborhood of angoisse came to feel accepted by that neighborhood and, consequently, safe enough to get by without those periodic, reconstructing fantasies?

Hard to tell.

The last work of fiction I wrote was my novel *What Dreams May Come* (1978). A story about life after death. One could, with justice, define this as the ultimate application of my leitmotif—a survival attempt against what is referred to, in the Bible, as "the last enemy to be destroyed." I think that I actually believe in afterlife, not because of panicked resistance to a dread of mortality but as a result of careful thought and conviction based on years of reading and thinking. Still, how can you believe me when I say that? How can I believe myself?

After all, this is Mr. Paranoia speaking.

Richard Matheson
April 1988
Los Angeles, California

GAUNTLET PRESS INTRODUCTION 2003

By Richard Matheson

It has been some time (fifteen years to be exact) since a collection of my stories (all of them) was published in one (huge) volume by Dream/Press (that name created because I asked the publisher to change it from his usual title—Scream Press).

Which means that it has been thirty-four years since (with a few exceptions when I had the time and slight inclination) the last story "Duel" was published in *Playboy*; soon to become a most excellent television movie scripted by me and directed by a very young novice director named Steven Spielberg.

Since 1970, my desire to write short stories has remained substantially the same—nil. *Not*, I must repeat, because I felt I had "conquered" the short story form and wanted to "move on" creatively. Far from it. I have an abiding respect for that form. It remains, historically, a complex and all-demanding challenge, its creators numbering among the most brilliant writers throughout the centuries.

Why have I left it "behind me", I cannot estimate. Why I leap-frogged from one genre to another—including westerns and metaphysics—indicates either a searching mind or an inability to stick to any field of endeavor for any appreciable length of time. I *did* stay with science-fiction and fantasy stories for two decades. But then I moved on—or should I say side-stepped—to other forms; in the last seven or eight years, stage plays. (None of which, at this writing, have been produced although one of them is very close to fruition; my creative fingers remain crossed.)

One of the areas I was drawn to most closely in the last fifteen years is metaphysics. I put together a book entitled *The Path* which consisted primarily of quotes by my candidate for the metaphysician of the twentieth (and more) century, Harold W. Percival, whose book *Thinking and Destiny* contains all the metaphysical truths I subscribe to at this time. And much more.

I also put together a book entitled *A Primer of Reality* which consists primarily of quotes by a multitude of important men and women on the subject of Reality.

A novel entitled *Hunted Past Reason* completes what (in my limited way) I have to say about Reality. I have no ideas for short stories on that subject.

All of which is noted only to explain why my collected stories (now to be published in three easier-to-lift volumes by Gauntlet Press) still remain, virtually, my only output in that form.

Do I still qualify my Mr. Paranoia (now that all of my children are grown and living most successful lives) in my thinking? To a lesser degree, I hope. At the age of 77, I have not achieved a sense of inner peace about the outside world. Hardly, the way things are faltering domestically and internationally. I *do* believe that my outlook has gone more *inward*. We are undoubtedly the major threat to our own lives.

However, my description of my mental state when all these stories were written remains accurate, needing no revision. Mr. Paranoia functioned at full gallop in those days.

Richard Matheson
September 2003
Los Angeles, California

BIG SURPRISE
1959

OLD MR. HAWKINS used to stand by his picket fence and call to the little boys when they were coming home from school.

"Lad!" he would call. "Come here, lad!"

Most of the little boys were afraid to go near him, so they laughed and made fun of him in voices that shook. Then they ran away and told their friends how brave they'd been. But once in a while a boy would go up to Mr. Hawkins when he called, and Mr. Hawkins would make his strange request.

> *Dig me a hole, he said,*
> *Winking his eyes,*
> *And you will find*
> *A big surprise.*

No one knew how long they'd heard the children chanting it. Sometimes the parents seemed to recall having heard it years ago.

Once a little boy started to dig the hole but he got tired after a while and he didn't find any big surprise. He was the only one who had every tried—

One day Ernie Willaker was coming home from school with two of his friends. They walked on the other side of the street when they saw Mr. Hawkins in his front yard standing by the picket fence.

"Lad!" they heard him call. "Come here, lad!"

"He means you, Ernie," teased one of the boys.

"He does not," said Ernie.

Mr. Hawkins pointed a finger at Ernie. "Come here, lad!" he called.

Ernie glanced nervously at his friends.

"Go on," said one of them. "What're ya scared of?"

"Who's scared?" said Ernie. "My ma says I have to come home right after school is all."

"Yella," said his other friend. "You're scared of old man Hawkins."

"Who's scared!"

"Go *on*, then."

"Lad!" called Mr. Hawkins. "Come here, lad."

"Well." Ernie hesitated. "Don't go nowhere," he said.

"We won't. We'll stick around."

"Well—" Ernie braced himself and crossed the street, trying to look casual. He shifted his books to his left hand and brushed back his hair with his right. *Dig me a hole, he says,* muttered in his brain.

Ernie stepped up to the picket fence. "Yes, sir?" he asked.

"Come closer, lad," the old man said, his dark eyes shining.

Ernie took a forward step.

"Now you aren't afraid of Mister Hawkins, are you?" said the old man winking.

"No, sir," Ernie said.

"Good," said the old man. "Now listen, lad. How would you like a big surprise?"

Ernie glanced across his shoulder. His friends were still there. He grinned at them. Suddenly he gasped as a gaunt hand clamped over his right arm. "Hey, leggo!" Ernie cried out.

"Take it easy, lad," soothed Mr. Hawkins. "No one's going to hurt you."

Ernie tugged. Tears sprang into his eyes as the old man drew him closer. From the corner of an eye Ernie saw his two friends running down the street.

"L-leggo," Ernie sobbed.

"Shortly," said the old man. "Now then, would you like a big surprise?"

"No-no, thanks, mister."

"Sure you would," said Mr. Hawkins. Ernie smelled his breath and tried to pull away, but Mr. Hawkins's grip was like iron.

"You know where Mr. Miller's field is?" asked Mr. Hawkins.

"Y-yeah."

"You know where the big oak tree is?"

"Yeah. Yeah, I know."

"You go to the oak tree in Mr. Miller's field and face towards the church steeple. You understand?"

"Y-y-yeah."

The old man drew him closer. "You stand there and you walk ten paces. You understand? Ten paces."

"Yeah—"

"You walk ten paces and you dig down ten feet. *How many feet?*" He prodded Ernie's chest with a boney finger.

"T-ten," said Ernie.

"That's it," said the old man. "Face the steeple, walk ten paces, dig ten feet—and there you'll find a big surprise." He winked at Ernie. "Will you do it, lad?"

"I—yeah, sure. *Sure.*"

Mr. Hawkins let go and Ernie jumped away. His arm felt completely numb.

"Don't forget, now," the old man said.

Ernie whirled and ran down the street as fast as he could. He found his friends waiting at the corner.

"Did he try and murder you?" one of them whispered.

"Nanh," said Ernie. "He ain't so m-much."

"What'd he want?"

"What d'ya s'pose?"

They started down the street, all chanting it.

Dig me a hole, he said,
Winking his eyes,
And you will find
A big surprise.

Every afternoon they went to Mr. Miller's field and sat under the big oak tree.

"You think there's somethin' down there really?"

"Nanh."

"What if there *was* though?"

"What?"

"Gold, maybe."

They talked about it every day, and every day they faced the steeple and walked ten paces. They stood on the spot and scuffed the earth with the tips of their sneakers.

"You s'pose there's gold down there really?"

"Why should he tell us?"

"Yeah, why not dig it up himself?"

"Because he's too old, stupid."

"Yeah? Well, if there's gold down there we split it three ways."

They became more and more curious. At night they dreamed about gold. They wrote *gold* in their schoolbooks. They thought about all the things they could buy with gold. They started walking past Mr. Hawkins's house to see if he'd call them again and they could ask him if it was gold. But he never called them.

Then, one day, they were coming home from school and they saw Mr. Hawkins talking to another boy.

"He told us *we* could have the gold!" said Ernie.

"Yeah!" they stormed angrily. "Let's go!"

They ran to Ernie's house and Ernie went down to the cellar and got shovels. They ran up the street, over lots, across the dump, and into Mr. Miller's field. They stood under the oak tree, faced the steeple, and paced ten times.

"Dig," said Ernie.

Their shovels sank into the black earth. They dug without speaking, breath whistling through their nostrils. When the hole was about three feet deep, they rested.

"You think there's gold down there really?"

"I don't know but we're gonna find out before that other kid does."

"Yeah!"

"Hey, how we gonna get out if we dig ten feet?" one of them said.

"We'll cut out steps," said Ernie.

They started digging again. For over an hour they shoveled out the cool, wormy earth and piled it high around the hole. It stained their clothes and their skin. When the hole was over their heads one of them went to get a pail and a rope. Ernie and the other boy kept digging and throwing the earth out of the hole. After a while the dirt rained back on their heads and they stopped. They sat on the damp earth wearily, waiting for the other boy to come back. Their hands and arms were brown with earth.

"How far're we down?" wondered the boy.

"Six feet," estimated Ernie.

The other boy came back and they started working again. They kept digging and digging until their bones ached.

"Aaah, the heck with it," said the boy who was pulling up the pail. "There ain't nothin' down there."

"He said ten feet," Ernie insisted.

"Well, I'm quittin'," said the boy.

"You're yella!"

"Tough," said the boy.

Ernie turned to the boy beside him. "You'll have to pull the dirt up," he said.

"Oh—okay," muttered the boy.

Ernie kept digging. When he looked up now, it seemed as if the sides of the hole were shaking and it was all going to cave in on him. He was trembling with fatigue.

"Come on," the other boy finally called down. "There ain't nothin' down there. You dug ten feet."

"Not yet," gasped Ernie.

"How deep ya goin', *China*?"

Ernie leaned against the side of the hole and gritted his teeth. A fat worm crawled out of the earth and tumbled to the bottom of the hole.

"I'm goin' home," said the other boy. "I'll catch it if I'm late for supper."

"You're yella too," said Ernie miserably.

"Aaaaah—*tough.*"

Ernie twisted his shoulders painfully. "Well, the gold is all mine," he called up.

"There ain't no gold," said the other boy.

"Tie the rope to something so I can get out when I find *the gold*," said Ernie.

The boy snickered. He tied the rope to a bush and let it dangle down into the hole. Ernie looked up and saw the crooked rectangle of darkening sky. The boy's face appeared, looking down.

"You better not get stuck down there," he said.

"I ain't gettin' stuck." Ernie looked down angrily and drove the shovel into the ground. He could feel his friend's eyes on his back.

"Ain't you scared?" asked the other boy.

"What of?" snapped Ernie without looking up.

"I dunno," said the boy.

Ernie dug.

"Well," said the boy, "I'll see ya."

Ernie grunted. He heard the boy's footsteps move away. He looked around the hole and a faint whimper sounded in his throat. He felt cold.

"Well, I ain't leavin'," he mumbled. The gold was his. He wasn't going to leave it for that other kid.

He dug furiously, piling the dirt on the other side of the hole. It kept getting darker.

"A little more," he told himself, gasping. "Then I'm goin' home with the gold."

He stepped hard on the shovel and there was a hollow sound beneath him. Ernie felt a shudder running up his back. He forced himself to keep on digging. Will I give *them* the horse laugh, he thought. Will I give *them*—

He had uncovered part of a box—a long box. He stood there looking down at the wood and shivering. *And you will find—*

Quivering, Ernie stood on top of the box and stamped on it. A deeply hollow sound struck his ears. He dug away more earth and his shovel scraped on the ancient wood. He couldn't uncover the entire box—it was too long.

Then he saw that the box had a two-part cover and there was a clasp on each part.

Ernie clenched his teeth and struck the clasp with the edge of his shovel. Half of the cover opened.

Ernie screamed. He fell back against the earth wall and stared in voiceless horror at the man who was sitting up.

"Surprise!" said Mr. Hawkins.

"Big Surprise" (as "What Was in the Box?") was first published in **Ellery Queen's Mystery Magazine**, *April 1959.*

"I believe that when it was first published, the editors left the ending open—and asked their readers to send in what they thought should be the conclusion of the story. Much later on, when I adapted it for **Night Gallery***, they naturally used my ending. I still really couldn't think of an ending except that maybe the guy who sent them there was a ghost and it was his body that was buried in that place. It doesn't really make much sense...but it had a good snappy ending! You could certainly believe it was John Carradine down there in the box." —RM*

Adapted by the author for an episode of the second season of Rod Serling's **Night Gallery***, it starred John Carradine and was directed by Jeannot Szwarc. It first aired on November 10, 1971.*

THE
CREEPING TERROR
1959

THESIS SUBMITTED AS PARTIAL
REQUIREMENT FOR MASTER OF ARTS
DEGREE

THE PHENOMENON KNOWN in scientific circles as the Los Angeles Movement came to light in the year 1982 when Doctor Albert Grimsby, A.B., B.S., A.M., Ph.D., professor of physics at the California Institute of Technology, made an unusual discovery.

"I have made an unusual discovery," said Doctor Grimsby.

"What is that?" asked Doctor Maxwell.

"Los Angeles is alive."

Doctor Maxwell blinked.

"I beg your pardon," he said.

"I can understand your incredulity," said Doctor Grimsby, "Nevertheless..."

He drew Doctor Maxwell to the laboratory bench.

RICHARD MATHESON

"Look into this microscope," he said, "under which I have iso-lated a piece of Los Angeles."

Doctor Maxwell looked. He raised his head, a look of aston-ishment on his face.

"It moves," he said.

Having made this strange discovery, Doctor Grimsby, oddly enough, saw fit to promulgate it only in the smallest degree. It appeared as a one-paragraph item in the *Science News Letter* of June 2, 1982, under the heading: CALTECH PHYSICIST FINDS SIGNS OF LIFE IN L.A.

Perhaps due to unfortunate phrasing, perhaps to normal lack of interest, the item aroused neither attention nor comment. This unfor-tunate negligence proved ever after a plague to the man originally responsible for it. In later years it became known as "Grimsby's Blunder."

Thus was introduced to a then unresponsive nation a phenome-non which was to become in the following years a most shocking threat to the nation's very existence.

Of late, researchers have discovered that knowledge concerning the Los Angeles Movement predates Doctor Grimsby's find by years. Indeed, hints of this frightening crisis are to be found in works pub-lished as much as fifteen years prior to the ill-fated "Caltech Disclosure."

Concerning Los Angeles, the distinguished journalist, John Gunther, wrote: "What distinguishes it is...its octopus-like growth."[1]

Yet another reference to Los Angeles mentions that: "In its amoeba-like growth it has spread in all directions..."[2]

Thus can be seen primitive approaches to the phenomenon which are as perceptive as they are unaware. Although there is no present evidence to indicate that any person during that early period actually knew of the fantastic process, there can hardly be any doubt that many *sensed* it, if only imperfectly.

Active speculation regarding freakish nature behavior began in July and August of 1982. During a period of approximately forty-

1. John Gunther, *Inside U.S.A.*, p. 44
2. Henry G. Alsbertg (ed.), *The American Guide*, p. 1200.

24

seven days the states of Arizona and Utah in their entirety and great portions of New Mexico and lower Colorado were inundated by rains that frequently bettered the ten-inch mark.

Such water fall in previously arid sections aroused great agitation and discussion. First theories placed responsibility for this uncommon rainfall on previous southwestern atomic tests.[3] Government disclaiming of this possibility seemed to increase rather than eliminate mass credulity to this later disproved supposition.

Other "precipitation postulations" as they were then known in investigative parlance can be safely relegated to the category of "crackpotia."[4] These include theories that excess commercial airflights were upsetting the natural balance of the clouds, that deranged Indian rain-makers had unwittingly come upon some lethal condensation factor and were applying it beyond all sanity, that strange frost from outer space was seeding Earth's overhead and causing this inordinate precipitation.

And, as seems an inevitable concomitant to all alien deportment in nature, hypotheses were propounded that this heavy rainfall presaged *Deluge II*. It is clearly recorded that several minor religious groups began hasty construction of "Salvation Arks." One of these arks can still be seen on the outskirts of the small town of Dry Rot, New Mexico, built on a small hill, "still waiting for the flood."[5]

Then came that memorable day when the name of farmer Cyrus Mills became a household word.

"Tarnation!" said farmer Mills.

He gaped in rustic amazement at the object he had come across in his corn field. He approached it cautiously. He prodded it with a sausage finger.

"Tarnation," he repeated, less volubly.

Jason Gullwhistle of the United States Experimental Farm

3. Symmes Chadwick, "Will We Drown the World?" *Southwestern Review IV* (Summer 1982), p. 698 ff.

4. Guilllaume Gaulte, "Les Théories de l'Eau de Ciel Sont Cuckoo," *Jaune Journale* (August 1982).

5. Harry L. Schuler, "Not Long for This World," *South Orange Literary Review,* XL (Sept. 1982), p. 214.

Station No. 3, *Nebraska, drove his station wagon out to farmer Mills's farm in answer to an urgent phone call. Farmer Mills took Mr. Gullwhistle out to the object.*

"That's odd," said Jason Gullwhistle. "It looks like an orange tree."

Close investigation revealed the truth of this remark. It was, indeed, an orange tree.

"Incredible," said Jason Gullwhistle. "An orange tree in the middle of a Nebraska corn field. I never."

Later they returned to the house for a lemonade and there found Mrs. Mills in halter and shorts wearing sunglasses and an old chewed-up fur jacket she had exhumed from her crumbling hope chest.

"Think I'll drive into Hollywood," said Mrs. Mills, sixty-five if she was a day.

By nightfall every wire service had embraced the item, every paper of any prominence whatever had featured it as a humorous insert on page one.

Within a week, however, the humor had vanished as reports came pouring in from every corner of the state of Nebraska as well as portions of Iowa, Kansas and Colorado; reports of citrus trees discovered in corn and wheat fields as well as more alarming reports relative to eccentric behavior in the rural populace.

Addition to the wearing of scanty apparel became noticeable, an inexplicable rise in the sales of frozen orange juice manifested itself and oddly similar letters were received by dozens of chambers of commerce; letters which heatedly demanded the immediate construction of condominiums, supermarkets, tennis courts, drive-in theaters and drive-in restaurants and which complained of smog.

But it was not until a marked decrease in daily temperatures and an equally marked increase of unfathomable citrus tree growth began to imperil the corn and wheat crop that serious action was taken. Local farm groups organized spraying operations but to little or no avail. Orange, lemon and grapefruit trees continued to flourish in geometric proliferation and a nation, at long last, became alarmed.

A seminar of the country's top scientists met in Ragweed, Nebraska, the geographical center of this multiplying plague, to discuss possibilities.

"Dynamic tremors in the alluvial substrata," said Doctor Kenneth Loam of the University of Denver.

"Mass chemical disorder in soil composition," said Spencer Smith of the Dupont Laboratories.

"Momentous gene mutation in the corn seed," said Professor Jeremy Brass of Kansas College.

"Violent contraction of the atmospheric dome," said Professor Lawson Hinkson of MIT.

"Displacement of orbit," said Roger Cosmos of the Hayden Planetarium.

"I'm scared," said a little man from Purdue.

What positive results emerged from this body of speculative genius is yet to be appraised. History records that a closer labeling of the cause of this unusual behavior in Nature and Man occurred in early October of 1982 when Associate Professor David Silver, young research physicist at the University of Missouri, published in *The Scientific American* an article entitled, "The Collecting of Evidences."

In this brilliant essay, Professor Silver first voiced the opinion that all the apparently disconnected occurrences were, in actuality, superficial revelations of one underlying phenomenon. To the moment of this article, scant attention had been paid to the erratic behavior of people in the affected areas. Professor Silver attributed this behavior to the same cause which had effected the alien growth of citrus trees.

The final deductive link was forged, oddly enough, in a Sunday supplement of the now defunct Hearst newspaper syndicate.[6] The author of this piece, a professional article writer, in doing research for an article, stumbled across the paragraph recounting Doctor Grimsby's discovery. Seeing in this a most salable feature, he wrote an article combining the theses of Doctor Grimsby and Professor Silver and emerging with his own amateur concept which, strange to say, was absolutely correct. (This fact was later obscured in the

6. H. Braham, "Is Los Angeles Alive?", *Los Angeles Sunday Examiner*, 29 Oct. 1982.

severe litigation that arose when Professors Grimsby and Silver brought suit against the author for not consulting them before writing the article.)

Thus did it finally become known that Los Angeles, like some gigantic fungus, was overgrowing the land.

A period of gestation followed during which various publications in the country slowly built up the import of the Los Angeles Movement, until it became a nation byword. It was during this period that a fertile-minded columnist dubbed Los Angeles "Ellie, the Meandering Metropolis,"[7] a title later reduced merely to "Ellie"—a term which became as common to the American mind as "ham and eggs" or "World War II."

Now began a cycle of data collection and an attempt by various of the prominent sciences to analyze the Los Angeles Movement with a regard to arresting its strange pilgrimage which had now spread into parts of South Dakota, Missouri, Arkansas and as far as the sovereign state of Texas. (To the mass convulsion this caused in the Lone Star State a separate paper might be devoted.)

REPUBLICANS DEMAND FULL INVESTIGATION
Claim L.A. Movement Subversive Camouflage

After a hasty dispatch of agents to all points in the infected area, the American Medical Association promulgated throughout the nation a list of symptoms by which all inhabitants might be forewarned of the approaching terror.

Symptoms Of "ELLIEITIS"[7]

1. An unnatural craving for any of the citrus fruits whether in solid or liquid form.
2. Partial or complete loss of geo-graphical distinction. (ie., A person in Kansas City might speak of driving down to San Diego for the weekend.)

7. "Ellieitis: Its Symptoms," AMA pamphlet, (fall 1982).

3. An unnatural desire to possess a motor vehicle.
4. An unnatural appetite for motion pictures and motion picture previews. (Including a subsidiary symptom, not all-inclusive but nevertheless a distinct menace. This is the insatiable hunger of young girls to become movie stars.)
5. A taste for weird apparel. (Including fur jackets, shorts, halters, slacks, sandals, blue jeans and bathing suits— all unusually of excessive color.)

This list, unfortunately, proved most inadequate for its avowed purpose. It did not mention, for one thing, the adverse effect of excess sunlight on residents of the northern states. With the expected approach to winter being forestalled indefinitely, numerous unfortunates, unable to adjust to this alternation, became neurotic and, often, lost their senses completely.

The story of Matchbox, North Dakota, a small town in the northernmost part of that state, is typical of accounts which flourished throughout the late fall and winter of 1982.

The citizens of this ill-fated town went berserk to a man waiting for the snow and, eventually running amuck, burned their village to the ground.

The pamphlet also failed to mention the psychological phenomenon known later as "Beach Seeking,"[8] a delusion under which masses of people, wearing bathing suits and carrying towels and blankets, wandered helplessly across the plains and prairies searching for the Pacific Ocean.

In October, the Los Angeles Movement (the process was given this more staid title in late September by Professor Augustus Wrench in a paper sent to the National Council of American Scientists) picked up momentum and, in a space of ten days, had engulfed Arkansas, Missouri and Minnesota and was creeping rapidly into the border-

8. Fritz Felix DerKatt, "Das Beachen Seeken," *Einzweidrei* (Nov. 1982)

lands of Illinois, Wisconsin, Tennessee, Mississippi and Louisiana. Smog drifted across the nation.

Up to this point, citizens on the east coast had been interested in the phenomenon but not overly perturbed since distance from the diseased territory had lent detachment. Now, however, as the Los Angeles city limits stalked closer and closer to them, the coastal region became alarmed.

Legislative activity in Washington was virtually terminated as Congressmen were inundated with letters of protest and demand. A special committee, heretofore burdened by general public apathy in the east, now became enlarged by the added membership of several distinguished Congressmen, and a costly probe into the problem ensued.

It was this committee that, during the course of its televised hearings, unearthed a secret group known as the L.A. Firsters.

This insidious organization seemed to have sprung almost spontaneously from the general chaos of the Los Angeles envelopment. General credence was given for a short time that it was another symptom of "Ellieitis." Intense interrogation, however, revealed the existence of L.A. Firster cells in east coast cities that could not possibly have been subject to the dread virus at that point.

This revelation struck terror into the heart of a nation. The presence of such calculated subversion in this moment of trial almost unnerved the national will. For it was not merely an organization loosely joined by emotional binds. This faction possessed a carefully wrought hierarchy of men and women which was plotting the overthrow of the national government. Nationwide distribution of literature had begun almost with the advent of the Los Angeles Movement. This literature, with the cunning of insurgent casuistry, painted a roseate picture of the future of—The United States of Los Angeles!

PEOPLE ARISE![9]
People arise! Cast off the shackles of reaction!
What sense is there is opposing the march of
PROGRESS! It is inevitable!—and you the
people of this glorious land—a land bought

9. *The Los Angeles Manifesto*, L.A. Firster Press, (Winter 1982).

dearly with *your* blood and *your* tears—should realize that *Nature herself* supports the L.A. FIRSTERS! How?—you ask. How does Nature support this glorious adventure? The question is simple enough to answer.

NATURE HAS SUPPORTED THE L.A.FIRSTER MOVEMENT FOR THE BETTERMENT OF YOU! AND *YOU*!

Here are a few facts:
In those states that have been blessed
1. Rheumatism has dropped 52%;
2. Pneumonia has dropped 61%;
3. Frostbite has *vanished*;
4. Incidence of the COMMON COLD has dropped 73%!

Is this bad news? Are these the changes brought about by anti-PROGRESS?

NO!!!

Wherever Los Angeles has gone, the deserts have fled, adding millions of new fertile acres to our beloved land. Where once there was only sand and cactus and *bleached bones*, are now plants and trees and FLOWERS!

This pamphlet closes with a couplet which aroused a nation to fury:

Sing out O land, with flag unfurled!
Los Angeles! Tomorrow's World!

The exposure of the L.A. Firsters caused a tide of reaction to sweep the country. Rage became the keynote of this counterrevolution; rage at the subtlety with which the L.A. Firsters had distorted truth in their literature; rage at their arrogant assumption that the country would inevitably fall to Los Angeles.

Slogans of "Down with the L.A. Lovers!" and "Send Them Back Where They Came From!" rang throughout the land. A measure was forced through Congress and presidential signature outlawing the group and making membership in it the offense of treason. Rabid groups attached a rider to this measure which would have enforced the outlawry, seizure and destruction of all tennis and beach supply manufacturing. Here, however, the N.A.M. stepped into the scene and, through the judicious use of various pressure means, defeated the attempt.

Despite this quick retaliation, the L.A. Firsters continued underground and at least one fatality of its persistent agitation was the state of Missouri.

In some manner, as yet undisclosed, the L.A. Firsters gained control of the state legislature and jockeyed through an amendment to the constitution of Missouri which was hastily ratified and made the Show-Me State the first area in the country to legally make itself a part of Los Angeles County.

UTTER MCKINLEY OPENS
FIVE NEW PARLORS
IN THE SOUTHWEST

In succeeding months there emerged a notable upsurge in the production of automobiles, particularly those of the convertible variety. In those states affected by the Los Angeles Movement, every citizen, apparently, had acquired that symptom of "Ellieitis" known as *automania*. The car industry entered accordingly upon a period of peak production, its factories turning out automobiles twenty-four hours a day, seven days a week.

In conjunction with this increase in automotive fabrication, there began a near maniacal splurge in the building of drive-in restaurants and theaters. These sprang up with mushroomlike celerity through western and midwestern United States, their planning going beyond all feasibility. Typical of these thoughtless projects was the endeavor to hollow out a mountain and convert it into a drive-in theater.[10]

As the month of December approached, the Los Angeles Movement engulfed Illinois, Wisconsin, Mississippi, half of Tennessee and was lapping at the shores of Indiana, Kentucky and Alabama. (No mention will be made of the profound effect this movement had on racial segregation in the South, this subject

10. L. Savage, "A Report on the Grand Teton Drive-In," *Fortune* (Jan. 1983).

demanding a complete investigation in itself.)

It was about this time that a wave of religious passion obsessed the nation. As is the nature of the human mind suffering catastrophe, millions turned to religion. Various cults had in this calamity grist for their metaphysical mills.

Typical of these were the San Bernardino Vine Worshipers who claimed Los Angeles to be the reincarnation of their deity Ochsalia— The Vine Divine. The San Diego Sons of the Weed claimed in turn that Los Angeles was a sister embodiment of their deity which they claimed had been creeping for three decades prior to the Los Angeles Movement.

Unfortunately for all concerned, a small fascistic clique began to usurp control of many of these otherwise harmless cults, emphasizing dominance through "power and energy." As a result, these religious bodies too often degenerated into mere fronts for political cells which plotted the overthrow of the government for purposes of self-aggrandizement. (Secret documents discovered in later years revealed the intention of one perfidious brotherhood of converting the Pentagon Building into an indoor race track.)

During a period beginning in September and extending for years, there also ensued a studied expansion of the motion-picture industry. Various of the major producers opened branch studios throughout the country (for example MGM built one in Terre Haute, Paramount in Cincinnati and Twentieth-Century Fox in Tulsa). The Screen Writer's Guild initiated branch offices in every large city and the term "Hollywood" became even more of a misnomer than it had previously been.

Motion picture output more than quadrupled as theaters of all description were hastily erected everywhere west of the Mississippi, sometimes wall to wall for blocks.[11] These buildings were rarely well constructed and often collapsed within weeks of their "grand openings."

Yet, in spite of the incredible number of theaters, motion pictures exceeded them in quantity (if not quality). It was in compensation for this economically dangerous situation that the studios inaugurated the expedient practice of burning films in order to maintain the stability

11. "Gulls Creek Get Its Forty-Eighth Theater." *The Arkansas Post-Journal*, 12 March 1983.

of the price floor. This aroused great antipathy among the smaller studios who did not produce enough films to burn any.

Another liability involved in the production of motion pictures was the geometric increase in difficulties raised by small but voluble pressure groups.

One typical coterie was the Anti-Horse League of Dallas which put up strenuous opposition to the utilization of horses in films. This, plus the increasing incidence of car owning which had made horse breeding unprofitable, made the production of Western films (as they had been known) an impossible chore. Thus was it that the so-called "Western" gravitated rapidly toward the "drawing room" drama.

SECTION OF A TYPICAL SCREENPLAY[12]

> *Tex D'Uverbille comes riding into*
> *Doomtown on the Colorado, his Jaguar*
> *raising a cloud of dust in the sleepy*
> *western town. He parks in front of the*
> *Golden Sovereign Saloon and steps out.*
> *He is a tall, rangy cowhand, impeccably*
> *attired in waistcoat and fawn-skin*
> *trousers with a ten-gallon hat, boots*
> *and pearl-gray spats. A heavy sixgun is*
> *belted at his waist. He carries a gold-*
> *topped Malacca cane.*
>
> *He enters the saloon and every man*
> *there scatters from the room, leaving*
> *only Tex and a scowling hulk of a man*
> *at the other end of the bar. This is Dirty*
> *Ned Updyke, local ruffian and gunman.*
> TEX *(Removing his white gloves and,*
>   *pretending he does not see Dirty*
>   *Ned, addressing the bartender): Pour*
>   *me a whiskey and seltzer will you,*
>   *Roger, there's a good fellow.*
> ROGER: *Yes sir.*

2. Maxwell Brande, "Altercation at Deadwood Spa," Epigram Studios (April 1983).

> *Dirty Ned scowls over his apéritif but*
> *does not dare to reach for his Webley*
> *automatic pistol which is concealed in*
> *a holster beneath his tweed jacket.*
>
> *Now Tex D'Uberville allows his icy*
> *blue eyes to move slowly about the*
> *room until they rest on the craven fea-*
> *tures of Dirty Ned.*
> TEX: *So...you're the beastly cad what*
> *shot my brother.*
> *Instantly they draw their cane swords*
> *and, approaching, salute each other*
> *grimly.*

An additional result not to be overlooked was the effect of increased film production on politics. The need for high-salaried workers such as writers, actors, directors and plumbers was intense and this mass of *nouveau riche*, having come upon good times so relatively abrupt-ly, acquired a definite guilt neurosis which resulted in their intensive participation in the so-called "liberal" and "progressive" groups. This swelling of radical activity did much to alter the course of American political history. (This subject being another which requires separate inquiry for a proper evaluation of its many and varied ramifications.)

Two other factors of this period which may be mentioned briefly are the increase in divorce due to the relaxation of divorce laws in every state affected by the Los Angeles Movement and the slow but even-tually complete bans placed upon tennis and beach supplies by a rabid but powerful group within the N.A.M. This ban led inexorably to a brief span of time which paralleled this so-called "Prohibition" period in the 1920's. During this infamous period, thrill seekers attended the many bootleg tennis courts throughout the country, which sprang up wherever perverse public demand made them prof-itable ventures for unscrupulous men.

In the first days of January of 1983 the Los Angeles Movement reached almost to the Atlantic shoreline. Panic spread through New England and the southern coastal region. The country and, ultimately,

Washington reverberated with cries of "*Stop Los Angeles*!" and all processes of government ground to a virtual halt in the ensuing chaos. Law enforcement atrophied, crime waves spilled across the nation and conditions became so grave that even the outlawed L.A. Firsters held revival meetings in the street.

On February 11, 1983, the Los Angeles Movement forded the Hudson River and invaded Manhattan Island. Flame-throwing tanks, proved futile against the invincible flux. Within a week the subways were closed and car purchases had trebled.

By March 1983 the only unaltered states in the union were Maine, Vermont, New Hampshire and Massachusetts. This was later explained by the lethargic adaptation of the fungi to the rocky New England soil and to the immediate inclement weather.

These northern states, cornered and helpless, resorted to extraordinary measures in a hopeless bid to ward off the awful incrustation. Several of them legalized the mercy killing of any person discovered to have acquired the taint of "Ellieitis." Newspaper reports of shootings, stabbings, poisonings and strangulations became so common in those days of "The Last-Ditch Defense" that newspapers inaugurated a daily section of their contents to such reports.

Boston, Mass. April 13, AP—Last rites were held today for Mr. Abner Scrounge who was shot after being found in his garage attempting to remove the top of his Rolls Royce with a can opener.

The history of the gallant battle of Boston to retain its essential dignity would, alone, make up a large work. The story of how the intrepid citizens of this venerable city refused to surrender their rights, choosing mass suicide rather than submission is a tale of enduring courage and majestic struggle against insurmountable odds.

What happened after the movement was contained within the boundaries of the United States (a name soon discarded) is data for another paper. A brief mention, however, may be made of the immense social endeavor which became known as the "Bacon and Waffles" movement, which sought to guarantee $750 per month for every person in Los Angeles over forty years of age.

With this incentive before the people, state legislatures were helpless before an avalanche of public demand and, within three years, the entire nation was a part of Los Angeles. The government seat was in Beverly Hills and ambassadors had been hastened to all foreign countries within a short period of time.

Ten years later the North American continent fell and Los Angeles was creeping rapidly down the Isthmus of Panama.

Then came that ill-fated day in 1994.

On the island of Pingo Pongo, Maona, daughter of Chief Luana, approached her father.

"Omu la golu si mongo," she said.

(Anyone for tennis?)

Whereupon her father, having read the papers, speared her on the spot and ran screaming from the hut.

"The Creeping Terror" (as "A Touch of Grapefruit") was first published in **Star Science Fiction Stories #5** (Ballantine Books, 1959), edited by Frederick Pohl.

"My original title was 'The Creeping Terror,' because I wanted it to sound like an honest to God horror story—when it wasn't at all. I had great fun writing it. All the footnotes—they were the names of people and writers that I knew. In one of the footnotes there's a 'Guillaume Gaulte' who was William Campbell Gault. He was a mystery writer whose house I stayed in when I first went to California. The whole story was done in documentary style to give a sense of reality to something that was patently unreal." —RM

DEADLINE
1959

THERE ARE AT LEAST two nights a year a doctor doesn't plan on and those are Christmas Eve and New Year's Eve. On Christmas Eve it was Bobby Dascouli's arm burns. I was salving and swathing them about the time I would have been nestled in an easy chair with Ruth, eyeing the Technicolor doings of the Christmas tree.

So it came as no surprise that ten minutes after we got to my sister Mary's house for the New Year's Eve party my answering service phoned and told me there was an emergency call downtown.

Ruth smiled at me sadly and shook her head. She kissed me on the cheek. "Poor Bill," she said.

"Poor Bill indeed," I said, putting down my first drink of the evening, two-thirds full. I patted her much-evident stomach.

"Don't have that baby till I get back," I told her.

"I'll do my bestest," she said.

I gave hurried goodbyes to everyone and left; turning up the collar of my overcoat and crunching over the snow-packed walk to the Ford; finally getting the engine started. Driving downtown with that look of dour reflection I've seen on many a GP's face at many a time.

It was after eleven when my tire chains rattled onto the dark desertion of East Main Street. I drove three blocks north to the address and parked in front of what had been a refined apartment dwelling when my father was in practice. Now it was a boarding-house, ancient, smelling of decay.

In the vestibule I lined the beam of my pencil flashlight over the mail boxes but couldn't find the name. I rang the landlady's bell and stepped over to the hall door. When the buzzer sounded I pushed it open.

At the end of the hall a door opened and a heavy woman emerged. She wore a black sweater over her wrinkled green dress, striped anklets over her heavy stockings, saddle shoes over the anklets. She had no make-up on; the only color in her face was a chapped redness in her cheeks. Wisps of steel-gray hair hung across her temples. She picked at them as she trundled down the dim hall-way towards me.

"You the doctor?" she asked.

I said I was.

"I'm the one called ya," she said. "There's an old guy up the fourth floor says he's dyin'."

"What room?" I asked.

"I'll show ya."

I followed her wheezing ascent up the stairs. We stopped in front of room 47 and she rapped on the thin paneling of the door, then pushed it open.

"In here," she said.

As I entered I saw him lying on an iron bed. His body had the flaccidity of a discarded doll. At his sides, frail hands lay motionless, topographed with knots of vein, islanded with liver spots. His skin was the brown of old page edges, his face a wasted mask. On the caseless pillow, his head lay still, its white hair straggling across the stripes like threading drifts of snow. There was a pallid stubble on his cheeks. His pale blue eyes were fixed on the ceiling.

As I slipped off my hat and coat I saw that there was no suffer-ing evident. His expression was one of peaceful acceptance. I sat down on the bed and took his wrist. His eyes shifted and he looked at me.

"Hello," I said, smiling.

"Hello." I was surprised by the cognizance in his voice.

The beat of his blood was what I expected however—a bare trickle of life, a pulsing almost lost beneath the fingers. I put down his hand and laid my palm across his forehead. There was no fever. But then he wasn't sick. He was only running down.

I patted the old man's shoulder and stood, gesturing towards the opposite side of the room. The landlady clumped there with me.

"How long has he been in bed?" I asked.

"Just since this afternoon," she said. "He come down to my room and said he was gonna die tonight."

I stared at her. I'd never come in contact with such a thing. I'd read about it; everyone has. An old man or woman announces that, at a certain time, they'll die and, when the time comes, they do. Who knows what it is; will or prescience or both. All one knows is that it is a strangely awesome thing.

"Has he any relatives?" I asked.

"None I know of," she said.

I nodded.

"Don't understand it," she said.

"What?"

"When he first moved in about a month ago he was all right. Even this afternoon he didn't look sick."

"You never know," I said.

"No. You don't." There was a haunted and uneasy flickering back deep in her eyes.

"Well, there's nothing I can do for him," I said. "He's not in pain. It's just a matter of time."

The landlady nodded.

"How old is he?" I asked.

"He never said."

"I see." I walked back to the bed.

"I heard you," the old man told me.

"Oh?"

"You want to know how old I am."

"How old are you?"

He started to answer, then began coughing dryly. I saw a glass of water on the bedside table and, sitting, I propped the old man while he drank a little. Then I put him down again.

"I'm one year old," he said.

It didn't register. I stared down at his calm face. Then, smiling nervously, I put the glass down on the table.

"You don't believe that," he said.

"Well—" I shrugged.

"It's true enough," he said.

I nodded and smiled again.

"I was born on December 31, 1958," he said. "At midnight."

He closed his eyes. "What's the use?" he said. "I've told a hundred people and none of them understood."

"Tell me about it," I said.

After a few moments, he drew in breath, slowly.

"A week after I was born," he said, "I was walking and talking. I was eating by myself. My mother and father couldn't believe their eyes. They took me to a doctor. I don't know what he thought but he didn't do anything. What could he do? I wasn't sick. He sent me home with my mother and father. Precocious growth, he said.

"In another week we were back again. I remember my mother's and father's faces when we drove there. They were afraid of me.

"The doctor didn't know what to do. He called in specialists and they didn't know what to do. I was a normal four-year-old boy. They kept me under observation. They wrote papers about me. I didn't see my father and mother any more."

The old man stopped for a moment, then went on in the same mechanical way.

"In another week I was six," he said. "In another week, eight. Nobody understood. They tried everything but there was no answer. And I was ten and twelve. I was fourteen and I ran away because I was sick of being stared at."

He looked at the ceiling for almost a minute.

"You want to hear more?" he asked then.

"Yes," I said, automatically. I was amazed at how easily he spoke.

"In the beginning I tried to fight it," he said. "I went to doctors and screamed at them. I told them to find out what was wrong with me. But there wasn't anything wrong with me. I was just getting two years older every week.

"Then I got the idea."

I started a little, twitching out the reverie of staring at him. "Idea?" I asked.

"This is how the story got started," the old man said.

"What story?"

"About the old year and the new year," he said. "The old year is an old man with a beard and a scythe. You know. And the new year is a little baby."

The old man stopped. Down in the street I heard a tire-screeching car turn a corner and speed past the building.

"I think there have been men like me all through time," the old man said. "Men who live for just a year. I don't know how it happens or why; but, once in a while, it does. That's how the story got started. After a while, people forgot how it started. They think it's a fable now. They think it's symbolic: but it isn't."

The old man turned his worn face towards the wall.

"And I'm 1959," he said, quietly. "That's who I am."

The landlady and I stood in silence looking down at him. Finally, I glanced at her. Abruptly, as if caught in guilt, she turned and hurried across the floor. The door thumped shut behind her.

I looked back at the old man. Suddenly, my breath seemed to stop. I leaned over and picked up his hand. There was no pulse. Shivering, I put down his hand and straightened up. I stood looking down at him. Then, from where I don't know, a chill laced up my back. Without thought, I extended my left hand and the sleeve of my coat slid back across my watch.

To the second.

I drove back to Mary's house unable to get the old man's story out of my mind—or the weary acceptance in his eyes. I kept telling myself it was only a coincidence, but I couldn't quite convince myself.

Mary let me in. The living room was empty.

"Don't tell me the party's broken up already?" I said.

Mary smiled. "Not broken up," she said. "Just continued at the hospital."

I stared at her, my mind swept blank. Mary took my arm.

    "And you'll never guess," she said, "what time Ruth had the sweetest little boy."

"Deadline" was first published in Rogue, December 1959.

*"Simple twist-ending tale in which a doctor meets an unusual patient—a dying old man who claims to be only one year old, and is in fact part of the old legend that each Year is represented by a Man who lives and dies in the space of that one year—and this man is 1959. Could have been a **Twilight Zone** story as well. Classic stinger at the end, too." —RM*

MANTAGE

1959

FADEOUT.

THE OLD MAN HAD SUCCUMBED. From its movie heaven, an ethereal choir paeaned. Amid roiling pink clouds they sang: *A Moment or Forever*. It was the title of the picture. Lights blinked on. The voices stopped abruptly, the curtain was lowered, the theater boomed with p.a. resonance; a quartet singing *A Moment or Forever* on the Decca label. Eight hundred thousand copies in a month.

Owen Crowley sat slumped in his seat, legs crossed, arms slackly folded. He stared at the curtain. Around him, people stood and stretched, yawned, chatted, laughed. Owen sat there, staring. Next to him, Carole rose and drew on her suede jacket. Softly, she was singing with the record, *"Your mind is the clock that ticks away a moment or forever."*

She stopped. "Honey?"

Owen grunted. "Are you coming?" she asked.

He sighed. "I suppose." He dragged up his jacket and followed her as she edged toward the aisle, shoes crunching over pale popcorn buds and candy wrappers. They reached the aisle and Carole took his arm.

"Well?" she asked. "What did you think?"

Owen had the burdening impression that she had asked him that question a million times; that their relationship consisted of an infinitude of movie-going and scant more. Was it only two years since they'd met; five months since their engagement? It seemed, momentarily, like the dreariest of eons.

"What's there to think?" he said. "It's just another movie."

"I thought you'd like it," Carole said, "being a writer yourself."

He trudged across the lobby with her. They were the last ones out. The snack counter was darkened, the soda machine stilled of technicolored bubblings. The only sound was the whisper of their shoes across the carpeting, then the click of them as they hit the outer lobby.

"What is it, Owen?" Carole asked when he'd gone a block without saying a word.

"They make me mad," he said.

"Who does?" Carole asked.

"The damn stupid people who make those damn stupid movies," he said.

"Why?" she asked.

"Because of the way they gloss over everything."

"What do you mean?"

"This writer the picture was about," said Owen. "He was a lot like I am; talented and with plenty of drive. But it took him almost ten years to get things going. Ten years. So what does the stupid picture do? Glosses over them in a few minutes. A couple of scenes of him sitting at his desk, looking broody, a couple of clock shots, a few trays of mashed-out butts, some empty coffee cups, a pile of manuscripts. Some bald-headed publishers with cigars shaking their heads no at him, some feet walking on the sidewalk; and that's it. *Ten years* of hard labor. It makes me mad."

"But they have to do that, Owen," Carole said. "That's the only way they have of showing it."

"Then life should be like that too," he said.

"Oh, you wouldn't like that," she said.

"You're wrong. I would," he said. "Why should I struggle ten years—or more—on my writing? Why not get it all over within a couple of minutes?"

"It wouldn't be the same," she said.

"That's for sure," he said.

An hour and forty minutes later, Owen sat on the cot in his furnished room staring at the table on which sat his typewriter and the half-completed manuscript of his third novel *And Now Gomorrah.*

Why not indeed? The idea had definite appeal. He knew that, someday, he'd succeed. It had to be that way. Otherwise, what was he working so hard for? But that transition—that was the thing. That indefinite transition between struggle and success. How wonderful if that part could be condensed, abbreviated.

Glossed over.

"You know what I wish?" he asked the intent young man in the mirror.

"No, what?" asked the man.

"I wish," said Owen Crowley, "that life could be as simple as a movie. All the drudgery set aside in a few flashes of weary looks, disappointments, coffee cups and midnight oil, trays of butts, no's and walking feet. Why not?"

On the bureau, something clicked. Owen looked down at his clock. It was 2:43 a.m.

Oh, well. He shrugged and went to bed. Tomorrow, another five pages, another night's work at the toy factory.

A year and seven months went by and nothing happened. Then, one morning, Owen woke up, went down to the mail box and there it was.

We are happy to inform you that we want to publish your novel Dream Within a Dream.

"Carole! Carole!" He pounded on her apartment door, heart drumming from the half-mile sprint from the subway, the leaping ascent of the stairs. "*Carole.*"

She jerked open the door, face stricken. "Owen, what—?" she began, then cried out, startled, as he swept her from the floor and whirled her around, the hem of her nightgown whipping silkenly. "Owen, what is it?" she gasped.

"Look! Look!" He put her down on the couch and, kneeling, held out the crumpled letter to her.

"*Oh, Owen!*"

They clung to each other and she laughed, she cried. He felt the unbound softness of her pressing at him through the filmy silk, the moist cushioning of her lips against his cheek, her warm tears trickling down his face. "Oh, Owen. *Darling.*"

She cupped his face with trembling hands and kissed him; then whispered, "And you were worried."

"No more," he said. "No more!"

The publisher's office stood aloofly regal above the city; draped, paneled, still. "If you'll sign here, Mr. Crowley," said the editor. Owen took the pen.

"*Hurray! Hurroo!*" He polkaed amid a debris of cocktail glasses, red-eyed olives, squashed hors d'oeuvres and guests. Who clapped and stamped and shouted and erected monumental furies in the neighbors' hearts. Who flowed and broke apart like noisy quicksilver through the rooms and halls of Carole's apartment. Who devoured regimental rations. Who flushed away Niagaras of converted alcohol. Who nuzzled in a fog of nicotine. Who gambled on the future census in the dark and fur-coat-smelling bedroom.

Owen sprang. He howled. "An Indian I am!" He grabbed the laughing Carole by her spilling hair. "An Indian I am, I'll scalp you! No, I won't, I'll kiss you!" He did to wild applause and whistles. She clung to him, their bodies molding. The clapping was like rapid fire. "And for an encore!" he announced.

Laughter. Cheers. Music pounding. A graveyard of bottles on the sink. Sound and movement. Community singing. Bedlam. A policeman at the door. "*Come in, come in, defender of the weal!*" "Now, let's be having a little order here, there's people want to sleep."

Silence in the shambles. They sat together on the couch, watching dawn creep in across the sills, a nightgowned Carole clinging to him, half asleep; Owen pressing his lips to her warm throat and feeling, beneath the satin skin, the pulsing of her blood.

"*I love you,*" whispered Carole. Her lips, on his, wanted, took. The electric rustle of her gown made him shudder. He brushed the straps and watched them slither from the pale curving of her shoulders. "Carole, Carole." Her hands were cat claws on his back.

The telephone rang, rang. He opened an eye. There was a heated pitchfork fastened to the lid. As the lid moved up it plunged the pitchfork into his brain. "*Ooh*!" He winced his eyes shut and the room was gone. "Go away," he muttered to the ringing, ringing; to the cleat-shoed, square-dancing goblins in his head.

Across the void, a door opened and the ringing stopped. Owen sighed.

"Hello?" said Carole. "Oh. Yes, he's here."

He heard the crackle of her gown, the nudging of her fingers on his shoulder. "Owen," she said. "Wake up, darling."

The deep fall of pink-tipped flesh against transparent silk was what he saw. He reached but she was gone. Her hand closed over his and drew him up. "The phone," she said.

"More," he said, pulling her against himself.

"The phone."

"Can wait," he said. His voice came muffled from her nape. "I'm breakfasting."

"Darling, the phone."

"Hello?" he said into the black receiver.

"This is Arthur Means, Mr. Crowley," said the voice.

"*Yes!*" There was an explosion in his brain but he kept on smiling anyway because it was the agent he'd called the day before.

"Can you make it for lunch?" asked Arthur Means.

Owen came back into the living room from showering. From the kitchen came the sound of Carole's slippers on linoleum, the sizzle of bacon, the dark odor of percolating coffee.

Owen stopped. He frowned at the couch where he'd been sleeping. How had he ended there? He'd been in bed with Carole.

The streets, by early morning, were a mystic lot. Manhattan after midnight was an island of intriguing silences, a vast acropolis of crouching steel and stone. He walked between the silent citadels, his footsteps like the ticking of a bomb.

"Which will explode!" he cried. "*Explode!*" cried back the streets of shadowed walls. "Which will explode and throw my shrapnel words through all the world!"

Owen Crowley stopped. He flung out his arms and held the universe. "You're mine!" he yelled.

"*Mine*," the echo came.

The room was silent as he shed his clothes. He settled on the cot with a happy sigh, crossed his legs and undid lace knots. What time was it? He looked over at the clock. 2:58 a.m.

Fifteen minutes since he'd made his wish.

He grunted in amusement as he dropped his shoe. Weird fancy, that. Yes, it was exactly fifteen minutes if you chose to ignore the one year, seven months and two days since he'd stood over there in his pajamas, fooling with a wish. Granted that, in thinking back, those nineteen months seemed quickly past; but not that quickly. If he wished to, he could tally up a reasonable itemization of every miserable day of them.

Owen Crowley chuckled. Weird fancy indeed. Well, it was the mind. The mind was a droll mechanism.

"Carole, let's get married!"

He might have struck her. She stood there, looking dazed.

"What?" she asked.

"*Married!*"

She stared at him. "You mean it?"

He slid his arms around her tightly. "Try me," he said.

"Oh, Owen." She clung to him a moment, then, abruptly, drew back her head and grinned.

"This," she said, "is not so sudden."

It was a white house, lost in summer foliage. The living room was large and cool and they stood together on the walnut floor, holding hands. Outside, leaves were rustling.

"Then by the authority vested in me," said Justice of the Peace Weaver, "by the sovereign state of Connecticut, I now pronounce you man and wife." He smiled. "You may kiss the bride" he said.

Their lips parted and he saw the tears glistening in her eyes.

"How do, Miz Crowley," he whispered.

The Buick hummed along the quiet country road. Inside, Carole leaned against her husband while the radio played, *A Moment or Forever*, arranged for strings. "Remember that?" he asked.

"Mmmm-hmmm." She kissed his cheek.

"Now where," he wondered, "is that motel the old man recommended?"

"Isn't that it up ahead?" she asked.

The tires crackled on the gravel path, then stopped. "Owen,

look," she said. He laughed. *Aldo Weaver, Manager*, read the bottom line of the rust-streaked wooden sign.

"Yes, brother George, he marries all the young folks around about," said Aldo Weaver as he led them to their cabin and unlocked the door. Then Aldo crunched away and Carole leaned her back against the door until the lock clicked. In the quiet room, dim from tree shade, Carole whispered, "Now you're mine."

They were walking through the empty, echoing rooms of a little house in Northport. "Oh, *yes*," said Carole happily. They stood before the living room window, looking out into the shadow-dark woods beyond. Her hand slipped into his. "Home," she said, "*sweet* home."

They were moving in and it was furnished. A second novel sold, a third. John was born when winds whipped powdery snow across the sloping lawn: Linda on a sultry, cricket-rasping summer night. Years cranked by, a moving backdrop on which events were painted.

He sat there in the stillness of his tiny den. He'd stayed up late correcting the galleys on his forthcoming novel. *One Foot in Sea*. Now, almost nodding, he twisted together his fountain pen and set it down. "My God, my God," he murmured, stretching. He was tired.

Across the room, standing on the mantel of the tiny fireplace, the clock buzzed once. Owen looked at it. 3:15 a.m. It was well past his—

He found himself staring at the clock and, like a slow-tapped tympani, his heart was felt. Seventeen minutes later than the last time, thought persisted; thirty-two minutes in all.

Owen Crowley shivered and rubbed his hands as if at some imaginary flame. Well, this is idiotic, he thought; idiotic to dredge up this fantasy every year or so. It was the sort of nonsense that could well become obsession.

He lowered his gaze and looked around the room. The sight of time-worn comforts and arrangements made him smile. This house, its disposition, that shelf of manuscripts at his left. These were measurable. The children alone were eighteen months of slow transition just in the making.

He clucked disgustedly at himself. This was absurd; rationalizing to himself as if the fancy merited rebuttal. Clearing his throat, he tidied up the surface of his desk with energetic movements. There. And there.

He leaned back heavily in his chair. Well, maybe it was a mistake to repress it. That the concept kept returning was proof enough it had a definite meaning. Certainly, the flimsiest of delusions fought against could disorient the reason. All men knew that.

Well, then, face it, he decided. Time was constant; that was the core. What varied was a person's outlook on it. To some it dragged by on tar-held feet, to others fled on blurring wings. It just happened he was one of those to whom time seemed overly transient. So transient that it fostered rather than dispelled the memory of that childish wish he'd made that night more than five years before.

That was it, of course. Months seemed a wink and years a breath because he viewed them so. And—

The door swung open and Carole came across the rug, holding a glass of warmed milk.

"You should be in bed," he scolded.

"So should you," she answered, "yet I see you sitting here. Do you know what time it is?"

"I know," he said.

She settled on his lap as he sipped the milk. "Galleys done?" she asked. He nodded and slid an arm around her waist. She kissed his temple. Out in the winter night, a dog barked once.

She sighed. "It seems like only yesterday, doesn't it?" she said.

He drew in faint breath. "I don't think so," he said.

"Oh, *you*." She punched him gently on the arm.

"This is Artie," said his agent. "Guess what?"

Owen gasped. "*No!*"

He found her in the laundry room, stuffing bedclothes into the washer. "Honey!" he yelled. Sheets went flying.

"It's happened!" he cried.

"What?"

"The movies, the movies! They're buying *Nobles and Heralds*!"

"No!"

"Yes! And—get this now—sit down and get it—go ahead and

sit or else you'll fall!—they're paying *twelve thousand, five hundred dollars* for it!"

"Oh!"

"And that's not all! They're giving me a ten-week guarantee to do the screenplay at—*get* this—*seven hundred and fifty dollars* a week!"

She squeaked. "We're rich."

"Not quite," he said, floor-pacing, "but it's only the beginning, folks, on-ly the beginning!"

October winds swept in like tides over the dark field. Spotlight ribbons wiped across the sky.

"I wish the kids were here," he said, his arm around her.

"They'd just be cold and cranky, darling," Carole said.

"Carole, don't you think—"

"Owen, you know I'd come with you if I could; but we'd have to take Johnny out of school and, besides, it would cost so much. It's only ten weeks, darling. Before you know it—"

"Flight twenty-seven for Chicago and Los Angeles," intoned the speaker, "Now boarding at Gate Three."

"*So soon,*" suddenly, her eyes were lost, she pressed her wind-chilled cheek to his. "Oh, darling, I'll miss you so."

The thick wheels squeaked below, the cabin walls shook. Outside, the engines roared faster and faster. The field rushed by. Owen looked back. Colored lights were distant now. Somewhere among them, Carole stood, watching his plane nose up into the black-ness. He settled back and closed his eyes a moment. A dream, he thought. Flying west to write a movie from his own novel. Good God, a veritable dream.

He sat there on a corner of the leather couch. His office was capa-cious. A peninsula of polished desk extended from the wall, an uphol-stered chair parked neatly against it. Tweed drapes concealed the humming air conditioner, tasteful reproductions graced the walls and, beneath his shoes, the carpet gave like sponge. Owen sighed.

A knocking broke his reverie. "Yes?" he asked. The snugly-sweatered blonde stepped in. "I'm Cora. I'm your secretary," she said. It was Monday morning.

"Eighty-five minutes, give or take," said Morton Zuckersmith,

Producer. He signed another notification. "That's a good length." He signed another letter. "You'll pick these things up as you go along." He signed another contract. "It's a world of its own." He stabbed the pen into its onyx sheath and his secretary exited, bearing off the sheaf of papers. Zuckersmith leaned back in his leather chair, hands behind his head, his polo-shirted chest broadening with air. "A world of its own, kiddy," he said. "Ah. Here's our girl."

Owen stood, his stomach muscles twitching as Linda Carson slipped across the room, one ivory hand extended. "Morton, dear," she said.

"Morning, darling." Zuckersmith engulfed her hand in his, then looked toward Owen. "Dear, I'd like you to meet your writer for *The Lady and the Herald*."

"I've been so anxious to meet you," said Linda Carson, neé Virginia Ostermeyer. "I loved your book. How can I tell you?"

He started up as Cora entered. "Don't get up," she said. "I'm just bringing you your pages. We're up to forty-five."

Owen watched her as she stretched across the desk. Her sweaters grew more skinlike every day. The tense expansion of her breathing posed threats to every fiber.

"How does it read?" he asked.

She took it for an invitation to perch across the couch arm at his feet. "I think you're doing *wonderfully*," she said. She crossed her legs and frothy slip lace sighed across her knees. "You're very talented." She drew in chest-enhancing air. "There's just a few things here and there," she said. "I'd tell you what they were right now but—well, it's lunchtime and—"

They went to lunch; that day and others after. Cora donned a mantle of stewardship, guiding him as though he were resourceless. Bustling in with smiles and coffee every morning, telling him what foods were best prepared at dinner and, fingering his arm, leading him to the commissary every afternoon for orange juice; hinting at a p.m. continuance of their relationship; assuming a position in his life he had no desire for. Actually sniffling one afternoon after he'd gone to lunch without her; and, as he patted her shoulder in rough commiseration, pressing against him suddenly, her firm lips taking their efficient due, the taut convexities of her indenting him. He drew back, startled. "*Cora*."

She patted his cheek: "Don't think about it, darling. You have important work to do." Then she was gone and Owen was sitting at his desk, alarm diffusing to his fingertips. A week, another week.

"Hi," said Linda. "How are you?"

"Fine," he answered as Cora entered, clad in hugging gabardine, in clinging silk. "Lunch? I'd love to. Shall I meet you at the—? Oh. All right!" He hung up. Cora at the gate, watching him grimly.

"Hello, Owen," Linda said. The Lincoln purred into the line of traffic. This is nonsense, Owen thought. He'd have to try a second time with Cora. The first discouragement she'd taken for nobility; the gesture of a gallant husband toward his wife and children. At least she seemed to take it so. Good God, what complication.

It was lunch together on the Strip; then, later, dinner, Owen trusting that enough hours devoted to Linda would convince Cora of his lack of interest. The next night it was dinner and the Philharmonic; two nights later, dancing and a drive along the shore; the next, a preview in Encino.

At what specific juncture the plan went wrong Owen never knew. It gained irrevocable form the night when, parked beside the ocean, radio music playing softly, Linda slipped against him naturally, her world-known body pressing close, her lips a succulence at his. "*Darling.*"

He lay starkly awake, thinking of the past weeks; of Cora and of Linda, of Carole whose reality had faded to the tenuous form of daily letters and a weekly voice emitting from the telephone, a smiling picture on his desk.

He'd almost finished with the screenplay. Soon he'd fly back home. So much time had passed. Where were the joints, the sealing place? Where was the evidence except in circumstantial shards of memory? It was like one of those effects they'd taught him at the studio; a *montage*—a series of quickly paced scenes. That's what life seemed like; a series of quickly paced scenes that flitted across the screen of one's attention, then were gone.

Across the hotel room, his traveling clock buzzed once. He would not look at it.

He ran against the wind, the snow, but Carole wasn't there. He stood, eyes searching, in the waiting room, an island of man and luggage.

Was she ill? There'd been no acknowledgement of his telegram but—

"Carole?" The booth was hot and stale.

"Yes," she said.

"My God, darling, did you *forget*?"

"No," she said.

The taxi ride to Northport was a jading travelogue of snow-cottoned trees and lawns, impeding traffic lights and tire chains rattling over slush-graviled streets. She'd been so deadly calm on the phone. No, I'm not sick. Linda has a little cold. John is fine. I couldn't get a sitter. A chill of premonitions troubled at him.

Home at last. He'd dreamed of it like this, standing silently among the skeletal trees, a mantle of snow across its roof, a rope of wood smoke spiraling from its chimney. He paid the driver with a shaking hand and turned expectantly. The door stayed shut. He waited but the door stayed shut.

He read the letter that she'd finally given him. *Dear Mrs. Crowley*, it began, *I thought you ought to know…*His eyes sought out the childish signature below. *Cora Bailey.*

"Why that dirty, little—"

"Dear God." She stood before the window, trembling. "To this very moment I've been praying it was a lie. But now…"

She shriveled at his touch. "*Don't.*"

"You wouldn't go with me," he charged. "You *wouldn't* go."

"*Is that your excuse?*" she asked.

"Wha'm I gonna do?" he asked, fumbling at his fourteenth Scotch and water. "*Wha'*? I don' wanna lose 'er, Artie. I don' wanna lose 'er an' the children. Wha'm I gonna do?"

"I don't know," said Artie.

"That dirty li'l—" Owen muttered. "Hadn't been for her…"

"Don't blame the silly little slut for this," said Artie. "She's just the icing. You're the one who baked the cake."

"*Wha'm I gonna do?*"

"Well, for one thing, start working at life a little more. It isn't just a play that's taking place in front of you. You're on the stage, you have a part. Either you play it or you're a pawn. No one's going to feed you dialogue or action, Owen. You're on your own. Remember that."

"*I wonder*," Owen said. Then and later in the silence of his hotel room.

A week, two weeks. Listless walks through a Manhattan that was only noise and loneliness. Movies stared at, dinners at the Automat, sleepless nights, the alcoholed search for peace. Finally, the desperate phone call. "Carole, take me back, *please* take me back."

"Oh, darling. *Come home to me.*"

Another cab ride, this time joyous. The porch light burning, the door flung open, Carole running to him. Arms around each other, walking back into their home together.

The Grand Tour! A dizzying whirl of places and events. Misted England in the spring; the broad, the narrow streets of Paris; Spree-bisected Berlin and Rhone-bisected Geneva. Milan of Lombardy, the hundred crumbling-castled islands of Venice, the culture trove of Florence, Marseilles braced against the sea, the Alps-protected Riviera, Dijon the ancient. A second honeymoon, a rush of desperate renewal, half seen, half felt like flashes of uncertain heat in a great, surrounding darkness.

They lay together on the river bank. Sunlight scattered glittering coins across the water, fish stirred idly in the thermal drift. The contents of their picnic basket lay in happy decimation. Carole rested on his shoulder, her breath a warming tickle on his chest.

"*Where has the time all gone to?*" Owen asked; not of her or anyone but to the sky.

"Darling, you sound upset," she said, raising on an elbow to look at him.

"I am," he answered. "Don't you remember the night we saw that picture *A Moment or Forever*? Don't you remember what I said?"

"No."

He told her; of that and of his wish and of the formless dread that sometimes came upon him. "It was just the first part I wanted fast, thought," he said, "*not the whole thing.*"

"Darling, darling," Carole said, trying not to smile, "I guess this must be the curse of having an imagination. Owen, it's been over seven years. *Seven years.*"

He held his watch up. "Or fifty-seven minutes," he said.

Home again. Summer, fall and winter. *Wind from the South* selling to the movies for $100,000; Owen turning down the screenplay offer. The aging mansion overlooking the Sound, the hiring of Mrs. Halsey as their housekeeper. John packed off to military academy, Linda to private school. As a result of the European trip, one blustery afternoon in March, the birth of George.

Another year. Another. Five years, ten. Books assured and flowing from his pen. *Lap of Legends Old*, *Crumbling Satires*, *Jiggery Pokery and The Dragon Fly*. A decade gone, then more. The National Book Award for *No Dying and No Tomb*. The Pulitzer Prize for *Bacchus Night*.

He stood before the window of his paneled office, trying to forget at least a single item of another paneled office he'd been in—that of his publisher the day he'd signed his first contract there. But he could forget nothing; not a single detail would elude him. As if, instead of twenty-three years before, it had been yesterday. How could he recall it all so vividly unless, actually—

"*Dad*?" He turned and felt a frozen trap jaw clamp across his heart. John strode across the room. "I'm going now," he said.

"What? *Going*?" Owen stared at him; at this tall stranger, at this young man in military uniform who called him Dad.

"Old Dad," laughed John. He clapped his father's arm. "Are you dreaming up another book?"

Only then, as if cause followed effect, Owen knew. Europe raged with war again and John was in the army, ordered overseas. He stood there, staring at his son, speaking with a voice not his; watching the seconds rush away. Where had *this* war come from? What vast and awful machinations had brought it into being? *And where was his little boy?* Surely he was not this stranger shaking hands with him and saying his goodbyes. The trap jaw tightened. Owen whimpered.

But the room was empty. He blinked. Was it all a dream, all flashes in an ailing mind? On leaden feet, he stumbled to the window and watched the taxi swallow up his son and drive away with him. "Goodbye," he whispered, "God protect you."

No one feeds you dialogue, he thought; but was that *he* who spoke?

The bell had rung and Carole answered it. Now, the handle of his office door clicked once and she was standing there, face bloodless, staring at him, in her hand the telegram. Owen felt his breath stop.

"*No*," he murmured; then, gasping, started up as, soundlessly, Carole swayed and crumpled to the floor.

"At least a week in bed," the doctor told him. "Quiet; lots of rest. The shock is most severe."

He shambled on the dunes; numbed, expressionless. Razored winds cut through him, whipped his clothes and lashed his gray-streaked hair to threads. With lightless eyes, he marked the course of foam-flecked waves across the Sound. Only yesterday that John went off to war, he thought; only yesterday he came home proudly rigid in his academy uniform; only yesterday he was in shorts and grammar school; only yesterday he thundered through the house leaving his wake of breathless laughter; only yesterday that he was born when winds whipped powdery snow across—

"Dear God!" Dead. *Dead*! Not twenty-one and *dead*; all his life a moment passed, a memory already slipping from the mind.

"*I take it back!*" Terrified, he screamed it to the rushing sky. "I take it back, I never meant it?" He lay there, scraping at the sand, weeping for his boy yet wondering if he ever had a boy at all.

"*Attendez, M'sieus, M'dames! Nice!*"

"Oh my, already?" Carole said. "That was quick now, children, wasn't it?"

Owen blinked. He looked at her; at this portly, gray-haired woman across the aisle from him. She smiled. She *knew* him?

"What?" he asked.

"Oh, why do I talk to you?" she grumbled. "You're always in your thoughts, your thoughts." Hissing, she stood and drew a wicker basket from the rack. *Was this some game*?

"Gee, Dad, look at *that*!"

He gaped at the teenaged boy beside him. And who was *he*? Owen Crowley shook his head a little. He looked around him. *Nice*? In France again? What about the war?

The train plunged into blackness. "Oh, *damn*!" snapped Linda. On Owen's other side she struck her match again and, in the flare, he saw, reflected in the window, the features of another middle-aged stranger and it was himself. The present flooded over him. The war over and he and his family abroad: Linda, twenty-two, divorced, bitter, slightly alcoholic: George, fifteen, chubby, flailing in the glandular limbo between women and erector sets; Carole, forty-six, newly risen from the sepulcher of menopause, pettish, somewhat bored; and he himself, forty-nine, successful, coldly handsome, still wondering if life were made of years or seconds. All this passing through his mind before Riviera sunlight flooded into their compartment again.

Out on the terrace it was darker, cooler. Owen stood there, smoking, looking at the spray of diamond pinpoints in the sky. Inside, the murmuring of gamblers was like a distant, insect hum.

"Hello, Mr. Crowley."

She was in the shadows, palely gowned; a voice, a movement.

"You know my name?" he asked.

"But you're famous," was her answer.

Awareness fluttered in him. The straining flattery of club women had turned his stomach more than once. But then she'd glided from the darkness and he saw her face and all awareness died. Moonlight creamed her arms and shoulders; it was incandescent in her eyes.

"My name is Alison," she said. "Are you glad to meet me?"

The polished cruiser swept a banking curve into the wind, its bow slashing at the waves, flinging up a rainbowed mist across them. "You little idiot!" he laughed. "You'll drown us yet!"

"You and I!" she shouted back. "Entwining under fathoms! I'd *love* that, wouldn't you?"

He smiled at her and touched her thrill-flushed cheek. She kissed his palm and held him with her eyes. *I love you.* Soundless; a movement of her lips. He turned his head and looked across the sun-jeweled Mediterranean. Just keep going on, he thought. Never turn. Keep going till the ocean swallows us. *I won't go back.*

Alison put the boat on automatic drive, then came up behind him, sliding warm arms around his waist, pressing her body to his. "You're off again," she murmured. "Where are you, darling?"

He looked at her. "How long have we known each other?" he asked.

"A moment, forever, it's all the same," she answered, teasing at his ear lobe with her lips.

"A moment or forever," he murmured. "Yes."

"What?" she asked.

"Nothing," he said. "Just brooding on the tyranny of clocks."

"Since time is so distressing to you, love," she said, pushing open the cabin door, "let's not waste another second of it."

The cruiser hummed across the silent sea.

"What, *hiking*?" Carole said. "At *your* age?"

"Though it may disturb you," Owen answered, tautly. "I, at least, am not yet prepared to surrender to the stodgy blandishments of old age."

"So I'm senile now!" she cried.

"*Please*," he said.

"She thinks you're *old*?" said Alison. "Good God, how little that woman knows you!"

Hikes, skiing, boat rides, swimming, horseback riding, dancing till sun dispersed the night. Him telling Carole he was doing research for a novel; not knowing if she believed him; not, either, caring much. Weeks and weeks of stalking the elusive dead.

He stood on the sun-drenched balcony outside Alison's room. Inside, ivory-limbed, she slept like some game-worn child. Owen's body was exhausted, each inadequate muscle pleading for surcease; but, for the moment, he was not thinking about that. He was wondering about something else; a clue that had occurred to him when he was lying with her.

In all his life, it seemed as if there never was a clear remembrance of physical love. Every detail of the moments leading to the act were vivid but the act itself was not. Equally so, all memory of his ever having cursed aloud was dimmed, uncertain.

And these were the very things that movies censored.

"Owen?" Inside, he heard the rustle of her body on the sheets. There was demand in her voice again; honeyed but authoritative. He turned. Then let me *remember* this, he thought. Let every second of it be with me; every detail of its fiery exaction, its flesh-born declarations, its drunken, sweet derangement. Anxiously, he stepped through the doorway.

Afternoon. He walked along the shore, staring at the mirror-flat blueness of the sea. It was true then. There was no distinct remembrance of it. From the second he'd gone through the doorway until now, all was a virtual blank. Yes, *true*! He knew it now. Interims were void; time was rushing him to his script-appointed end. He was a player, yes, as Artie said, but the play had already been written.

He sat in the dark train compartment, staring out the window. Far below slept moon-washed Nice and Alison; across the aisle slept George and Linda, grumbled Carole in a restless sleep. How angry they had been at his announcement of their immediate departure for home.

And now, he thought, and *now*. He held his watch up and marked the posture of its luminous hands. *Seventy-four minutes.*

How much left?

"You know, George," he said, "when I was young—and not so young—I nursed a fine delusion. I thought my life was being run out like a motion picture. It was never certain, mind you, only nagging doubt but it dismayed me; oh, indeed it did. Until, one day—a little while ago—it came to me that everyone has an uncontrollable aversion to the inroads of mortality. Especially old ones like myself, George. How we are inclined to think that time has, somehow, tricked us, making us look the other way a moment while, low unguarded, it rushes by us, bearing on its awful, tracking shoulders, our lives."

"I can see that," said George and lit his pipe again.

Owen Crowley chuckled: "George, George," he said. "Give full humor to your nutty sire. He'll not be with you too much longer."

"Now stop that talk," said Carole, knitting by the fire. "Stop that silly talk."

"Carole?" he called. "My dear?" Wind from the Sound obscured his trembling voice. He looked around. "Here, *you*! *Here*!"

The nurse primped mechanically at his pillow. She chided, "Now, now, Mr. Crowley. You mustn't tire yourself."

"Where's my wife? For pity's sake go fetch her. I can't—"

"Hush now, Mr. Crowley, don't start in again."

He stared at her; at this semi-mustached gaucherie in white who fussed and wheedled. "What?" he murmured. "*What*?" Then something drew away the veil and he knew. Linda was getting her fourth divorce, shuttling between her lawyer's office and the cocktail lounges; George was a correspondent in Japan, a brace of critic-feted books to his name. And Carole, Carole?

Dead.

"No," he said, quite calmly. "No, no, that's not true. I tell you, fetch her. Oh, there's a pretty thing." He reached out for the falling leaf.

The blackness parted; it filtered into unmarked grayness. Then his room appeared, a tiny fire in the grate, his doctor by the bed consulting with the nurse; at the foot of it, Linda standing like a sour wraith.

Now, thought Owen. Now was just about the time. His life, he thought, had been a brief engagement; a flow of scenes across what cosmic retina? He thought of John, of Linda Carson, of Artie, of Morton Zuckersmith and Cora; of George and Linda and Alison; of Carole; of the legioned people who had passed him during his performance. They were all gone, almost faceless now.

"What…time?" he asked.

The doctor drew his watch. "Four-oh-eight," he said, "a.m."

Of course. Owen smiled. He should have known it all along. A dryness in his throat thinned the laugh to a rasping whisper. They stood there, staring at him.

"Eighty-five minutes," he said. "A good length. Yes; *a good length*."

Then, just before he closed his eyes, he saw them—letters floating in the air, imposed across their faces and the room. And they were words but words seen in a mirror, white and still.

THE END

Or was it just imagination?
Fadeout.

"Mantage" was first published in **Science Fiction Showcase** *(Curtis Books, 1959), edited by Cyril Kornbluth.*

"Do you know the cinematic term which ends with '-age?' It's called 'montage.' I just thought: what if this guy discovers—as he got older and older—that his entire life was really a montage. That he remembered important events from his life, but the time sequence of them

was not clear at all. He wondered which events really happened—or was he just part of a movie? I guess that was the original idea: that this man's entire life was a montage in a movie. And even when he was dying, the length of his life was the same length in years as the minutes in the length of a perfect movie's running time." —RM

NO SUCH THING
AS A VAMPIRE
1959

IN THE EARLY AUTUMN of the year 18—Madame Alexis Gheria awoke one morning to a sense of utmost torpor. For more than a minute, she lay inertly on her back, her dark eyes staring upward. How wasted she felt. It seemed as if her limbs were sheathed in lead. Perhaps she was ill, Petre must examine her and see.

Drawing in a faint breath, she pressed up slowly on an elbow. As she did, her nightdress slid, rustling, to her waist. How had it come unfastened? She wondered, looking down at herself.

Quite suddenly, Madame Gheria began to scream.

In the breakfast room, Dr. Petre Gheria looked up, startled, from his morning paper. In an instant, he had pushed his chair back, slung his napkin on the table and was rushing for the hallway. He dashed across its carpeted breadth and mounted the staircase two steps at a time.

It was a near hysterical Madame Gheria he found sitting on the edge of her bed looking down in horror at her breasts. Across the dilated whiteness of them, a smear of blood lay drying.

Dr. Gheria dismissed the upstairs maid, who stood frozen in the open doorway, gaping at her mistress. He locked the door and hurried to his wife.

"Petre!" she gasped.

"Gently." He helped her lie back across the blood-stained pillow.

"Petre, what *is* it?" she begged.

"Lie still, my dear." His practiced hands moved in swift search over her breasts. Suddenly, his breath choked off. Pressing aside her head, he stared down dumbly at the pinprick lancinations on her neck, the ribbon of tacky blood that twisted downward from them.

"My *throat*," Alexis said.

"No, it's just a—" Dr. Gheria did not complete the sentence. He knew exactly what it was.

Madame Gheria began to tremble. "Oh, my God, my *God*," she said.

Dr. Gheria rose and foundered to the washbasin. Pouring in water, he returned to his wife and washed away the blood. The wound was clearly visible now—two tiny punctures close to the jugular. A grimacing Dr. Gheria touched the mounds of inflamed tissue in which they lay. As he did, his wife groaned terribly and turned her face away.

"Now listen to me," he said, his voice apparently calm. "We will not succumb, immediately, to superstition, do you hear? There are any number of—"

"I'm going to die," she said.

"Alexis, do you hear me?" He caught her harshly by the shoulders.

She turned her head and stared at him with vacant eyes. "You know what it is," she said.

Dr. Gheria swallowed. He could still taste coffee in his mouth.

"I know what it appears to be," he said, "and we shall—not ignore the possibility. However—"

"I'm going to die," she said.

"Alexis!" Dr. Gheria took her hand and gripped it fiercely. "*You shall not be taken from me*," he said.

Solta was a village of some thousand inhabitants situated in the foothills of Rumania's Bihor Mountains. It was a place of dark traditions.

People, hearing the bay of distant wolves, would cross themselves without a thought. Children would gather garlic buds as other children gather flowers, bringing them home for the windows. On every door there was a painted cross, at every throat a metal one. Dread of the vampire's blighting was as normal as the dread of fatal sickness. It was always in the air.

Dr. Gheria thought about that as he bolted shut the windows of Alexis' room. Far off, molten twilight hung above the mountains. Soon it would be dark again. Soon the citizens of Solta would be barricaded in their garlic-reeking houses. He had no doubt that every soul of them knew exactly what had happened to his wife. Already the cook and upstairs maid were pleading for discharge. Only the inflexible discipline of the butler, Karel, kept them at their jobs. Soon, even that would not suffice. Before the horror of the vampire, reason fled.

He'd seen the evidence of it that very morning when he'd ordered Madame's room stripped to the walls and searched for rodents or venomous insects. The servants had moved about the room as if on a floor of eggs, their eyes more white than pupil, their fingers twitching constantly to their crosses. They had known full well no rodent or insects would be found. And Gheria had known it. Still, he'd raged at them for their timidity, succeeding only in frightening them further.

He turned from the window with a smile.

"There now," said he, "nothing alive will enter this room tonight."

He caught himself immediately, seeing the flare of terror in her eyes.

"Nothing at *all* will enter," he amended.

Alexis lay motionless on her bed, one pale hand at her breast, clutching at the worn silver cross she'd taken from her jewel box. She hadn't worn it since he'd given her the diamond-studded one when they were married. How typical of her village background that, in this moment of dread, she should seek protection from the unadorned cross of her church. She was such a child. Gheria smiled down gently at her.

"You won't be needing that, my dear," he said, "you'll be safe tonight."

Her fingers tightened on the crucifix.

"No, no, wear it if you will," he said. "I only meant that I'll be at your side all night."

"You'll stay with me?"

He sat on the bed and held her hand.

"Do you think I'd leave you for a moment?" he said.

Thirty minutes later, she was sleeping. Dr. Gheria drew a chair beside the bed and seated himself. Removing his glasses, he massaged the bridge of his nose with the thumb and forefinger of his left hand. Then, sighing, he began to watch his wife. How incredibly beautiful she was. Dr. Gheria's breath grew strained.

"There is no such thing as a vampire," he whispered to himself.

There was a distant pounding. Dr. Gheria muttered in his sleep, his fingers twitching. The pounding increased; an agitated voice came swirling from the darkness. "Doctor!" it called.

Gheria snapped awake. For a moment, he looked confusedly towards the locked door.

"Dr. Gheria?" demanded Karel.

"What?"

"Is everything all right?"

"Yes, everything is—"

Dr. Gheria cried out hoarsely, springing for the bed. Alexis' nightdress had been torn away again. A hideous dew of blood covered her chest and neck.

Karel shook his head.

"Bolted windows cannot hold away the creature, sir," he said.

He stood, tall and lean, beside the kitchen table on which lay the cluster of silver he'd been polishing when Gheria had entered.

"The creature has the power to make itself a vapor which can pass through any opening however small," he said.

"But the cross!" cried Gheria. "It was still at her throat—untouched! Except by—blood," he added in a sickened voice.

"This I cannot understand," said Karel, grimly. "The cross should have protected her."

"But why did I see nothing?"

"You were drugged by its mephitic presence," Karel said. "Count yourself fortunate that you were not also attacked."

"I do not count myself fortunate!" Dr. Gheria struck his palm, a look of anguish on his face. "What am I to do, Karel?" he asked.

"Hang garlic," said the old man. "Hang it at the windows, at the doors. Let there be no opening unblocked by garlic."

Gheria nodded distractedly. "Never in my life have I seen this thing," he said, brokenly. "Now, my own wife—"

"I have seen it," said Karel. "I have, myself, put to its rest one of these monsters from the grave."

"The stake—?" Gheria looked revolted.

The old man nodded slowly.

Gheria swallowed. "Pray God you may put this one to rest as well," he said.

"Petre?"

She was weaker now, her voice a toneless murmur. Gheria bent over her. "Yes, my dear," he said.

"It will come again tonight," she said.

"No." He shook his head determinedly. "It cannot come. The garlic will repel it."

"My cross didn't," she said, "you didn't."

"The garlic will," he said. "And see?" He pointed at the bedside table. "I've had black coffee brought for me. I won't sleep tonight."

She closed her eyes, a look of pain across her sallow features.

"I don't want to die," she said. "Please don't let me die, Petre."

"You won't," he said. "I promise you; the monster shall be destroyed."

Alexis shuddered feebly. "But if there is no way, Petre," she murmured.

"There is always a way," he answered.

Outside the darkness, cold and heavy, pressed around the house. Dr. Gheria took his place beside the bed and began to wait. Within the hour, Alexis slipped into a heavy slumber. Gently, Dr. Gheria released her hand and poured himself a cup of steaming coffee. As he sipped it hotly, bitter, he looked around the room. Door locked, windows bolted, every opening sealed with garlic, the cross at Alexis' throat. He nodded slowly to himself. It will work, he thought. The monster would be thwarted.

He sat there, waiting, listening to his breath.

Dr. Gheria was at the door before the second knock.

"Michael!" He embraced the younger man. "Dear Michael, I was sure you'd come!"

Anxiously, he ushered Dr. Vares towards his study. Outside darkness was just falling.

"Where on earth are all the people of the village?" asked Vares. "I swear, I didn't see a soul as I rode in."

"Huddling, terror-stricken, in their houses," Gheria said, "and all my servants with them save for one."

"Who is that?"

"My butler, Karel," Gheria answered. "He didn't answer the door because he's sleeping. Poor fellow, he is very old and has been doing the work of five." He gripped Vares' arm. "Dear Michael," he said, "you have no idea how glad I am to see you."

Vares looked at him worriedly. "I came as soon as I received your message," he said.

"And I appreciate it," Gheria said. "I know how long and hard a ride it is from Cluj."

"What's wrong?" asked Vares. "Your letter only said—"

Quickly, Gheria told him what had happened in the past week.

"I tell you, Michael, I stumble at the brink of madness," he said. "Nothing works! Garlic, wolfsbane, crosses, mirrors, running water—useless! No, don't say it! This isn't superstition nor imagination! This is *happening*! A vampire is destroying her! Each day she sinks yet deeper into that—deadly torpor from which—"

Gheria clinched his hands. "And yet I cannot understand it."

"Come, sit, sit." Doctor Vares pressed the older man into a chair, grimacing at the pallor of him. Nervously, his fingers sought for Gheria's pulse beat.

"Never mind me," protested Gheria. "It's Alexis we must help." He pressed a sudden, trembling hand across his eyes. "Yet how?" he said.

He made no resistance as the younger man undid his collar and examined his neck.

"You, too," said Vares, sickened.

"What does that matter?" Gheria clutched at the younger man's hand. "My friend, my dearest friend," he said, "tell me that it is not I! Do *I* do this hideous thing to her?"

Vares looked confounded. "*You*?" he said. "But—"

"I know, I know," said Gheria. "I, myself, have been attacked. Yet nothing follows, Michael! What breed of horror is this which cannot be impeded? From what unholy place does it emerge? I've had the countryside examined foot by foot, every graveyard ransacked, every crypt inspected! There is no house within the village that has not yet been subjected to my search. I tell you, Michael, there is nothing! Yet, there is something—something which assaults us nightly, draining us of life. The village is engulfed by terror—and I as well! I never see this creature, never hear it! Yet, every morning, I find my beloved wife—"

Vares's face was drawn and pallid now. He stared intently at the older man.

"What am I to do, my friend?" pleaded Gheria. "How am I to save her?"

Vares had no answer.

"How long has she—been like this?" asked Vares. He could not remove his stricken gaze from the whiteness of Alexis' face.

"For many days," said Gheria. "The retrogression has been constant."

Dr. Vares put down Alexis' flaccid hand. "Why did you not tell me sooner?" he asked.

"I thought the matter could be handled," Gheria answered, faintly. "I know now that it—cannot."

Vares shuddered. "But, surely—" he began.

"There is nothing left to be done," said Gheria. "Everything has been tried, *everything*!" He stumbled to the window and stared out bleakly into the deepening night. "And now it comes again," he murmured, "and we are helpless before it."

"Not helpless, Petre." Vares forced a cheering smile to his lips and laid his hand upon the older man's shoulder. "I will watch her tonight."

"It's useless."

"Not at all, my friend," said Vares, nervously. "And now you must sleep."

"I will not leave her," said Gheria.

"But you need rest."

"I cannot leave," said Gheria. "I will not be separated from her."

Vares nodded. "Of course," he said. "We will share the hours of watching then."

Gheria sighed. "We can try," he said, but there was no sound of hope in his voice.

Some twenty minutes later, he returned with an urn of steaming coffee which was barely possible to smell through the heavy mist of garlic fumes which hung in the air. Trudging to the bed, Gheria set down the tray. Dr. Vares had drawn a chair up beside the bed.

"I'll watch first," he said. "You sleep, Petre."

"It would do no good to try," said Gheria. He held a cup beneath the spigot and the coffee gurgled out like smoking ebony.

"Thank you," murmured Vares as the cup was handed to him. Gheria nodded once and drew himself a cupful before he sat.

"I do not know what will happen to Solta if this creature is not destroyed," he said. "The people are paralyzed by terror."

"Has it—been elsewhere in the village?" Vares asked him.

Gheria sighed exhaustedly. "Why need it go elsewhere?" he said. "It is finding all it—craves within these walls." He stared despondently at Alexis. "When we are gone," he said, "it will go elsewhere. The people know that and are waiting for it."

Vares set down his cup and rubbed his eyes.

"It seems impossible," he said, "that we, practitioners of a science, should be unable to—"

"What can science effect against it?" said Gheria. "Science which will not even admit its existence? We could bring, into this very room, the foremost scientists of the world and they would say—my friends, you have been deluded. There is no vampire. All is mere trickery."

Gheria stopped and looked intently at the younger man. He said, "Michael?"

Vares' breath was slow and heavy. Putting down his cup of untouched coffee, Gheria stood and moved to where Vares sat slumped in his chair. He pressed back an eyelid, looked down briefly at the sightless pupil, then withdrew his hand. The drug was quick, he thought. And most effective. Vares would be insensible for more than time enough.

Moving to the closet, Gheria drew down his bag and carried it to the bed. He tore Alexis's nightdress from her upper body and, within seconds, had drawn another syringe full of her blood; this would be the last withdrawal, fortunately. Staunching the wound, he took the syringe to Vares and emptied it into the young man's mouth, smearing it across his lips and teeth.

That done, he strode to the door and unlocked it. Returning to Vares, he raised and carried him into the hall. Karel would not awaken; a small amount of opiate in his food had seen to that. Gheria labored down the steps beneath the weight of Vares' body. In the darkest corner of the cellar, a wooden casket waited for the younger man. There he would lie until the following morning when the distraught Dr. Petre Gheria would, with sudden inspiration, order Karel to search the attic and cellar on the remote, nay fantastic possibility that—

Ten minutes later, Gheria was back in the bedroom checking Alexis's pulse beat. It was active enough; she would survive. The pain and torturing horror she had undergone would be punishment enough for her. As for Vares—

Dr. Gheria smiled in pleasure for the first time since Alexis and he had returned from Cluj at the end of the summer. Dear spirits in heaven, would it not be sheer enchantment to watch old Karel drive a stake through Michael Vares' damned cuckolding heart!

*"No Such Thing as a Vampire" was first published in **Playboy**, October 1959.*

*"In those days, the only things that editor Ray Russell would publish of mine were horror stories with surprise endings. So for him, this was the perfect **Playboy** story. Dan Curtis later used it in one of his three-part movies of the week. Curtis and I were always trying to put together these three-part movies to get a television series going. We never got a weekly series, but as I recall the story came*

out fine in that movie. I was usually pleased with whatever Dan did of mine." —RM

*Adapted by the author for a segment of **Dead of Night**, first broadcast on March 29, 1977. It starred Patrick Macnee and was directed by Dan Curtis.*

FROM
HARLAN ELLISON

When I reached page 108 of the Summer 1950 issue of *The Magazine of Fantasy & Science Fiction*, I was fifteen years old, maybe just turned sixteen. I read the title of the story that began on that page, it was "Born of Man and Woman"; and I read the name of the author, it was Richard Matheson.

It was a short piece, the author's first published effort, according to the editorial note. But when I finished reading, this is *exactly* how I felt:

Empty.

I was suspended in darkness, looking straight down into an abyss that fell away beneath me without shape or limit. Not as though I were lying out face-down across the mouth of a well, or a pit, or a mineshaft, but as if I had been miraculously made weightless, had been transported in an instant without any sense of having moved, to find myself floating in deepest space, turning, turning, and staring down into a darkness empty even of the faintest scintillance. It was the void, indeed.

I had been trying to write. I had been doing up my little sophomoric stories and had been sending them out. What had been coming back was, I'm certain, the sound of the wind between the stars. It was the void, indeed.

And now I had read this *first sale* from this name I had never encountered before, and it was—do you understand what I'm trying to *say* here—it was his *first* sale, for godsake. And I was as empty as any cicada husk. I turned slowly in the abyss and saw how far away in darkness it all lay. Impossibly beyond my grasp, forever denied me; the thing I most wanted. To be able to write like that. No better, just that wonderfully.

A year later, in the back of an issue of *Startling Stories*, Matheson had a short piece called "Witch War" and again I had the *frisson*, but not quite as severely. I'd read several of his stories between "Born of Man and Woman" and "Witch War", including one of his most well-known, most often-reprinted killers, "Third From the Sun" (which blew everyone away when it first appeared), but they had only been terrific and original and memorable. They hadn't destroyed me. Then came "Witch War" and I looked down into emptiness again. Not for as long, and not as intensely this time—no Cheyne-Stokes breathing—but long and painfully enough to remind me of the previous infarct.

Well, I recovered. I became and stayed a writer. And in time got over the paralysis that followed in the wake of discovering Matheson.

But the feeling swallows its own tail, and here I come thirty-five years later, to set down a few words about Richard Matheson. In 1950 I could never had dreamed such an impertinent dream. Matheson was, and is, and continues to be, a giant to those of us who look for the perfect beacon. He is the writer of whose work one finds oneself most often saying, "God, I wish I'd written that."

"Duel", "To Fit the Crime", "Little Girl Lost", "Shipshape Home" and "Steel"…the novels and "The Splendid Source"…all those segments of *The Twilight Zone* and…

I have known Richard Matheson personally for more than twenty years. Not as closely as I might wish, but that can never be. Because he does a thing, through his work, that sets him apart from the rest of us trying as hard as we can to put it all down precisely and with passion; he does a thing that a few writers can do.

He humbles us with his brilliance.

And that is why he is loved, respected, and the object of our curses.

—*Harlan Ellison*

CRICKETS
1960

AFTER SUPPER, they walked down to the lake and looked at its moon-reflecting surface.

"Pretty, isn't it?" she said.

"Mmm-hmm."

"It's been a nice vacation."

"Yes, it has," he said.

Behind them, the screen door on the hotel porch opened and shut. Someone started down the gravel path towards the lake. Jean glanced over her shoulder.

"Who is it?" asked Hal without turning.

"That man we saw in the dining room," she said.

In a few moments, the man stood nearby on the shoreline. He didn't speak or look at them. He stared across the lake at the distant woods.

"Should we talk to him?" whispered Jean.

"I don't know," he whispered back.

They looked at the lake again and Hal's arm slipped around her waist.

Suddenly the man asked:

"Do you hear them?"

"Sir?" said Hal.

The small man turned and looked at them. His eyes appeared to glitter in the moonlight.

"I asked if you heard them," he said.

There was a brief pause before Hal asked, "Who?"

"The crickets."

The two of them stood quietly. Then Jean cleared her throat. "Yes, they're nice," she said.

"*Nice?*" The man turned away. After a moment, he turned back and came walking over to them.

"My name is John Morgan," he said.

"Hal and Jean Galloway," Hal told him and then there was an awkward silence.

"It's a lovely night," Jean offered.

"It would be if it weren't for them," said Mr. Morgan. "The crickets."

"Why don't you like them?" asked Jean.

Mr. Morgan seemed to listen for a moment, his face rigid. His gaunt throat moved. Then he forced a smile.

"Allow me the pleasure of buying you a glass of wine," he said.

"Well—" Hal began.

"Please." There was a sudden urgency in Mr. Morgan's voice.

The dining hall was like a vast shadowy cavern. The only light came from the small lamp on their table which cast up formless shadows of them on the walls.

"Your health," said Mr. Morgan, raising his glass.

The wine was dry and tart. It trickled in chilly drops down Jean's throat, making her shiver.

"So what about the crickets?" asked Hal.

Mr. Morgan put his glass down.

"I don't know whether I should tell you," he said. He looked at them carefully. Jean felt restive under his surveillance and reached out to take a sip from her glass.

Suddenly, with a movement so brusque that it made her hand

twitch and spill some wine, Mr. Morgan drew a small, black notebook from his coat pocket. He put it on the table carefully.

"There," he said.

"What is it?" asked Hal.

"A code book," said Mr. Morgan.

They watched him pour more wine into his glass, then set down the bottle and the bottle's shadow on the table cloth. He picked up the glass and rolled its stem between his fingers.

"It's the code of the crickets," he said.

Jean shuddered. She didn't know why. There was nothing terrible about the words. It was the way Mr. Morgan had spoken them.

Mr. Morgan leaned forward, his eyes glowing in the lamp-light.

"Listen," he said. "They aren't just making indiscriminate noises when they rub their wings together." He paused. *They're sending messages*," he said.

Jean felt as if she were a block of wood. The room seemed to shift balance around her, everything leaning towards her.

"Why are you telling us?" asked Hal.

"Because now I'm sure," said Mr. Morgan. He leaned in close. "Have you ever really listened to the crickets?" he asked. "I mean really? If you had you'd have heard a rhythm to their noises. A pace—a definite beat.

"I've listened," he said. "For seven years I've listened. And the more I listened the more I became convinced that their noise was a code; that they were sending messages in the night.

"Then—about a week ago—I suddenly heard the pattern. It's like Morse code only, of course, the sounds are different."

Mr. Morgan stopped talking and looked at his black notebook.

"And there it is," he said. "After seven years of work, here it is. I've deciphered it."

His throat worked convulsively as he picked up his glass and emptied it with a swallow.

"Well—what are they saying?" Hal asked, awkwardly.

Mr. Morgan looked at him.

"Names," he said. "Look, I'll show you."

He reached into one of his pockets and drew out a stubby pencil. Tearing a blank page from his notebook, he started to write on it, muttering to himself.

"Pulse, pulse—silence—pulse, pulsepulse—silence—pulse—silence—"

Hal and Jean looked at each other. Hal tried to smile but couldn't. Then they were looking back at the small man bent over the table, listening to the crickets and writing.

Mr. Morgan put down the pencil. "It will give you some idea," he said, holding out the sheet to them. They looked at it.

MARIE CADMAN, it read. JOHN JOSEPH ALSTER. SAMUEL—

"You see," said Mr. Morgan. "Names."

"Whose?" Jean had to ask it even though she didn't want to.

Mr. Morgan held the book in a clenching hand.

"*The names of the dead*," he answered.

Later that night, Jean climbed into bed with Hal and pressed close to him. "I'm cold," she murmured.

"You're scared."

"Aren't you?"

"Well," he said, "if I am, it isn't in the way you think."

"How's that?"

"I don't believe what he said. But he might be a dangerous man. That's what I'm afraid of."

"Where'd he get those names?"

"Maybe they're friends of his," he said. "Maybe he got them from tombstones. He might have just made them up." He grunted softly. "But I don't think the crickets told him," he said.

Jean snuggled against him.

"I'm glad you told him we were tired," she said. "I don't think I could have taken much more."

"Honey," he said, "here that nice little man was giving us the lowdown on crickets and you disparage him."

"Hal," she said, "I'll never be able to enjoy crickets for the rest of my life."

They lay close to each other and slept. And, outside in the still darkness, crickets rubbed their wings together until morning came.

Mr. Morgan came rapidly across the dining room and sat down at their table.

"I've been looking for you all day," he said. "You've got to help me."

Hal's mouth tightened. "Help you how?" he asked, putting down his fork.

"They know I'm on to them," said Mr. Morgan. "They're after me."

"Who, the crickets?" Hal asked, jadedly.

"I don't know," said Mr. Morgan. "Either them or—"

Jean held her knife and fork with rigid fingers. For some reason, she felt a chill creeping up her legs.

"Mr. Morgan." Hal was trying to sound patient.

"Understand me," Mr. Morgan pleaded. "The crickets are under the command of the dead. The dead send out these messages."

"Why?"

"They're compiling a list of all their names," said Mr. Morgan. "They keep sending the names through the crickets to let the others know."

"*Why?*" repeated Hal.

Mr. Morgan's hands trembled. "I don't know, I don't know," he said. "Maybe when there are enough names, when enough of them are ready, they'll—" His throat moved convulsively. "*They'll come back*," he said.

After a moment, Hal asked, "What makes you think you're in any danger?"

"Because while I was writing down more names last night," said Mr. Morgan, "*they spelled out my name*."

Hal broke the heavy silence.

"What can we do?" he asked in a voice that bordered on uneasiness.

"Stay with me," said Mr. Morgan, "so they can't get me."

Jean looked nervously at Hal.

"I won't bother you," said Mr. Morgan. "I won't even sit here, I'll sit across the room. Just so I can see you."

He stood up quickly and took out his notebook.

"Will you watch this?" he asked.

Before they could say another word, he left their table and walked across the dining room, weaving in and out among the white-clothed tables. About fifty feet from them, he sat down, facing them.

They saw him reach forward and turn on the table lamp.

"What do we do now?" asked Jean.

"We'll stay here a little while," said Hal. "Nurse the bottle along. When it's empty, we'll go to bed."

"Do we have to stay?"

"Honey, who knows what's going on in that mind of his? I don't want to take any chances."

Jean closed her eyes and exhaled wearily. "What a way to polish off a vacation," she said.

Hal reached over and picked up the notebook. As he did, he became conscious of the crickets rasping outside. He flipped through the pages. They were arranged in alphabetical order, on each page three letters with their pulse equivalents.

"He's watching us," said Jean.

"Forget him."

Jean leaned over and looked at the notebook with him. Her eyes moved over the arrangements of dots and dashes.

"You think there's anything to this?" she asked.

"Let's hope not," said Hal.

He tried to listen to the crickets' noise and find some point of comparison with the notes. He couldn't. After several minutes, he shut the book.

When the wine bottle was empty, Hal stood. "Beddy-bye," he said.

Before Jean was on her feet, Mr. Morgan was halfway to their table. "You're leaving?" he asked.

"Mr. Morgan, it's almost eleven," Hal said. "We're tired. I'm sorry but we have to go to bed."

The small man stood wordless, looking from one to the other with pleading, hopeless eyes. He seemed about to speak, then his narrow shoulders slumped and his gaze dropped to the floor. They heard him swallowing.

"You'll take care of the book?" he asked.

"Don't you want it?"

"No." Mr. Morgan turned away. After a few paces, he stopped and glanced back across his shoulder. "Could you leave your door open so I can—call?"

"All right, Mr. Morgan," he said.

A faint smile twitched Mr. Morgan's lips.

"Thank you," he said and walked away.

It was after four when the screaming woke them. Hal felt Jean's fingers clutching at his arm as they both jolted to a sitting position, staring into the darkness.

"*What is it?*" gasped Jean.

"I don't know." Hal threw off the covers and dropped his feet to the floor.

"Don't leave me!" said Jean.

"Come on then!"

The hall had a dim bulb burning overhead. Hal sprinted over the floorboards towards Mr. Morgan's room. The door to it was closed although it had been left open before. Hal banged his fist on it. "Mr. Morgan!" he called.

Inside the room, there was a sudden, rustling, crackling sound—like that of a million, wildly shaken tambourines. The noise made Hal's hand jerk back convulsively from the door knob.

"What's *that?*" Jean asked in a terrified whisper.

He didn't answer. They stood immobile, not knowing what to do. Then, inside, the noise stopped. Hal took a deep breath and pushed open the door.

The scream gagged in Jean's throat.

Lying in a pool of blood-splotched moonlight was Mr. Morgan, his skin raked open as if by a thousand tiny razor blades. There was a gaping hole in the window screen.

Jean stood paralyzed, a fist pressed against her mouth while Hal moved to Mr. Morgan's side. He knelt down beside the motionless man and felt at Mr. Morgan's chest where the pajama top had been sliced to ribbons. The faintest of heartbeats pulsed beneath his trembling fingers.

Mr. Morgan opened his eyes. Wide, staring eyes that recognized nothing, that looked right through Hal.

"P-H-I-L-I-P M-A-X-W-E-L-L." Mr. Morgan spelled out the name in a bubbling voice.

"M-A-R-Y G-A-B-R-I-E-L," spelled Mr. Morgan, eyes stark and glazed.

His chest lurched once. His eyes widened.

"J-O-H-N M-O-R-G-A-N," he spelled.

Then his eyes began focusing on Hal. There was a terrible rattling in his throat. As though the sounds were wrenched from him one by one by a power beyond his own, he spoke again.

"H-A-R-O-L-D G-A-L-L-O-W-A-Y," he spelled, "J-E-A-N G-A-L-L-O-W-A-Y."

Then they were alone with a dead man. And outside in the night, a million crickets rubbed their wings together.

*"Crickets" was first published in **Shock**, May 1960.*

"I got that idea one night at the Hollywood Bowl when I heard these crickets. And I thought, 'Geez, what if they were sending messages?' So that was the basis of the story. A man finds out their secret, and then because he's blown the whistle on them, it gets him killed. Classic paranoia once again. Always—always paranoia. That's why I stopped writing short stories in 1970, because I had just run paranoia into the ground. At least to my taste." —RM

DAY OF
RECKONING
1960

Dₑₐᵣ Pₐ:

I am sending you this note under Rex's collar because I got to stay here. I hope this note gets to you all right.

I couldn't deliver the tax letter you sent me with because the Widow Blackwell is killed. She is upstairs. I put her on her bed. She looks awful. I wish you would get the sheriff and the coroner Wilks.

Little Jim Blackwell, I don't know where he is right now. He is so scared he goes running around the house and hiding from me. He must have got awful scared by whoever killed his ma. He don't say a word. He just runs around like a scared rat. I see his eyes sometimes in the dark and then they are gone. They got no electric power here you know.

I came out toward sundown bringing that note. I rung the bell but there was no answer so I pushed open the front door and looked in.

All the shades was down. And I heard someone running light in the front room and then feet running upstairs. I called around for the Widow but she didn't answer me.

I started upstairs and saw Jim looking down through the banister posts. When he saw me looking at him, he run down the hall and I ain't seen him since.

I looked around the upstairs rooms. Finally, I went in the Widow Blackwell's room and there she was dead on the floor in a puddle of blood. Her throat was cut and her eyes was wide open and looking up at me. It was an awful sight.

I shut her eyes and searched around some and I found the razor. The Widow has all her clothes on so I figure it were only robbery that the killer meant.

Well, Pa, please come out quick with the sheriff and the coroner Wilks. I will stay here and watch to see that Jim don't go running out of the house and maybe get lost in the woods. But come as fast as you can because I don't like sitting here with her up there like that and Jim sneaking around in the dark house.

LUKE

Dear George:

We just got back from your sister's house. We haven't told the papers yet so I'll have to be the one to let you know.

I sent Luke out there with a property tax note and he found your sister murdered. I don't like to be the one to tell you but somebody has to. The sheriff and his boys are scouring the countryside for the killer. They figure it was a tramp or something. She wasn't raped though and, far as we can tell, nothing was stolen.

What I mean more to tell you about is little Jim.

That boy is fixing to die soon from starvation and just plain scaredness. He won't eat nothing. Sometimes, he gulps down a piece of bread or a piece of candy but as soon as he starts to chewing, his face gets all twisted and he gets violent sick and throws up. I don't understand it at all.

Luke found your sister in her room with her throat cut ear to ear. Coroner Wilks says it was a strong, steady hand that done it because the cut is deep and sure. I am terribly sorry to be the one to tell you all this but I think it is better you know. The funeral will be in a week.

Luke and I had a long time rounding up the boy. He was like lightning. He ran around in the dark and squealed like a rat. He showed his teeth at us when we'd corner him with a lantern. His skin is all white and the way he rolls his eyes back and foams at his mouth is something awful to see.

We finally caught him. He bit us and squirmed around like an eel. Then he got all stiff and it was like carrying a two-by-four, Luke said.

We took him into the kitchen and tried to give him something to eat. He wouldn't take a bite. He gulped down some milk like he felt guilty about it. Then, in a second, his face twists and he draws back his lips and the milk comes out.

He kept trying to run away from us. Never a single word out of him. He just squeaks and mutters like a monkey talking to itself.

We finally carried him upstairs to put him to bed. He froze soon as we touched him and I thought his eyes would fall out he opened them so wide. His jaw fell slack and he stared at us like we was boogie men or trying to slice open his throat like his ma's.

He wouldn't go into his room. He screamed and twisted in our hands like a fish. He braced his feet against the wall and tugged and pulled and scratched. We had to slap his face and then his eyes got big and he got like a board again and we carried him in his room.

When I took off his clothes, I got a shock like I haven't had in years, George. That boy is all scars and bruises on his back and chest like someone has strung him up and tortured him with pliers or hot irons or God knows what all. I got a downright chill seeing that. I know they said the widow wasn't the same in her head after her husband died, but I can't believe she done this. It is the work of a crazy person.

Jim was sleepy but he wouldn't shut his eyes. He kept looking around the ceiling and the window and his lips kept moving like he was trying to talk. He was moaning kind of low and shaky when Luke and I went out in the hall.

No sooner did we leave him than he's screaming at the top of his voice and thrashing in his bed like someone was strangling him. We rushed in and I held the lantern high but we couldn't see anything. I thought the boy was sick with fear and seeing things.

Then, as if it was meant to happen, the lantern ran out of oil and all of a sudden we saw white faces staring at us from the walls and ceiling and the window.

It was a shaky minute there, George, with the kid screaming out his lungs and twisting on his bed but never getting up. And Luke trying to find the door and me feeling for a match but trying to look at those horrible faces at the same time.

Finally, I found a match and I got it lit and we couldn't see the faces any more, just part of one on the window.

I sent Luke down to the car for some oil and when he come back we lit the lantern again and looked at the window and saw that the face was painted on it so's to light up in the dark. Same thing for the faces on the walls and the ceiling. It was enough to scare a man half out of his wits to think of anybody doing that inside a little boy's room.

We took him to another room and put him down to bed. When we left him he was squirming in his sleep and muttering words we couldn't understand. I left Luke in the hall outside the room to watch. I went and looked around the house some more.

In the Widow's room I found a whole shelf of psychology books. They was all marked in different places. I looked in one place and it told about a thing how they can make rats go crazy by making them think there is food in a place when there isn't. And another one about how they can make a dog lose its appetite and starve to death by hitting big pieces of pipe together at the same time when the dog is trying to eat.

I guess you know what I think. But it is so terrible I can hardly believe it. I mean that Jim might have got so crazy that he cut her. He is so small I don't see how he could.

You are her only living kin, George, and I think you should do something about the boy. We don't want to put him in an orphan home. He is in no shape for it. That is why I am telling you all about him so you can judge.

There was another thing. I played a record on a phonograph in the boy's room. It sounded like wild animals all making terrible noises and even louder than them was a terrible high laughing.

That is about all, George. We will let you know if the sheriff finds the one who killed your sister because no one really believes that Jim could have done it. I wish you would take the boy and try to fix him up.

Until I hear,

SAM DAVIS

Dear Sam:

I got your letter and am more upset than I can say.

I knew for a long time that my sister was mentally unbalanced after her husband's death, but I had no idea in the world she was gone so far.

You see, when she was a girl she fell in love with Phil. There was never anyone else in her life. The sun rose and descended on her love for him. She was so jealous that, once, because he had taken another girl to a party, she crashed her hands through a window and nearly bled to death.

Finally, Phil married her. There was never a happier couple, it seemed. She did anything and everything for him. He was her whole life.

When Jim was born I went to see her at the hospital. She told me she wished it had been born dead because she knew that the boy meant so much to Phil and she hated to have Phil want anything but her.

She never was good to Jim. She always resented him. And, that day, three years ago, when Phil drowned saving Jim's life, she went out of her mind. I was with her when she heard about it. She ran into the kitchen and got a carving knife and took it running through the streets, trying to find Jim so she could kill him. She finally fainted in the road and we took her home.

She wouldn't even look at Jim for a month. Then she packed up and took him to that house in the woods. Since then I never saw her.

You saw yourself, the boy is terrified of everyone and everything. Except one person. My sister planned that. Step by step she planned it—God help me for never realizing it before. In a whole, monstrous world of horrors she built around that boy she left him trust and need for only one person—*her*. She was Jim's only shield against those horrors. She knew that, when she died, Jim would go completely mad because there wouldn't be anyone in the world he could turn to for comfort.

I think you see now why I say there's isn't any murderer.

Just bury her quick and send the boy to me. I'm not coming to the funeral.

GEORGE BARNES

*"Day of Reckoning" (as "The Faces") was first published in **Ed McBain's Mystery Book #1**, 1960.*

"I just thought it was an interesting idea that a woman hated her child so much for causing the death of her husband that she turns his life into a nightmare. A nightmare in which she was the only one the child could depend on, could count on. And then she'd kill herself and leave him totally alone in the world. A radical revenge.

"I enjoyed writing stories in the form of letters, or in a diary. In a lot of the great old classic stories they almost never were told in the straight third person. It was often someone meets someone on a train, and that stranger on the train is the person who tells the story." —RM

FIRST
ANNIVERSARY
1960

JUST BEFORE HE LEFT the house on Thursday morning, Adeline asked him, "Do I still taste sour to you?"

Norman looked at her reproachfully.

"Well, do I?"

He slipped his arms around her waist and nibbled at her throat.

"Tell me now," said Adeline.

Norman looked submissive.

"Aren't you going to let me live it down?" he asked.

"Well, you *said* it, darling. And on our first anniversary, too!"

He pressed his cheek to hers. "So I said it," he murmured. "Can't I be allowed a faux pas now and then?"

"You haven't answered me."

"Do you taste sour? Of course you don't." He held her close and breathed the fragrance of her hair. "Forgiven?"

She kissed the tip of his nose and smiled and, once more, he could only marvel at the fortune which had bestowed on him such a magnificent wife. Starting their second year of marriage, they were still like honeymooners.

Norman raised her face and kissed her.

"Be damned," he said.

"What's wrong? Am I sour again?"

"No." He looked confused. "Now I can't taste you at all."

"Now you can't taste her at all," said Dr. Phillips.

Norman smiled. "I know it sounds ridiculous," he said.

"Well, it's unique, I'll give it that," said Phillips.

"More than you think," added Norman, his smile grown a trifle labored.

"How so?"

"I have no trouble tasting anything else."

Dr. Phillips peered at him awhile before he spoke. "Can you smell her?" he asked then.

"Yes."

"You're sure."

"*Yes*. What's that got to do with—" Norman stopped. "You mean that the senses of taste and smell go together." He said.

Phillips nodded. "If you can smell her, you should be able to taste her."

"I suppose," said Norman, "but I can't."

Dr. Phillips grunted wryly. "Quite a poser."

"No idea?" asked Norman.

"Not offhand," said Phillips, "though I suspect it's allergy of some kind."

Norman looked disturbed.

"I hope I find out soon," he said.

Adeline looked up from her stirring as he came into the kitchen. "What did Dr. Phillips say?"

"That I'm allergic to you."

"He didn't say that," she scolded.

"Sure he did."

"Be serious now."

"He said I have to take some allergy tests."

"He doesn't think it's anything to worry about, does he?" asked Adeline.

"No."

"Oh, good." She looked relieved.

"Good, nothing," he grumbled. "The taste of you is one of the few pleasures I have in life."

"You stop that." She removed his hands and went on stirring. Norman slid his arm around her and rubbed his nose on the back of her neck. "Wish I could taste you," he said. "I like your flavor."

She reached up and caressed his cheek. "I love you," she said.

Norman twitched and made a startled noise.

"What's wrong?" she asked.

He sniffed. "What's that?" He looked around the kitchen. "Is the garbage out?" he asked.

She answered quietly. "Yes, Norman."

"Well, something sure as hell smells awful in here. Maybe—" He broke off, seeing the expression on her face. She pressed her lips together and, suddenly, it dawned on him. "Honey, you don't think I'm saying—"

"Well, *aren't* you?" Her voice was faint and trembling.

"Adeline, come on."

"First, I taste sour. Now—"

He stopped her with a lingering kiss.

"I love you," he said, "understand? I *love* you. Do you think I'd try to hurt you?"

She shivered in his arms. "You *do* hurt me," she whispered.

He held her close and stroked her hair. He kissed her gently on the lips, the cheeks, the eyes. He told her again how much he loved her.

He tried to ignore the smell.

Instantly, his eyes were open and he was listening. He stared up sightlessly into the darkness. Why had he woken up? He turned his head and reached across the mattress. As he touched her, Adeline stirred a little in her sleep.

Norman twisted over on his side and wriggled close to her. He pressed against the yielding warmth of her body, his hand slipping languidly across her hip. He lay his cheek against her back and started drifting downward into sleep again.

Suddenly, his eyes flared open. Aghast, he put his nostrils to her skin and sniffed. An icy barb of dread hooked at his brain; *my God, what's wrong?* He sniffed again, harder. He lay against her, motionless, trying not to panic.

If his senses of taste and smell were atrophying, he could understand, accept. They weren't, though. Even as he lay there, he could taste the acrid flavor of the coffee that he'd drunk that night. He could smell the faint odor of mashed-out cigarettes in the ashtray on his bedside table. With the least effort, he could smell the wool of the blanket over them.

Then *why?* She was the most important thing in his life. It was torture to him that, in bits and pieces, she was fading from his senses.

It had been a favorite restaurant since their days of courtship. They liked the food, the tranquil atmosphere, the small ensemble which played for dining and for dancing. Searching in his mind, Norman had chosen it as the place where they could best discuss this problem. Already, he was sorry that he had. There was no atmosphere that could relieve the tension he was feeling; and expressing.

"What *else* can it be?" he asked, unhappily. "It's nothing physical." He pushed aside his untouched supper. "It's got to be my mind."

"But why, Norman?"

"*If I only knew,*" he answered.

She put her hand on his. "Please don't worry," she said.

"How can I help it?" he asked. "It's a nightmare. I've *lost* part of you, Adeline."

"Darling, don't," she begged, "I can't bear to see you unhappy."

"I *am* unhappy," he said. He rubbed a finger on the table cloth. "And I've just about made up my mind to see an analyst." He looked up. "It's got to be my mind," he repeated. "And—damnit!—I resent it. I want to root it out."

He forced a smile, seeing the fear in her eyes.

"Oh, the hell with it," he said. "I'll go to an analyst; he'll fix me up. Come on, let's dance."

She managed to return his smile.

"Lady, you're just plain gorgeous," he told her as they came together on the dance floor.

"*Oh, I love you so,*" she whispered.

It was in the middle of their dance that the feel of her began to change. Norman held her tightly, his cheek forced close to hers so that she wouldn't see the sickened expression on his face.

"And now it's gone?" finished Dr. Bernstrom.

Norman expelled a burst of smoke and jabbed out his cigarette in the ashtray. "Correct," he said, angrily.

"When?"

"This morning," answered Norman. The skin grew taut across his cheeks. "No taste. No smell." He shuddered fitfully. "And now no sense of touch."

His voice broke. "What's wrong?" he pleaded. "What kind of breakdown *is* this?"

"Not an incomprehensible one," said Bernstrom.

Norman looked at him anxiously. "What then?" he asked. "Remember what I said: it has to do only with my wife. Outside of her—"

"I understand," said Bernstrom.

"*Then what is it?*"

"You've heard of hysterical blindness."

"Yes."

"Hysterical deafness."

"Yes, but—"

"Is there any reason, then, there couldn't be an hysterical restraint of the other senses as well?"

"All right, but why?"

Dr. Bernstrom smiled.

"That, I presume," he said, "is why you came to see me."

Sooner or later, the notion had to come. No amount of love could stay it. It came now as he sat alone in the living room, staring at the blur of letters on a newspaper page.

Look at the facts. Last Wednesday night, he'd kissed her and, frowning, said. "You taste sour, honey." She'd tightened, drawn away. At the time, he'd taken her reaction at its obvious value: she felt insulted. Now, he tried to summon up a detailed memory of her behavior afterward.

Because, on Thursday morning, he'd been unable to taste her at all.

Norman glanced guiltily toward the kitchen where Adeline was cleaning up. Except for the sound of her occasional footsteps, the house was silent.

Look at the facts, his mind persisted. He leaned back in the chair and started to review them.

Next, on Saturday, had come that dankly fetid stench. Granted, she should feel resentment if he'd accused her of being its source. But he hadn't; he was sure of it. He'd looked around the kitchen, asked her if she'd put the garbage out. Yet, instantly, she'd assumed that he was talking about her.

And, that night, when he'd woken up, he couldn't smell her.

Norman closed his eyes. His mind must really be in trouble if he could justify such thoughts. He loved Adeline; needed her. How could he allow himself to believe that *she* was, in any way, responsible for what had happened?

Then, in the restaurant, his mind went on, unbidden, while they were dancing, she'd suddenly felt cold to him. She'd suddenly felt— he could not evade the word—*pulpy*.

And, then, this morning—

Norman flung aside the paper. *Stop it*! Trembling, he stared across the room with angry, frightened eyes. It's *me*, he told himself, me! He wasn't going to let his mind destroy the most beautiful thing in his life. He wasn't going to let—

It was as if he'd turned to stone, lips parted, eyes widened, blank. Then, slowly—so slowly that he heard the delicate crackling of bones in his neck—he turned to look toward the kitchen. Adeline was moving around.

Only it wasn't footsteps he heard.

He was barely conscious of his body as he stood. Compelled, he drifted from the living room and across the dining alcove, slippers noiseless on the carpeting. He stopped outside the kitchen door, his face a mask of something like revulsion as he listened to the sounds she made in moving.

Silence then. Bracing himself, he pushed open the door.

Adeline was standing at the opened refrigerator. She turned and smiled.

"I was just about to bring you—" She stopped and looked at him uncertainly. "Norman?" she said.

He couldn't speak. He stood frozen in the doorway, staring at her.

"Norman, what is it?" she asked.

He shivered violently.

Adeline put down the dish of chocolate pudding and hurried toward him. He couldn't help himself; he shrank back with a tremulous cry, his face twisted, stricken.

"Norman, what's the matter?"

"I don't know," he whimpered.

Again, she started for him, halting at his cry of terror. Suddenly, her face grew hard as if with angry understanding.

"What is it now?" she asked. "I want to know."

He could only shake his head.

"I want to know, Norman!"

"No." Faintly, frightenedly.

She pressed trembling lips together. "I can't take much more of this," she said. "I mean it, Norman."

He jerked aside as she passed him. Twisting around, he watched her going up the stairs, his expression one of horror as he listened to the noises that she made. Jamming palsied hands across his ears, he stood shivering uncontrollably. *It's me!* He told himself again, again; until the words began to lose their meaning—*me, it's me, it's me, it's me!*

Upstairs, the bedroom door slammed shut. Norman lowered his hands and moved unevenly to the stairs. She had to know that he loved her, that he wanted to believe it was his mind. She had to understand.

Opening the bedroom door, he felt his way through the darkness and sat on the bed. He heard her turn and knew that she was looking at him.

"I'm sorry," he said, "I'm...sick."

"No," she said. Her voice was lifeless.

Norman stared at her. "What?"

"There's no problem with other people, our friends, trades-men…" she said. "They don't see me enough. With you, it's differ-ent. We're together too often. The strain of hiding it from you hour after hour, day after day, for a whole year, is too much for me. I've lost the power to control your mind. All I can do is—blank away your senses one by one."

"You're not—"

"—telling you those things are real? I am. They're real. The taste, the smell, the—and what you heard tonight."

He sat immobile, staring at the dark form of her.

"I should have taken all your senses when it started," she said. "It would have been easy then. Now it's too late."

"What are you talking about?" He could barely speak.

"It isn't fair!" cried her voice. "I've been a good wife to you! Why should I have to go back? I *won't* go back! I'll find somebody else. I won't make the same mistake next time!"

Norman jerked away from her and stood on wavering legs, his fingers clutching for the lamp.

"*Don't touch it!*" ordered the voice.

The light flared blindingly into his eyes. He heard a thrashing on the bed and whirled. He couldn't even scream. Sound coagulated in his throat as he watched the shapeless mass rear upward, dripping decay.

"All right!" the words exploded in his brain with the illusion of sound. "All right, then *know* me!"

All his senses flooded back at once. The air was clotted with the smell of her. Norman recoiled, lost balance, fell. He saw the molder-ing bulk rise from the bed and start for him. Then his mind was swal-lowed in consuming blackness and it seemed as if he fled along a night-swept hall pursued by a suppliant voice which kept repeating endlessly, "Please! I don't want to go back! *None of us want to go back*! Love me, let me stay with you! Love me, love me, love me…"

"First Anniversary" was first published in **Playboy**, *July 1960.*

"My characters were always men who were single because when I started writing, I was single. Before I was married, the idea of get-ting married daunted me, and so I had nothing but unsuccessful

marriages in my stories. Then, after I got married, I had successful marriages in my stories—so now it was the couple who got involved in scary situations. And then, after I had children, it was the family who got involved in scary situations. You just use what you know. It's all environmental; either from personality or location." —RM

Adapted by the author's daughter, Ali Marie Matheson, and her husband, Jon Cooksey, for an episode of the cable revival of **The Outer Limits**. *It starred Matt Frewer and was directed by Brad Turner. The episode first aired on February 16, 1996.*

FROM SHADOWED PLACES

1960

Dr. JENNINGS HOOKED in toward the curb, the tires of his Jaguar spewing out a froth of slush. Braking hard, he jerked the key loose with his left hand while his right clutched for the satchel at his side. In a moment, he was on the street, waiting for a breach in traffic.

His gaze leaped upward to the windows of Peter Lang's apartment. Was Patricia all right? She'd sounded awful on the phone—tremulous, near to panic. Jennings lowered his eyes and frowned uneasily at the line of passing cars. Then, as an opening appeared in the procession, he lunged forward.

The glass door swung pneumatically shut behind him as he strode across the lobby. *Father, hurry! Please! I don't know what to do with him!* Patricia's stricken voice re-echoed in his mind. He stepped into the elevator and pressed the tenth-floor button. *I can't tell you on the phone! You've go to come!* Jennings stared ahead with sightless eyes, unconscious of the whispering closure of the doors.

Patricia's three-month engagement to Lang had certainly been a troubled one. Even so, he wouldn't feel justified in telling her to break it off. Lang could hardly be classified as one of the idle rich. True, he'd never had to face a job of work in his entire twenty-seven years. Still, he wasn't indolent or helpless. One of the world's ranking hunter-sportsmen, he handled himself and his chosen world with graceful authority. There was a readily mined vein of humor in him and a sense of basic justice despite his air of swagger. Most of all, he seemed to love Patricia very much.

Still, all this trouble—

Jennings twitched, blinking his eyes into focus. The elevator doors were open. Realizing that the tenth floor had been reached, he lurched into the corridor, shoe heels squeaking on the polished tile. Without thinking, he thrust the satchel underneath his arm and began pulling off his gloves. Before he'd reached the apartment, they were in his pocket and his coat had been unbuttoned.

A penciled note was tacked unevenly to the door. *Come in.* Jennings felt a tremor at the sight of Pat's misshapen scrawl. Bracing himself, he turned the knob and went inside.

He froze in unexpected shock. The living room was a shambles, chairs and tables overturned, lamps broken, a clutter of books hurled across the floor, and, scattered everywhere, a debris of splintered glasses, matches, cigarette butts. Dozens of liquor stains islanded the white carpeting. On the bar, an upset bottle trickled Scotch across the counter edge while, from the giant wall speakers, a steady rasping flooded the room. Jennings stared, aghast. *Peter must have gone insane.*

Thrusting his bag onto the hall table, he shed his hat and coat, then grabbed his bag again, and hastened down the steps into the living room. Crossing to the built-in sound system, he switched it off.

"*Father?*"

"Yes." Jennings heard his daughter sob with relief and hurried towards the bedroom.

They were on the floor beneath the picture window. Pat was on her knees embracing Peter who had drawn his naked body into a heap, arms pressed across his face. As Jennings knelt beside them, Patricia looked at him with terror-haunted eyes.

"He tried to jump," she said. "He tried to kill himself." Her voice was fitful, hoarse.

"All right." Jennings drew away the rigid quiver of her arms and tried to raise Lang's head. Peter gasped, recoiling from his touch, and bound himself again into a ball of limbs and torso. Jennings stared at his constricted form. Almost in horror, he watched the crawl of muscles in Peter's back and shoulders. Snakes seemed to writhe beneath the sun-darkened skin.

"How long has he been like this?" he asked.

"I don't know." Her face was a mask of anguish. "I don't know."

"Go in the living room and pour yourself a drink," her father ordered, "I'll take care of him."

"He tried to jump right through the window."

"*Patricia.*"

She began to cry and Jennings turned away; tears were what she needed. Once again, he tried to uncurl the inflexible knot of Peter's body. Once again, the young man gasped and shrank away from him.

"Try to relax," said Jennings, "I want to get you on your bed."

"*No!*" said Peter, his voice a pain-thickened whisper.

"I can't help you, boy, unless—"

Jennings stopped, his face gone blank. In an instant, Lang's body had lost its rigidity. His legs were straightening out, his arms were slipping from their tense position at his face. A stridulous breath swelled out his lungs.

Peter raised his head.

The sight made Jennings gasp. If ever a face could be described as tortured, it was Lang's. Darkly bearded, bloodless, stark-eyed, it was the face of a man enduring inexplicable torment.

"What *is* it?" Jennings asked, appalled.

Peter grinned; it was the final, hideous touch that made the doctor shudder. "Hasn't Patty told you?" Peter answered.

"Told me what?"

Peter hissed, apparently amused. "I'm being hexed," he said. "Some scrawny—"

"Darling, *don't,*" begged Pat.

"What are you talking about?" demanded Jennings.

"Drink?" asked Peter. "Darling?"

Patricia pushed unsteadily to her feet and started for the living room. Jennings helped Lang to his bed.

"What's this all about?" he asked.

Lang fell back heavily on his pillow. "What I said," he answered. "Hexed. Cursed. Witch doctor." He snickered feebly. "Bastard's killing me. Been three months now—almost since Patty and I met."

"Are you—?" Jennings started.

"Codeine ineffectual," said Lang. "Even morphine—got some. Nothing." He sucked in at the air. "No fever, no chills, No symptoms for the AMA. Just—someone killing me." He peered up through slitted eyes. "Funny?"

"*Are you serious?*"

Peter snorted. "Who the hell knows?" he said. "Maybe it's delirium tremens. God knows I've drunk enough today to—" The tangle of his dark hair rustled on the pillow as he looked towards the window. "Hell, it's night," he said. He turned back quickly. "Time?" he asked.

"After ten," said Jennings. "What about—?"

"Thursday, isn't it?" asked Lang.

Jennings stared at him.

"No, I see it isn't." Lang started coughing dryly. "Drink!" he called. As his gaze jumped towards the doorway, Jennings glanced across his shoulder. Patricia was back.

"It's all spilled," she said, her voice like that of a frightened child.

"All right, don't worry," muttered Lang. "Don't need it. I'll be dead soon anyways."

"*Don't talk like that!*"

"Honey, I'd be glad to die right now," said Peter, staring at the ceiling. His broad chest hitched unevenly as he breathed. "Sorry, darling, I don't mean it. Uh-oh, here we go again." He spoke so mildly that his seizure caught them by surprise.

Abruptly, he was floundering on the bed, his muscle-knotted legs kicking like pistons, his arms clamped down across the drumhide tautness of his face. A noise like the shrilling of a violin wavered in his throat, and Jennings saw saliva running from the corners of his mouth. Turning suddenly, the doctor lurched across the room for his bag.

Before he'd reached it, Peter's thrashing body had fallen from the bed. The young man reared up, screaming, on his face the wide-mouthed, slavering frenzy of an animal. Patricia tried to hold him back but, with a snarl, he shoved her brutally aside and staggered for the window.

Jennings met him with the hypodermic. For several moments, they were locked in reeling struggle, Peter's distended, teeth-bared face inches from the doctor's, his vein-corded hands scrabbling for Jennings's throat. He cried out hoarsely as the needle pierced his skin and, springing backwards, lost his balance, fell. He tried to stand, his crazed eyes looking towards the window. Then the drug was in his blood and he was sitting with the flaccid posture of a rag doll. Torpor glazed his eyes. "Bastard's killing me," he muttered.

They laid him on the bed and covered up the sluggish twitching of his body.

"Killing me," said Lang. "Black bastard."

"Does he really *believe* this?" Jennings asked.

"Father, *look* at him," she answered.

"You believe it too?"

"*I* don't know." She shook her head impotently. "All I know is that I've seen him change from what he was to—*this*. He isn't sick, father. There's nothing wrong with him." She shuddered. "Yet he's dying."

"Why didn't you call me sooner?"

"I couldn't," she said. "I was afraid to leave him for a second."

Jennings drew his fingers from the young man's fluttering pulse. "Has he been examined at all?"

She nodded tiredly. "Yes," she answered, "when it started getting worse, he went to see a specialist. He thought, perhaps his brain—" She shook her head. "There's nothing wrong with him."

"But why does he say he's being—?" Jennings found himself unable to speak the word.

"*I don't know*," she said. "Sometimes, he seems to believe it. Mostly he jokes about it."

"But on what grounds—?"

"Some incident on his last safari," said Patricia. "I don't really know what happened. Some—Zulu native threatened him; said he was a witch doctor and was going to—" Her voice broke into a wracking sob. "Oh, God, how can such a thing be true? How can it *happen?*"

"The point, I think, is whether Peter, actually, believes it's happening," said Jennings. He turned to Lang. "And, from the look of him—"

"Father, I've been wondering if—" Patricia swallowed. "If maybe Doctor Howell could help him."

Jennings stared at her for a moment. Then he said, "You *do* believe it, don't you?"

"Father, *try to understand.*" There was a trembling undertone of panic in her voice, "You've only seen Peter now and then. I've watched it happening to him almost day by day. Something is destroying him! I don't know what it is, but I'll try anything to stop it. *Anything.*"

"All right." He pressed a reassuring hand against her back. "Go phone while I examine him."

After she'd gone into the living room—the telephone connected in the bedroom had been ripped from the wall—Jennings drew the covers down and looked at Peter's bronzed and muscular body. It was trembling with minute vibrations—as if, within the chemical imprisoning of the drug, each separate nerve still pulsed and throbbed.

Jennings clenched his teeth in vague distress. Somewhere, at the core of his perception, where the rationale of science had yet to filter, he sensed that medical inquiry would be pointless. Still, he felt distaste for what Patricia might be setting up. It went against the grain of learned acceptance. It offended mentality.

It, also, frightened him.

The drug's effect was almost gone now, Jennings saw. Ordinarily, it would have rendered Lang unconscious for six to eight hours. Now—in *forty minutes*—he was in the living room with them, lying on the sofa in his bathrobe, saying, "Patty, it's ridiculous. What good's another doctor going to do?"

"All right then, it's ridiculous!" she said. "What would you *like* for us to do—just stand around and watch you—?" She couldn't finish.

"Shhh." Lang stroked her hair with trembling fingers. "Patty, Patty. Hang on, darling. Maybe I can beat it."

"You're *going* to beat it." Patricia kissed his hand. "It's both of us, Peter. I won't go on without you."

"Don't *you* talk like that." Lang twisted on the sofa. "Oh, Christ, it's starting up again." He forced a smile. "No, I'm all right," he told her, "just—crawly, sort of." His smile flared into a sudden grimace of pain. "So this Doctor Howell is going to solve my problem is he? How?"

Jennings saw Patricia bite her lip. "It's a—*her*, darling," she told Lang.

"Great," he said. He twitched convulsively. "That's what we need. What is she, a chiropractor?"

"She's an anthropologist."

"*Dandy*. What's she going to do, explain the ethnic origins of superstition to me?" Lang spoke rapidly as if trying to outdistance pain with words.

"She's been to Africa," said Pat. "She—"

"So have I," said Peter. "Great place to visit. Just don't screw around with witch doctors." His laughter withered to a gasping cry. "Oh, God, you scrawny, black bastard, if I had you here!" His hands clawed out as if to throttle some invisible assailant.

"I beg your pardon—"

They turned in surprise. A young black woman was looking down at them from the entrance hall.

"There was a card on the door," she said.

"Of course; we'd forgotten." Jennings was on his feet now. He heard Patricia whispering to Lang. "I *meant* to tell you. Please don't be biased." Peter looked at her sharply, his expression even more surprised now. "*Biased*?" he said.

Jennings and his daughter moved across the room.

"Thank you for coming." Patricia pressed her cheek to Dr. Howell's.

"It's nice to see you, Pat," said Dr. Howell. She smiled across Patricia's shoulder at the doctor.

"Had you any trouble getting here?" he asked.

"No, no, the subway never fails me." Lurice Howell unbuttoned her coat and turned as Jennings reached to help her. Pat looked at the overnight bag that Lurice had set on the floor, then glanced at Peter.

Lang did not take his eyes from Lurice Howell as she approached him, flanked by Pat and Jennings.

"Peter, this is Dr. Howell," said Pat. "She and I went to Columbia together. She teaches anthropology at City College."

Lurice smiled. "Good evening," she said.

"Not so very," Peter answered. From the corners of his eyes Jennings saw the way Patricia stiffened.

Dr. Howell's expression did not alter. Her voice remained the same. "And who's the scrawny, black bastard you wish you had here?" she asked.

Peter's face went momentarily blank. Then, his teeth clenched against the pain, he answered, "What's that supposed to mean?"

"A question," said Lurice.

"If you're planning to conduct a seminar on race relations, skip it," muttered Lang, "I'm not in the mood."

"*Peter*."

He looked at Pat through pain-filmed eyes. "What do you want?" he demanded. "You're already convinced I'm prejudiced, so—" He dropped his head back on the sofa arm and jammed his eyes shut. "Jesus, stick a *knife* in me," he rasped.

The straining smile had gone from Dr. Howell's lips. She glanced at Jennings gravely as he spoke. "I've examined him," he told her. "There's not a sign of physical impairment, not a hint of brain injury."

"How could there be?" she answered, quietly. "It's not disease. It's juju."

Jennings stared at her. "You—"

"*There* we go," said Peter, hoarsely. "Now we've got it." He was sitting up again, whitened fingers digging at the cushions. "That's the answer. *Juju*."

"Do you doubt it?" asked Lurice.

"I *doubt* it."

"The way you doubt your prejudice?"

"Oh, Jesus. *God*." Lang filled his lungs with a guttural, sucking noise. "I was hurting and I wanted something to hate so I picked on that lousy savage to—" He fell back heavily. "The hell with it. Think what you like." He clamped a palsied hand across his eyes. "Just let me die. Oh, Jesus, Jesus God, sweet Jesus, *let me die*." Suddenly, he looked at Jennings. "Another shot?" he begged.

"Peter, your heart can't—"

"*Damn* my heart!" Peter's head was rocking back and forth now. "Half strength then! You can't refuse a dying man!"

Pat jammed the edge of a shaking fist against her lips, trying not to cry.

"*Please!*" said Peter.

After the injection had taken effect, Lang slumped back, his face and neck soaked with perspiration. "Thanks," he gasped. His pale lips twitched into a smile as Patricia knelt beside him and began to dry his face with a towel. "Greetings, love," he muttered. She couldn't speak.

Peter's hooded eyes turned to Dr. Howell. "All right, I'm sorry, I apologize," he told her curtly. "I thank you for coming, but I don't believe it."

"Then why is it working?" asked Lurice.

"I don't even know what's happening!" snapped Lang.

"I think you do," said Dr. Howell, an urgency rising in her voice, "and I know, Mr. Lang. Juju is the most fearsome pagan sorcery in the world. Centuries of mass belief alone would be enough to give it terrifying power. It *has* that power, Mr. Lang. You know it does."

"And how do *you* know, Dr. Howell?" he countered.

"When I was twenty-two," she said, "I spent a year in a Zulu village doing field work for my Ph.D. While I was there, the *ngombo* took a fancy to me and taught me almost everything she knew."

"*Ngombo*?" asked Patricia.

"*Witch doctor*," said Peter, in disgust.

"I thought witch doctors were men," said Jennings.

"No, most of them are women," said Lurice. "Shrewd, observant women who work very hard at their profession."

"*Frauds*," said Peter.

Lurice smiled at him. "Yes," she said, "they are. Frauds. Parasites, Loafers. Scaremongers. Still—" Her smile grew hard. "—what do you suppose is making you feel as though a thousand spiders were crawling all over you?"

For the first time since he'd entered the apartment, Jennings saw a look of fear on Peter's face. "*You know that*?" Peter asked her.

"I know everything you're going through," said Dr. Howell. "I've been through it myself."

"*When*?" demanded Lang. There was no derogation in his voice now.

"During that year," said Dr. Howell, "a witch doctor from a nearby village put a death curse on me. Kuringa saved me from it."

"Tell me," said Peter, breaking in on her. Jennings noticed that the young man's breath was quickening. It appalled him to realize that the second injection was already beginning to lose its effect.

"Tell you what?" said Lurice. "About the long-nailed fingers scraping at your insides? About the feeling that you have to pull yourself into a ball in order to crush the snake uncoiling in your belly?"

Peter gaped at her.

"The feeling that your blood has turned to acid?" said Lurice. "That, if you move, you'll crumble because your bones have all been sucked hollow?"

Peter's lips began to shake.

"The feeling that your brain is being eaten by a pack of furry rats? That your eyes are just about to melt and dribble down your cheeks like jelly? That—?"

"That's enough." Lang's body seemed to jolt, he shuddered so spasmodically.

"I only said these things to convince you that I know," said Lurice, "I remember my own pain as if I'd suffered it this morning instead of seven years ago. I can help you if you'll let me, Mr. Lang. Put aside your skepticism. You *do* believe it or it couldn't hurt you, don't you see that?"

"Darling, *please*," said Patricia.

Peter looked at her. Then his gaze moved back to Dr. Howell.

"We mustn't wait much longer, Mr. Lang," she warned.

"All *right*!" He closed his eyes. "All right then, *try*. I sure as hell can't get any worse."

"*Quickly*," begged Patricia.

"Yes." Lurice Howell turned and walked across the room to get her overnight bag.

It was as she picked it up that Jennings saw the look cross her face—as if some formidable complication had just occurred to her. She glanced at them. "Pat," she said.

"*Yes.*"

"Come here a moment."

Patricia pushed up hurriedly and moved to her side. Jennings watched them for a moment before his eyes shifted to Lang. The young man was starting to twitch again. It's *coming*, Jennings thought. *Juju is the most fearsome pagan sorcery in the world—*

"What?"

Jennings glanced at the women. Pat was staring at Dr. Howell in shock.

"I'm sorry," said Lurice, "I should have told you from the start, but there wasn't any opportunity."

Pat hesitated. "It has to be that way?" she asked.

"Yes. It does."

Patricia looked at Peter with a questioning apprehension in her eyes. Abruptly, then, she nodded. "All right," she said, "but *hurry.*"

Without another word, Lurice Howell went into the bedroom. Jennings watched his daughter as she looked intently at the door behind which the black woman had closeted herself. He could not fathom the meaning of her look. For now the fear in Pat's expression was of a different sort.

****

The bedroom door opened and Dr. Howell came out. Jennings, turning from the sofa, caught his breath. Lurice was naked to the waist and garbed below with a skirt composed of several colored handkerchiefs knotted together. Her legs and feet were bare. Jennings gaped at her. The blouse and skirt she'd worn had revealed nothing of her voluptuous breasts, the sinuous abundance of her hips. Suddenly conscious of his blatant observation, Jennings turned his eyes towards Pat. Her expression, as she stared at Dr. Howell, was unmistakable now.

Jennings looked back at Peter. Due to its masking of pain, the young man's face was more difficult to read.

"Please understand, I've never done this before," said Lurice, embarrassed by their staring silence.

"We understand," said Jennings, once more unable to take his eyes from her.

A bright red spot was painted on each of her tawny cheeks and, over her twisted, twine-held hair, she wore a helmet-like plume of feathers, each of a chestnut hue with a vivid white eye at the tip. Her breasts thrust out from a tangle of necklaces made of animals teeth, skeins of brightly colored yarn, beads, and strips of snake skin. On her left arm—banded at the biceps with a strip of angora fleece—was slung a small shield of dappled oxhide.

The contrast between the bag and her outfit was marked enough. The effect of her appearance in the Manhattan duplex created a ripple of indefinable dread in Jennings as she moved towards them with a shy, almost childlike defiance—as if her shame were balanced by a knowledge of her physical wealth. Jennings was startled to see that her stomach was tattooed, hundreds of tiny welts forming a design of concentric circles around her navel.

"Kuringa insisted on it," said Lurice as if he'd asked. "It was her price for teaching me her secrets." She smiled fleetingly. "I managed to dissuade her from filing my teeth to a point."

Jennings sensed that she was talking to hide her embarrassment and he felt a surge of empathy for her as she set her bag down, opened it and started to remove its contents.

"The welts are raised by making small incisions in the flesh," she said, "and pressing into each incision a dab of paste." She put, on the coffee table, a vial of grumous liquid, a handful of small, polished bones. "The paste I had to make myself. I had to catch a land crab with my bare hands and tear off one of its claws. I had to tear the skin from a living frog and the jaw from a monkey." She put on the table a bundle of what looked like tiny lances. "The claws, the skin, and the jaw, together with some plant ingredients, I pounded into the paste."

Jennings looked surprised as she withdrew an LP from the bag and set it on the turntable.

"When I say '*Now*,' Doctor," she asked, "will you put on the turntable arm?"

Jennings nodded mutely, watching her with what was close to fascination. She seemed to know exactly what she was doing. Ignoring the slit-eyed stare of Lang, the uncertain surveillance of Patricia, Lurice set the various objects on the floor. As she squatted,

Pat could not restrain a gasp. Underneath the skirt of handkerchiefs, Lurice's loins were uncovered.

"Well, I may not live," said Peter—his face was almost white now—"but it looks as if I'm going to have a fascinating death."

Lurice interrupted him. "If the three of you will sit in a circle," she said. The prim refinement of her voice coming from the lips of what seemed a pagan goddess struck Jennings forcibly as he moved to assist Lang.

The seizure came as Peter tried to stand. In an instant, he was in the throes of it, groveling on the floor, his body doubled, his knees and elbows thumping at the rug. Abruptly, he flopped over, forcing back his head, the muscles of his spine tensed so acutely that his back arched upward from the floor. Pale foam ribboned from the slash of his mouth, his staring eyes seemed frozen in their sockets.

"Lurice!" screamed Pat.

"There's nothing we can do until it passes," said Lurice. She stared at Lang with sickened eyes. Then, as his bathrobe came undone and he was thrashing naked on the rug, she turned away, her face tightening with a look that Jennings, glancing at her, saw, to his added disquietude, was a look of fear. Then he and Pat were bent across Lang's afflicted body, trying to hold him in check.

"*Let him go*," said Lurice. "There's nothing you can do."

Patricia glared at her in frightened animosity. As Peter's body finally shuddered into immobility, she drew the edges of his robe together and refastened the sash.

"*Now*. Into the circle, quickly," said Lurice, clearly forcing herself against some inner dread. "No, he has to sit alone," she said, as Patricia braced herself beside him, supporting his back.

"He'll *fall*," said Pat, an undercurrent of resentment in her voice.

"Patricia, if you want my help—!"

Uncertainly, her eyes drifting from Peter's pain-wasted features to the harried expression on Lurice's face, Patricia edged away and settled herself.

"Cross-legged, please," said Lurice. "Mr. Lang?"

Peter grunted, eyes half-closed.

"During the ceremony, I'll ask you for a token of payment. Some unimportant personal item will suffice."

Peter nodded. "All right; let's *go*," he said, "I can't take much more."

Lurice's breasts rose, quivering, as she drew in breath. "No talking now," she murmured. Nervously, she sat across from Peter and bowed her head. Except for Lang's stentorian breathing, the room grew deathly still. Jennings could hear, faintly, in the distance, the sounds of traffic. It seemed impossible to adjust his mind to what was about to happen; an attempted ritual of jungle sorcery—in a New York City apartment.

He tried, in vain, to clear his mind of misgivings. He didn't believe in this. Yet here he sat, his crossed legs already beginning to cramp. Here sat Peter Lang, obviously close to death with not a symptom to explain it. Here sat his daughter, terrified, struggling mentally against that which she herself had initiated. And there most bizarre of all, sat—not Dr. Howell, an intelligent professor of anthropology, a cultured, civilized woman—but a near-naked African witch doctor with her implements of barbarous magic.

There was a rattling noise. Jennings blinked his eyes and looked at Lurice. In her left hand, she was clutching the sheaf of what looked like miniature lances. With her right, she was picking up the cluster of tiny, polished bones. She shook them in her palm like dice and tossed them onto the rug, her gaze intent on their fall.

She stared at their pattern on the carpeting, then picked them up again. Across from her, Peter's breath was growing tortured. What if he suffered another attack? Jennings wondered. Would the ceremony have to be restarted?

He twitched as Lurice broke the silence.

"Why do you come here?" she asked. She looked at Peter coldly, almost glaring at him. "Why do you consult me? Is it because you have no success with women?"

"What?" Peter stared at her bewilderedly.

"Is someone in your house sick? Is that why you come to me?" asked Lurice, her voice imperious. Jennings realized abruptly that she was—completely now—a witch doctor questioning her male client, arrogantly contemptuous of his inferior status.

"Are *you* sick?" She almost spat the words, her shoulders jerking back so that her breasts hitched upwards. Jennings glanced involuntarily at his daughter. Pat was sitting like a statue, cheeks pale, lips a narrow, bloodless line.

"Speak up, man!" ordered Lurice—ordered the scowling *ngombo*.

"Yes! I'm sick!" Peter's chest lurched with breath. "I'm *sick*."

"Then speak of it," said Lurice. "Tell me how this sickness came upon you."

Either Peter was in such pain now that any notion of resistance was destroyed—or else he had been captured by the fascination of Lurice's presence. Probably it was a combination of the two, thought Jennings as he watched Lang begin to speak, his voice compelled, his eyes held by Lurice's burning stare.

"One night, this man came sneaking into camp," he said. "He tried to steal some food. When I chased him, he got furious and threatened me. He said he'd kill me." Jennings wondered if Lurice had hypnotized Peter, the young man's voice was so mechanical.

"And he carried, in a sack at his side—" Lurice's voice seemed to prompt like a hypnotist's.

"He carried a doll," said Peter. His throat contracted as he swallowed. "It spoke to me," he said.

"The fetish spoke to you," said Lurice. "What did the fetish say?"

"It said that I would die. It said that, when the moon was like a bow, I would die."

Abruptly, Peter shivered and closed his eyes. Lurice threw down the bones again and stared at them. Abruptly, she flung down the tiny lances.

"It is not Mbwiri nor Hebiezo," she said. "It is not Atando nor Fuofuo nor Sovi. It is not Kundi or Sogbla. It is not a demon of the forest that devours you. It is an evil spirit that belongs to a *ngombo* who has been offended. The *ngombo* has brought evil to your house. The evil spirit of the *ngombo* has fastened itself upon you in revenge for your offense against its master. Do you understand?"

Peter was barely able to speak. He nodded jerkily. "Yes."

"Say—*Yes, I understand*."

"Yes." He shuddered. "Yes. I understand."

"You will pay me now," she told him.

Peter stared at her for several moments before lowering his

eyes. His twitching fingers reached into the pockets of his robe and came out empty. Suddenly, he gasped, his shoulders hitching forward as a spasm of pain rushed through him. He reached into his pockets a second time as if he weren't sure that they were empty. Then, frantically, he wrenched the ring from the third finger of his left hand and held it out. Jennings's gaze darted to his daughter. Her face was like stone as she watched Peter handing over the ring she'd given him.

"*Now*," said Lurice.

Jennings pushed to his feet and, stumbling because of the numbness in his legs, he moved to the turntable and lowered the stylus in place. Before he'd settled back into the circle, the record started playing.

In a moment, the room was filled with drumbeats, with a chanting of voices and a slow, uneven clapping of hands. His gaze intent on Lurice, Jennings had the impression that everything was fading at the edges of his vision, that Lurice, alone, was visible, standing in a dimly nebulous light.

She had left her oxhide shield on the floor and was holding the bottle in her hand. As Jennings watched, she pulled the stopper loose and drank the contents with a single swallow. Vaguely, through the daze of fascination that gripped his mind, Jennings wondered what it was she'd drunk.

The bottle thudded on the floor.

Lurice began to dance.

She started languidly. Only her arms and shoulders moved at first, their restless sinuating timed to the cadence of drumbeats. Jennings stared at her, imagining that his heart had altered its rhythm to that of the drums. He watched the writhing of her shoulders, the serpentine gestures she was making with her arms and hands. He heard the rustling of her necklaces. Time and place were gone for him. He might have been sitting in a jungle glade, watching the somnolent twisting of her dance.

"Clap hands," said the *ngombo*.

Without hesitation, Jennings started clapping in time with the drums. He glanced at Patricia. She was doing the same, her eyes still fixed on Lurice. Only Peter sat motionless, looking straight ahead, the muscles of his jaw quivering as he ground his teeth together. For a fleeting moment, Jennings was a doctor once again, looking at his patient in concern. Then turning back, he was redrawn into the mindless captivation of Lurice's dance.

The drumbeats were accelerating now, becoming louder. Lurice began to move within the circle, turning slowly, arms and shoulders still in undulant motion. No matter where she moved, her eyes remained on Peter, and Jennings realized that her gesturing was exclusively for Lang—drawing, gathering gestures as if she sought to lure him to her side.

Suddenly, she bent over, her breasts dropping heavily, then jerking upward as their muscles caught. She shook herself with feverish abandon, swinging her breasts from side to side and rattling her necklaces, her wild face hovering inches over Peter's. Jennings felt his stomach muscles pulling in as Lurice drew her talon-shaped fingers over Peter's cheeks, then straightened up and pivoted, her shoulders thrust back carelessly, her teeth bared in a grimace of savage zeal. In a moment, she had spun around to face her client again.

A second time she bent herself, this time stalking back and forth in front of Peter with a catlike gait, a rabid crooning in her throat. From the corners of his eyes, Jennings saw his daughter straining forward and he glanced at her. The expression on her face was terrible.

Suddenly, Patricia's lips flared back as in a soundless cry and Jennings looked back quickly at Lurice. His breath choked off. Leaning over, she had clutched her breasts with digging fingers and was thrusting them at Peter's face. Peter stared at her, his body trembling. Crooning again, Lurice drew back. She lowered her hands and Jennings tightened as he saw that she was pulling at the skirt of handkerchiefs. In a moment, it had fluttered to the carpeting and she was back at Peter. It was then that Jennings knew exactly what she'd drunk.

"*No.*" Patricia's venom-thickened voice made him twist around, his heart-beat lurching. She was starting to her feet.

"*Pat!*" he whispered.

She looked at him and, for a moment, they were staring at each other. Then, with a violent shudder, she sank to the floor again and Jennings turned away from her.

Lurice was on her knees in front of Peter now, rocking back and forth and rubbing at her thighs with flattened hands. She couldn't seem to breathe. Her open mouth kept sucking at the air with wheezing noises. Jennings saw perspiration trickling down her cheeks; he saw it glistening on her back and shoulders. No, he thought. The word came automatically, the voicing of some alien dread that seemed to rise up, choking, in him. No. He watched Lurice's hand clutch upwards at her breasts again, proferring them to Peter. *No.* The word was lurking terror in his mind. He kept on staring at Lurice, fearing what was going to happen, fascinated at its possibility. Drumbeats throbbed and billowed in his ears. His heartbeat pounded.

No!

Lurice's hands had clawed out suddenly and torn apart the edges of Lang's robe. Patricia's gasp was hoarse, astounded. Jennings only caught a glimpse of her distorted face before his gaze was drawn back to Lurice. Swallowed by the frenzied thundering of the drums, the howl of chanting voices, the explosive clapping, he felt as if his head were going numb, as if the room were tilting. In a dreamlike haze, he saw Lurice's hands begin to rub at Peter's flesh. He saw a look of nightmare on the young man's face as torment closed a vise around him—torment that was just as much carnality as agony. Lurice moved closer to him. Closer. Now her writhing, sweat-laved body pendulated inches from his own, her hands caressing wantonly.

"Come into me." Her voice was bestial, gluttonous. "Come into me."

"*Get away from him.*" Patricia's guttural warning tore Jennings from entrancement. Jerking around, he saw her reaching for Lurice—who, in that instant, clamped herself on Peter's body.

Jennings lunged at Pat, not understanding why he should restrain her, only sensing that he must. She twisted wildly in his grip, her hot breath spilling on his cheeks, her body violent in rage.

"Get away from him!" she screamed at Lurice. "*Get your hands away from him.*"

"Patricia!"

"Let me *go!*"

Lurice's scream of anguish paralyzed them. Stunned, they watched her flinging back from Peter and collapsing on her back, her legs jerked in, arms flung across her face. Jennings felt a burst of horror in himself. His gaze leaped up to Peter's face. The look of pain had vanished from it. Only stunned bewilderment remained.

"What *is* it?" gasped Patricia.

Jennings's voice was hollow, awed. "*She's taken it away from him,*" he said.

"Oh, my God—" Aghast, Patricia watched her friend.

The feeling that you have to pull yourself into a ball in order to crush the snake uncoiling in your belly. The words assaulted Jennings's mind. He watched the rippling crawl of muscles underneath Lurice's flesh, the spastic twitching of her legs. Across the room, the record stopped and, in the sudden stillness, he could hear a shrill whine quavering in Lurice's throat. *The feeling that your blood has turned to acid, that, if you move, you'll crumble because your bones have all been sucked hollow.* Eyes haunted, Jennings watched her suffering Peter's agony. *The feeling that your brain is being eaten by a pack of furry rats, that your eyes are just about to melt and dribble down your cheeks like jelly.* Lurice's legs kicked out. She twisted onto her back and started rolling on her shoulders. Her legs jerked in until her feet were resting on the carpet. Convulsively, she reared her hips. Her stomach heaved with tortured breath, her swollen breasts lolled from side to side.

"*Peter.*"

Lang tried to shove him aside but Jennings tightened his grip. "*For God's sake—*Peter!"

The noise Lang uttered made Jennings's skin crawl. He clamped his fingers brutally in Peter's hair and jerked him around so that they faced each other.

"Use your mind, man!" Jennings ordered. "Your *mind!*"

Peter blinked. He stared at Jennings with the eyes of a newly awakened man. Jennings pulled his hands away and turned back quickly.

Lurice was lying motionless on her back, her dark eyes staring at the ceiling. With a gasp, Jennings leaned over and pressed a finger underneath her left breast. Her heartbeat was nearly imperceptible. He looked at her eyes again. They had the glassy stare of a corpse. He gaped at them in disbelief. Suddenly, they closed and a protracted, body-wracking shudder passed through Lurice. Jennings watched her, open-mouthed, unable to move. No, he thought. It was impossible. She couldn't be—

"*Lurice!*" he cried.

She opened her eyes and looked at him. After several moments, her lips stirred feebly as she tried to smile.

"It's over now," she whispered.

The car moved along Seventh Avenue, its tires hissing on the slush. Across the seat from Jennings, Dr. Howell slumped, motionless, in her exhaustion. A shamed, remorseful Pat had bathed and dressed her, after which Jennings had helped her to his car. Just before they'd left the apartment, Peter had attempted to thank her, then, unable to find the words, had kissed her hand and turned away in silence.

Jennings glanced at her. "You know," he said, "if I hadn't actually seen what happened tonight, I wouldn't believe it for a moment. I'm still not sure that I do."

"It isn't easy to accept," she said.

Jennings drove in silence for a while before he spoke again. "Dr. Howell?"

"Yes?"

He hesitated. Then he asked, "Why did you do it?"

"If I hadn't," said Lurice, "your future son-in-law would have died before the night was over. You have no idea how close he came."

"Granting that," said Jennings, "what I mean is—why did you deliberately subject yourself to such—abasement?"

"There was no alternative," she answered. "Mr. Lang couldn't possibly have coped with what was happening to him. I could. It was as simple as that. Everything else was—unfortunate necessity."

"And something of a Pandora's box as well," he said.

"I know," she said, "I was afraid of it but there was nothing I could do."

"You told Patricia what was going to happen?"

"No," said Lurice, "I couldn't tell her everything. I tried to brace her for the shock of what was coming but, of course, I had to withhold some of it. Otherwise she might have refused my help—and her fiancé would have died."

"It was the aphrodisiac in that bottle, wasn't it?"

"Yes," she answered, "I had to lose myself. If I hadn't, personal inhibitions would have kept me from doing what was necessary."

"What happened just before the end of it—" Jennings began.

"Mr. Lang's apparent lust for me?" said Lurice. "It was only a derangement of the moment. The sudden extraction of the pain left him, for a period of seconds, without conscious volition. Without, if you will, civilized restraint. It was an animal who wanted me, not a man. You saw that, when you ordered him to use his mind, the lust was controlled."

"But the animal was there," said Jennings, grimly.

"It's always there," she answered. "The trouble is that people forget it."

Minutes later, Jennings parked in front of Dr. Howell's apartment house and turned to her.

"I think we both know how much sickness you exposed—and cured tonight," he said.

"I hope so," said Lurice. "Not for myself but—" She smiled a little. *"Not for myself I make this prayer,"* she recited. "Are you familiar with that?"

"I'm afraid I'm not."

He listened quietly as Dr. Howell recited again. Then, as he started to get out of the car, she held him back. "Please don't," she said, "I'm fine now." Pushing open the door, she stood on the sidewalk. For several moments, they looked at each other. Then Jennings reached over and squeezed her hand.

"Good night, my dear," he said.

Lurice Howell returned his smile. "Good night, Doctor." She closed the door and turned away.

Jennings watched her walk across the sidewalk and enter her apartment house. Then, drawing his car into the street again, he made a U-turn and started back towards Seventh Avenue. As he drove, he began remembering the Countee Cullen poem that Lurice had spoken for him.

> *Not for myself I made this prayer*
> *But for this race of mine*
> *That stretches forth from shadowed places*
> *Dark hands for bread and wine.*

Jennings's fingers tightened on the wheel.

"Use your mind, man," he said. "Your *mind*."

RICHARD MATHESON

"From Shadowed Places" was first published in **The Magazine of Fantasy & Science Fiction**, *October 1960.*

"That was a story in which I spent a lot of effort on the way that it was told, the way it was written. Ordinarily when I had a good idea I just sort of blasted my way right through it—and it seemed to work out in the end. But occasionally, like in 'Dance of the Dead' and with this one, I wanted it to be really well-delineated. It was a story of possession, but also of race prejudice." —RM

NIGHTMARE AT
20,000 FEET
1962

"SEAT BELT, PLEASE," said the stewardess cheerfully as she passed him.

Almost as she spoke, the sign above the archway which led to the forward compartment lit up—FASTEN SEAT BELT—with, below, its attendant caution—NO SMOKING. Drawing in a deep lungful, Wilson exhaled it in bursts, then pressed the cigarette into the armrest tray with irritable stabbing motions.

Outside, one of the engines coughed monstrously, spewing out a cloud of fume which fragmented into the night air. The fuselage began to shudder and Wilson, glancing through the window, saw the exhaust of flame jetting whitely from the engine's nacelle. The second engine coughed, then roared, its propeller instantly a blur of revolution. With a tense submissiveness, Wilson fastened the belt across his lap.

Now all the engines were running and Wilson's head throbbed in unison with the fuselage. He sat rigidly, staring at the seat ahead as the DC-7 taxied across the apron, heating the night with the thundering blast of its exhausts.

At the edge of the runway, it halted. Wilson looked out through the window at the leviathan glitter of the terminal. By late morning, he thought, showered and cleanly dressed, he would be sitting in the office of one more contact discussing one more specious deal the net result of which would not add one jot of meaning to the history of mankind. It was all so damned—

Wilson gasped as the engines began their warm-up race preparatory to takeoff. The sound, already loud, became deafening— waves of sound that crashed against Wilson's ears like club blows. He opened his mouth as if to let it drain. His eyes took on the glaze of a suffering man, his hands drew in like tensing claws.

He started, legs retracting, as he felt a touch on his arm. Jerking aside his head, he saw the stewardess who had met him at the door. She was smiling down at him.

"Are you all right?" he barely made out her words.

Wilson pressed his lips together and agitated his hand at her as if pushing her away. Her smile flared into excess brightness, then fell as she turned and moved away.

The plane began to move. At first lethargically, like some behemoth struggling to overthrow the pull of its own weight. Then with more speed, forcing off the drag of friction.Wilson, turning to the window, saw the dark runway rushing by faster and faster. On the wing edge, there was a mechanical whining as the flaps descended. Then, imperceptibly, the giant wheels lost contact with the ground, the earth began to fall away. Trees flashed underneath, buildings, the darting quicksilver of car lights. The DC-7 banked slowly to the right, pulling itself upward toward the frosty glitter of the stars.

Finally, it leveled off and the engines seemed to stop until Wilson's adjusting ear caught the murmur of their cruising speed. A moment of relief slackened his muscles, imparting a sense of well-being. Then it was gone. Wilson sat immobile, staring at the NO SMOKING sign until it winked out, then, quickly, lit a cigarette. Reaching into the seat-back pocket in front of him, he slid free his newspaper.

As usual, the world was in a state similar to his. Friction in diplomatic circles, earthquakes and gunfire, murder, rape, tornadoes and collisions, business conflicts, gangsterism. God's in his heaven, all's right with the world, thought Arthur Jeffrey Wilson.

Fifteen minutes later, he tossed the paper aside. His stomach felt awful. He glanced up at the signs beside the two lavatories. Both, illuminated, read OCCUPIED. He pressed out his third cigarette since takeoff and, turning off the overhead light, stared out through the window.

Along the cabin's length, people were already flicking out their lights and reclining their chairs for sleep. Wilson glanced at his watch. Eleven-twenty. He blew out tired breath. As he'd anticipated, the pills he'd taken before boarding hadn't done a bit of good.

He stood abruptly as the woman came out of the lavatory and, snatching up his bag, he started down the aisle.

His system, as expected, gave no cooperation. Wilson stood with a tired moan and adjusted his clothing. Having washed his hands and face, he removed the toilet kit from the bag and squeezed a filament of paste across his toothbrush.

As he brushed, one hand braced for support against the cold bulkhead, he looked out through the port. Feet away was the pale blue of the inboard propeller. Wilson visualized what would happen if it were to tear loose and, like a tri-bladed cleaver, come slicing in at him.

There was a sudden depression in his stomach. Wilson swallowed instinctively and got some paste-stained saliva down his throat. Gagging, he turned and spat into the sink, then, hastily, washed out his mouth and took a drink. Dear God, if only he could have gone by train; had his own compartment, taken a casual stroll to the club car, settled down in an easy chair with a drink and a magazine. But there was no such time or fortune in this world.

He was about to put the toilet kit away when his gaze caught on the oilskin envelope in the bag. He hesitated, then, setting the small briefcase on the sink, drew out the envelope and undid it on his lap.

He sat staring at the oil-glossed symmetry of the pistol. He'd carried it around with him for almost a year now. Originally, when he'd thought about it, it was in terms of money carried, protection from holdup, safety from teenage gangs in the cities he had to attend. Yet, far beneath, he'd always known there was no valid reason except one. A reason he thought more of every day. How simple it would be—here, now—

Wilson shut his eyes and swallowed quickly. He could still taste the toothpaste in his mouth, a faint nettling of peppermint on the buds. He sat heavily in the throbbing chill of the lavatory, the oily gun resting in his hands. Until, quite suddenly, he began to shiver without control. God, let me go! His mind cried out abruptly.

"Let me go, *let me go*." He barely recognized the whimpering in his ears.

Abruptly, Wilson sat erect. Lips pressed together, he rewrapped the pistol and thrust it into his bag, putting the briefcase on top of it, zipping the bag shut. Standing, he opened the door and stepped outside, hurrying to his seat and sitting down, sliding the overnight bag precisely into place. He indented the armrest button and pushed himself back. He was a business man and there was business to be conducted on the morrow. It was as simple as that. The body needed sleep, he would give it sleep.

Twenty minutes later, Wilson reached down slowly and depressed the button, sitting up with the chair, his face a mask of vanquished acceptance. Why fight it? he thought. It was obvious he was going to stay awake. So that was that.

He had finished half of the crossword puzzle before he let the paper drop to his lap. His eyes were too tired. Sitting up, he rotated his shoulders, stretching the muscles of his back. Now what? he thought. He didn't want to read, he couldn't sleep. And there were still—he checked his watch—seven to eight hours left before Los Angeles was reached. How was he to spend them? He looked along the cabin and saw that, except for a single passenger in the forward compartment, everyone was asleep.

A sudden, overwhelming fury filled him and he wanted to scream, to throw something, to hit somebody. Teeth jammed together so rabidly it hurt his jaws, Wilson shoved aside the curtains with a spastic hand and stared out murderously through the window.

Outside, he saw the wing lights blinking off and on, the lurid flashes of exhaust from the engine cowlings. Here he was, he thought; twenty-thousand feet above the earth, trapped in a howling shell of death, moving through polar night toward—

Wilson twitched as lightning bleached the sky, washing its false daylight across the wing. He swallowed. Was there going to be a storm? The thought of rain and heavy winds, of the plane a chip in the sea of sky was not a pleasant one. Wilson was a bad flyer. Excess motion always made him ill. Maybe he should have taken another few Dramamines to be on the safe side. And, naturally, his seat was next to the emergency door. He thought about it opening accidentally; about himself sucked from the plane, falling, screaming.

Wilson blinked and shook his head. There was a faint tingling at the back of his neck as he pressed close to the window and stared out. He sat there motionless, squinting. He could have sworn—

Suddenly, his stomach muscles jerked in violently and he felt his eyes strain forward. There was something crawling on the wing.

Wilson felt a sudden, nauseous tremor in his stomach. Dear God, had some dog or cat crawled onto the plane before takeoff and, in some way managed to hold on? It was a sickening thought. The poor animal would be deranged with terror. Yet, how, on the smooth, wind-blasted surface, could it possibly discover gripping places? Surely that was impossible. Perhaps, after all, it was only a bird or—

The lightning flared and Wilson saw that it was a man.

He couldn't move. Stupefied, he watched the black form crawling down the wing. *Impossible*. Somewhere, cased in layers of shock, a voice declared itself but Wilson did not hear. He was conscious of nothing but the titanic, almost muscle-tearing leap of his heart—and of the man outside.

Suddenly, like ice-filled water thrown across him, there was a reaction; his mind sprang for the shelter of explanation. A mechanic had, through some incredible oversight, been taken up with the ship and had managed to cling to it even though the wind had torn his clothes away, even though the air was thin and close to freezing.

Wilson gave himself no time for refutation. Jarring to his feet, he shouted: "Stewardess! Stewardess!" his voice a hollow, ringing sound in the cabin. He pushed the button for her with a jabbing finger.

"*Stewardess!*"

She came running down the aisle, her face tightened with alarm. When she saw the look on his face, she stiffened in her tracks.

"There's a man out there! A man!" cried Wilson

"*What?*" Skin constricted on her cheeks, around her eyes.

"Look, *look!*" Hand shaking, Wilson dropped back into his seat and pointed out the window. "He's crawling on the—"

The words ended with a choking rattle in his throat. There was nothing on the wing.

Wilson sat there trembling. For a while, before he turned back, he looked at the reflection of the stewardess on the window. There was a blank expression on her face.

At last, he turned and looked up at her. He saw her red lips part as though she meant to speak but she said nothing, only placing the lips together again and swallowing. An attempted smile distended briefly at her features.

"I'm sorry," Wilson said. "It must have been a—"

He stopped as though the sentence were completed. Across the aisle a teenage girl was gaping at him with sleepy curiosity.

The stewardess cleared her throat. "Can I get you anything?" she asked.

"A glass of water," Wilson said.

The stewardess turned and moved back up the aisle.

Wilson sucked in a long breath of air and turned away from the young girl's scrutiny. He felt the same. That was the thing that shocked him most. Where were the visions, the cries, the pummeling of fists on temples, the tearing out of hair?

Abruptly he closed his eyes. There had been a man, he thought. There had, actually, been a man. That's why he felt the same. And yet, there couldn't have been. He knew that clearly.

Wilson sat with his eyes closed, wondering what Jacqueline would be doing now if she were in the seat beside him. Would she be silent, shocked beyond speaking? Or would she, in the more accepted manner, be fluttering around him, smiling, chattering, pretending that she hadn't seen? What would his sons think? Wilson felt a dry sob threatening in his chest. Oh, God—

Behind him, as he sat with the untouched cup of water in his hand, he heard the muted voices of the stewardess and one of the passengers. Wilson tightened with resentment. Abruptly, he reached down and, careful not to spill the water, pulled out the overnight bag. Unzipping it, he removed the box of sleeping capsules and washed two of them down. Crumpling the empty cup, he pushed it into the seat-pocket in front of him, then, not looking, slid the curtains shut.

There—it was ended. One hallucination didn't make insanity.

Wilson turned onto his right side and tried to set himself against the fitful motion of the ship. He had to forget about this, that was the most important thing. He mustn't dwell on it. Unexpectedly, he found a wry smile forming on his lips. Well, by God, no one could accuse him of mundane hallucinations anyway. When he went at it, he did a royal job. A naked man crawling down a DC-7's wing at twenty-thousand feet—there was a chimera worthy of the noblest lunatic.

The humor faded quickly. Wilson felt chilled. It had been so clear, so vivid. How could the eyes see such a thing when it did not exist? How could what was in his mind make the physical act of seeing work to its purpose so completely? He hadn't been groggy, in a daze—nor had it been a shapeless, gauzy vision. It had been sharply three-dimensional, fully a part of the things he saw which he *knew* were real. That was the frightening part of it. It had not been dreamlike in the least. He had looked at the wing and—

Impulsively, Wilson drew aside the curtain.

He did not know, immediately, if he would survive. It seemed as if all the contents of his chest and stomach were bloating horribly, the excess pushing up into his throat and head, choking away breath, pressing out his eyes. Imprisoned in this swollen mass, his heart pulsed strickenly, threatening to burst its case as Wilson sat, paralyzed.

Only inches away, separated from him by the thickness of a piece of glass, the man was staring at him.

It was a hideously malignant face, a face not human. Its skin was grimy, of a wide-pored coarseness; its nose a squat, discolored lump; its lips misshapen, cracked, forced apart by teeth of a grotesque size and crookedness; its eyes recessed and small—unblinking. All framed by shaggy, tangled hair which sprouted, too in furry tufts from the man's ears and nose, in birdlike down across his cheeks.

Wilson sat riven to his chair, incapable of response. Time stopped and lost its meaning. Function and analysis ceased. All were frozen in an ice of shock. Only the beat of heart went on—alone, a frantic leaping in the darkness. Wilson could not so much as blink. Dull-eyed, breathless, he returned the creature's vacant stare.

Abruptly then, he closed his eyes and his mind, rid of the sight, broke free. It isn't there, he thought. He pressed his teeth together, breath quavering in his nostrils. It isn't there, *it simply is not there.*

Clutching at the armrests with pale-knuckled fingers, Wilson braced himself. There is no man out there, he told himself. It was impossible that there should be a man out there crouching on the wing looking at him.

He opened his eyes—

—to shrink against the seat back with a gagging inhalation. Not only was the man still there but he was grinning. Wilson turned his fingers in and dug the nails into his palms until pain flared. He kept it there until there was no doubt in his mind that he was fully conscious.

Then, slowly, arm quivering and numb, Wilson reached up for the button which would summon the stewardess. He would not make the same mistake again—cry out, leap to his feet, alarm the creature into flight. He kept reaching upward, a tremor of aghast excitement in his muscles now because the man was watching him, the small eyes shifting with the movement of his arm.

He pressed the button carefully once, twice. Now come, he thought. Come with your objective eyes and see what I see—but hurry.

In the rear of the cabin, he heard a curtain being drawn aside and, suddenly, his body stiffened. The man had turned his caliban head to look in that direction. Paralyzed, Wilson stared at him. Hurry, he thought. For God's sake, *hurry*!

It was over in a second. The man's eyes shifted back to Wilson, across his lips a smile of monstrous cunning. Then with a leap, he was gone.

"Yes, sir?"

For a moment, Wilson suffered the fullest anguish of madness. His gaze kept jumping from the spot where the man had stood to the stewardess's questioning face, then back again. Back to the stewardess, to the wing, to the stewardess, his breath caught, his eyes stark with dismay.

"What *is* it?" asked the stewardess.

It was the look on her face that did it. Wilson closed a vise on his emotions. She couldn't possibly believe him. He realized it in an instant.

"I'm—I'm sorry," he faltered. He swallowed so dryly that it made a clicking noise in his throat. "It's nothing. I—apologize."

The stewardess obviously didn't know what to say. She kept leaning against the erratic yawing of the ship, one hand holding on to the back of the seat beside Wilson's, the other stirring limply along the seam of her skirt. Her lips were parted slightly as if she meant to speak but could not find the words.

"Well," she said finally and cleared her throat, "if you—need anything."

"Yes, yes. Thank you. Are we—going into a storm?"

The stewardess smiled hastily. "Just a small one," she said. "Nothing to worry about."

Wilson nodded with little twitching movements. Then, as the stewardess turned away, breathed in suddenly, his nostrils flaring. He felt certain that she already thought him mad but didn't know what to do about it because, in her course of training, there had been no instruction on the handling of passengers who thought they saw small men crouching on the wing.

Thought?

Wilson turned his head abruptly and looked outside. He stared at the dark rise of the wing, the spouting flare of the exhausts, the blinking lights. He'd *seen* the man—to that he'd swear. How could he be completely aware of everything around him—be, in all ways, sane and still imagine such a thing? Was it logical that the mind, in giving way, should, instead of distorting all reality, insert, within the still intact arrangement of details, one extraneous sight?

No, not logical at all.

Suddenly, Wilson thought about war, about the newspaper stories which recounted the alleged existence of creatures in the sky who plagued the Allied pilots in their duties. They called them gremlins, he remembered. Were there, actually, such beings? Did they, truly, exist up here, never falling, riding on the wind, apparently of bulk and weight, yet impervious to gravity?

He was thinking that when the man appeared again.

One second the wing was empty. The next, with an arcing descent, the man came jumping down to it. There seemed no impact. He landed almost fragilely, short, hairy arms outstretched as if for balance. Wilson tensed. Yes, there was knowledge in his look. The man—was he to think of it as a man?—somehow understood that he had tricked Wilson into calling the stewardess in vain. Wilson felt himself tremble with alarm. How could he prove the man's existence to others? He looked around desperately. That girl across the aisle. If he spoke to her softly, woke her up, would she be able to—

No, the man would jump away before she could see. Probably to the top of the fuselage where no one could see him, not even the pilots in their cockpit. Wilson felt a sudden burst of self-condemnation that he hadn't gotten that camera Walter had asked for. Dear Lord, he thought, to be able to take a picture of the man.

He leaned in close to the window. What was the man doing?

Abruptly, darkness seemed to leap away as the wing was chalked with lightning and Wilson saw. Like an inquisitive child, the man was squatted on the hitching wing edge, stretching out his right hand toward one of the whirling propellers.

As Wilson watched, fascinatedly appalled, the man's hand drew closer and closer to the blurring gyre until, suddenly, it jerked away and the man's lips twitched back in a soundless cry. He's lost a finger! Wilson thought, sickened. But, immediately, the man reached forward again, gnarled finger extended, the picture of some monstrous infant trying to capture the spin of a fan blade.

If it had not been so hideously out of place it would have been amusing for, objectively seen, the man, at that moment, was a comic sight—a fairy tale troll somehow come to life, wind whipping at the hair across his head and body, all of his attention centered on the turn of the propeller. How could this be madness? Wilson suddenly thought. What self-revelation could this farcial little horror possibly bestow on him?

Again and again, as Wilson watched, the man reached forward. Again and again jerked back his fingers, sometimes, actually, putting them in his mouth as if to cool them. And, always, apparently checking, he kept glancing back across at his shoulder looking at Wilson. *He knows*, thought Wilson. Knows that this is a game between us. If I am able to get someone else to see him, then he loses. If I am the only witness, then he wins. The sense of faint amusement was gone now. Wilson clenched his teeth. Why in hell didn't the pilots see!

Now the man, no longer interested in the propeller, was settling himself across the engine cowling like a man astride a bucking horse. Wilson stared at him. Abruptly a shudder plaited down his back. The little man was picking at the plates that sheathed the engine, trying to get his nails beneath them.

Impulsively, Wilson reached up and pushed the button for the stewardess. In the rear of the cabin, he heard her coming and, for a second, thought he'd fooled the man, who seemed absorbed with his efforts. At the last moment, however, just before the stewardess arrived, the man glanced over at Wilson. Then, like a marionette jerked upward from its stage by wires, he was flying up into the air.

"Yes?" She looked at him apprehensively.

"Will you—sit down, please?" he asked.

She hesitated. "Well, I—"

"Please."

She sat down gingerly on the seat beside his.

"What is it, Mr. Wilson?" she asked.

He braced himself.

"That man is still outside," he said.

The stewardess stared at him.

"The reason I'm telling you this," Wilson hurried on, "is that he's starting to tamper with one of the engines."

She turned her eyes instinctively toward the window.

"No, no, don't look," he told her. "He isn't there now." He cleared his throat viscidly. "He—jumps away whenever you come here."

A sudden nausea gripped him as he realized what she must be thinking. As he realized what he, himself, would think if someone told him such a story. A wave of dizziness seemed to pass across him and he thought—I *am* going mad!

"The point is this," he said, fighting off the thought. "If I'm not imagining this thing, the ship is in danger."

"Yes," she said.

"I know," he said. "You think I've lost my mind."

"Of course not," she said.

"All I ask is this," he said, struggling against the rise of anger. "Tell the pilots what I've said. Ask them to keep an eye on the wings. If they see nothing—all right. But if they do—"

The stewardess sat there quietly, looking at him. Wilson's hands curled into fists that trembled in his lap.

"*Well?*" he asked.

She pushed to her feet. "I'll tell them," she said.

Turning away, she moved along the aisle with a movement that was, to Wilson, poorly contrived—too fast to be normal yet, clearly, held back as if to reassure him that she wasn't fleeing. He felt his stomach churning as he looked out at the wing again.

Abruptly, the man appeared again, landing on the wing like some grotesque ballet dancer. Wilson watched him as he set to work again, straddling the engine casing with his thick, bare legs and picking at the plates.

Well, what was he so concerned about? thought Wilson. That miserable creature couldn't pry up rivets with his fingernails. Actually, it didn't matter if the pilots saw him or not—at least so far as the safety of the plane was concerned. As for his own personal reasons—

It was at that moment that the man pried up one edge of a plate.

Wilson gasped. "Here, quickly!" he shouted, noticing, up ahead, the stewardess and the pilot coming through the cockpit doorway.

The pilot's eyes jerked up to look at Wilson, then abruptly, he was pushing past the stewardess and lurching up the aisle.

"*Hurry!*" Wilson cried. He glanced out the window in time to see the man go leaping upward. That didn't matter now. There would be evidence.

"What's going on?" the pilot asked, stopping breathlessly beside his seat.

"He's torn up one of the engine plates!" said Wilson in a shaking voice.

"He's what?"

"The man outside!" said Wilson. "I tell you he's—!"

"Mister Wilson, keep your voice down!" ordered the pilot.

Wilson's jaw went slack.

"I don't know what's going on here," said the pilot, "But—"

Drawing in an agitated breath, the pilot bent over. In a moment, his gaze shifted coldly to Wilson's. "Well?" he asked.

Wilson jerked his head around. The plates were in their normal position.

"Oh, now wait," he said before the dread could come. "I saw him pry that plate up."

"Mister Wilson, if you don't—"

"*I said I saw him pry it up*," said Wilson.

The pilot stood there looking at him in the same withdrawn, almost aghast way as the stewardess had. Wilson shuddered violently.

"Listen, I *saw* him!" he cried. The sudden break in his voice appalled him.

In a second, the pilot was down beside him. "Mister Wilson, please," he said. "All right, you saw him. But remember there are other people aboard. We mustn't alarm them."

Wilson was too shaken to understand at first.

"You—mean you've *seen* him then?" he asked.

"Of course," the pilot said, "but we don't want to frighten the passengers. You can understand that."

"Of course, of course. I don't want to—"

Wilson felt a spastic coiling in his groin and lower stomach. Suddenly, he pressed his lips together and looked at the pilot with malevolent eyes.

"I understand," he said.

"The thing we have to remember—" began the pilot.

"You can stop now," Wilson said.

"Sir?"

Wilson shuddered. "Get out of here," he said.

"Mister Wilson, what—?"

"*Will you stop?*" Face whitening, Wilson turned from the pilot and stared out at the wing, eyes like stone.

He glared back suddenly.

"Rest assured I'll not say another word!" he snapped.

"Mr. Wilson, try to understand our—"

Wilson twisted away and stared out venomously at the engine. From a corner of vision, he saw two passengers standing in the aisle looking at him. *Idiots*! his mind exploded. He felt his hands begin to tremble and, for a few seconds, was afraid that he was going to vomit. It's the motion, he told himself. The plane was bucking in the air now like a storm-tossed boat.

He realized that the pilot was still talking to him and, refocusing his eyes, he looked at the man's reflection in the window. Beside him, mutely somber, stood the stewardess. Blind idiots, both of them, thought Wilson. He did not indicate his notice of their departure. Reflected on the window, he saw them heading toward the rear of the cabin. They'll be discussing me now, he thought. Setting up plans in case I grow violent.

He wished now that the man would reappear, pull off the cowling plate and ruin the engine. It gave him a sense of vengeful pleasure to know that only he stood between catastrophe and the more than thirty people aboard. If he chose, he could allow that catastrophe to take place. Wilson smiled without humor. There would be a royal suicide, he thought.

The little man dropped down again and Wilson saw that what he'd thought was correct—the man had pressed the plate back into place before jumping away. For, now, he was prying it up again and it was raising easily, peeling back like skin excised by some grotesque surgeon. The motion of the wing was very broken but the man seemed to have no difficulty staying balanced.

Once more Wilson felt panic. What was he to do? No one believed him. If he tried to convince them any more they'd probably restrain him by force. If he asked the stewardess to sit by him it would be, at best, only a momentary reprieve. The second she departed or, remaining, fell asleep, the man would return. Even if she stayed awake beside him, what was to keep the man from tampering with the engines on the other wing? Wilson shuddered, a coldness of dread misting along his bones.

Dear God, there was nothing to be done.

He twitched as, across the window through which he watched the little man, the pilot's reflection passed. The insanity of the moment almost broke him—the man and the pilot within feet of each other, both seen by him yet not aware of one another. No, that was wrong. The little man had glanced across his shoulder as the pilot passed. As if he knew there was no need to leap off any more, that Wilson's capacity for interfering was at an end. Wilson suddenly trembled with mind-searing rage. I'll kill you! he thought. You filthy little animal, I'll *kill* you!

Outside, the engine faltered.

It lasted only for a second, but, in that second, it seemed to Wilson as if his heart had, also, stopped. He pressed against the window, staring. The man had bent the cowling plate far back and now was on his knees, poking a curious hand into the engine.

"Don't." Wilson heard the whimper of his own voice begging. *"Don't…"*

Again, the engine failed. Wilson looked around in horror. Was everyone deaf? He raised his hand to press the button for the stewardess, then jerked it back. No, they'd lock him up, restrain him somehow. And he was the only one who knew what was happening, the only one who could help.

"God…" Wilson bit his lower lip until the pain made him whimper. He twisted around again and jolted. The stewardess was hurrying down the rocking aisle. She'd heard it! He watched her fixedly and saw her glance at him as she passed his seat.

She stopped three seats down the aisle. Someone else had heard! Wilson watched the stewardess as she leaned over, talking to the unseen passenger. Outside, the engine coughed again. Wilson jerked his head around and looked out with horror-pinched eyes.

"Damn you!" he whined.

He turned again and saw the stewardess coming back up the aisle. She didn't look alarmed. Wilson stared at her with unbelieving eyes. It wasn't possible. He twisted around to follow her swaying movement and saw her turn in at the kitchen.

"No." Wilson was shaking so badly now he couldn't stop. No one had heard.

No one knew.

Suddenly, Wilson bent over and slid his overnight bag out from under the seat. Unzipping it, he jerked out his briefcase and threw it on the carpeting. Then, reaching in again, he grabbed the oilskin envelope and straightened up. From the corners of his eyes, he saw the stewardess coming back and pushed the bag beneath the seat with his shoes, shoving the oilskin envelope beside himself. He sat there rigidly, breath quavering in his chest, as she went by.

Then he pulled the envelope into his lap and untied it. His movements were so feverish that he almost dropped the pistol. He caught it by the barrel, then clutched at the stock with white-knuckled fingers and pushed off the safety catch. He glanced outside and felt himself grow cold.

The man was looking at him.

Wilson pressed his shaking lips together. It was impossible that the man knew what he intended. He swallowed and tried to catch his breath. He shifted his gaze to where the stewardess was handing some pills to the passenger ahead, then looked back at the wing. The man was turning to the engine once again, reaching in. Wilson's grip tightened on the pistol. He began to raise it.

Suddenly, he lowered it. The window was too thick. The bullet might be deflected and kill one of the passengers. He shuddered and stared out at the little man. Again the engine failed and Wilson saw an eruption of sparks cast light across the man's animal features. He braced himself. There was only one answer.

He looked down at the handle of the emergency door. There was a transparent cover over it. Wilson pulled it free and dropped it. He looked outside. The man was still there, crouched and probing at the engine with his hand. Wilson sucked in trembling breath. He put his left hand on the door handle and tested. It wouldn't move downward. Upward there was play.

Abruptly, Wilson let go and put the pistol in his lap. No time for argument, he told himself. With shaking hands, he buckled the belt across his thighs. When the door was opened, there would be a tremendous rushing out of air. For the safety of the ship, he must not go with it.

Now. Wilson picked the pistol up again, his heartbeat staggering. He'd have to be sudden, accurate. If he missed, the man might jump onto the other wing—worse, onto the tail assembly where, inviolate, he could rupture wires, mangle flaps, destroy the balance of the ship. No, this was the only way. He'd fire low and try to hit the man in the chest or stomach. Wilson filled his lungs with air. Now, he thought. *Now*.

The stewardess came up the aisle as Wilson started pulling at the handle. For a moment, frozen in her steps, she couldn't speak. A look of stupefied horror distended her features and she raised one hand as if imploring him. Then, suddenly, her voice was shrilling above the noise of the engines.

"*Mr. Wilson, no!*"

"Get back!" cried Wilson and he wrenched the handle up.

The door seemed to disappear. One second it was by him, in his grip. The next, with a hissing roar, it was gone.

In the same instant, Wilson felt himself enveloped by a monstrous suction which tried to tear him from his seat. His head and shoulders left the cabin and, suddenly, he was breathing tenuous, freezing air. For a moment, eardrums almost bursting from the thunder of the engines, eyes blinded by the artic winds, he forgot the man. It seemed he heard a prick of screaming in the maelstrom that surrounded him, a distant shout.

Then Wilson saw the man.

He was walking across the wing, gnarled from leaning forward, talon-twisted hands outstretched in eagerness. Wilson flung his arm up, fired. The explosion was like a popping in the roaring violence of the air. The man staggered, lashed out and Wilson felt a streak of pain across his head. He fired again at immediate range and saw the man go flailing backward—then, suddenly, disappear with no more solidity than a paper doll swept in a gale. Wilson felt a bursting numbness in his brain. He felt the pistol torn from failing fingers.

Then all was lost in winter darkness.

He stirred and mumbled. There was a warmness trickling in his veins, his limbs felt wooden. In the darkness, he could hear a shuffling sound, a delicate swirl of voices. He was lying, face up, on something—moving, joggling. A cold wind sprinkled on his face, he felt the surface tilt beneath him.

He sighed. The plane was landed and he was being carried off on a stretcher. His head wound, likely, plus an injection to quiet him.

"Nuttiest way of tryin' to commit suicide *I* ever heard of," said a voice somewhere.

Wilson felt the pleasure of amusement. Whoever spoke was wrong, of course. As would be established soon enough when the engine was examined and they checked his wound more closely. Then they'd realize that he'd saved them all.

Wilson slept without dreams.

"Nightmare at 20,000 Feet" was first published in **Alone by Night** *(Ballantine Books, 1962), edited by Michael Congdon & Don Congdon.*

"When I first wrote that, I think the story was something like twenty pages longer at the beginning. I followed him going from his office, to taking a cab, going to the airport—he was analyzing his marriage, his life—the whole thing. I don't recall if I decided or it was one of

*the editors who asked me if I could get into the story sooner, so I just—bang!—put him into the airplane and started from there. It was one of my first **Twilight Zone** scripts that I adapted from one my stories instead of being an original script. I've always been glad that I kept writing prose, because if I had just gone into writing scripts entirely, by now I would have died from a broken heart." —RM*

*Adapted by the author into an episode of **The Twilight Zone**, starring William Shatner. Directed by Richard Donner, it was first telecast on October 11, 1963. It was also adapted by RM as a segment of the feature film **Twilight Zone—The Movie** (1983), starring John Lithgow and directed by George Miller.*

FINGER PRINTS
1962

WHEN I GOT ON THE BUS, the two of them were sitting in the third row on the right-hand side. The small woman in the aisle seat was staring into her lap where her hands were resting limply. The other one was staring out the window. It was almost dark.

There were two empty seats across the aisle from them, so I put my suitcase up on the rack and sat down. The heavy door was pulled shut and the bus pulled out of the depot.

For awhile I contented myself with looking out the window and browsing through a magazine I'd brought with me.

Then I looked over at the two women.

The one on the aisle had dry, flat colored blonde hair. It looked like the wig from a doll that had fallen on the floor and gotten dusty. Her skin was tallow white and her face looked as if it had been formed of this tallow with two fingers, a pinch for the chin, one for the lips, one for the nose, one each for the ears, and finally two savage pokes for her beady eyes.

She was talking with her hands.

I had never seen that before. I'd read about it and I'd seen pictures of the various hand positions that deaf-mutes use for communication, but I'd never actually seen them used.

Her short, colorless fingers moved energetically in the air as though her mind were teeming with interesting things she must say and was afraid to lose. The hands contracted and expanded; they assumed a dozen different shapes in the space of a few moments. She drew the taut hand figures one over the other, pulling and squeezing out her deathly still monologue.

I looked at the other woman.

Her face was thin and weary. She was leaning back on the head rest with her eyes fixed dispassionately on her gesticulating companion. I had never seen such eyes before. They never moved; they were without a glimmer of life. She stared dully at the mute woman and kept nodding her head in an endless jerky motion as if it were on rockers.

Once in a while she'd try to turn away and look out the window or close her eyes. But the moment she did, the other woman would reach out her pudgy right hand and pluck at her dress, tugging at it until her companion was forced to look once more at the endless patterns of shapes created by the white hands.

To me it was phenomenal that it could be understood at all. The hands moved so quickly that I could hardly see them. They were a blur of agitating flesh. But the other woman kept nodding and nodding.

In her soundless way, the deaf-mute woman was a chatterbox.

She wouldn't stop moving her hands. She acted as though she had to keep it up at top speed or perish. It got to a point where I almost could hear what she was talking about, almost could imagine in my mind the splatter of insensate trivia and gossip.

Every once in a while, she seemed to come up with something very amusing to herself, so overpoweringly amusing that she would push her hands away quickly, palms out, as though physically repulsing this outstandingly funny bit of business, lest, in retaining it, she should destroy herself with hilarity.

I must have stared at them a long time, because suddenly they were conscious of it and the two of them were looking at me.

I don't know which of their looks was the more repelling.

The small deaf-mute woman looked at me with her eyes like hard black beads, her buttonlike nose twitching and her mouth arced into a dimpling bowlike smirk, and in her lap her white fingers plucked like leprous bird beaks at the skirt of her flowered dress. It was the look of a hideous life-sized doll somehow come to life.

The other woman's look was one of strange hunger.

Her dark-rimmed eyes ran over my face, then abruptly down over my body, and I saw the shallow rise of her breasts swell suddenly under her dark dress before I turned to the window.

I pretended to look out at the fields, but I could still feel the two of them looking at me steadily.

Then, from the corner of an eye I saw the deaf-mute woman throw up her hands again and begin weaving her silent tapestries of communication. After a few minutes I glanced over at them.

The gaunt woman was watching the hands again in stolid silence. Yes, she nodded wearily, yes, yes, yes.

I fell into a half-sleep, seeing the flashing hands, the rocking head. Yes, yes, yes...

I woke up suddenly, feeling a furtive pluck of fingers on my jacket.

I looked up and saw the deaf-mute woman weaving in the aisle over me. She was tugging at my jacket, trying to pull me up. I stared up at her in sleepy bewilderment.

"What are you doing?" I whispered, forgetting that she couldn't hear.

She kept tugging resolutely and every time the bus passed a street lamp, I could see her pale white face and her dark eyes glittering like jewels set in the waxy flesh.

I had to get up. She kept pulling, and I was so sleepy I couldn't get my mind awake enough to combat her insistent efforts.

As I stood up in the aisle, she plumped down where I had been and drew up her feet so that she covered both seats. I stared down at her uncomprehendingly. Then, as she pretended to be suddenly asleep, I turned and looked at her companion.

She was sitting quietly, looking out the window.

With a lethargic movement I dropped down beside her. Seeing that she was not going to say anything I asked, "Why did your friend do that?"

She turned and looked at me. She was even more gaunt than I had thought. I saw her scrawny throat contract.

"It was her own idea," she said. "I didn't tell her to."

"What idea?" I asked.

She looked more closely at me, and again I saw that look of hunger. It was intense. It burned out from her like an arc of drawing flame. I felt my heart jolt.

"Are you sisters?" I asked for no other reason than to break the silence.

She didn't answer for a moment. Then her face grew tight.

"I'm her companion," she said. "I'm her paid companion."

"Oh," I said, "I guess it—" I forgot what I was going to say.

"You don't have to talk to me," she said. "It was her idea. I didn't tell her to."

We sat in awkward, painful silence, me looking at her groggily, her watching the dark streets pass by. Then she turned and her eyes glittered once from the light of a street lamp.

"She keeps talking all the time," she said.

"What?"

"She keeps talking all the time."

"That's funny," I said awkwardly, "to call it talking, I mean. I mean—"

"I don't see her mouth anymore," she said. "Her hands are her mouth. I can hear her talking with her hands. Her voice is like a squeaky machine." She drew in hurried breath. "God, how she talks," she said.

I sat without speaking, watching her face.

"I never talk," she said. "I'm with her all the time and we never talk because she can't. It's always quiet. I get surprised when I hear people really talking. I get surprised when I hear *myself* really talking. I forget how it is to talk. I feel like I'm going to forget everything I know about talking."

Her voice was jerky and rapid, of indefinite pitch. It plunged from a guttural croak to a thin falsetto, more so since she was trying to speak under her breath. There was mounting unrest in it, too, which I began to feel in myself, as though at any moment something in her was going to explode.

"She never lets me have any time to myself," she said. "She's always with me. I keep telling her I'm leaving. I can talk a little with my hands, too. I tell her I'm going to leave. And she cries and moans around and says she's going to kill herself if I go away. God, it's awful to watch her begging. It makes me sick.

"Then I feel sorry for her and I don't leave. And she's happy as a lark and her father gives me a raise and sends us on another trip to see some of her relatives. Her father hates her. He likes to get rid of her. I hate her, too. But it's like she has some power over us all. We can't argue with her. You can't yell with your hands. And it isn't enough for you to close your eyes and turn away so you can't see her hands anymore."

Her voice grew heavier and I noticed how she kept pressing her palms into her lap as she spoke. The more she pressed down against herself, the harder it was to keep my eyes off her hands. After a while I couldn't stop. Even when I knew she saw me looking I couldn't stop. It was like the complete abandon one feels in a dream, when any desire is allowable.

She kept on talking, her voice trembling a little as she spoke.

"She knows I want to get married," she said. "Any girl wants that. But she won't let me leave her. Her father pays me good and I don't know anything else. Besides, even when I hate her most, I feel sorry for her when she cries and begs. It's not like real crying and real begging. It's so quiet, and all you see are tears running down her cheeks. She keeps begging me until I stay."

Now I felt my own hands trembling in my lap. Somehow her words seemed to mean something more than they said on the surface. It seemed that what was coming grew more and more apparent. But I was hypnotized. With the lights flashing over us in the pitch blackness as the bus sped on through the night, it was like being inextricably bound in some insane nightmare.

"Once she said she'd get me a boyfriend," she said, and I shuddered. "I told her to stop making fun of me, but she said she'd get me a boyfriend. So when we went on a trip to Indianapolis, she went across the aisle in the bus and brought a sailor to talk to me. He was just a boy. He told me he was twenty, but I bet he was eighteen. He was nice though. He sat with me and we talked. At first I was embarrassed and I didn't know what to say. But he was nice, and it was nice talking to him except for *her* sitting across the way."

Instinctively I turned, but the deaf-mute woman seemed to be asleep. Yet I had the feeling that the moment I turned my back, her beady eyes popped open again and refocused on us. "Never mind her," said the woman beside me.

I turned back.

"Do you think it's wrong?" she said suddenly, and I shuddered again as her hot, damp hand closed over mine.

"I—I don't know."

"The sailor was so nice," she said in a heavy voice. "He was so nice. I don't care if she's watching. It doesn't matter, does it? It's dark and she can't really see. She can't hear anything."

I must have drawn back, because her fingers tightened on mine.

"I'm clean," she whined pathetically. "It's not all the time. I only did it with the sailor, I swear I only did. I'm not lying."

As she spoke more and more excitedly, her hand slipped off mine and dropped, quivering, on my leg. It made my stomach lurch. I couldn't move. I guess I didn't want to move. I was paralyzed by the sound of her thickening voice and the flaring sensation of her hand beginning to move over my leg, sensuously caressing.

"*Please*," she said, almost gasping the word.

I tried to say something but nothing came.

"I'm always alone," she said, starting in again. "She won't let me get married because she gets afraid and she doesn't want to let me leave her. It's all right, no one can see us."

Now she was clutching at my leg, digging her hand in fiercely. She put her other hand in my lap and as a blaze of light splashed over us, I saw her mouth as a dark gaping wound, her starved eyes shining.

"You have to," she said, moving closer.

Suddenly, she threw herself against me. Her mouth was burning hot, shaking under mine. Her breath was hot in my throat and her hands were wild and throbbing on my suddenly exposed flesh. Her frail, hot limbs seemed to wrap themselves around me again and again like writhing tentacles. The heat of her body blasted me into submission. I'll never know how the other passengers slept through it. But they didn't all sleep through it. One of them was watching.

Suddenly, the night had chilled; it was over, and she drew back quickly and her dress rustled angrily as she pulled it down like an outraged old lady who has inadvertently exposed her legs. She turned and looked out the window as if I wasn't there any longer. Stupidly, I watched her back rise and fall, feeling drained of strength, feeling as if my muscles had become fluid.

Then, shakily, I adjusted my clothing and struggled up into the aisle. Instantly, the deaf-mute woman jumped up and pushed past me roughly, wide awake. I caught a glimpse of her excited face as she moved.

As I slumped down on the other seat, I looked across the aisle again and saw her stubby white fingers grasping and fluttering, milking greedy questions from the air. And the gaunt woman was nodding and nodding and the deaf woman wouldn't let her turn away.

"Finger Prints" was first published in **The Fiend in You** *(Ballantine Books, 1962), edited by Charles Beaumont.*

"When I first came out to California, all I could afford at the time was to come out on a Greyhound bus, and there was a woman who looked something like that traveling with another woman. She appeared exhausted, and she couldn't talk, but just by using sign language, she just went on and on and the other woman just nodded rarely. So I just added my twist to it, and it worked out pretty well.

"I showed it to Chuck Beaumont, who happened at the time to be putting together an anthology. He liked it—a lot—and so I think it went in that anthology before I ever submitted it to anyone else.

"It's just what I've always liked to do—take simple, real situations, and tweak it a little." —RM

THE LIKENESS
OF JULIE
1962

October

Eddy Foster had never noticed the girl in his English class until that day.

It wasn't because she sat behind him. Any number of times, he'd glanced around while Professor Euston was writing on the blackboard or reading to them from *College Literature*. Any number of times, he'd seen her as he left or entered the classroom. Occasionally, he'd passed her in the hallways or on the campus. Once, she'd even touched him on the shoulder during class and handed him a pencil which had fallen from his pocket.

Still, he'd never noticed her the way he noticed other girls. First of all, she had no figure—or if she did she kept it hidden under loose-fitting clothes. Second, she wasn't pretty and she looked too young. Third, her voice was faint and high-pitched.

Which made it curious that he should notice her that day. All through class, he'd been thinking about the redhead in the first row.

In the theater of his mind he'd staged her—and himself—through an endless carnal play. He was just raising the curtain on another act when he heard the voice behind him.

"Professor?" it asked.

"Yes, Miss Eldridge."

Eddy glanced across his shoulder as Miss Eldridge asked a question about *Beowulf*. He saw the plainness of her little girl's face, heard her faltering voice, noticed the loose yellow sweater she was wearing. And, as he watched, the thought came suddenly to him.

Take her.

Eddy turned back quickly, his heartbeat jolting as if he'd spoken the words aloud. He repressed a grin. What a screwy idea that was. Take *her*? With no figure? With that kid's face of hers?

That was when he realized it was her face which had given him the idea. The very childishness of it seemed to needle him perversely.

There was a noise behind him. Eddy glanced back. The girl had dropped her pen and was bending down to get it. Eddy felt a crawling tingle in his flesh as he saw the strain of her bust against the tautening sweater. Maybe she had a figure after all. That was more exciting yet. A child afraid to show her ripening body. The notion struck dark fire in Eddy's mind.

Eldridge, Julie, read the yearbook. *St. Louis, Arts & Sciences.*

As he'd expected, she belonged to no sorority or organizations. He looked at her photograph and she seemed to spring alive in his imaginations—shy, withdrawn, existing in a shell of warped repressions.

He had to have her.

Why? He asked himself the question endlessly but no logical answer ever came. Still, visions of her were never long out of his mind—the two of them locked in a cabin at the *Hiway Motel*, the wall heater crowding their lungs with oven air while they rioted in each other's flesh; he and this degraded innocent.

The bell had rung and, as the students left the classroom, Julie dropped her books.

"Here, let me pick them up," said Eddy.

"Oh." She stood motionless while he collected them. From the corners of his eyes, he saw the ivory smoothness of her legs. He shuddered and stood with the books.

"Here," he said.

"Thank you." Her eyes lowered and the faintest of color touched her cheeks. She wasn't so bad-looking, Eddy thought. And she did have a figure. Not much of one but a figure.

"What is it we're supposed to read for tomorrow?" he heard himself asking.

"The—'Wife of Bath's Tale', isn't it?" she asked.

"Oh, is that it?" Ask her for a date, he thought.

"Yes. I think so."

He nodded. Ask her now, he thought.

"Well," said Julie. She began to turn away.

Eddy smiled remotely at her and felt his stomach muscles trembling.

"Be seeing you," he said.

He stood in the darkness staring at her window. Inside the room, the light went on as Julie came back from the bathroom. She wore a terrycloth robe and was carrying a towel, a washcloth, and a plastic soap box. Eddy watched her put the washcloth and soap box on her bureau and sit down on the bed. He stood there rigidly, watching her with eyes that did not blink. What was he doing here? he thought. If anybody caught him, he'd be arrested. He had to leave.

Julie stood. She undid the sash at her waist and the bathrobe slipped to the floor. Eddy froze. He parted his lips, sucking at the damp air. She had the body of a woman—full-hipped with breasts that both jutted and hung. And with that pretty child's face—

Eddy felt hot breath forcing out between his lips. He muttered, "*Julie, Julie, Julie—*"

Julie turned away to dress.

The idea was insane. He knew it but he couldn't get away from it. No matter how he tried to think of something else, it kept returning.

He'd invite her to a drive-in movie, drug her coke there, take her to the *Hiway Motel*. To guarantee his safety afterward, he'd take photographs of her and threaten to send them to her parents if she said anything.

The idea was insane. He knew it but he couldn't fight it. He had to do it now—now when she was still a stranger to him; an unknown female with a child's face and a woman's body. That was what he wanted; not an individual.

No! It was insane! He cut his English class twice in succession. He drove home for the weekend. He saw a lot of movies. He read magazines and took long walks. He could beat this thing.

"Miss Eldridge?"

Julie stopped. As she turned to face him, the sun made ripples on her hair. She looked very pretty, Eddy thought.

"Can I walk with you?" he asked.

"All right," she said.

They walked along the campus path.

"I was wondering," said Eddy, "if you'd like to go to the drive in movie Friday night." He was startled at the calmness of his voice.

"Oh," said Julie. She glanced at him shyly. "What's playing?" she asked.

He told her.

"That sounds very nice," she said.

Eddy swallowed. "Good," he answered. "What time shall I pick you up?"

He wondered, later, if it made her curious that he didn't ask her where she lived.

There was a light burning on the porch of the house she roomed in. Eddy pushed the bell and waited, watching two moths flutter around the light. After several moments, Julie opened the door. She looked almost beautiful, he thought. He'd never seen her dressed so well.

"Hello," she said.

"Hi," he answered. "Ready to go?"

"I'll get my coat." She went down the hall and into her room. In there, she'd stood naked that night, her body glowing in the light. Eddy pressed his teeth together. He'd be all right. She'd never tell anyone when she saw the photographs he was going to take.

Julie came back down the hallway and they went out to the car. Eddy opened the door for her.

"Thank you," she murmured. As she sat down, Eddy caught a glimpse of stockinged knees before she pulled her skirt down. He slammed the door and walked around the car. His throat felt parched.

Ten minutes later, he nosed the car onto an empty ramp in the last row of the drive-in theater and cut the engine. He reached outside and lifted the speaker off its pole and hooked it over the window. There was a cartoon playing.

"You want some popcorn and coke?" he asked, feeling a sudden bolt of dread that she might say no.

"Yes. Thank you," Julie said.

"I'll be right back." Eddy pushed out of the car and started for the snack bar. His legs were shaking.

He waited in the milling crowd of students, seeing only his thoughts. Again and again, he shut the cabin door and locked it, pulled the shades down, turned on all the lights, switched on the wall heater. Again and again, he walked over to where Julie lay stupefied and helpless on the bed.

"Yours?" said the attendant.

Eddy started. "Uh—two popcorns and a large and a small coke," he said.

He felt himself begin to shiver convulsively. He couldn't do it. He might go to jail the rest of his life. He paid the man mechanically and moved off with the cardboard tray. The photographs, you idiot, he thought. They're your protection. He felt angry desire shudder through his body. Nothing was going to stop him. On the way back to the car, he emptied the contents of the packet into the small coke.

Julie was sitting quietly when he opened the door and slid back in. The feature had begun.

"Here's your coke," he said. He handed her the small cup with her box of popcorn.

"Thank you," said Julie.

Eddy sat watching the picture. He felt his heart thud slowly like a beaten drum. He felt bugs of perspiration running down his back and sides. The popcorn was dry and tasteless. He kept drinking coke to wet his throat. Soon now, he thought. He pressed his lips together and stared at the screen. He heard Julie eating popcorn, he heard her drinking coke.

The thoughts were coming faster now: the door locked, the shades drawn, the room a bright-lit oven as they twisted on the bed together. Now they were doing things that Eddy almost never thought of—wild, demented things. It was her face, he thought; that damned angel's face of hers. It made the mind seek out every black avenue it could find.

Eddy glanced over at Julie. He felt his hands retract so suddenly that he spilled coke on his trousers. Her empty cup had fallen on the floor, the box of popcorn turned over on her lap. Her head was lying on the seat back and, for one hideous moment, Eddy thought she was dead.

Then she inhaled raspingly and turned her head towards him. He saw her tongue move, dark and sluggish, on her lips.

Suddenly, he was deadly calm again. He picked the speaker off the window and hung it up outside. He threw out the cups and boxes. He started the engine and backed out into the aisle. He turned on his parking lights and drove out of the theater.

Hiway Motel. The sign blinked off and on a quarter of a mile away. For a second, Eddy thought he read *No Vacancy* and he made a frightened sound. Then he saw that he was wrong. He was still trembling as he circled the car around the drive and parked to one side of the office.

Bracing himself, he went inside and rang the bell. He was very calm and the man didn't say a word to him. He had Eddy fill out the registration card and gave him the key.

Eddy pulled his car into the breezeway beside the cabin. He put his camera in the room, then went out and looked around. There was no one in sight. He ran to the car and opened the door. He carried Julie to the cabin door, his shoes crunching quickly on the gravel. He carried her into the dark room and dropped her on the bed.

Then it was his dream coming true. The door was locked. He moved around the room on quivering legs, pulling down the shades. He turned on the wall heater. He found the light switch by the door and pushed it up. He turned on all the lamps and pulled their shades off. He dropped one of them and it rolled across the rug. He left it there. He went over to where Julie lay.

In falling on the bed, her skirt had pulled up to her thighs. He could see the tops of her stockings and the garter buttons fastened to them. Swallowing, Eddy sat down and drew her up into a sitting position. He took her sweater off. Shakily, he reached around her and unhooked her bra; her breasts slipped free. Quickly, he unzipped her skirt and pulled it down.

In seconds, she was naked. Eddy propped her against the pillows, posing her. *Dear God, the body on her.* Eddy closed his eyes and shuddered. *No,* he thought, this is the important part. First get the photographs and you'll be safe. She can't do anything to you then; she'll be too scared. He stood up, tensely, and got his camera. He set the dials. He got her centered on the viewer. Then he spoke.

"Open your eyes," he said.

Julie did.

He was at her house before six the next morning, moving up the alley cautiously and into the yard outside her window. He hadn't slept all night. His eyes felt dry and hot.

Julie was on her bed exactly as he'd placed her. He looked at her a moment, his heartbeat slow and heavy. Then he raked a nail across the screen. "Julie," he said.

She murmured indistinctly and turned onto her side. She faced him now.

"Julie."

Her eyes fluttered open. She stared at him dazedly. "Who's that?" she asked.

"Eddy. Let me in."

"Eddy?"

Suddenly, she caught her breath and shrank back and he knew that she remembered.

"Let me in or you're in trouble," he muttered. He could feel his legs begin to shake.

Julie lay motionless a few seconds, eyes fixed on his. Then she pushed to her feet and weaved unsteadily towards the door. Eddy turned for the alley. He strode down it nervously and started up the porch steps as she came outside.

"What do you want?" she whispered. She looked exciting, half asleep, her clothes and hair all mussed.

"Inside," he said.

Julie stiffened. "No."

"All right, come on," he said, taking her hand roughly. "We'll talk in my car."

She walked with him to the car and, as he slid in beside her, he saw that she was shivering.

"I'll turn on the heater," he said. It sounded stupidly inane. He was here to threaten her, not comfort. Angrily, he started the engine and drove away from the curb.

"Where are we going?" Julie asked.

He didn't know at first. Then, suddenly, he thought of the place outside of town where dating students always parked. It would be deserted at this hour. Eddy felt a swollen tingling in his body and he pressed down on the accelerator. Sixteen minutes later, the car was standing in the silent woods. A pale mist hung across the ground and seemed to lap at the doors.

Julie wasn't shivering now; the inside of the car was hot.

"What is it?" she asked, faintly.

Impulsively, Eddy reached into his inside coat pocket and pulled out the photographs. He threw them on her lap.

Julie didn't make a sound. She just stared down at the photographs with frozen eyes, her fingers twitching as she held them.

"Just in c-ase you're thinking of calling the police," Eddy faltered. He clenched his teeth. *Tell her*! He thought savagely. In a dull, harsh voice, he told her everything he'd done the night before. Julie's face grew pale and rigid as she listened. Her hands pressed tautly at each other. Outside, the mist appeared to rise around the windows like a chalky fluid. It surrounded them.

"You want money?" Julie whispered.

"Take off your clothes," he said. It wasn't his voice, it occurred to him. The sound of it was too malignant, too inhuman.

Then Julie whimpered and Eddy felt a surge of blinding fury boil upward in him. He jerked his hand back, saw it flail out in a blur of movement, heard the sound of it striking her on the mouth, felt the sting across his knuckles.

"*Take them off*!" His voice was deafening in the stifling closeness of the car. Eddy blinked and gasped for breath. He stared dizzily at Julie as, sobbing, she began to take her clothes off. There was a thread of blood trickling from a corner of her mouth. *No, don't*, he heard a voice in his mind. *Don't do this*. It faded quickly as he reached for her with alien hands.

When he got home at ten that morning there was blood and skin under his nails. The sight of it made him violently ill. He lay trembling on his bed, lips quivering, eyes staring at the ceiling. I'm through, he thought. He had the photographs. He didn't have to see her any more. It would destroy him if he saw her any more. Already, his brain felt like rotting sponge, so bloated with corruption that the pressure of his skull caused endless overflow into his thoughts. Trying to sleep, he thought, instead, about the bruises on her lovely body, the ragged scratches, and the bite marks. He heard her screaming in his mind.

He would not see her any more.

December

Julie opened her eyes and saw tiny falling shadows on the wall. She turned her head and looked out through the window. It was beginning to snow. The whiteness of it reminded her of the morning Eddy had first shown her the photographs.

The photographs. That was what had woken her. She closed her eyes and concentrated. They were burning. She could see the prints and negatives scattered on the bottom of a large enamel pan—the kind used for developing film. Bright flames crackled on them and the enamel was smudging.

Julie held her breath. She pushed her mental gaze further—to scan the room that was lit by the flaming enamel pan—until it came to rest upon the broken thing that dangled and swayed, suspended from the closet hook.

She sighed. It hadn't lasted very long. That was the trouble with a mind like Eddy's. The very weakness which made it vulnerable to her soon broke it down. Julie opened her eyes, her ugly child's face puckered in a smile. Well, there were others.

She stretched her scrawny body languidly. Posing at the window, the drugged coke, the motel photographs—these were getting dull by now although that place in the woods was wonderful. Especially in the early morning with the mist outside, the car like an oven. That she'd keep for a while; and the violence of course. The rest would have to go. She'd think of something better next time.

Philip Harrison had never noticed the girl in his Physics class until that day—

*"The Likeness of Julie" (as by "Logan Swanson") was first published in **Alone by Night** (Ballantine Books, 1962), edited by Michael Congdon & Don Congdon.*

"I had two stories in the anthology, which was why I didn't want to use my name twice. I had created the pen name previously to cover some terrible movie script where I told the Writers Guild, 'I don't even want my name on this thing.' And they said, 'Well, you lose the residuals if you have no credit at all,' so that's where I changed my mind and created 'Logan Swanson.' I took the maiden name of my wife's mother, which was Logan, and the maiden name of my mother—and so Logan Swanson.

"I liked this idea of a plain-looking girl—I didn't even know the term 'succubus' at the time I wrote it—managing to lure men into this situation and finally destroy them. And then she would go on—just like 'The Distributor'—to the next location." —RM

*It was later adapted by William F. Nolan as "Julie," a segment of **Trilogy of Terror**, first broadcast on March 4, 1975. Each segment starred Karen Black, and all were directed by Dan Curtis.*

MUTE
1962

THE MAN IN THE DARK RAINCOAT arrived in German Corners at two-thirty that Friday afternoon. He walked across the bus station to a counter behind which a plump, gray-haired woman was polishing glasses.

"Please," he said, "where might I find authority?"

The woman peered through rimless glasses at him. She saw a man in his late thirties, a tall, good-looking man.

"Authority?" she asked.

"Yes—how do you say it? The constable? The—?"

"Sheriff?"

"Ah." The man smiled. "Of course. The sheriff. Where might I find him?"

After being directed, he walked out of the building into the overcast day. The threat of rain had been constant since he'd woken up that morning as the bus was pulling over the mountains into Casca Valley. The man drew up his collar, then slid both hands into the pockets of his raincoat and started briskly down Main Street.

Really, he felt tremendously guilty for not having come sooner; but there was so much to do, so many problems to overcome with his own two children. Even knowing that something was wrong with Holger and Fanny, he'd been unable to get away from Germany until now—almost a year since they'd last heard from the Nielsens. It was a shame that Holger had chosen such an out of the way place for his corner of the four-sided experiment.

Professor Werner walked more quickly, anxious to find out what had happened to the Nielsens and their son. Their progress with the boy had been phenomenal—really an inspiration to them all. Although, Werner felt, deep within himself, that something terrible had happened he hoped they were all alive and well. Yet, if they were, how to account for the long silence?

Werner shook his head worriedly. Could it have been the town? Elkenberg had been compelled to move several times in order to avoid the endless prying—sometimes innocent, more often malicious—into *his* work. Something similar might have happened to Nielsen. The workings of the small town composite mind could, sometimes, be a terrible thing.

The sheriff's office was in the middle of the next block. Werner strode more quickly along the narrow sidewalk, then pushed open the door and entered the large, warmly heated room.

"Yes?" the sheriff asked, looking up from his desk.

"I have come to inquire about a family," Werner said, "the name of Nielsen."

Sheriff Harry Wheeler looked blankly at the tall man.

Cora was pressing Paul's trousers when the call came. Setting the iron on its stand, she walked across the kitchen and lifted the receiver from the wall telephone.

"Yes?" she said.

"Cora, it's me."

Her face tightened. "Is something wrong, Harry?"

He was silent.

"Harry?"

"*The one from Germany is here.*"

Cora stood motionless, staring at the calendar on the wall, the numbers blurred before her eyes.

"Cora, did you hear me?"

She swallowed dryly. "Yes."

"I—I have to bring him out to the house," he said.

She closed her eyes.

"I know," she murmured and hung up.

Turning, she walked slowly to the window. It's going to rain, she thought. Nature was setting the scene well.

Abruptly, her eyes shut, her fingers drew in tautly, the nails digging at her palms.

"No." It was almost a gasp. "*No.*"

After a few moments she opened her tear-glistening eyes and looked out fixedly at the road. She stood there numbly, thinking of the day the boy had come to her.

If the house hadn't burned in the middle of the night there might have been a chance. It was twenty-one miles from German Corners but the state highway ran fifteen of them and the last six—the six miles of dirt road that led north into the wood-sloped hills—might have been navigated had there been more time.

As it happened, the house was a night-lashing sheet of flame before Bernhard Klaus saw it.

Klaus and his family lived some five miles away on Skytouch Hill. He had gotten out of bed around one-thirty to get a drink of water. The window of the bathroom faced north and that was why, entering, Klaus saw the tiny flaring blaze out in the darkness.

"*Gott'n'immel!*" he slung startled words together and was out of the room before he'd finished. He thumped heavily down the carpeted steps, then, feeling at the wall for guidance, hurried for the living room.

"Fire at Nielsen house!" he gasped after agitated cranking had roused the night operator from her nap.

The hour, the remoteness, and one more thing doomed the house. German Corners had no official fire brigade. The security of its brick and timbered dwellings depended on voluntary effort. In the town itself this posed no serious problem. It was different with those houses in the outlying areas.

By the time Sheriff Wheeler had gathered five men and driven them to the fire in the ancient truck, the house was lost. While four of the six men pumped futile streams of water into the leaping, crackling inferno, Sheriff Wheeler and his deputy, Max Ederman, circuited the house.

There was no way in. They stood in back, raised arms warding off the singeing buffet of heat, grimacing at the blaze.

"They're done for!" Ederman yelled above the windswept roar.

Sheriff Wheeler looked sick. "The *boy*," he said but Ederman didn't hear.

Only a waterfall could have doused the burning of the old house. All the six men could do was prevent ignition of the woods that fringed the clearing. Their silent figures prowled the edges of the glowing aura, stamping out sparks, hosing out the occasional flare of bushes and tree foliage.

They found the boy just as the eastern hill peaks were being edged with gray morning.

Sheriff Wheeler was trying to get close enough to see into one of the side windows when he heard a shout. Turning, he ran towards the thick woods that sloped downwards a few dozen yards behind the house. Before he'd reached the underbrush, Tom Poulter emerged from them, his thin frame staggering beneath the weight of Paal Nielsen.

"Where'd you find him?" Wheeler asked, grabbing the boy's legs to ease weight from the older man's back.

"Down the hill," Poulter gasped. "Lyin' on the ground."

"Is he burned?"

"Don't look it. His pajamas ain't touched."

"Give him here," the sheriff said. He shifted Paal into his own strong arms and found two large, green-pupiled eyes staring blankly at him.

"You're awake," he said, surprised.

The boy kept staring at him without making a sound.

"You all right, son?" Wheeler asked. It might have been a statue he held, Paal's body was so inert, his expression so dumbly static.

"Let's get a blanket on him," the sheriff muttered aside and started for the truck. As he walked he noticed how the boy stared at the burning house now, a look of mask-like rigidity on his face.

"*Shock*," murmured Poulter and the sheriff nodded grimly.

They tried to put him down on the cab seat, a blanket over him but he kept sitting up, never speaking. The coffee Wheeler tried to give him dribbled from his lips and across his chin. The two men stood beside the truck while Paal stared through the windshield at the burning house.

"Bad off," said Poulter. "Can't talk, cry nor nothing."

"He isn't burned," Wheeler said, perplexed. "How'd he get out of the house without getting burned?"

"Maybe his folks got out too," said Poulter.

"Where are they then?"

The older man shook his head. "Dunno, Harry."

"Well, I better take him home to Cora," the sheriff said. "Can't leave him sitting out here."

"Think I'd better go with you," Poulter said. "I have t'get the mail sorted for delivery."

"All right."

Wheeler told the other four men he'd bring back food and replacements in an hour or so. Then Poulter and he climbed into the cab beside Paal and he jabbed his boot toe on the starter. The engine coughed spasmodically, groaned over, then caught. The sheriff raced it until it was warm, then eased it into gear. The truck rolled off slowly down the dirt road that led to the highway.

Until the burning house was no longer visible, Paal stared out the back window, face still immobile. Then, slowly, he turned, the blanket slipping off his thin shoulders. Tom Poulter put it back over him.

"Warm enough?" he asked.

The silent boy looked at Poulter as if he'd never heard a human voice in his life.

As soon as she heard the truck turn off the road, Cora Wheeler's quick right hand moved along the stove-front switches. Before her husband's bootfalls sounded on the back porch steps, the bacon lay neatly in strips across the frying pan, white moons of pancake batter were browning on the griddle, and the already-brewed coffee was heating.

"*Harry.*"

There was a sound of pitying distress in her voice as she saw the boy in his arms. She hurried across the kitchen.

"Let's get him to bed," Wheeler said. "I think maybe he's in shock."

The slender woman moved up the stairs on hurried feet, threw open the door of what had been David's room, and moved to the bed. When Wheeler passed through the doorway she had the covers peeled back and was plugging in an electric blanket.

"Is he hurt?" she asked.

"No." He put Paal down on the bed.

"Poor darling," she murmured, tucking in the bedclothes around the boy's frail body. "Poor little darling." She stroked back the soft blond hair from his forehead and smiled down at him.

"There now, go to sleep, dear. It's all right. Go to sleep."

Wheeler stood behind her and saw the seven-year-old boy staring up at Cora with that same dazed, lifeless expression. It hadn't changed once since Tom Poulter had brought him out of the woods.

The sheriff turned and went down to the kitchen. There he phoned for replacements, then turned the pancakes and bacon, and poured himself a cup of coffee. He was drinking it when Cora came down the back stairs and returned to the stove.

"Are his parents—?" she began.

"I don't know," Wheeler said, shaking his head. "We couldn't get near the house."

"But the boy—?"

"Tom Poulter found him outside."

"*Outside.*"

"We don't know how he got out," he said. "All we know's he was there."

His wife grew silent. She slid pancakes on a dish and put the dish in front of him. She put her hand on his shoulder.

"You look tired," she said. "Can you go to bed?"

"Later," he said.

She nodded, then, patting his shoulder, turned away. "The bacon will be done directly," she said.

He grunted. Then, as he poured maple syrup over the stack of cakes, he said, "I expect they are dead, Cora. It's an awful fire; still going when I left. Nothing we could do about it."

"That poor boy," she said.

She stood by the stove watching her husband eat wearily.

"I tried to get him to talk," she said, shaking her head, "but he never said a word."

"Never said a word to us either," he told her, "just stared."

He looked at the table, chewing thoughtfully.

"Like he doesn't even know how to talk," he said.

A little after ten that morning the waterfall came—a waterfall of rain—and the burning house sputtered and hissed into charred, smoke-fogged ruins.

Red-eyed and exhausted, Sheriff Wheeler sat motionless in the truck cab until the deluge had slackened. Then, with a chest-deep groan, he pushed open the door and slid to the ground. There, he raised the collar of his slicker and pulled down the wide-brimmed Stetson more tightly on his skull. He walked around to the back of the covered truck.

"Come on," he said, his voice hoarsely dry. He trudged through the clinging mud towards the house.

The front door still stood. Wheeler and the other men by-passed it and clambered over the collapsed living room wall. The sheriff felt thin waves of heat from the still-glowing timbers and the throat-clogging reek of wet, smoldering rugs and upholstery turned his edgy stomach.

He stepped across some half-burned books on the floor and the roasted bindings crackled beneath his tread. He kept moving, into the hall, breathing through gritted teeth, rain spattering off his shoulders and back. I hope they got out, he thought, I hope to God they got out.

They hadn't. They were still in their bed, no longer human, blackened to a hideous, joint-twisted crisp. Sheriff Wheeler's face was taut and pale as he looked down at them.

One of the men prodded a wet twig at something on the mattress.

"Pipe," Wheeler heard him say above the drum of rain. "Must have fell asleep smokin'."

"Get some blankets," Wheeler told them. "Put them in the back of the truck."

Two of the men turned away without a word and Wheeler heard them clump away over the rubble.

He was unable to take his eyes off Professor Holger Nielsen and his wife Fanny, scorched into grotesque mockeries of the handsome couple he remembered—the tall, big-framed Holger, calmly imperious; the slender, auburn-haired Fanny, her face a soft, rose-cheeked—

Abruptly, the sheriff turned and stumped from the room, almost tripping over a fallen beam.

The boy—what would happen to the boy now? That day was the first time Paal had ever left this house in his life. His parents were the fulcrum of his world; Wheeler knew that much. No wonder there had been that look of shocked incomprehension on Paal's face.

Yet how did he know his mother and father were dead?

As the sheriff crossed the living room, he saw one of the men looking at a partially charred book.

"Look at this," the man said, holding it out.

Wheeler glanced at it, his eyes catching the title: *The Unknown Mind*.

He turned away tensely. "Put it down!" he snapped, quitting the house with long, anxious strides. The memory of how the Nielsens looked went with him; and something else. A question.

How did Paal get out of the house?

Paal woke up.

For a long moment he stared up at the formless shadows that danced and fluttered across the ceiling. It was raining out. The wind was rustling tree boughs outside the window, causing shadow movements in this strange room. Paal lay motionless in the warm center of the bed, air crisp in his lungs, cold against his pale cheeks.

Where were they? Paal closed his eyes and tried to sense their presence. They weren't in the house. Where then? Where were his mother and father?

Hands of my mother. Paal washed his mind clean of all but the trigger symbol. They rested on the ebony velvet of his concentration—pale, lovely hands, soft to touch and be touched by, the mechanism that could raise his mind to the needed level of clarity.

In his own home it would be unnecessary. His own home was filled with the sense of them. Each object touched by them possessed a power to bring their minds close. The very air seemed charged with their consciousness, filled with a constancy of attention.

Not here. He needed to lift himself above the alien drag of here.

Therefore, I am convinced that each child is born with this instinctive ability. Words given to him by his father appearing again like dew-jewelled spider web across the fingers of his mother's hands. He stripped it off. The hands were free again, stroking slowly at the darkness of his mental focus. His eyes were shut; a tracery of lines and ridges scarred his brow, his tightened jaw was bloodless. The level of awareness, like waters, rose.

His senses rose along, unbidden.

Sound revealed its woven maze—the rushing, thudding, drumming, dripping rain; the tangled knit of winds through air and tree and gabled eave; the crackling settle of the house; each whispering transcience of process.

Sense of smell expanded to a cloud of brain-filling odors— wood and wool, damp brick and dust and sweet starched linens. Beneath his tensing fingers weave became apparent—coolness and warmth, the weight of covers, the delicate, skin-scarring press of rumpled sheet. In his mouth the taste of cold air, old house. Of sight, only the hands.

Silence; lack of response. He'd never had to wait so long for answers before. Usually, they flooded on him easily. His mother's hands grew clearer. They pulsed with life. Unknown, he climbed beyond. *This bottom level sets the stage for more important phenomena.* Words of his father. He'd never gone above that bottom level until now.

Up, up. Like cool hands drawing him to rarified heights. Tendrils of acute consciousness rose towards the peak, searching desperately for a holding place. The hands began breaking into clouds. The clouds dispersed.

It seemed he floated towards the blackened tangle of his home, rain a glistening lace before his eyes. He saw the front door standing, waiting for his hand. The house drew closer. It was engulfed in licking mists. Closer, closer—

Paal, no.

His body shuddered on the bed. Ice frosted his brain. The house fled suddenly, bearing with itself a horrid image of two black figures lying on—

Paal jolted up, staring and rigid. Awareness maelstromed into its hiding place. One thing alone remained. He knew that they were gone. He knew that they had guided him, sleeping, from the house.

Even as they burned.

That night they knew he couldn't speak.

There was no reason for it, they thought. His tongue was there, his throat looked healthy. Wheeler looked into his opened mouth and saw that. But Paal did not speak.

"So *that's* what it was," the sheriff said, shaking his head gravely. It was near eleven. Paal was asleep again.

"What's that, Harry?" asked Cora, brushing her dark blonde hair in front of the dressing table mirror.

"Those times when Miss Frank and I tried to get the Nielsens to start the boy in school." He hung his pants across the chair back. "The answer was always no. Now I see why."

She glanced up at his reflection. "There must be something wrong with him, Harry," she said.

"Well, we can have Doc Steiger look at him but I don't think so."

"But they were college people," she argued. "There was no earthly reason why they shouldn't teach him how to talk. Unless there was some reason he *couldn't*."

Wheeler shook his head again.

"They were strange people, Cora," he said. "Hardly spoke a word themselves. As if they were too good for talking—or something." He grunted disgustedly. "No wonder they didn't want that boy to school."

He sank down on the bed with a groan and shucked off boots and calf-high stockings. "What a day," he muttered.

"You didn't find anything at the house?"

"Nothing. No identification papers at all. The house is burned to a cinder. Nothing but a pile of books and they don't lead us anywhere."

"Isn't there any way?"

"The Nielsens never had a charge account in town. And they weren't even citizens so the professor wasn't registered for the draft."

"Oh." Cora looked a moment at her face reflected in the oval mirror. Then her gaze lowered to the photograph on the dressing table—David as he was when he was nine. The Nielsen boy looked a great deal like David, she thought. Same height and build. Maybe David's hair had been a trifle darker but—

"What's to be done with him?" she asked.

"Couldn't say, Cora," he answered. "We have to wait till the end of the month, I guess. Tom Poulter says the Nielsens got three letters the end of every month. Come from Europe, he said. We'll just have to wait for them, then write back to the addresses on them. May be the boy has relations over there."

"Europe," she said, almost to herself. "That far away."

Her husband grunted, then pulled the covers back and sank down heavily on the mattress.

"Tired," he muttered.

He stared at the ceiling. "Come to bed," he said.

"In a little while."

She sat there brushing distractedly at her hair until the sound of his snoring broke the silence. Then, quietly, she rose and moved across the hall.

There was a river of moonlight across the bed. It flowed over Paal's small, motionless hands. Cora stood in the shadows a long time looking at the hands. For a moment she thought it was David in his bed again.

It was the sound.

Like endless club strokes across his vivid mind, it pulsed and throbbed into him in an endless, garbled din. He sensed it was communication of a sort but it hurt his ears and chained awareness and locked incoming thoughts behind dense, impassable walls.

Sometimes, in an infrequent moment of silence he would sense a fissure in the walls and, for that fleeting moment, catch hold of fragments—like an animal snatching scraps of food before the trap jaws clash together.

But then the sound would start again, rising and falling in rhythmless beat, jarring and grating, rubbing at the live, glistening surface of comprehension until it was dry and aching and confused.

"Paal," she said.

A week had passed; another week would pass before the letters came.

"Paal, didn't they ever talk to you? Paal?"

Fists striking at delicate acuteness. Hands squeezing sensitivity from the vibrant ganglia of his mind.

"Paal, don't you know your name? Paal? *Paal.*"

There was nothing physically wrong with him. Doctor Steiger had made sure of it. There was no reason for him not to talk.

"We'll teach you, Paal. It's all right, darling. We'll teach you." Like knife strokes across the weave of consciousness. "*Paal. Paal.*"

Paal. It was himself; he sensed that much. But it was different in the ears, a dead, depressive sound standing alone and drab, without the host of linked associations that existed in his mind. In thought, his name was more than letters. It was *him*, every facet of his person and its meaning to himself, his mother and his father, to his life. When they had summoned him or thought his name it had been more than just the small hard core which sound made of it. It had been everything interwoven in a flash of knowing, unhampered by sound.

"Paal, don't you understand? It's your name. Paal Nielsen. Don't you understand?"

Drumming, pounding at raw sensitivity. Paal. The sound kicking at him. *Paal. Paal.* Trying to dislodge his grip and fling him into the maw of sound.

"Paal. *Try*, Paal. Say it after me. Pa-al. *Pa-al.*"

Twisting away, he would run from her in panic and she would follow him to where he cowered by the bed of her son.

Then, for long moments, there would be peace. She would hold him in her arms and, as if she understood, would not speak. There would be stillness and no pounding clash of sound against his mind. She would stroke his hair and kiss away sobless tears. He would lie against the warmth of her, his mind, like a timid animal, emerging from its hiding place again—to sense a flow of understanding from this woman. Feeling that needed no sound.

Love—wordless, unencumbered, and beautiful.

Sheriff Wheeler was just leaving the house that morning when the phone rang. He stood in the front hallway, waiting until Cora picked it up.

"Harry!" He heard her call. "Are you gone yet?"

He came back into the kitchen and took the receiver from her. "Wheeler," he said into it.

"Tom Poulter, Harry," the postmaster said. "Them letters is in."

"Be right there," Wheeler said and hung up.

"The letters?" his wife asked.

Wheeler nodded.

"*Oh*," she murmured so that he barely heard her.

When Wheeler entered the post office twenty minutes later, Poulter slid the three letters across the counter. The sheriff picked them up.

"Switzerland," he read the postmarks, "Sweden, Germany."

"That's the lot," Poulter said, "like always. On the thirtieth of the month."

"Can't open them, I suppose," Wheeler said.

"Y'know I'd say yes if I could, Harry," Poulter answered. "But law's law. You know that. I got t'send them back unopened. That's the law."

"All right." Wheeler took out his pen and copied down the return addresses in his pad. He pushed the letters back. "Thanks."

When he got home at four that afternoon, Cora was in the front room with Paal. There was a look of confused emotion on Paal's face—a desire to please coupled with a frightened need to flee the disconcertion of sound. He sat beside her on the couch looking as if he were about to cry.

"Oh *Paal*," she said as Wheeler entered. She put her arms around the trembling boy. "There's nothing to be afraid of, darling."

She saw her husband.

"What did they *do* to him?" she asked, unhappily.

He shook his head. "Don't know," he said. "He should have been put in school though."

"We can't very well put him in school when he's like *this*," she said.

"We can't put him anywhere till we see what's what," Wheeler said. "I'll write those people tonight."

In the silence, Paal felt a sudden burst of emotion in the woman and he looked up quickly at her stricken face.

Pain. He felt it pour from her like blood from a mortal wound.

And while they ate supper in an almost silence, Paal kept sensing tragic sadness in the woman. It seemed he heard sobbing in a distant place. As the silence continued he began to get momentary flashes of remembrance in her pain-opened mind. He saw the face of another boy. Only it swirled and faded and there was *his* face in her thoughts. The two faces, like contesting wraiths, lay and overlay upon each other as if fighting for the dominance of her mind.

All fleeing, locked abruptly behind black doors as she said, "You have to write to them, I suppose."

"You know I do, Cora," Wheeler said.

Silence. Pain again. And when she tucked him into bed, he looked at her with such soft, apparent pity on his face that she turned quickly from the bed and he could feel the waves of sorrow break across his mind until her footsteps could no longer be heard. And, even then, like the faint fluttering of bird wings in the night, he felt her pitiable despair moving in the house.

"What are you writing?" she asked.

Wheeler looked over from his desk as midnight chimed its seventh stroke in the hall. Cora came walking across the room and set the tray down at his elbow. The steamy fragrance of freshly brewed coffee filled his nostrils as he reached for the pot.

"Just telling them the situation," he said, "about the fire, the Nielsens dying. Asking them if they're related to the boy or know any of his relations over there."

"And what if his relations don't do any better than his parents?"

"Now, Cora," he said, pouring cream, "I thought we'd already discussed that. It's not our business."

She pressed pale lips together.

"A frightened child *is* my business," she said angrily. "Maybe you—"

She broke off as he looked up at her patiently, no argument in his expression.

"*Well*," she said, turning from him, "it's true."

"It's not our business, Cora." He didn't see the tremor of her lips.

"So he'll just go on not talking, I suppose! Being afraid of shadows!"

She whirled. "It's *criminal!*" she cried, love and anger bursting from her in a twisted mixture.

"It's got to be done, Cora," he said quietly. "It's our duty."

"*Duty.*" She echoed it with an empty lifelessness in her voice.

She didn't sleep. The liquid flutter of Harry's snoring in her ears, she lay staring at the jump of shadows on the ceiling, a scene enacted in her mind.

A summer's afternoon; the back doorbell ringing. Men standing on the porch, John Carpenter among them, a blanket-covered stillness weighing down his arms, a blank look on his face. In the silence, a drip of water on the sunbaked boards—slowly, unsteadily, like the beats of a dying heart. *He was swimming in the lake, Miz Wheeler and—*

She shuddered on the bed as she had shuddered then—numbly, mutely. The hands beside her were a crumpled whiteness, twisted by remembered anguish. All these years waiting, waiting for a child to bring life into her house again.

At breakfast she was hollow-eyed and drawn. She moved about the kitchen with a willful tread, sliding eggs and pancakes on her husband's plate, pouring coffee, never speaking once.

Then he had kissed her goodbye and she was standing at the living room window watching him trudge down the path to the car. Long after he'd gone, staring at the three envelopes he'd stuck into the side clip of the mailbox.

When Paal came downstairs he smiled at her. She kissed his cheek, then stood behind him, wordless and watching, while he drank his orange juice. The way he sat, the way he held his glass; it was so like—

While Paal ate his cereal she went out to the mailbox and got the three letters, replacing them with three of her own—just in case her husband ever asked the mailman if he'd picked up three letters at their house that morning.

While Paal was eating his eggs, she went down into the cellar and threw the letters into the furnace. The one to Switzerland burned, then the ones to Germany and Sweden. She stirred them with a poker until the pieces broke and disappeared like black confetti in the flames.

Weeks passed: and, with every day, the service of his mind grew weaker.

"Paal, dear, don't you understand?" The patient, loving voice of the woman he needed but feared. "Won't you say it once for me? Just for me? *Paal?*"

He knew there was only love in her but sound would destroy him. It would chain his thoughts—like putting shackles on the wind.

"Would you like to go to school, Paal? Would you? *School?*"

Her face a mask of worried devotion.

"Try to talk, Paal. Just *try.*"

He fought it off with mounting fear. Silence would bring him scraps of meaning from her mind. Then sound returned and grossed each meaning with unwieldy flesh. Meanings joined with sounds. The links formed quickly, frighteningly. He struggled against them. Sounds could cover fragile, darting symbols with a hideous, restraining dough, dough that would be baked in ovens of articulation, then chopped into the stunted lengths of words.

Afraid of the woman, yet wanting to be near the warmth of her, protected by her arms. Like a pendulum he swung from dread to need and back to dread again.

And still the sounds kept shearing at his mind.

"We can't wait any longer to hear from them," Harry said. "He'll have to go to school, that's all."

"No," she said.

He put down his newspaper and looked across the living room at her. She kept her eyes on the movements of her knitting needles.

"What do you mean, no?" he asked, irritably. "Every time I mention school you say no. Why *shouldn't* he go to school?"

The needles stopped and were lowered to her lap. Cora stared at them.

"I don't know," she said, "it's just that—" A sigh emptied from her. "I don't know," she said.

"He'll start on Monday," Harry said.

"But he's frightened," she said.

"Sure he's frightened. You'd be frightened too if you couldn't talk and everybody around you was talking. He needs education, that's all."

"But he's not *ignorant*, Harry. I—I swear he understands me sometimes. *Without* talking."

"*How?*"

"I don't know. But—well, the Nielsens weren't stupid people. They wouldn't just *refuse* to teach him."

"Well, whatever they taught him," Harry said, picking up his paper, "it sure doesn't show."

When they asked Miss Edna Frank over that afternoon to meet the boy she was determined to be impartial.

That Paal Nielsen had been reared in miserable fashion was beyond cavil, but the maiden teacher had decided not to allow the knowledge to affect her attitude. The boy needed understanding. The cruel mistreatment of his parents had to be undone and Miss Frank had elected herself to the office.

Striding with a resolute quickness down German Corners' main artery, she recalled that scene in the Nielsen house when she and Sheriff Wheeler had tried to persuade them to enter Paal in school.

And such a smugness in their faces, thought Miss Frank, remembering. Such a polite disdain. *We do not wish our boy in school*, she heard Professor Nielsen's words again. Just like that, Miss Frank recalled. Arrogant as you please. *We do not wish—* Disgusting attitude.

Well, at least the boy was out of it now. The fire was probably the blessing of his life, she thought.

"We wrote to them four, five weeks ago," the sheriff explained, "and we haven't gotten an answer yet. We can't just let the boy go on the way he is. He needs schooling."

"He most certainly does," agreed Miss Frank, her pale features drawn into their usual sum of unyielding dogmatism. There was a wisp of mustache on her upper lip, her chin came almost to a point. On Halloween the children of German Corners watched the sky above her house.

"He's very shy," Cora said, sensing that harshness in the middle-aged teacher. "He'll be terribly frightened. He'll need a lot of understanding."

"He shall receive it," Miss Frank declared. "But let's see the boy."

Cora led Paal down the steps speaking to him softly. "Don't be afraid, darling. There's nothing to be afraid of."

Paal entered the room and looked into the eyes of Miss Edna Frank.

Only Cora felt the stiffening of his body—as though, instead of the gaunt virgin, he had looked into the petrifying gaze of the Medusa. Miss Frank and the sheriff did not catch the flare of iris in his bright, green eyes, the minute twitching at one corner of his mouth. None of them could sense the leap of panic in his mind.

Miss Frank sat smiling, holding out her hand.

"Come here, child," she said and, for a moment, the gates slammed shut and hid away the writhing shimmer.

"Come on, darling," Cora said, "Miss Frank is here to help you." She led him forward, feeling beneath her fingers the shuddering of terror in him.

Silence again. And, in the moment of it, Paal felt as though he were walking into a century-sealed tomb. Dead winds gushed out upon him, creatures of frustration slithered on his heart, strange flying jealousies and hates rushed by—all obscured by clouds of twisted memory. It was the purgatory that his father had pictured to him once in telling him of myth and legend. This was no legend though.

Her touch was cool and dry. Dark wrenching terrors ran down her veins and poured into him. Inaudibly, the fragment of a scream tightened his throat. Their eyes met again and Paal saw that, for a second, the woman seemed to know that he was looking at her brain.

Then she spoke and he was free again, limp and staring.

"I think we'll get along just fine," she said.

Maelstrom!

He lurched back on his heels and fell against the sheriff's wife.

All the way across the grounds, it had been growing, growing—as if he were a Geiger counter moving towards some fantastic pulsing strata of atomic force. Closer, yet closer, the delicate controls within him stirring, glowing, trembling, reacting with increasing violence to the nearness of power. Even though his sensitivity had been weakened by over three months of sound he felt this now, strongly. As though he walked into a center of vitality.

It was *the young*.

Then the door opened, the voices stopped, and all of it rushed through him like a vast, electric current—all wild and unharnessed. He clung to her, fingers rigid in her skirt, eyes widened, quick breaths falling from his parted lips. His gaze moved shakily across the rows of staring children faces and waves of distorted energies kept bounding out from them in a snarled, uncontrolled network.

Miss Frank scraped back her chair, stepped down from her six-inch eminence and started down the aisle towards them.

"Good morning," she said, crisply. "We're just about to start our classes for the day."

"I—do hope everything will be all right," Cora said. She glanced down. Paal was looking at the class through a welling haze of tears. "Oh, *Paal.*" She leaned over and ran her fingers through his blond hair, a worried look on her face. "Paal, don't be afraid, dear," she whispered.

He looked at her blankly.

"Darling, there's nothing to be—"

"Now just you leave him here," Miss Frank broke in, putting her hand on Paal's shoulder. She ignored the shudder that rippled through him. "He'll be right at home in no time, Mrs. Wheeler. But you've got to leave him by himself."

"Oh, but—" Cora started.

"No, believe me, it's the only way," Miss Frank insisted. "As long as you stay he'll be upset. Believe me. I've seen such things before."

At first he wouldn't let go of Cora but clung to her as the one familiar thing in this whirlpool of frightening newness. It was only when Miss Frank's hard, thin hands held him back that Cora backed off slowly, anxiously, closing the door and cutting off from Paal the sight of her soft pity.

He stood there trembling, incapable of uttering a single word to ask for help. Confused, his mind sent out tenuous shoots of communication but in the undisciplined tangle they were broken off and lost. He drew back quickly and tried, in vain, to cut himself off. All he could manage to do was let the torrent of needling thoughts continue unopposed until they had become a numbing, meaningless surge.

"Now, Paal," he heard Miss Frank's voice and looked up gingerly at her. The hand drew him from the door. *Come along.*"

He didn't understand the words but the brittle sound of them was clear enough, the flow of irrational animosity from her was unmistakable. He stumbled along at her side, threading a thin path of consciousness through the living undergrowth of young, untrained minds; the strange admixture of them with their retention of born sensitivity overlaid with the dulling coat of formal inculcation.

She brought him to the front of the room and stood him there, his chest laboring for breath as if the feelings around him were hands pushing and constraining on his body.

"This is Paal Nielsen, class," Miss Frank announced, and sound drew a momentary blade across the stunted weave of thoughts. "We're going to have to be very patient with him. You see his mother and father never taught him how to talk."

She looked down at him as a prosecuting lawyer might gaze upon exhibit A.

"He can't understand a word of English," she said.

Silence a moment, writhing. Miss Frank tightened her grip on his shoulder.

"Well, we'll help him learn, won't we, class?"

Faint mutterings arose from them; one thin, piping. "*Yes*, Miss Frank."

"Now, Paal," she said. He didn't turn. She shook his shoulder. "*Paal*," she said.

He looked at her.

"Can you say your name?" she asked. "Paal? Paal Nielsen? Go ahead. Say your name."

Her fingers drew in like talons.

"Say it. Paal. *Pa-al.*"

He sobbed. Miss Frank released her hand.

"You'll learn," she said calmly.

It was not encouragement.

He sat in the middle of it like hooked bait in a current that swirled with devouring mouths, mouths from which endlessly came mind-deadening sounds.

"This is a boat. A boat sails on the water. The men who live on the boat are called sailors."

And, in the primer, the words about the boat printed under a picture of one.

Paal remembered a picture his father had shown him once. It had been a picture of a boat too; but his father had not spoken futile words about the boat. His father had created about the picture every sight and sound heir to it. Great blue rising swells of tide. Gray-green mountain waves, their white tops lashing. Storm winds whistling through the rigging of a bucking, surging, shuddering vessel. The quiet majesty of an ocean sunset, joining, with a scarlet seal, sea and sky.

"This is a farm. Men grow food on the farm. The men who grow food are called farmers."

Words. Empty, with no power to convey the moist, warm feel of earth. The sound of grain fields rustling in the wind like golden seas. The sight of sun setting on a red barn wall. The smell of soft lea winds carrying, from afar, the delicate clank of cowbells.

"This is a forest. A forest is made of trees."

No sense of presence in those black, dogmatic symbols whether sounded or looked upon. No sound of winds rushing like eternal rivers through the high green canopies. No smell of pine and birch, oak and maple and hemlock. No feel of treading on the century-thick carpet of leafy forest floors.

Words. Blunt, sawed-off lengths of hemmed-in meaning; incapable of evocation, of expansion. Black figures on white. This is a cat. This is a dog. Cat, dog. This is a man. This is a woman. Man, woman. Car. Horse. Tree. Desk. Children. Each word a trap, stalking his mind. A snare set to enclose fluid and unbounded comprehension.

Every day she stood him on the platform.

"Paal," she would say, pointing at him. "Paal. Say it. Paal."

He couldn't. He stared at her, too intelligent not to make the connection, to much afraid to seek further.

"Paal," A boney finger prodding at his chest. "Paal. Paal. *Paal*."

He fought it. He had to fight it. He blanked his gaze and saw nothing of the room around him, concentrating only on his mother's hands. He knew it was a battle. Like a jelling of sickness, he had felt each new encroachment on his sensitivity.

"You're not listening, Paal Nielsen!" Miss Frank would accuse, shaking him. "You're a stubborn, ungrateful boy. Don't you want to be like *other* children?"

Staring eyes; and her thin, never-to-be-kissed lips stirring, pressing in.

"Sit down," she's say. He didn't move. She'd move him off the platform with rigid fingers.

"Sit *down*," she'd say as if talking to a mulish puppy.

Every day.

She was awake in an instant; in another instant, on her feet and hurrying across the darkness of the room. Behind her, Harry slept with laboring breaths. She shut away the sound and let her hand slip off the door knob as she started across the hall.

"*Darling.*"

He was standing by the window, looking out. As she spoke, he whirled and, in the faint illumination of the night light, she could see the terror written on his face.

"Darling, come to bed." She led him there and tucked him in, then sat beside him, holding his thin, cold hands.

"What is it, dear?"

He looked at her with wide, pained eyes.

"*Oh*—" She bent over and pressed her warm cheek to his. "What are you afraid of?"

In the dark silence it seemed as if a vision of the schoolroom and Miss Frank standing in it crossed her mind.

"Is it the school?" she asked, thinking it only an idea which had occurred to her.

The answer was in his face.

"But school is nothing to be afraid of, darling," she said. "You—"

She saw tears welling in his eyes, and abruptly she drew him up and held him tightly against herself. *Don't be afraid*, she thought. *Darling, please don't be afraid. I'm here and I love you just as much as they did. I love you even more—*

Paal drew back. He stared at her as if he didn't understand.

As the car pulled up in back of the house, Werner saw a woman turn away from the kitchen window.

"If we'd only heard from you," said Wheeler, "but there was never a word. You can't blame us for adopting the boy. We did what we thought was best."

Werner nodded with short, distracted movements of his head.

"I understand," he said quietly. "We received no letters however."

They sat in the car in silence, Werner staring through the windshield, Wheeler looking at his hands.

Holger and Fanny *dead*, Werner was thinking. A horrible discovery to make. The boy exposed to the cruel blunderings of people who did not understand. That was, in a way, even more horrible.

Wheeler was thinking of those letters and of Cora. He should have written again. Still, those letters should have reached Europe. Was it possible they were all missent?

"Well," he said, finally, "you'll—want to see the boy."

"Yes," said Werner.

The two men pushed open the car doors and got out. They walked across the backyard and up the wooden porch steps. Have you taught him how to speak?—Werner almost said but couldn't bring himself to ask. The concept of a boy like Paal exposed to the blunt, deadening forces of usual speech was something he felt uncomfortable thinking about.

"I'll get my wife," said Wheeler. "The living room's in there."

After the sheriff had gone up the back stairs, Werner walked slowly through the hall and into the front room. There he took off his raincoat and hat and dropped them over the back of a wooden chair. Upstairs he could hear the faint sound of voices—a man and woman. The woman sounded upset.

When he heard footsteps, he turned from the window.

The sheriff's wife entered beside her husband. She was smiling politely, but Werner knew she wasn't happy to see him there.

"Please sit down," she said.

He waited until she was in a chair, then settled down on the couch.

"What is it you want?" asked Mrs. Wheeler.

"Did your husband tell you—?"

"He told me who you were," she interrupted, "but not why you want to see Paul."

"*Paul?*" asked Werner, surprised.

"We—" Her hands sought out each other nervously. "—We changed it to Paul. It—seemed more appropriate. For a Wheeler, I mean."

"I see." Werner nodded politely.

Silence.

"Well," Werner said then, "you wish to know why I am here to see—the boy. I will explain as briefly as possible.

"Ten years ago, in Heidelbert, four married couples—the Elkenbergs, the Kalders, the Nielsens, and my wife and I—decided to try an experiment on our children—some not yet born. An experiment of the mind.

"We had accepted, you see, the proposition that ancient man, deprived of the dubious benefit of language, had been telepathic."

Cora started in her chair.

"Further," Werner went on, not noticing, "that the basic organic source of this ability is still functioning though no longer made use of—a sort of ethereal tonsil, a higher appendix—not used but neither useless.

"So we began our work, each searching for physiological facts while, at the same time, developing the ability in our children. Monthly correspondence was exchanged, a systematic methodology of training was arrived at slowly. Eventually, we planned to establish a colony with the grown children, a colony to be gradually consolidated until these abilities would become second nature to its members.

"*Paal is one of these children.*"

Wheeler looked almost dazed.

"This is a *fact?*" he asked.

"A fact," said Werner.

Cora sat numbly in her chair staring at the tall German. She was thinking about the way Paal seemed to understand her without words. Thinking of his fear of the school and Miss Frank. Thinking of how many times she had woken up and gone to him even though he didn't make a sound.

"What?" she asked, looking up as Werner spoke.

"I say—may I see the boy now?"

"He's in school," she said. "He'll be home in—"

She stopped as a look of almost revulsion crossed Werner's face.

"*School?*" he asked.

"Paal Nielsen, stand."

The young boy slid from his seat and stood beside the desk. Miss Frank gestured to him once and, more like an old man than a boy, he trudged up to the platform and stood beside her as he always did.

"Straighten up," Miss Frank demanded. "Shoulders back."

The shoulders moved, the back grew flat.

"What's your name?" asked Miss Frank.

The boy pressed his lips together slightly. His swallowing made a dry, rattling noise.

"*What is your name?*"

Silence in the classroom except for the restive stirring of the young. Erratic currents of their thought deflected off him like random winds.

"*Your name*," she said.

He made no reply.

The virgin teacher looked at him and, in the moment that she did, through her mind ran memories of her childhood. Of her gaunt, mania-driven mother keeping her for hours at a time in the darkened front parlor, sitting at the great round table, her fingers arched over the smoothly worn ouija board—making her try to communicate with her dead father.

Memories of those terrible years were still with her—always with her. Her minor sensitivity being abused and twisted into knots until she hated every single thing about perception. Perception was an evil, full of suffering and anguish.

The boy must be freed of it.

"Class," she said, "I want you all to think of Paal's name." (This was his name no matter what Mrs. Wheeler chose to call him.) "Just think of it. Don't say it. Just think: Paal, Paal, Paal. When I count three. Do you understand?"

They stared at her, some nodding. "*Yes*, Miss Frank," piped up her only faithful.

"All right," she said, "One—two—*three*."

It flung into his mind like the blast of a hurricane, pounding and tearing at his hold on wordless sensitivity. He trembled on the platform, his mouth fallen ajar.

The blast grew stronger, all the power of the young directed into a single, irresistible force. Paal, *Paal, PAAL*!! It screamed into the tissues of his brain.

Until, at the very peak of it, when he thought his head would explode, it was all cut away by the voice of Miss Frank scalpelling into his mind.

"*Say it*! *Paal*!"

"Here he comes," said Cora. She turned from the window. "Before he gets here, I want to apologize for my rudeness."

"Not at all," said Werner, distractedly, "I understand perfectly. Naturally, you would think that I had come to take the boy away. As I have said, however, I have no legal powers over him—being no relation. I simply want to see him as the child of my two colleagues—whose shocking death I have only now learned of."

He saw the woman's throat move and picked out the leap of guilty panic in her mind. She had destroyed the letters her husband wrote. Werner knew it instantly but said nothing. He sensed that the husband also knew it; she would have enough trouble as it was.

They heard Paal's footsteps on the bottom step of the front porch.

"I *will* take him out of school," Cora said.

"Perhaps not," said Werner, looking towards the door. In spite of everything he felt his heartbeat quicken, felt the fingers of his left hand twitch in his lap. Without a word, he sent out the message. It was a greeting the four couples had decided on; a sort of password.

Telepathy, he thought, *is the communication of impressions of any kind from one mind to another independently of the recognized channels of sense.*

Werner sent it twice before the front door opened.

Paal stood there, motionless.

Werner saw recognition in his eyes, but, in the boy's mind, was only confused uncertainty. The misted vision of Werner's face crossed it. In his mind, all the people had existed—Werner, Elkenberg, Kalder, all their children. But now it was locked up and hard to capture. The face disappeared.

"Paul, this is Mister Werner," Cora said.

Werner did not speak. He sent the message out again—with such force that Paal could not possibly miss it. He saw a look of uncomprehending dismay creep across the boy's features, as if Paal suspected that something was happening yet could not imagine what.

The boy's face grew more confused. Cora's eyes moved concernedly from him to Werner and back again. Why didn't Werner speak? She started to say something, then remembered what the German had said.

"Say, what—?" Wheeler began until Cora waved her hand and stopped him.

Paal, think!—Werner thought desperately—*Where is your mind?*

Suddenly, there was a great, wracking sob in the boy's throat and chest. Werner shuddered.

"My name is Paal," the boy said.

The voice made Werner's flesh crawl. It was unfinished, like a puppet voice, thin, wavering, and brittle.

"My name is Paal."

He couldn't stop saying it. It was as if he were whipping himself on, knowing what had happened and trying to suffer as much as possible with the knowledge.

"My name is Paal. My name is Paal." An endless, frightening babble; in it, a panic-stricken boy seeking out an unknown power which had been torn from him.

"My name is Paal." Even held tightly in Cora's arms, he said it. "My name is Paal." Angrily, pitiably, endlessly. *"My name is Paal. My name is Paal."*

Werner closed his eyes.

Lost.

Wheeler offered to take him back to the bus station, but Werner told him he'd rather walk. He said goodbye to the sheriff and asked him to relay his regrets to Mrs. Wheeler, who had taken the sobbing boy up to his room.

RICHARD MATHESON

Now, in the beginning fall of a fine, mistlike rain, Werner walked away from the house, from Paal.

It was not something easily judged, he was thinking. There was no right and wrong of it. Definitely, it was not a case of evil versus good. Mrs. Wheeler, the sheriff, the boy's teacher, the people of German Corners—they had, probably, all meant well. Understandably, they had been outraged at the idea of a seven-year-old boy not having been taught to speak by his parents. Their actions were, in light of that, justifiable and good.

It was simply that, so often, evil could come of misguided good.

No, it was better left as it was. To take Paal back to Europe—back to the others—would be a mistake. He could if he wanted to; all the couples had exchanged papers giving each other the right to take over rearing of the children should anything happen to the parents. But it would only confuse Paal further. He had been a trained sensitive, not a born one. Although, by the principle they all worked on, all children were born with the atavistic ability to telepath, it was so easy to lose, so difficult to recapture.

Werner shook his head. It was a pity. The boy was without his parents, without his talent, even without his name.

He had lost everything.

Well, perhaps, not everything.

As he walked, Werner sent his mind back to the house to discover them standing at the window of Paal's room, watching sunset cast its fiery light on German Corners. Paal was clinging to the sheriff's wife, his cheek pressed to her side. The final terror of losing his awareness had not faded but there was something else counterbalancing it. Something Cora Wheeler sensed yet did not fully realize.

Paal's parents had not loved him. Werner knew this. Caught up in the fascination of their work they had not had the time to love him as a child. Kind, yes, affectionate, always; still, they had regarded Paal as their experiment in flesh.

Which was why Cora Wheeler's love was, in part, as strange a thing to Paal as all the crushing horrors of speech. It would not remain so. For, in that moment when the last of his gift had fled, leaving his mind a naked rawness, she had been there with her love, to soothe away the pain. And always would be there.

"Did you find who you were looking for?" the gray-haired

woman at the counter asked Werner as she served him coffee.

"Yes. Thank you," he said.

"Where was he?" asked the woman.

Werner smiled.

"At home," he said.

*"Mute" was first published in **The Fiend in You** (Ballantine Books, 1962), edited by Charles Beaumont.*

*"That was another story that I spent a lot of time trying to get it right with the research. It was almost a short novel when you think of it. I have no idea why I turned the young boy into a girl for **The Twilight Zone**. I've been told over the years that the ending was cruel; that for the little girl to lose her telepathic abilities at the end was something 'bad.' But to me it was not 'bad' at all; she was going to find something instead, which her parents—as relatively nice as they were—had never really showered on her. And that was love. She was going to be much better off with the new family." —RM*

*"Mute" was adapted by the author into an hour-long episode of **The Twilight Zone**, and first telecast on January 31, 1963. It starred Ann Jillian and was directed by Stuart Rosenberg.*

DEUS EX
MACHINA
1963

IT BEGAN WHEN he cut himself with a razor.

Until then, Robert Carter was typical. He was thirty-four, an accountant with a railroad firm. He lived in Brooklyn with his wife, Helen, and their two daughters, Mary, ten, and Ruth. Ruth was five and not tall enough to reach the bathroom sink. A box for her to stand on was kept under the sink. Robert Carter shifted his feet as he leaned in toward the mirror to shave his throat, stumbled on the box and fell. As he did, his arms flailed out for balance, his grip clamping on the straight razor. He grunted as his knee banged on the tile floor. His forehead hit the sink. And his throat was driven against the hair-thin edge of the razor.

He lay sprawled and gasping on the floor. Out in the hall, he heard running feet.

"*Daddy*?" asked Mary.

He said nothing because he was staring at his reflection, at the wound on his throat. Vision seemed composed of overlays. In one, he saw blood running. In the other—

"Daddy?" Her voice grew urgent.

"I'm all right," he said. The overlays had parted now. Carter heard his daughter walk back to the bedroom as he watched the reddish-brown oil pulse from his neck and spatter on the floor.

Suddenly, with a convulsive shudder, he pulled a towel off its rack and pressed it to the wound. There was no pain. He drew the towel away, and in the moment before bubbling oil obscured the wound again, he saw red-cased wires as thin as threads.

Robert Carter staggered back, eyes round with shock. Reaction made him jerk away the towel again. Wires still, and metal.

Robert Carter looked around the bathroom dazedly. The details of reality crowded him in—the sink, the mirror-faced cabinet, the wooden bowl of shaving soap, its edge still frothed, the brush dripping snowy lather, the bottle of green lotion. All real.

Tight-faced, he wrapped the wound with jerking motions and pushed to his feet.

The face he saw in the mirror looked the same. He leaned in close, searching for some sign of difference. He prodded at the sponginess of his cheeks, ran a forefinger along the length of his jaw-bone. He pressed at the softness of this throat caked with drying lather. Nothing was different.

Nothing?

He twisted away from the mirror and stared at the wall through a blur of tears. Tears? He touched the corner of an eye.

It was a drop of oil on his finger.

Reaction hit him violently. He began to shake without control. Downstairs, he could hear Helen moving in the kitchen. In their room, he could hear the girls talking as they dressed. It was like any other morning—all of them preparing for another day. Yet it wasn't just another day. The night before he'd been a businessman, a father, husband, man. This morning—

"Bob?"

He twitched as Helen called up from the foot of the stairs. His lips moved as though he were about to answer her.

"Almost seven-fifteen," she said, and he heard her start back for the kitchen. "Hurry up, Mary!" she called before the kitchen door swung shut behind her.

It was then that Robert Carter had his premonition. Abruptly, he was on his knees, mopping at the oil with another towel. He wiped until the floor was spotless. He cleaned off the smeared razor blade. Then he opened the hamper and pushed the towel to the bottom of the clothes pile.

He jumped as they banged against the door.

"Daddy, I have to get in!" they said.

"Wait a second," he heard himself reply. He looked into the mirror. Lather. He wiped it off. There was still the bluish-dark beard on his face. *Or was it wire?*

"Daddy, I'm *late*," said Mary.

"All right." His voice was very calm as he drew the neck of his robe over the cut on his throat, flattening the makeshift bandage so it wouldn't be seen. He drew in a deep breath—could it be called breath?—and opened the door.

"I have to wash first," said Mary, pushing to the sink. "I have to go to school."

Ruth pouted. "Well, I have a lot of work to do," she said.

"That's enough," he told them. The words were leftovers from the yesterdays when he was their human father. "Behave," he said.

"Well, I have to wash first," Mary said, twisting the HOT faucet.

Carter stood looking at his children.

"What's that, Daddy?" asked Ruth.

He twitched in surprise. She was looking at the drops of oil on the side of the bathtub. He'd missed them.

"I cut myself," he said. If he wiped them away fast enough they couldn't see that they weren't drops of blood. He mopped at them with a piece of tissue paper and dropped it into the toilet, flushing it away.

"Is it a bad cut?" asked Mary, soaping her cheeks.

"No," he said. He couldn't bear to look at them. He walked quickly into the hall.

"Bob, breakfast!"

"All right," he mumbled.

"*Bob?*"

"I'll be right down," he said.

Helen, Helen…

Robert Carter stood in front of the bedroom mirror looking at his body, a host of impenetrables rushing over him. Tonsils out, appendix out, dental work, vaccination, injections, blood tests, x-rays. The entire background against which he had acted out his seemingly mortal drama—a background of blood, tissue, muscles, glands and hormones, arteries, veins—

No answer. He dressed with quick, erratic motions, trying not to think. He took off the towel and placed a large Band-aid against the wound on his throat.

"Bob, come *on*!" she called.

He finished knotting his tie as he had knotted it thousands of times before. He was dressed now. He looked like a man. He stared at his reflection in the mirror and saw how exactly he looked like a man.

Bracing himself, he turned and went into the hall. He descended the stairs and walked across the dining room. He'd made up his mind. He wasn't going to tell her.

"There you are," she said. She looked him over. "Where did you cut yourself?"

"What?"

"The girls said you cut yourself. Where?"

"On my neck. It's fine now."

"Well, let me see."

"It's all right, Helen."

She peered at his neck, where the bandage was slightly visible above his shirt collar.

"It's still bleeding," she said.

Carter jolted. He reached up to touch his wound. The Bank-aid was stained with a spot of oil. He looked back at Helen, startled. A second premonition came. He had to leave, *now*.

He left the kitchen and got his suit coat from the closet by the front door.

She'd seen blood.

His shoes made a fast, clicking sound on the sidewalk as he fled his house. It was a cold morning, gray and overcast. It was probably going to rain in a while. He shivered. He felt chilly. It was absurd now that he knew what he was; but he felt chilly.

She'd seen blood. Somehow, that terrified him even more than knowing what he was. That it was oil staining the bandage was painfully obvious. Blood didn't look like that, didn't smell like that. Yet she'd seen blood. *Why?*

Hatless, blond hair ruffling slightly in the breeze, Robert Carter walked along the street, trying to think. He was a robot; there was that to begin with. If there ever had been a human Robert Carter, he was now replaced. But why? *Why?*

He moved down the subway steps, lost in thought. People milled about him. People with explicable lives, people who knew that they were flesh and blood and did not have to think about it.

On the subway platform, he passed a newsstand and saw the headlines in a morning paper: THREE DIE IN HEAD-ON CRASH. There was a photograph—mangled automobiles, inert, partly covered bodies on a dark highway. Streams of blood. Carter thought, with a shudder, of himself lying in the photograph, a stream of oil running from his body.

He stood at the edge of the platform staring at the tracks. Was it possible that his human self *had* been replaced by a robot? Who would go to such trouble? And, having gone to it, who would allow it to be so easily discovered? A cut, a nick, a nosebleed even, and the fraud was revealed. Unless that blow on his head had jarred something loose. Maybe if he had cut himself without that blow, he would have seen only blood and tissue.

As he thought, unconsciously he took a penny from his trouser pocket and slipped it into a gum machine. He pulled at the knob and the gum thumped down. He had it half unwrapped before it struck him. Chew gum now? He grimaced, visualizing a turn of gears in his head, levers attached to curved bars attached to artificial teeth; all moving in response to a synaptic impulse.

He shoved the gum into his pocket. The station was trembling with the approach of a train. Carter's eyes turned to the left. Far in the distance, he saw the red and green eyes of the Manhattan express. He turned back front. Replaced when? Last night, the night before, last year? No, it was impossible to believe.

The train rushed by him with a blur of windows and doors. He felt the warmish, stale wind rush over him. He could smell it. His eyes blinked to avoid the swirl of dust. All this in seconds. As a machine, his reactions were so close to being human that it was incredible.

The train screeched to a halt in front of him. He moved over and entered the car with the pushing crowd. He stood by a pole, his left hand gripping it for balance. The doors slid shut again, the train rolled forward. Where was he going? he wondered suddenly. Surely not to work. Where then? To think, he told himself. He had to think.

That was when he found himself staring at a man standing near him.

The man had a bandage on his left hand and the bandage was stained with oil.

That sense of being frozen again—of his brain petrified by shock, his body still and numbed.

He wasn't the only one.

The neon sign above the door read EMERGENCY. Robert Carter's hand shook as he reached for the handle and pulled open the door.

It took no more than a moment to find out. There had been a traffic accident—a man driving to work, a flat tire, a truck. Robert Carter stood in the hallway staring in at the man on the table. He was being bandaged. There was a deep cut over his eye and oil was running down his cheek and dripping onto his suit.

"You'll have to go in the waiting room."

"What?" Carter started at the sound of the nurse's voice.

"I say you'll have to—"

She stopped as he turned away suddenly and pushed out into the April morning.

Carter walked along the sidewalk slowly, barely able to hear the sounds of the city.

There were other robots then—God only knew how many. They walked among men and were never known. Even if they were hurt they weren't known. That was the insane part. That man had been covered with oil. Yet no one had noticed it except him.

Robert Carter stopped. He felt so heavy. He had to sit down and rest a while.

The bar had only one customer, a man sitting at the far end of the counter, drinking beer and reading a newspaper. Carter pushed onto a leather stool and hooked his feet tiredly around its legs. He sat there, shoulders lumped, staring at the counter's dark, glossy wood.

Pain, confusion, dread and apprehension mixed and writhed in him. Was there a solution? Or was he just to wander like this, hopeless? Already it seemed a month since he'd left his house. But then it wasn't his house anymore.

Or was it? He sat up slowly. If there were others like him, could Helen and the girls be among that number? The idea repelled and appealed at once. He wanted them back desperately—yet how could he feel the same toward them if he knew that they, too, were wire and metal and electric current? How could he tell them about it since, if they were robots, they obviously didn't know it?

His left hand thumped down heavily on the bar. God, he was so tired. If only he could rest.

The bartender came out of the back room. "What'll it be?" he asked.

"Scotch on the rocks," said Robert Carter automatically.

Sitting alone and quiet as the bartender made the drink, it came to him. *How could he drink*? Liquid would rust metal, short out circuits. Carter sat there, tightening fearfully, watching the bartender pour. A wave of terror broke across him as the bartender came back and put the glass on the counter.

No, this wouldn't rust him. Not this.

Robert Carter shuddered and stared down into the glass while the bartender walked off to make change for a five-dollar bill. *Oil*. He felt like screaming. A glass of oil.

"*Oh, my God…*" Carter slipped off the stool and stumbled for the door.

Outside, the street seemed to move about him. What's happening to me? he thought. He leaned weakly against a plate-glass window, blinking dizzily.

His eyes focused. Inside the cafeteria, a man and woman were sitting, eating. Robert Carter gaped at them.

Plates of grease. Cups of oil.

People walked around him, making him an island in their swirling midst. How many of them? he thought. Dear God, *how many of them*?

What about agriculture? What about grain fields, vegetable patches, fruit orchards? What about beef and lamp and pork? What about processing, canning, baking? No, he had to go back, to retrench, to recapture simple possibility. He'd struck his head and was losing contact with reality. Things were still as they had always been. It was him.

Robert Carter began to smell the city.

It was a smell of hot oils and machinery turning, the smell of a great, unseen factory. His head snapped around, his face a mask of terror. Dear God, *how many*? He tried to run but couldn't. He could hardly move at all.

Robert Carter cried out.

He was running down.

He moved across the hotel lobby very slowly, with a halting, mechanical motion.

"Room," he said.

The clerk eyed him suspiciously, this man with the ruffled hair, the strangely haunted look in his eyes. He was given a pen to sign the register.

Robert Carter, he wrote very slowly, as if he had forgotten how to spell it.

In the room, Carter locked the door and slumped down on the bed. He sat, staring at his hands. Running down like a clock. A clock that never knew its builder nor its fate.

One last possibility—wild, fantastic, yet all he could manage now.

Earth was being taken over, each person replaced by mechanical duplicates. Doctors would be first, undertakers, policemen, anyone who would come in contact with exposed bodies. And they would be conditioned to see nothing. He, as an accountant, would be high on the list. He was part of the basic commerce system. He was—

Robert Carter closed his eyes. How stupid, he thought. How stupid and impossible.

It took him minutes just to stand. Lethargically, he took out an envelope and a piece of paper from a desk drawer. For a moment his eye was caught by the Gideon Bible in the drawer. Written by robots? he thought. The idea repelled him. No, there must have been humans *then*. This had to be a contemporary horror.

He drew out his fountain pen and tried to write a letter to Helen. As he fumbled, he reached into his pocket for the gum. It was a habit. Just as he was going to put it in his mouth, he became conscious of it. It wasn't gum. It was a piece of solid grease.

It fell from his hand. The pen slipped from his failing grip and dropped to the rug, and he knew he wouldn't have the strength to pick it up again.

The gum. The drink in the bar. The food in the cafeteria. His eyes raised, impelled.

And what was beginning to rain down from the sky?

The truth crushed down on him.

Just before he fell, his staring gaze was fastened to the Bible once again. *And God said let us make man in our image,* he thought.

Then the darkness came.

"Deus Ex Machina" was first published in **Gamma***, November 1963.*

"The critics always say that when a writer just drags in something by the heels to explain things, he's using 'deus ex machina.' But this is just one of those stories that starts in an ordinary way as possible, in a tract neighborhood, where a guy is shaving before he goes to work. The paranoia begins there. You certainly don't need an exotic beginning to have that occur." —RM

GIRL OF
MY DREAMS
1963

He woke up, grinning, in the darkness. Carrie was having a nightmare. He lay on his side and listened to her breathless moaning. Must be a good one, he thought. He reached out and touched her back. The nightgown was wet with her perspiration. Great, he thought. He pulled his hand away as she squirmed against it, starting to make faint noises in her throat; it sounded as if she were trying to say "No."

No, hell, Greg thought. Dream, you ugly bitch; what else are you good for? He yawned and pulled his left arm from beneath the covers. Three-sixteen. He wound the watch stem sluggishly. Going to get me one of those electric watches one of these days, he thought. Maybe this dream would do it. Too bad Carrie had no control over them. If she did, he could really make it big.

He rolled onto his back. The nightmare was ending now; or coming to its peak, he was never sure which. What difference did it make anyway? He wasn't interested in the machinery, just the product. He grinned again, reaching over to the bedside table for his cigarettes. Lighting one, he blew out smoke. Now he'd have to comfort her, he thought with a frown. That was the part he could live without. Dumb little creep. Why couldn't she be blonde and beautiful? He expelled a burst of smoke. Well, you couldn't ask for everything. If she were good-looking, she probably wouldn't have these dreams. There were plenty of other women to provide the rest of it.

Carrie jerked violently and sat up with a cry, pulling the covers from his legs. Greg looked at her outline in the darkness. She was shivering. "Oh, no," she whispered. He watched her head begin to shake. "No. No." She started to cry, her body hitching with sobs. Oh, Christ, he thought, this'll take hours. Irritably, he pressed his cigarette into the ashtray and sat up.

"Baby?" he said.

She twisted around with a gasp and stared at him. "Come 'ere," he told her. He opened his arms and she flung herself against him. He could feel her narrow fingers gouging at his back, the soggy weight of her breasts against his chest. Oh, boy, he thought. He kissed her neck, grimacing at the smell of her sweat-damp skin. Oh, boy, what I go through. He caressed her back. "Take it easy, baby," he said. "I'm here." He let her cling to him, sobbing weakly. He tried to sound concerned.

"Oh, Greg." She could barely speak. "It was horrible, oh, God, how horrible."

He grinned. It *was* a good one.

"Which way?" he asked.

Carrie perched stiffly on the edge of the seat, looking through the windshield with troubled eyes. Any second now, she'd pretend she didn't know; she always did. Greg's fingers tightened slowly on the wheel. One of these days, by God, he'd smack her right across her ugly face and walk out, free. Damn freak. He felt the skin begin to tighten across his cheeks. "Well?" he asked.

"I don't—"

"*Which way, Carrie?*" God, he'd like to twist back one of her scrawny arms and break the damn thing; squeeze that skinny neck until her breath stopped.

Carrie swallowed dryly. "Left," she murmured.

Bingo! Greg almost laughed aloud, slapping down the turn

indicator. *Left*—right into the Eastridge area, the money area. You dreamed it right this time, you dog, he thought; this is *It*. All he had to do now was play it smart and he'd be free of her for good. He'd sweated it out and now it was payday!

The tires made a crisp sound on the pavement as he turned the car onto the quiet, tree-lined street. "How far?" he asked. She didn't answer and he looked at her threateningly. Her eyes were shut.

"How far? I said."

Carrie clutched her hands together. "Greg, please—" she started. Tears were squeezing out beneath her lids.

"Damn it!"

Carrie whimpered and said something. "What?" he snapped. She drew in wavering breath. "The middle of the next block," she said.

"Which side?"

"The right."

Greg smiled. He leaned back against the seat and relaxed. That was more like it. Dumb bitch tried the same old "I-forget" routine every time. When would she learn that he had her down cold? He almost chuckled. She never would, he thought; because, after this one, he'd be gone and she could dream for nothing.

"Tell me when we reach it," he said.

"Yes," she answered. She had turned her face to the window and was leaning her forehead against the cold glass. Don't cool it too much, he thought, amused; keep it hot for Daddy. He pressed away the rising smile as she turned to look at him. Was she picking up on him? Or was it just the usual? It was always the same. Just before they reached wherever they were going, she'd look at him intently as if to convince herself that it was worth the pain. He felt like laughing in her face. Obviously, it was worth it. How else could a beast like her land someone with his class? Except for him, her bed would be the emptiest, her nights the longest.

"Almost there?" he asked.

Carrie looked to the front again. "The white one," she said.

"With the half-circle drive?"

She nodded tightly. "Yes."

Greg clenched his teeth, a spasm of avidity sweeping through him. Fifty thousand if it was worth a nickel, he thought. Oh, you bitch, you crazy bitch, you really nailed it for me this time! He turned the wheel and pulled in at the curb. Cutting the engine, he glanced across the street. The convertible would come from that direction, he thought. He wondered who'd be driving it. Not that it mattered.

"Greg?"

He turned and eyed her coldly. "What?"

She bit her lip, then started to speak.

"*No*," he said, cutting her off. He pulled out the ignition key and shoved open the door. "Let's go," he said. He slid out, shut the door and walked around the car. Carrie was still inside. "Let's *go*, baby," he said, the hint of venom in his voice.

"Greg, please—"

He shuddered at the cost of repressing an intense desire to scream curses at her, jerk open the door and drag her out by her hair. His rigid fingers clamped on the handle and he opened the door, waited. Christ, but she was ugly—the features, the skin, the body. She'd never looked so repugnant to him. "*I said let's go*," he told her. He couldn't disguise the tremble of fury in his voice.

Carrie got out and he shut the door. It was getting colder. Greg drew up the collar of his topcoat, shivering as they started up the drive toward the front door of the house. He could use a heavier coat, he thought; with a nice, thick lining. A real sharp one, maybe black. He'd get one one of these days—and maybe real soon too. He glanced at Carrie, wondering if she had any notion of his plans. He doubted it even though she looked more worried than ever. What the hell was with her? She'd never been this bad before. Was it because it was a kid? He shrugged. What difference did it make? She'd perform.

"Cheer up," he said. "It's a school day. You won't have to see him." She didn't answer.

They went up two steps onto the brick porch and stopped before the door. Greg pushed the button and, deep inside the house, melodic chimes sounded. While they waited, he reached inside his topcoat pocket and touched the small leather notebook. Funny how he always felt like some kind of weird salesman when they were operating. A salesman with a damned closed market, he thought, amused. No one else could offer what he had to sell, that was for sure.

He glanced at Carrie. "Cheer *up*," he told her. "We're helping them, aren't we?"

Carrie shivered. "It won't be too much, will it, Greg?"

"I'll decide on—"

He broke off as the door was opened. For a moment, he felt angry disappointment that the bell had not been answered by a maid. Then he thought: Oh, what the hell, the money's still here—and he smiled at the woman who stood before them. "Good afternoon," he said.

The woman looked at him with that half polite, half suspicious smile most women gave him at first. "Yes?" she asked.

"It's about Paul," he said.

The smile disappeared, the woman's face grew blank. "What?" she asked.

"That's your son's name, isn't it?"

The woman glanced at Carrie. Already, she was disconcerted, Greg could see.

"He's in danger of his life," he told her. "Are you interested in hearing more about it?"

"*What's happened to him?*"

Greg smiled affably. "Nothing yet," he answered. The woman caught her breath as if, abruptly, she were being strangled.

"You've taken him," she murmured.

Greg's smile broadened. "Nothing like that," he said.

"Where is he then?" the woman asked.

Greg looked at his wristwatch, feigning surprise. "Isn't he at school?" he asked.

Uneasily confused, the woman stared at him for several moments before she twisted away, pushing at the door. Greg caught hold of it before it shut. "Inside," he ordered.

"Can't we wait out—?"

Carrie broke off with a gasp as he clamped his fingers on her arm and pulled her into the hall. While he shut the door, Greg listened to the rapid whir and click of a telephone being dialed in the kitchen. He smiled and took hold of Carrie's arm again, guiding her into the living room. "Sit," he told her.

Carrie settled gingerly on the edge of a chair while he appraised the room. Money was in evidence wherever he looked, in the carpeting and drapes, the period furniture, the accessories. Greg pulled in a tight, exultant breath and tried to keep from grinning like an eager kid; this was *It* all right. Dropping onto the sofa, he stretched luxuriously, leaned back and crossed his legs, glancing at the name on a magazine lying on the end table beside him. In the kitchen, he could hear the woman saying, "He's in Room Fourteen; Mrs. Jennings' class."

A sudden clicking sound made Carrie gasp. Greg turned his head and saw, through the back drapes, a collie scratching at the sliding-glass door; beyond, he noted, with renewed pleasure, the glint of swimming pool water. Greg watched the dog. It must be the one that would—

"*Thank* you," said the woman gratefully. Greg turned back and looked in that direction. The woman hung up the telephone receiver and her footsteps tapped across the kitchen floor, becoming soundless as she stepped onto the hallway carpeting. She started cautiously toward the front door.

"We're in here, Mrs. Wheeler," said Greg.

The woman caught her breath and whirled in shock. "What *is* this?" she demanded.

"Is he all right?" Greg asked.

"*What do you want?*"

Greg drew the notebook from his pocket and held it out. "Would you like to look at this?" he asked.

The woman didn't answer but peered at Greg through narrowing eyes. "That's right," he said. "We're selling something."

The woman's face grew hard.

"*Your son's life,*" Greg completed.

The woman gaped at him, momentary resentment invaded by fear again. Jesus, you look stupid, Greg felt like telling her. He forced a smile. "Are you interested?" he asked.

"Get out of here before I call the police." The woman's voice was husky, tremulous.

"You're not interested in your son's life then?"

The woman shivered with fear-ridden anger. "Did you hear me?" she said.

Greg exhaled through clenching teeth.

"Mrs. Wheeler," he said, "unless you listen to us—*carefully*—

your son will soon be dead." From the corners of his eyes, he noticed Carrie wincing and felt like smashing in her face. That's right, he thought with savage fury. Show her how scared you are, you stupid bitch!

Mrs. Wheeler's lips stirred falteringly as she stared at Greg. "What are you talking about?" she finally asked.

"Your son's life, Mrs. Wheeler."

"Why should you want to hurt my boy?" the woman asked, a sudden quaver in her voice. Greg felt himself relax. She was almost in the bag.

"Did I say that we were going to hurt him?" he asked, smiling at her quizzically. "I don't remember saying that, Mrs. Wheeler."

"Then—?"

"Sometime before the middle of the month," Greg interrupted, "Paul will be run over by a car and killed."

"What?"

Greg did not repeat.

"What car?" asked the woman. She looked at Greg in panic. "What car?" she demanded.

"We don't know exactly."

"Where?" the woman asked. "When?"

"That information," Greg replied, "is what we're selling."

The woman turned to Carrie, looking at her frightenedly. Carrie lowered her gaze, teeth digging at her lower lip. The woman looked back at Greg as he continued.

"Let me explain," he said. "My wife is what's known as a 'sensitive.' You may not be familiar with the term. It means she has visions and dreams. Very often, they have to do with real people. Like the dream she had last night—about your son."

The woman shrank from his words and, as Greg expected, an element of shrewdness modified her expression; there was now, in addition to fear, suspicion.

"I know what you're thinking," he informed her. "Don't waste your time. Look at this notebook and you'll see—"

"Get out of here," the woman said.

Greg's smile grew strained. "That again?" he asked. "You mean you really don't care about your son's life?"

The woman managed a smile of contempt. "Shall I call the police now?" she asked. "The *bunco* squad?"

"If you really want to," answered Greg, "but I suggest you listen to me first." He opened the notebook and began to read. "*January twenty-second: Man named Jim to fall from roof while adjusting television aerial. Ramsay Street. Two-story house, green with white trim.* Here's the news item."

Greg glanced at Carrie and nodded once, ignoring her pleading look as he stood and walked across the room. The woman cringed back apprehensively but didn't move. Greg held up the notebook page. "As you can see," he said, "the man didn't believe what we told him and did fall off his roof on January twenty-second; it's harder to convince them when you can't give any details so as not to give it all away." He clucked as if disturbed. "He should have paid us, though," he said. "It would have been a lot less expensive than a broken back."

"Who do you think you're —?"

"Here's another," Greg said, turning a page. "This should interest you. *February twelfth, afternoon: boy, 13, name unknown, to fall into abandoned well shaft, fracture pelvis. Lives on Darien Circle,* etcetera, etcetera, you can see the details here," he finished, pointing at the page. "Here's the newspaper clipping. As you can see, his parents were just in time. They'd refused to pay at first, threatened to call the police like you did." He smiled at the woman. "Threw us out of the house as a matter of fact," he said. "On the afternoon of the twelfth, though, when I made a last-minute phone check, they were out of their minds with worry. Their son had disappeared and they had no idea where he was—I hadn't mentioned the well shaft, of course."

He paused for a moment of dramatic emphasis, enjoying the moment fully. "I went over to their house," he said. "They made their payment and I told them where their son was." He pointed at the clipping. "He was found, as you see—down in an abandoned well shaft. With a broken pelvis."

"Do you really—?"

"—expect you to believe all this?" Greg completed her thought. "Not completely; no one ever does at first. Let me tell you what you're thinking right now. You're thinking that we cut out these newspaper items and made up this story to fit them. You're entitled to believe that if you want to—" his face hardened "—but, if you do, you'll have a dead son by the middle of the month, you can count on that."

He smiled cheerfully. "I don't believe you'd enjoy hearing how it's going to happen," he said.

The smile began to fade. "And it *is* going to happen, Mrs. Wheeler, whether you believe it or not."

The woman, still too dazed by fright to be completely sure of her suspicion, watched Greg as he turned to Carrie. "Well?" he said.

"I don't—"

"*Let's have it,*" he demanded.

Carrie bit her lower lip and tried to restrain the sob.

"What are you going to do?" the woman asked.

Greg turned to her with a smile. "Make our point," he said. He looked at Carrie again. "*Well?*"

She answered, eyes closed, voice pained and feeble. "There's a throw rug by the nursery door," she said. "You'll slip on it while you're carrying the baby."

Greg glanced at her in pleased surprise; he hadn't known there was a baby. Quickly, he looked at the woman as Carrie continued in a troubled voice, "There's a black widow spider underneath the playpen on the patio, it will bite the baby, there's a—"

"Care to check these items, Mrs. Wheeler?" Greg broke in. Suddenly, he hated her for her slowness, for her failure to accept. "Or shall we just walk out of here," he said, sharply, "*and let that blue convertible drag Paul's head along the street until his brains spill out?*"

The woman looked at him in horror. Greg felt a momentary dread that he had told her too much, then relaxed as he realized that he hadn't. "I suggest you check," he told her, pleasantly. The woman backed away from him a little bit, then turned and hurried toward the patio door. "Oh, incidentally," Greg said, remembering. She turned. "That dog out there will try to save your son but it won't succeed; the car will kill it, too."

The woman stared at him, as if uncomprehending, then turned away and, sliding open the patio door, went outside. Greg saw the collie frisking around her as she moved across the patio. Leisurely, he returned to the sofa and sat down.

"Greg—?"

He frowned grimacingly, jerking up his hand to silence her. Out on the patio, there was a scraping noise as the woman overturned the playpen. He listened intently. There was a sudden gasp, then the stamping of the woman's shoe on concrete, an excited barking by the dog. Greg smiled and leaned back with a sigh. Bingo.

When the woman came back in, he smiled at her, noticing how heavily she breathed.

"That could happen any place," she said, defensively.

"Could it?" Greg's smile remained intact. "And the throw rug?"

"Maybe you looked around while I was in the kitchen."

"We didn't."

"*Maybe you guessed.*"

"And maybe we didn't," he told her, chilling his smile. "Maybe everything we've said is true. You want to gamble on it?"

The woman had no reply. Greg looked at Carrie. "Anything else?" he asked. Carrie shivered fitfully. "An electric outlet by the baby's crib," she said. "She has a bobby pin beside her, she's been trying to put it in the plug and—"

"Mrs. Wheeler?" Greg looked inquisitively at the woman. He snickered as she turned and hurried from the room. When she was gone, he smiled and winked at Carrie. "You're really on today, baby," he said. She returned his look with glistening eyes. "Greg, please don't make it too much," she murmured.

Greg turned away from her, the smile withdrawn. Relax, he told himself; relax. After today, you'll be free of her. Casually, he slipped the notebook back into his topcoat pocket.

The woman returned in several minutes, her expression now devoid of anything but dread. Between two fingers of her right hand she was carrying a bobby pin. "*How did you know?*" she asked. Her voice was hollow with dismay.

"I believe I explained that, Mrs. Wheeler," Greg replied. "My wife has a gift. She knows exactly where and when the accident will occur. Do you care to buy that information?"

The woman's hands twitched at her sides. "What do you want?" she asked.

"Ten thousand dollars in cash," Greg answered. His fingers flexed reactively as Carrie gasped but he didn't look at her. He fixed his gaze on the woman's stricken face. "Ten thousand…" she repeated dumbly.

"That's correct. Is it a deal?"

"But we don't—"

"*Take it or leave it, Mrs. Wheeler.* You're not in a bargaining position. Don't think for a second that there's anything you can do to prevent the accident. Unless you know the exact time and place, it's going to happen." He stood abruptly, causing her to start. "Well?" he snapped, "what's it going to be? Ten thousand dollars or your son's life?"

The woman couldn't answer. Greg's eyes flicked to where Carrie sat in mute despair. "Let's go," he said. He started for the hall.

"*Wait.*"

Greg turned and looked at the woman. "Yes?"

"How—do I know—?" she faltered.

"You don't," he broke in, "you don't know a thing. *We* do."

He waited another few moments for her decision, then walked into the kitchen and, removing his memo pad from an inside pocket, slipped the pencil free and jotted down the telephone number. He heard the woman murmuring pleadingly to Carrie and, shoving the pad and pencil into his topcoat pocket, left the kitchen. "Let's go," he said to Carrie who was standing now. He glanced disinterestedly at the woman. "I'll phone this afternoon," he said. "You can tell me then what you and your husband have decided to do." His mouth went hard. "*It'll be the only call you'll get,*" he said.

He turned and walked to the front door, opened it. "Come on, come on," he ordered irritably. Carrie slipped by him, brushing at the tears on her cheeks. Greg followed and began to close the door, then stopped as if remembering something.

"Incidentally," he said. He smiled at the woman. "I wouldn't call the police if I were you. There's nothing they could charge us with even if they found us. And, of course, we couldn't tell you then—and your son would have to die." He closed the door and started for the car, a picture of the woman printed in his mind: standing, dazed and trembling, in her living room, looking at him with haunted eyes. Greg grunted in amusement.

She was hooked.

Greg drained his glass and fell back heavily on the sofa arm, making a face. It was the last cheap whiskey he'd ever drink; from now on, it was exclusively the best. He turned his head to look at Carrie. She was standing by the window of their hotel living room, staring at the city. What the hell was she brooding about now? Likely, she was wondering where that blue convertible was. Momentarily, Greg wondered himself. Was it parked?—moving? He grinned drunkenly. It gave him a feeling of power to know something about that car that even its owner didn't know: namely, that, in eight days, at two-sixteen on a Thursday afternoon, it would run down a little boy and kill him.

He focused his eyes and glared at Carrie. "All right, say it," he demanded. "Get it out."

She turned and looked at him imploringly. "Does it have to be so much?" she asked.

He turned his face away from her and closed his eyes.

"Greg, does it—"

"*Yes*!" He drew in shaking breath. God, would he be glad to get away from her!

"What if they can't pay?"

"*Tough.*"

The sound of her repressed sob set his teeth on edge. "Go in and lie down," he told her.

"Greg, he hasn't got a chance!"

He twisted around, face whitening. "Did he have a better chance before we came?" he snarled. "Use your head for once, God damn it! If it wasn't for us, he'd be as good as dead already!"

"Yes, but—"

"I said go in and lie down!"

"You haven't seen the way it's going to happen, Greg!"

He shuddered violently, fighting back the urge to grab the whiskey bottle, leap at her and smash her head in. "*Get out of here*," he muttered.

She stumbled across the room, pressing the back of a hand against her lips. The bedroom door thumped shut and he heard her fall across the bed, sobbing. Damn wet-eye bitch! He gritted his teeth until his jaws hurt, then poured himself another inch of whiskey, grimacing as it burned its way into his stomach. They'll come through, he told himself. Obviously, they had the money and, obviously, the woman had believed him. He nodded to himself. They'll come through, all right. Ten thousand; his passport to another life. Expensive clothes. A class hotel. Good-looking women; maybe one of them for keeps. He kept nodding. One of these days, he thought.

He was reaching for his glass when he heard the muffled sound of Carrie talking in the bedroom. For several moments, his outstretched hand hovered between the sofa and the table. Then, in an instant, he was on his feet, lunging for the bedroom door. He flung it open. Carrie jerked around, the phone receiver in her hand, her face a mask of dread. "Thursday, the fourteenth!" she blurted into the mouthpiece. "Two-sixteen in the afternoon!" She screamed as Greg wrenched the receiver from her hand and slammed his palm on the cradle, breaking the connection.

He stood quivering before her, staring at her face with widened, maniac eyes. Slowly, Carrie raised her hand to avert the blow. "Greg, please don't—"

Fury deafened him. He couldn't hear the heavy, thudding sound the earpiece made against her cheek as he slammed it across her face with all his might. She fell back with a strangled cry. "You bitch," he gasped. "You bitch, you bitch, you bitch!" He emphasized each repetition of the word with another savage blow across her face.He couldn't see her clearly either; she kept wavering behind a film of blinding rage. Everything was finished! She'd blown the deal! The Big One was gone! *God damn it, I'll kill you!* He wasn't certain if the words exploded in his mind or if he was shouting them into her face.

Abruptly, he became aware of the telephone receiver clutched in his aching hand; of Carrie lying, open-mouthed and staring on the bed, her features mashed and bloody. He lost his grip and heard, as if it were a hundred miles below, the receiver thumping on the floor. He stared at Carrie, sick with horror. Was she dead? He pressed his ear against her chest and listened. At first, he could hear only the pulse of his own heart throbbing in his ears. Then, as he concentrated, his expression tautly rabid, he became aware of Carrie's heartbeat, faint and staggering. She wasn't dead! He jerked his head up.

She was looking at him, mouth slack, eyes dumbly stark. "Carrie?'

No reply. Her lips moved soundlessly. She kept on staring at him. "What?" he asked. He recognized the look and shuddered. "*What?*"

"Street," she whispered.

Greg bent over, staring at her mangled features. "Street," she whispered, "...night." She sucked in wheezing, blood-choked breath. "Greg." She tried to sit up but couldn't. Her expression was becoming one of terrified concern. She whispered, "Man...razor...you—oh, *no!*"

Greg felt himself enveloped in ice. He clutched at her arm. "Where?" he mumbled. She didn't answer and his fingers dug convulsively into her flesh. "Where?" he demanded. "When?" He began to shiver uncontrollably. "Carrie, *when*?!"

It was the arm of a dead woman that he clutched. With a gagging sound, he jerked his hand away. He gaped at her, unable to speak or think. Then, as he backed away, his eyes were drawn to the calendar on the wall and a phrase crept leadenly across his mind: *one of these days.* Quite suddenly, he began to laugh and cry. And before he fled, he stood at the window for an hour and twenty minutes, staring out, wondering who the man was, where he was right now and just what he was doing.

"Girl of My Dreams" was first published in **The Magazine of Fantasy & Science Fiction***, October 1963.*

"Well, I believe I wrote that story very carefully, too. I seem to have written quite a few stories very carefully. I liked the idea that for once the really rotten guy gets his comeuppance. And the girl isn't doing it out of viciousness; she just can't help it. And why they didn't later ask me to adapt it myself for television I don't know." —RM

The story was later adapted by Robert Bloch and Michael J. Bird for the ABC anthology series produced in England, **Journey to the Unknown***. Directed by Peter Sasdy and starring Michael Callan, it was first telecast on December 5, 1968.*

THE
JAZZ MACHINE
1963

I HAD THE WEIGHT THAT NIGHT
I mean I had the lubes and no one hides the blues away
You got to wash them out
Or you end up riding a slow drag to nowhere
You got to let them fly
I mean you got to

I play trumpet in this barrelhouse off Main Street
Never mind the name of it
It's like scumpteen other cellar drink dens
Where the downtown ofays bring their loot and jive talk
And listen to us try to blow out notes
As free and pure as we can never be

Like I told you, I was gully low that night
Brassing at the great White way

Lipping back a sass in jazz that Rone got off in words
And died for
Hitting at the jug and loaded
Spiking gin and rage with shaking miseries
I had no food in me and wanted none
I broke myself to pieces in a hungry night

This white I'm getting off on showed at ten
Collared him a table near the stand
And sat there nursing at a glass of wine
Just casing us
All the way into the late watch he was there
He never budged or spoke a word
But I could see that he was picking up
On what was going down
He got into my mouth, man
He bothered me

At four I crawled down off the stand
And that was when this ofay stood and put his grabber on my arm
"May I speak to you?" he asked
The way I felt I took no shine
To pink hands wrinkling up my gaberdine
"Broom off, stud," I let him know
"Please," he said, "I have to speak to you."

Call me blowtop, call me Uncle Tom
Man, you're not far wrong
Maybe my brain was nowhere
But I sat down with Mister Pink
And told him—lay his racket
"You've lost someone," he said.

It hit me like a belly chord
"What do you know about it, white man?"
I felt that hating pick up tempo in my guts again
"I don't know anything about it," he replied
"I only know you've lost someone

"*You've told it to me with your horn a hundred times.*"
I felt evil crawling in my belly
"Let's get this straight," I said
"Don't hype me, man; don't give me stuff"
"Listen to me then," he said.

"Jazz isn't only music
"It's a language too
"A language born of protest
"Torn in bloody ragtime from the womb of anger and despair
"A secret tongue with which the legions of abused
"Cry out their misery and their troubled hates.
"This language has a million dialects and accents
"It may be a tone of bitter sweetness whispered in a brass-lined
throat
"Or rush of frenzy screaming out of reed mouths
"Or hammering at strings in vibrant piano hearts
"Or pulsing, savage, under taut-drawn hides.

"In dark-peaked stridencies it can reveal the aching core of sorrow
"Or cry out the new millennium
"Its voices are without number
"Its forms beyond statistic
"It is, in very fact, *an endless tonal revolution*
"The pleading furies of the damned
"Against the cruelty of their damnation
"I know this language, friend," he said.

"What about my—?" I began and cut off quick
"Your—*wha*t, friend?" he inquired
"Someone near to you; I know that much
"Not a woman though; your trumpet wasn't grieving for a woman
loss
"Someone in your family; your father maybe
"Or your brother."

I gave him words that tiger-prowled behind my teeth
"You're hanging over trouble, man

"Don't break the thread
"Give it to me straight."
So Mister Pink leaned in and laid it down
"I have a sound machine," he said
"Which can convert the forms of jazz
"Into the sympathies which made them
"If, into my machine, I play a sorrowing blues
"From out the speaker comes the human sentiment
"Which felt those blues
"And fashioned them into the secret tongue of jazz."

He dug the same old question stashed behind my eyes
"How do I know you've lost someone?" he asked
"I've heard so many blues and stomps and strutting jazzes
"Changed, in my machine, to sounds of anger, hopelessness and joy
"That I can understand the language now
"The story that you told was not a new one
"Did you think you were inviolate behind your tapestry of woven
brass?"

"Don't hype me, man," I said
I let my fingers rigor mortis on his arm
He didn't ruffle up a hair
"If you don't believe me, come and see," he said
"Listen to my machine
"Play your trumpet into it.
"You'll see that everything I've said is true."
I felt shivers like a walking bass inside my skin
"Well, will you come?" he asked.

***

Rain was pressing drum rolls on the roof
As Mister Pink turned tires onto Main Street
I sat dummied in his coupe
My sacked-up trumpet on my lap
Listening while he rolled off words

Like Stacy runnings on a tinkle box

"Consider your top artists in the genre
"Armstrong, Bechet, Waller, Hines
"Goodman, Mezzrow, Spanier, dozens more both male and female
"Jews and Negroes all and why?
"Why are the greatest jazz interpreters
"Those who live beneath the constant gravity of prejudice?
"I think because the scaldings of external bias
"Focus all their vehemence and suffering
"To a hot, explosive core
"And, from this nucleus of restriction
"Comes all manner of fissions, violent and slow
"Breaking loose in brief expression
"Of the tortures underneath
"Crying for deliverance in the unbreakable code of jazz."
He smiled. "*Unbreakable till now*," he said.
"Rip bop doesn't do it
"Jump and mop-mop only cloud the issue
"They're like jellied coatings over true response
"Only the authentic jazz can break the pinions of repression
"Liberate the heart-deep mournings
"Unbind the passions, give freedom to the longing essence
"You understand?" he asked.
"I understand," I said, knowing why I came.

Inside the room, he flipped the light on, shut the door
Walked across the room and slid away a cloth that covered his machine
"Come here," he said
I suspicioned him of hyping me but good
His jazz machine was just a jungleful of scraggy tubes and wheels
And scrumpteen wires boogity-boogity
Like a black-snake brawl
I double-o'ed the heap
"That's really in there, man," I said
And couldn't help but smile a cutting smile

Right off he grabbed a platter, stuck it down
"Heebie-Jeebies: Armstrong
"First, "I'll play the record by itself," he said

***

Any other time I'd bust my conk on Satchmo's scatting
But I had the crawling heavies in me
And I couldn't even loosen up a grin
I stood there feeling nowhere
While Daddy-O was tromping down the English tongue
Rip-bip-dee-doo-dee-doot-doo!
The Satch recited in his Model T baritone
Then white man threw a switch

In one hot second all the crazy scat was nixed
Instead, all pounding in my head
There came a sound like bottled blowtops scuffling up in jamboree
Like twenty tongue-tied hipsters in the next apartment
Having them a ball
Something frosted up my spine
I felt the shakes do get-off chorus in my gut
And even though I knew that Mister Pink was smiling at me
I couldn't look him back
My heart was set to knock a doorway through my chest
Before he cut his jazz machine

"You see?" he asked.
I couldn't talk. He had the up on me
"Electrically, I've caught the secret heart of jazz
"Oh, I could play you many records
"That would illustrate the many moods
"Which generate this complicated tongue
"But I would like for you to play in my machine
"Record a minute's worth of solo
"Then we'll play the record through the other speaker
"And we'll hear exactly what you're feeling

"Stripped of every sonic superficial. Right?"

I had to know
I couldn't leave that place no more than fly
So, while white man set his record maker up,
I unsacked my trumpet, limbering up my lip
All the time the heebies rising in my craw
Like ice cubes piling

Then I blew it out again
The weight
The dragging misery
The bringdown blues that hung inside me
Like twenty irons on a string
And the string stuck to my guts with twenty hooks
That kept on slicing me away
I played for Rone, my brother
Rone who could have died a hundred different times and ways
Rone who died, instead, down in the Murder Belt
Where he was born
Rone who thought he didn't have to take that same old stuff
Rone who forgot and rumbled back as if he was a man
Rone who died without a single word
Underneath the boots of Mississippi peckerwoods
Who hated him for thinking he was human
And kicked his brains out for it

That's what I played for
I blew it hard and right
And when I finished and it all came rushing back on me
Like screaming in a black-walled pit
I felt a coat of evil on my back
With every scream a button that held the dark coat closer
Till I couldn't get the air

That's when I crashed my horn on his machine
That's when I knocked it on the floor

And crouched it down and kicked it to a thousand pieces
"You fool!" That's what he called me
"*You damned black fool*!"
All the time until I left

I didn't know it then
I thought that I was kicking back for every kick
That took away my only brother
But now it's done and I can get off all the words
I should have given Mister Pink

Listen, white man; listen to me good
Buddy ghee, it wasn't you
I didn't have no hate for you
Even though it was your kind that put my brother
In his final place
I'll knock it to you why I broke your jazz machine

I broke it 'cause I had to
'Cause it did just what you said it did
And, if I let it stand,
It would have robbed us of the only thing we have
That's ours alone
The thing no boot can kick away
Or rope can choke

You cruel us and you kill us
But listen, white man,
These are only needles in our skin
But if I'd let you keep on working your machine
You'd know all our secrets
And you'd steal the last of us
And we'd blow away and never be again
Take everything you want, man
You will because you have
But don't come scuffling for our souls.

*"The Jazz Machine" was first published in **The Magazine of Fantasy & Science Fiction**, February 1963.*

"Originally I wrote it as a short story. I used this book by Mess Mezzore, who is a jazz great, and I used all this phraseology, and as a prose story it was so thick. But when I turned it into a poem it worked fine. I've always hoped that someone would put music to it. There's some phraseology in it that I really like. When I was young I wrote quite a few poems, but I never tried to do anything with them."
—RM

FROM
STEPHEN KING

To SAY THAT RICHARD MATHESON invented the horror story would be as ridiculous as it would be to say that Elvis Presley invented rock and roll—what, the purist would scream, about Chuck Berry, Little Richard, Stick McGhee, The Robins, and a dozen others? The same is true in the horror genre, which is the literary equivalent of rock and roll—a quick hit to the head that bops your nerves and makes them hurt so good.

Before Matheson came dozens, going back to the author of the Grendel story, and Mary Shelley, and Horace Walpole, and Edgar Allan Poe, and Bram Stoker, and J. P. Lovecraft, and...

But like rock and roll, or any other genre that skates across the nerve-endings, horror must constantly regenerate and renew itself or die.

In the early 1950s, when *Weird Tales* was dying its slow death and Robert Bloch, horror's greatest writer at the time, had turned to psychological tales (and at this same time Fritz Leiber, easily Bloch's equal, had fallen oddly silent for a time) and the genre was languishing in the horse latitudes, Richard Matheson came like a bolt of pure ozone lightning.

He single-handedly regenerated a stagnant genre, rejecting the conventions of the pulps which were already dying, incorporating sexual impulses and images into his work as Theodore Sturgeon had already begun to do in his science fiction, and writing a series of gut-bucket short stories that were like shots of white lightning.

What do I remember about those stories.

I remember what they taught me; the same thing rock's most recent regenerator, Bruce Springsteen, articulates in one of his songs: No retreat, baby, no surrender. I remember that Matheson would never give ground.When you thought it *had* to be over, that your nerves couldn't stand any more, *that* was when Matheson turned on the afterburners and went into overdrive. He wouldn't quit. He was relentless. The baroque intonations of Lovecraft, the perfervid prose of the pulps, the sexual innuendoes were all absent. You were faced with so much pure drive that only re-readings showed Matheson's wit, cleverness, and control.

When people talk about the genre, I guess they mention my name first, but without Richard Matheson, I wouldn't be around. He is as much my father as Bessie Smith was Elvis Presley's mother. He came when he was needed, and these stories hold all their original hypnotic appeal

Be warned: you are in the hands of a writer who asks no quarter and gives none. He will wring you dry...and when you close this volume he will leave you with the greatest gift a writer can give: he will leave you wanting more.

—*Stephen King*

SHOCK WAVE
1963

"I TELL YOU THERE'S something wrong with her," said Mr. Moffat.

Cousin Wendall reached for the sugar bowl.

"Then they're right," he said. He spooned the sugar into his coffee.

"They are *not*," said Mr. Moffat, sharply. "They most certainly are *not*."

"If she isn't working," Wendall said.

"She *was* working until just a month or so ago," said Mr. Moffat. "She was working *fine* when they decided to replace her the first of the year."

His fingers, pale and yellowed, lay tensely on the table. His eggs and coffee were untouched and cold before him.

"Why are you so upset?" asked Wendall. "She's just an organ."

"*She is more*," Mr. Moffat said. "She was in before the church was even finished. Eighty years she's been there. *Eighty*."

"That's pretty long," said Wendall, crunching jelly-smeared toast. "Maybe too long."

"There's nothing wrong with her," defended Mr. Moffat. "Leastwise, there never was before. That's why I want you to sit in the loft with me this morning."

"How come you haven't had an organ man look at her?" Wendall asked.

"He'd just agree with the rest of them," said Mr. Moffat, sourly. "He'd just say she's too old, too worn."

"Maybe she is," said Wendall.

"*She is not.*" Mr. Moffat trembled fitfully.

"Well, I don't know," said Wendall, "she's pretty old though."

"She worked fine before," said Mr. Moffat. He stared into the blackness of his coffee. "The gall of them," he muttered. "Planning to get rid of her. The *gall*."

He closed his eyes.

"Maybe she knows," he said.

***

The clock-like tapping of his heels perforated the stillness in the lobby.

"This way," Mr. Moffat said.

Wendall pushed open the arm-thick door and the two men spiraled up the marble staircase. On the second floor, Mr. Moffat shifted the briefcase to his other hand and searched his keyring. He unlocked the door and they entered the musty darkness of the loft. They moved through the silence, two faint, echoing sounds.

"Over here," said Mr. Moffat.

"Yes, I see," said Wendall.

The old man sank down on the glass-smooth bench and turned the small lamp on. A wedge of bulb light forced aside the shadows.

"Think the sun'll show?" asked Wendall.

"Don't know," said Mr. Moffat.

He unlocked and rattled up the organ's rib-skinned top, then raised the music rack. He pushed the finger-worn switch across its slot.

In the brick room to their right there was a sudden hum, a mounting rush of energy. The air-gauge needle quivered across its dial.

"She's alive now," Mr. Moffat said.

Wendall grunted in amusement and walked across the loft. The old man followed.

"What do you think?" he asked inside the brick room.

Wendall shrugged.

"Can't tell," he said. He looked at the turning of the motor. "Single-phase induction," he said. "Runs by magnetism."

He listened. "Sounds all right to me," he said.

He walked across the small room.

"What's this?" he asked, pointing.

"Relay machines," said Mr. Moffat. "Keep the channels filled with wind."

"And this is the fan?" asked Wendall.

The old man nodded.

"Mmm-hmm." Wendall turned. "Looks all right to me," he said.

They stood outside looking up at the pipes. Above the glossy wood of the enclosure box, they stood like giant pencils painted gold.

"Big," said Wendall.

"She's *beautiful*," said Mr. Moffat.

"Let's hear her," Wendall said.

They walked back to the keyboards and Mr. Moffat sat before them. He pulled out a stop and pressed a key into its bed.

A single tone poured out into the shadowed air. The old man pressed a volume pedal and the note grew louder. It pierced the air, tone and overtones bouncing off the church dome like diamonds hurled from a sling.

Suddenly, the old man raised his hand.

"*Did you hear?*" he asked.

"Hear what?"

"It *trembled*," Mr. Moffat said.

As people entered the church, Mr. Moffat was playing Bach's chorale-prelude *Aus der Tiefe rufe ich* (*From the Depths, I cry*). His fingers moved certainly on the manual keys, his sprinkling shoes walked a dance across the pedals; and the air was rich with moving sound.

Wendall leaned over to whisper, "There's the sun."

Above the old man's gray-wreathed pate, the sunlight came filtering through the stained-glass window. It passed across the rack of pipes with a mistlike radiance.

Wendall leaned over again.

"Sounds all right to me," he said.

"*Wait*," said Mr. Moffat.

Wendall grunted. Stepping to the loft edge, he looked down at the nave. The three-aisled flow of people was branching off into rows. The echoing of their movements scaled up like insect scratchings. Wendall watched them as they settled in the brown-wood pews. Above and all about them moved the organ's music.

"*Sssst.*"

Wendall turned and moved back to his cousin.

"What is it?" he asked.

"*Listen.*" Wendall cocked his head.

"Can't hear anything but the organ and the motor," he said.

"That's *it*," the old man whispered. "*You're not supposed to hear the motor.*"

Wendall shrugged. "So?" he said.

The old man wet his lips. "I thing it's starting," he murmured.

Below, the lobby doors were being shut. Mr. Moffat's gaze fluttered to his watch propped against the music rack, thence to the pulpit where the Reverend had appeared. He made of the chorale-prelude's final chord a shimmering pyramid of sound, paused, then modulated, *mezzo forte*, to the key of G. He played the opening phrase of the Doxology.

Below, the Reverend stretched out his hands, palms up, and the congregation took its feet with a rustling and crackling. An instant of silence filled the church. Then the singing began.

Mr. Moffat led them through the hymn, his right hand pacing off the simple route. In the third phrase an adjoining key moved down with the one he pressed and an alien dissonance blurred the chord. The old man's fingers twitched; the dissonance faded.

"*Praise Father, Son and Holy Ghost.*"

The people capped their singing with a lingering Amen. Mr.

Moffat's fingers lifted from the manuals, he switched the motor off, the nave remurmured with the crackling rustle and the dark-robed Reverend raised his hands to grip the pulpit railing.

"Dear Heavenly Father," he said, "we, Thy children, meet with Thee today in reverent communion."

Up in the loft, a bass note shuddered faintly.

Mr. Moffat hitched up, gasping. His gaze jumped to the switch (off), to the air-gauge needle (motionless), toward the motor room (still).

"*You heard that?*" he whispered.

"Seems like I did," said Wendall.

"*Seems?*" said Mr. Moffat tensely.

"Well…" Wendall reached over to flick a nail against the air dial. Nothing happened. Grunting, he turned and started toward the motor room. Mr. Moffat rose and tiptoed after him.

"Looks dead to me," said Wendall.

"*I hope so*," Mr. Moffat answered. He felt his hands begin to shake.

The offertory should not be obtrusive but form a staidly moving background for the clink of coins and whispering of bills. Mr. Moffat knew this well. No man put holy tribute to music more properly than he.

Yet, that morning…

The discords surely were not his. Mistakes were rare for Mr. Moffat. The keys resisting, throbbing beneath his touch like things alive; was that imagined? Cords thinned to fleshless octaves, then, moments later, thick with sound; was it he? The old man sat, rigid, hearing the music stir unevenly in the air. Ever since the Responsive Reading had ended and he'd turned the organ on again, it seemed to possess almost a willful action.

Mr. Moffat turned to whisper to his cousin.

Suddenly, the needle of the other gauge jumped from *mezzo* to *forte* and the volume flared. The old man felt his stomach muscles clamped. His pale hands jerked from the keys and, for a second, there was only the muffled sound of usher's feet and money falling into baskets.

Then Mr. Moffat's hands returned and the offertory murmured

once again, refined and inconspicuous. The old man noticed, below, faces turning, tilting upward curiously and a jaded pressing rolled in his lips.

"Listen," Wendall said when the collection was over, "how do you *know* it isn't you?"

"Because it isn't," the old man whispered back. "It's *her*."

"That's crazy," Wendall answered. "Without you playing, she's just a contraption."

"No," said Mr. Moffat, shaking his head. "*No*. She's more."

"Listen," Wendall said, "you said you were bothered because they're getting rid of her."

The old man grunted.

"So," said Wendall, "I think you're doing these things yourself, unconscious-like."

The old man thought about it. Certainly, she was an instrument; he knew that. Her soundings were governed by his feet and fingers, weren't they? Without them, she was, as Wendall had said, a contraption. Pipes and levers and static rows of keys; knobs without function, arm-long pedals and pressuring air.

"Well, what do you think?" asked Wendall.

Mr. Moffat looked down at the nave.

"Time for the Benediction," he said.

In the middle of the Benediction postlude, the *swell to great* stop pushed out and, before Mr. Moffat's jabbing hand had shoved it in again, the air resounded with a thundering of horns, the church air was gorged with swollen, trembling sound.

"*It wasn't me*," he whispered when the postlude was over, "*I saw it move by itself.*"

"Didn't see it," Wendall said.

Mr. Moffat looked below where the Reverend had begun to read the words of the next hymn.

"*We've got to stop the service*," he whispered in a shaking voice.

"We can't do that," said Wendall.

"But something's going to happen, I know it," the old man said.

"What can happen?" Wendall scoffed. "A few bad notes is all."

The old man sat tensely, staring at the keys. In his lap his hands wrung silently together. Then, as the Reverend finished reading, Mr.

Moffat played the opening phrase of the hymn. The congregation rose and, following that instant's silence, began to sing.

This time no one noticed but Mr. Moffat.

Organ tone possesses what is called "inertia," an impersonal character. The organist cannot change this tonal quality; it is inviolate.

Yet, Mr. Moffat clearly heard, reflected in the music, his own disquiet. Hearing it sent chills of prescience down his spine. For thirty years he had been organist here. He knew the workings of the organ better than any man. Its pressures and reactions were in the memory of his touch.

That morning, it was a strange machine he played on.

A machine whose motor, when the hymn was ended, would not stop.

"Switch it off again," Wendall told him.

"I *did*," the old man whispered frightenedly.

"*Try it again.*"

Mr. Moffat pushed the switch. The motor kept running. He pushed the switch again. The motor kept running. He clenched his teeth and pushed the switch a seventh time.

The motor stopped.

"*I don't like it,*" said Mr. Moffat faintly.

"Listen, I've seen this before," said Wendall. "When you push the switch across the slot, it pushes a copper contact across some porcelain. That's what joins the wires so the current can flow.

"Well, you push that switch enough times, it'll leave a copper residue on the porcelain so's the current can move across it. Even when the switch is off. I've seen it before."

The old man shook his head.

"She *knows*," he said.

"That's *crazy*," Wendall said.

"*Is it?*"

They were in the motor room. Below, the Reverend was delivering his sermon.

"Sure it is," said Wendall. "She's an organ, not a person."

"I don't know any more," said Mr. Moffat hollowly.

"Listen," Wendall said, "you want to know what it probably is?"

"She knows they want her out of here," the old man said. "That's what it is."

"Oh, come on," said Wendall, twisting impatiently, "I'll tell you what it is. This is an old church—and this old organ's been shaking the walls for eighty years. Eighty years of that and walls are going to start warping, floors are going to start settling. And when the floor settles, this motor here starts tilting and wires go and there's arcing."

"Arcing?"

"Yes," said Wendall. "Electricity jumping across gaps."

"I don't see," said Mr. Moffat.

"All this here extra electricity gets into the motor," Wendall said. "There's electromagnets in these relay machines. Put more electricity into them, there'll be more force. Enough to cause those things to happen maybe."

"Even if it's so," said Mr. Moffat, "Why is she fighting me?"

"Oh, stop talking like that," said Wendall.

"But I know," the old man said, "I *feel*."

"It needs repairing is all," said Wendall. "Come on, let's go outside. It's hot in here."

Back on his bench, Mr. Moffat sat motionless, staring at the keyboard steps.

Was it true, he wondered, that everything was as Wendall had said—partly due to faulty mechanics, partly due to him? He mustn't jump to rash conclusions if this were so. Certainly, Wendall's explanations made sense.

Mr. Moffat felt a tingling in his head. He twisted slightly, grimacing.

Yet, there were these things which happened: the keys going down by themselves, the stop pushing out, the volume flaring, the sound of emotion in what should be emotionless. Was this mechanical defect; or was this defect on his part? It seemed impossible.

The prickling stir did not abate. It mounted like a flame. A restless murmur fluttered in the old man's throat. Beside him, on the bench, his fingers twitched.

Still, things might not be so simple, he thought. Who could say conclusively that the organ was nothing but inanimate machinery? Even if what Wendall had said were true, wasn't it feasible that these very factors might have given strange comprehension to the organ?

Tilting floors and ruptured wires and arcing and overcharged electromagnets—mightn't these have bestowed cognizance?

Mr. Moffat sighed and straightened up. Instantly, his breath was stopped.

The nave was blurred before his eyes. It quivered like a gelatinous haze. The congregation had been melted, run together. They were welded substance in his sight. A cough he heard was hollow detonation miles away. He tried to move but couldn't. Paralyzed, he sat there.

And it came.

It was not thought in words so much as raw sensation. It pulsed and tremored in his mind electrically. *Fear—Dread—Hatred*—all cruelly unmistakable.

Mr. Moffat shuddered on the bench. Of himself, there remained only enough to think, in horror—*She does know*! The rest was lost beneath overcoming power. It rose up higher, filling him with black contemplations. The church was gone, the congregation gone, the Reverend and Wendall gone. The old man pendulumed above a bottomless pit while fear and hatred, like dark winds, tore at him possessively.

"Hey, what's wrong?"

Wendall's urgent whisper jarred him back. Mr. Moffat blinked.

"What happened?" he asked.

"You were turning on the organ."

"Turning on—?"

"And *smiling*," Wendall said.

There was a trembling sound in Mr. Moffat's throat. Suddenly, he was aware of the Reverend's voice reading the words of the final hymn.

"*No*," he murmured.

"What is it?" Wendall asked.

"*I can't turn her on.*"

"What do you mean?"

"I *can't.*"

"Why?"

"I don't know. I just—"

The old man felt his breath thinned as, below, the Reverend

ceased to speak and looked up, waiting. No, thought Mr. Moffat. No, I *mustn't*. Premonition clamped a frozen hand on him. He felt a scream rising in his throat as he watched his hand reach forward and push the switch.

The motor started.

Mr. Moffat began to play. Rather, the organ seemed to play, pushing up or drawing down his fingers at its will. Amorphous panic churned the old man's insides. He felt an overpowering urge to switch the organ off and flee.

He played on.

He started as the singing began. Below, armied in their pews, the people sang, elbow to elbow, the wine-red hymnals in their hands.

"*No*," gasped Mr. Moffat.

Wendall didn't hear him. The old man sat staring as the pressure rose. He watched the needle of the volume gauge move past *mezzo* toward *forte*. A dry whimper filled his throat. No, please, he thought, *please*.

Abruptly, the *swell to great* stop slid out like the head of some emerging serpent. Mr. Moffat thumbed it in desperately. The *swell unison* button stirred. The old man held it in; he felt it throbbing at his finger pad. A dew of sweat broke out across his brow. He glanced below and saw the people squinting up at him. His eyes fled to the volume needle as it shook toward *grand crescendo*.

"Wendall, try to—!"

There was no time to finish. The *swell to great stop* slithered out again, the air ballooned with sound. Mr. Moffat jabbed it back. He felt keys and pedals dropping in their beds. Suddenly, the *swell unison* button was out. A peal of unchecked clamor filled the church. No time to speak.

The organ was alive.

He gasped as Wendall reached over to jab a hand across the switch. Nothing happened. Wendall cursed and worked the switch back and forth. The motor kept on running.

Now pressure found its peak, each pipe shuddering with storm winds. Tones and overtones flooded out in a paroxysm of sound. The hymn fell mangled underneath the weight of hostile chords.

"Hurry!" Mr. Moffat cried.

"It won't go off!" Wendall shouted back.

Once more, the *swell to great* stop jumped forward. Coupled with the volume pedal, it clubbed the walls with dissonance. Mr. Moffat lunged for it. Freed, the *swell unison* button jerked out again. The raging sound grew thicker yet. It was a howling giant shouldering the church.

Grand crescendo. Slow vibrations filled the floors and walls.

Suddenly, Wendall was leaping to the rail and shouting, "Out! Get Out!"

Bound in panic, Mr. Moffat pressed at the switch again and again; but the loft still shook beneath him. The organ still galed out music that was no longer music but attacking sound.

"Get out!" Wendall shouted at the congregation. "*Hurry!*"

The windows went first.

They exploded from their frames as though cannon shells had pierced them. A hail of shattered rainbow showered on the congregation. Women shrieked, their voices pricking at the music's vast ascension. People lurched from their pews. Sound flooded at the walls in tidelike waves, breaking and receding.

The chandeliers went off like crystal bombs.

"*Hurry!*" Wendall yelled.

Mr. Moffat couldn't move. He sat staring blankly at the manual keys as they fell like toppling dominoes. He listened to the screaming of the organ.

Wendall grabbed his arm and pulled him off the bench. Above them, two last windows were disintegrated into clouds of glass. Beneath their feet, they felt the massive shudder of the church.

"*No!*" The old man's voice was inaudible; but his intent was clear as he pulled his hand from Wendall's and stumbled backward toward the railing.

"*Are you crazy?*" Wendall leaped forward and grabbed the old man brutally. They spun around in battle. Below, the aisles were swollen. The congregation was a fear-mad boil of exodus.

"Let me go!" screamed Mr. Moffat, his face a bloodless mask. "I have to stay!"

"No, you don't!" Wendall shouted. He grabbed the old man bodily and dragged him from the loft. The storming dissonance rushed after them on the staircase, drowning out the old man's voice.

"You don't understand!" screamed Mr. Moffat. "*I have to stay!*"

Up in the trembling loft, the organ played alone, its stops all out, its volume pedals down, its motor spinning, its bellows shuddering, its pipe mouths bellowing and shrieking.

Suddenly, a wall cracked open. Arch frames twisted, grinding stone on stone. A jagged block of plaster crumbled off the dome, falling to the pews in a cloud of white dust. The floors vibrated.

Now the congregation flooded from the doors like water. Behind their screaming, shoving ranks, a window frame broke loose and somersaulted to the floor. Another crack ran crazily down a wall. The air swam thick with plaster dust.

Bricks began to fall.

Out on the sidewalk, Mr. Moffat stood motionless staring at the church with empty eyes.

He was the one. How could he have failed to know it? His fear, his dread, his hatred. His fear of being also scrapped, replaced; his dread of being shut out from the things he loved and needed; his hatred of a world that had no use for aged things.

It had been he who turned the overcharged organ into a maniac machine.

Now, the last of the congregation was out. Inside the first wall collapsed.

It fell in a clamorous rain of brick and wood and plaster. Beams tottered like trees, then fell quickly, smashing down the pews like sledges. The chandeliers tore loose, adding their explosive crash to the din.

Then, up in the loft, the bass notes began.

The notes were so low they had no audible pitch. They were vibrations in the air. Mechanically, the pedals fell, piling up a mountainous chord. It was the roar of some titanic animal, the thundering of a hundred, storm-tossed oceans, the earth sprung open to swallow every life. Floors buckled, walls caved in with crumbling roars. The dome hung for an instant, then rushed down and mangled half the nave. A monstrous cloud of plaster and mortar dust enveloped everything. Within its swimming opacity, the church, with a crackling, splintering, crashing, thundering explosion, went down.

Later, the old man stumbled dazedly across the sunlit ruins and heard the organ breathing like some unseen beast dying in an ancient forest.

"Shock Wave" (originally titled "Crescendo") was first published in **Gamma**, *July 1963.*

"After I first got the idea, I didn't have all the details that I wanted. So my cousin, who played the organ in the church, took me up to where the organ was. I wrote down in vivid description everything I saw while he told me how the organ worked. I liked the idea that the organ itself felt it was rejected, put out of the way. If my cousin had not been able to take me up into the loft and showed me exactly how this instrument worked, and what could happen if it malfunctioned, I never could have effectively done it." —RM

TIS THE SEASON
TO BE JELLY
1963

PA'S NOSE FELL OFF at breakfast. It fell right into Ma's coffee and displaced it. Prunella's wheeze blew out the gut lamp.

"Land o' Goshen, Dad," Ma said, in the gloom, "if ya know'd it was ready t'plop, whyn't ya tap it off y'self?"

"Didn't know," said Pa.

"That's what ya said the last time, Paw," said Luke, choking on his bark bread. Uncle Rock snapped his fingers beside the lamp. Prunella's wheezing shot the flicker out.

"Shet off ya laughin', gal," scolded Ma. Prunella toppled off her rock in a flurry of stumps, spilling liverwort mush.

"Tarnation take it!" said Uncle Eyes.

"Well, combust the wick, combust the wick!" demanded Grampa, who was reading when the light went out. Prunella wheezed, thrashing on the dirt.

Uncle Rock got sparks again and lit the lamp.

"Where was I now?" said Grampa.

"Git back up here," Ma said. Prunella scrabbled back onto her rock, eye streaming tears of laughter. "Giddy chile," said Ma. She slung another scoop of mush on Prunella's board. "Go to," she said. She picked Pa's nose out of her corn coffee and pitched it at him.

"Ma, I'm fixin' t'ask 'er t'*day*," said Luke.

"Be ya, son?" said Ma. "Thet's nice."

"Ain't no pu'pose to it!" Grampa said. "The dang force o' life is spent!"

"Now, Pa," said Pa, "don't fuss the young 'uns' mind-to."

"Says right hyeh!" said Grampa, tapping at the journal with his wrist. "We done let in the wavelen'ths of anti-life, that's what we done!"

"*Manure*," said Uncle Eyes. "Ain't we living'?"

"I'm talkin' 'bout the coming gene-rations, ya dang fool!" Grampa said. He turned to Luke. "Ain't no pu'pose to it, boy!" he said. "You cain't have no young 'uns nohow!"

"Thet's what they tole Pa 'n' me too," soothed Ma, "an' we got two lovely cillun. Don't ya pay no mind t'Grampa, son."

"We's comin' apart!" said Grampa. "Our cells is unlockin'! Man says right hyeh! We's like jelly, breakin'-down jelly!"

"Not me," said Uncle Rock.

"When you fixin' t'ask 'er, son?" asked Ma.

"We done bollixed the protective canopee!" said Grampa.

"Can o' what?" said Uncle Eyes.

"This mawnin'," said Luke.

"We done pregnayted the clouds!" said Grampa.

"She'll be might glad," said Ma. She rapped Prunella on the skull with a mallet. "Eat with ya mouth, chile," she said.

"We'll get us hitched up come May," said Luke.

"We done low-pressured the weather system!" Grampa said.

"We'll get ya corner ready," said Ma.

Uncle Rock, cheeks flaking, chewed mush.

"We done screwed up the dang master plan!" said Grampa.

"Aw, shet your ravin' craw!" said Uncle Eyes.

"Shet yer own!" said Grampa.

"Let's have a little ear-blessin' harminy round hyeh," said Pa, scratching his nose. He spat once and downed a flying spider. Prunella won the race.

"Dang leg," said Luke, hobbling back to the table. He punched the thigh bone back into play. Prunella ate wheezingly.

"Leg aloosenin' agin, son?" asked Ma.

"She'll hold, I reckon," said Luke.

"Says right hyeh!" said Grampa, "we'uns clompin' round under a killin' umbreala. A umbrella o' death!"

"*Bull*," said Uncle Eyes. He lifted his middle arm and winked at Ma with the blue one. "Go 'long," said Ma, gumming off a chuckle. The east wall fell in.

"Thar she goes," observed Pa.

Prunella tumbled off her rock and rolled out, wheezing, through the opening. "High-speerited gal," said Ma, brushing cheek flakes off the table.

"What about my corner now?" asked Luke.

"Says right hyeh!" said Grampa, "'lectric charges is afummadiddled! 'Tomic structure's unseamin'!!"

"We'll prop'er up again," said Ma. "Don't ya fret none, Luke."

"Have us a wing-ding," said Uncle Eyes. "Juste beer 'n' all."

"Ain't no pu'pose to it!" said Grampa. "We done smithereened the whole kiboodle!"

"Now, Pa," said Ma, "ain't no pu'pose in apreachin' doom nuther. Ain't they been apreachin' it since I was a tyke? Ain't no reason in the wuld why Luke hyeh shouldn't hitch hisself up with Annie Lou. Ain't he got him two strong arms and four strong legs? Ain't no sense in settin' out the dance o' life."

"We'uns ain't got naught t'fear but fear its own self," observed Pa.

Uncle Rock nodded and raked a sulphur match across his jaw to light his punk.

"Ya gotta have faith," said Ma. "Ain't no sense in Godless gloomin' like them signtist fellers."

"Stick 'em in the army, I say," said Uncle Eyes. "Poke a Z-bomb down their britches an' send 'em jiggin' at the enemy!"

"Spray 'em with fire acids," said Pa.

"Stick'em in a jug o' germ juice," said Uncle Eyes. "Whiff a fog o' vacuum viriss up their snoots. Give 'em hell Columbia."

"That'll teach 'em," Pa observed.

"We wawked t'gether through the yallar rain.
Our luv was stronger than the blisterin' pain
The sky was boggy and yer skin was new
My hearts was beatin'—Annie, I luv you."

Luke raced across the mounds, phantomlike in the purple light of his gut-bucket. His voice swirled in the soup as he sang the poem he'd made up in the well one day. He turned left at Fallout Ridge, followed Missile Gouge to Shockwave Slope, posted to Radiation Cut and galloped all the way to Mushroom Valley. He wished there were horses. He had to stop three times to reinsert his leg.

Annie Lou's folks were hunkering down to dinner when Luke arrived. Uncle Slow was still eating breakfast.

"Howdy, Mister Mooncalf," said Luke to Annie Lou's pa.

"Howdy, Hoss," said Mr. Mooncalf.

"Pass," said Uncle Slow.

"Draw up sod," said Mr. Mooncalf. "Plenty chow fer all."

"Jest et," said Luke. "Whar's Annie Lou?"

"Out the well fetchin' whater," Mr. Mooncalf said, ladling bitter vetch with his flat hand.

"The," said Uncle Slow.

"Reckon I'll help 'er lug the bucket then," said Luke.

"How's ya folks?" asked Mrs. Mooncalf, salting pulse-seeds.

"Jest fine," said Luke. "Top o' the heap."

"Mush," said Uncle Slow.

"Glad t'hear it, Hoss," said Mr. Mooncalf.

"Give 'em our crawlin' best," said Mrs. Mooncalf.

"Sure will," said Luke.

"Dammit," said Uncle Slow.

Luke surfaced through the air hole and cantered toward the well, kicking aside three littles and one big that squished irritably.

"How is yo folks?" asked the middle little.

"None o' yo dang business," said Luke.

Annie Lou was drawing up the water bucket and holding on the side of the well. She had an armful of loose bosk blossoms.

Luke said, "Howdy."

"Howdy, Hoss," she wheezed, flashing her tooth in a smile of love.

"What happened t'yer other ear?" asked Luke.

"Aw, Hoss," she giggled. Her April hair fell down the well. "Aw, pshaw," said Annie Lou.

"Tell ya," said Luke. "Somep'n on my cerebeelum. Got that wud from Grampa," he said, proudly. "Means I got me a mindful."

"That right?" said Annie Lou, pitching bosk blossoms in his face to hide her rising color.

"Yep," said Luke, grinning shyly. He punched at his thigh bone. "Dang leg," he said.

"Givin' ya trouble agin, Hoss?" asked Annie Lou.

"Don't matter none," said Luke. He picked a swimming spider from the bucket and plucked at its legs. "Sh'luvs me," he said, blushing. "Sh'luvs me not. Ow!" The spider flipped away, teeth clicking angrily.

Luke gazed at Annie Lou, looking from eye to eye.

"Well," he said, "will ya?"

"Oh, Hoss!" She embraced him at the shoulders and waist. "I thought you'd never ask!"

"Ya *will*?"

"*Sho*!"

"Creeps!" cried Luke. "I'm the happiest Hoss wot ever lived!"

At which he kissed her hard on the lip and went off racing across the flats, curly mane streaming behind, yelling and whooping.

"Ya-hoo! I'm so happy! I'm so happy, happy, happy!"

His leg fell off. He left it behind, dancing.

*"Tis the Season to Be Jelly" was first published in **The Magazine of Fantasy & Science Fiction**, June 1963.*

"I really like this story—it's a nutty as it can be. I remember amusing myself greatly with the writing of it. It's the Terry Gilliam approach to being serious. At a science fiction convention which took place in Connecticut, I believe, the organizers asked for recordings from us, and so I recorded a section of that story in which I read and acted it out. But they never did anything with it as far as I know; it's since disappeared." —RM

INTEREST
1965

"I'M SORRY," Cathryn said, lowering her eyes in embarrassment, "I shouldn't gape so. It's just that I've never been in such a beautiful home before."

She looked across the wide snowy-clothed table for support. But Gerald's returned smile was as tight and restrained as hers. She glanced at his father from the corners of her eyes. Mr. Cruickshank seemed to be absorbed in running his silver-handled knife through the butter-soft filet mignon.

"We understand, my dear," said Mrs. Cruickshank. "I felt the same when when I first…" Her voice broke off.

Cathryn glanced aside involuntarily and saw Mr. Cruickshank's head lower again over the gilted plate. A slight shudder ran down her back. She pretended not to notice, picking up her delicate gold-rimmed wine glass in a shaky hand.

"The steak is delicious," she said, putting down the glass. Mrs. Cruickshank nodded and smiled weakly. Then it was silent except for the clink of silver on dishes and the tiny explosions of log bits in the huge marble fireplace that stood at one end of the great dining room.

Cathryn looked at Gerald again.

His gaze was fixed on his plate. His jaws moved slowly and irregularly as though he were thinking and, at odd moments, drifted so far away that he forgot he was eating too.

Her mouth tightened as she watched his restive movements. She took a sip of water to clear her throat. I'm marrying *him*, she thought, not this house, not his parents. He's all right when his father isn't around.

She flushed a little as if her thoughts were audible to Mr. Cruickshank. She lowered her eyes and ate again. She felt the old man's eyes on her, and unconsciously, she drew her feet together under the chair. The grating of her heels on the smooth inlaid wood floor made Mr. Cruickshank's shoulders twitch.

She kept her eyes on her food. Stop looking at me like that, she thought, her mind snapping the words. Then, resolutely, she raised her eyes and looked at him. She saw the flesh on his right cheek pulsate for a moment. Her throat contracted.

"How high is the ceiling, Mr. Cruickshank?" she blurted out, unable to face him in silence. She noticed his shirt, as snowy white as the table cloth, the impeccably-set bow tie standing out against it like a complementary pair of jet-black triangles. She put her shaking hands in her lap for a moment. I couldn't call him Father if I lived a million years, she thought.

"Mmm?" Mr. Cruickshank finally grunted. *You heard me*! Her mind cried out.

"How high is the ceiling?" she asked with a trembling smile.

"Seventy-five feet," he said as though reading off the measurement to a surveyor.

She glanced up as if checking, glad to avoid his pale blue eyes and the sight of the tic which sprang in his cheek like a tiny imprisoned insect.

Her eyes ran up the tapestried walls, past the high, wide-paned windows, to the dark curving beams that arched to the ceiling. Gerald take me away, she thought. I can't go on with this. I can't.

"Seventy-five," she said. "My."

Mr. Cruickshank was no longer watching her. Nor was his wife.

Only Gerald's eyes met her's as she looked down. They looked at each other a moment. *Don't be afraid*; she seemed to see the message in his look.

She began to eat again, unable to keep the trembling from her hands. What is it about this house, she wondered. I can't help feeling it isn't me. It's the house. It's too big. Everything about it is too big. And there's something else about it. Something I can't explain. But I feel it. I feel it every second.

She glanced up at the two giant chandeliers that hung over their heads like great bracelets of glowing gold nuggets. Involuntarily her eyes moved to the length of marble wall between the top of the tapestried panels and the bottom of the windows.

Deer heads, she thought with a shudder, lowering her gaze quickly; a row of decapitations looking down at us while we eat. And, on the floor, what's left of a grizzly bear, staring up, mouth gaping in a forever snarl.

She closed her eyes, the feeling swelling up in her again. It's the house, the house, she thought.

When she opened her eyes, after a moment, Gerald was looking at her, his lean mouth set concernedly. Are you all right? he asked soundlessly, with his lips.

She smiled at him, wanting to run around the table and hold on to him forever. Oh God, don't look at me like that, she begged in her mind, not with such pity and anguish in your eyes. I need strength now, not looks of unhappiness.

She started violently, her heart thudded against her chest as Mr. Cruickshank cleared his throat and put down his silver. He leaned back in the chair, his eyes running imperiously down the length of the table.

Abruptly, Mrs. Cruickshank put down her silverware and sat rigidly. Gerald put his down too, and looked over at Cathryn, his face a mask of sudden pain. She didn't understand. She glanced at his father.

Mr. Cruickshank sat waiting, his lean blue-veined hands planted on each knee. He stared ahead as though he sat alone. Cathryn felt her stomach muscles tighten. She put down her silver quietly and sat staring at the row of white candles jutting out from the shining silver centerpiece.

Mr. Cruickshank raised one half-palsied hand then and wrapped the fingers of it around a crown-topped silver bell. He shook it precisely, twice, as though to ring it more or less would profane a ritual.

The high jingle echoed in the long room. Oh my God, this is so ridiculous, Cathryn thought, are we at dinner or at worship?

She looked at Mrs. Cruickshank, at Gerald. They sat mutely. Gerald was looking at his father with a look of tight bitterness marring his features.

Before the sound of the bell had died, the thick oak door which led to the kitchen opened noiselessly and the two maids came filing in silently. As they took away the main course, Cathryn watched Gerald.

He was holding one blood-drained fist against his chin. She could sense the endless unrest in him. I've never seen him like this before, she thought. Not so upset.

She shifted on the red plush chair as a maid set the tall dish of lemon ice before her.

She kept her head down as she ate, wishing that Gerald would say something, anything. The ice made her shiver as it slid wetly down her throat and into her stomach.

"Too cold," muttered Mr. Cruickshank.

She glanced aside with a questioning look on her face. Mr. Cruickshank was staring at the table cloth. His colorless lips were pursed as he ran the ice around his mouth to take off the chill before swallowing it.

As she watched him, she suddenly wanted to throw back the chair, jump up and run away as far as she could. She shivered.

Again Mr. Cruickshank cleared his throat. Cathryn started and her spoon clinked loudly against the dish. Mrs. Cruickshank smiled in vague pleasantness.

The bell again. She sat primly. The maids entered with the butler following.

"Coffee in the library," specified Mr. Cruickshank abruptly. His heavy chair grated back on the floor, setting Cathryn's teeth on edge. She noticed how the old man's body wavered as he stood.

Gerald was up and around the table. He helped her up and she clung gratefully to his arm.

"You've been fine," he said quietly. "Just fine."

She didn't say anything. She kept her hand on his arm as they walked across the wide room to the hall.

In silence, they crossed the great hall. The click of their footsteps seemed lost in its immensity. Cathryn glanced up the long wide staircase with the gold-framed oil paintings hung along its length.

"Do you…" she started and then stopped when she saw Gerald wasn't listening. He was staring ahead at his father, his face pale and absorbed in thought. She looked at him as she might view a stranger. *What is it?* Her mind asked it again and again.

She looked around the hall and felt fear creeping over her. She wanted to shrink, draw into herself, away from the very walls. There's something terrible about it. She was sure of it. Something hidden from her mind as knowledge but not as trembling premonition.

As they entered the library another thought jolted her. Was it possible that his parents were against the marriage now? After they'd given their word?

What am I doing to myself? she thought. I'm just making this up. All of it.

Gerald turned and looked at her and she realized she'd been staring at him all the time she was thinking.

"What is it, Cathryn?" he asked.

"Darling, you're so quiet."

He smiled sadly and pressed her hand in his.

"Am I?" he said. "I'm sorry. It's…well I'll tell you after. I…" He finished in a whisper as they approached his parents.

There were heavy chairs and couches arranged before the fireplace. Mr. Cruickshank's sparse frame was on a couch. His wife was getting settled on a nearby chair.

Mr. Cruickshank patted the couch beside him.

"Sit here, Cathryn," he said.

She sat down nervously. She could smell the clean starchiness of his shirt and the pomade he had on his thin gray hair.

She tried not to shiver. Heat waves from the fireplace played against her legs. She glanced up. Another seventy-five-foot ceiling, she thought. And books, millions of them. Shadowy marble busts peering down glumly from the tops of bookcases. The ceiling covered with a gigantic green-tinted painting. All around, she could see the shapes of fresh tropical plants sticking out of their huge pots, the leaves like sharpened green knives.

"You are twenty-five, Cathryn," said Mr. Cruickshank. It was only half question.

She folded her hands. "Yes." Her throat contracted and she waited for more questions. First dinner with my fiancé's parents, she thought. She waited tensely.

But Mr. Cruickshank said nothing more. From the corner of an eye she noticed his gaunt fingers drumming restlessly on a knee cap.

"Father, I…" Gerald suddenly started to say. His voice broke off as the door opened behind him and the butler entered, carrying a tray.

The night will never end, Cathryn thought as the butler proferred the tray toward her. She took a cup of coffee. She poured a little cream from the silver pitcher, put a half teaspoon of sugar in the cup and stirred as quietly as she could.

Mr. Cruickshank was sipping the black coffee without cream or sugar. The cup rattled a little on the saucer while he held it. Cathryn tried hard not to hear it. She tried to concentrate on the popping splutter of the fire. But she kept hearing the slight jiggling of the cup and saucer that the old man held.

She looked at Gerald, then at his mother. They were both staring into their coffee. Her muscles tightened suddenly. I don't know why I'm so afraid, she thought. Afraid of his father and his mother and his house. It's terrible to be afraid of everything that's a part of him but I can't help it. I want him to take me far away from them.

Again, she looked at Gerald. Something was rising in him. Like a fanned fire. She could tell it. She sat waiting, knowing that something was going to happen, that he would speak or shout or hurl his cup on the floor. Her throat moved as he put down his cup and ran the edge of his tongue quickly over his lips. She waited tensely, her hands trembling. She realized she wasn't breathing and the room seemed to have whirled away except for Gerald sitting there.

Then as the moments passed, she noticed the marble bust *behind him in the distance*. *The marble bust of Pallas just above my chamber door*, her mind ranted inanely. *And with many and flirt and…*

"Father," Gerald said quickly and her eyes were riveted on his face. He was sitting on the edge of the chair, hands pressed together in his lap.

She felt numb, waiting for Mr. Cruickshank's answer.

"Gerald," he said and, taking a sudden breath, Cathryn put down her cup and saucer with nervous fingers.

Gerald stared at his father. Oh my God, *speak*! Her mind cried out.

"I...I think," Gerald said falteringly, "I think that Cathryn has a right to know. Before we're married."

There was silence for a horrible moment. Then Mr. Cruickshank said, "Know?" His voice was cold. She glanced at him and was revolted and frightened by the twitching under his right eye.

She looked away and noticed how pale Gerald's mother had become. She was looking fearfully at her son.

Gerald clenched his fists. "You know what I mean," he said, "about..."

"That will do," said his father in a threatening tone.

Gerald was silent. He pressed his lips together. Then suddenly he drove one fist against his leg.

"No!" he said, all the withheld nerves exploding in his voice, "I'm not going to shock her as mother was..."

"I said that will do!"

Mr. Cruickshank's voice was rising and shrill. Cathryn felt the couch cushion move as the old man lurched forward and back with a spasmodic movement.

Gerald stood up quickly, his face taut. He turned and started toward one end of the room.

"Gerald, no!" cried his mother, starting half to her feet. She stumbled, righted herself and hurried after her son. She caught his sleeve. Cathryn watched in astonishment, hearing the shaking urgency in Mrs. Cruickshank's voice.

Mr. Cruickshank stood up.

"This is no concern of yours," he said hastily. "It's not as important as it seems." She avoided his eyes and heard his black shoes moving rapidly over the rug.

She raised her eyes and watched the three of them standing at the end of the room. Gerald was gesturing rabidly, seemingly unable to control himself. His movements were erratic. His voice broke often as he spoke. Three times he made a move for the bookcase of red leather volumes at his side. Three times his father restrained him.

"No!" his voice billowed up in fury, "I won't ask it of her. You had no right to…"

The voices became muffled again. She turned away and stared at the fire, her teeth chattering. What is it, what *is* it? She wanted to scream the question at them. It was unnerving her not to know but to feel it every second.

What was the terrible menace that filled the very air of the house? Why did Gerald always seem to have this fear in him and terribly so in his own home?

No, she thought. It was worse than fear. It was like a deep corroding sense of guilt. Guilt like a never-healing wound, self-broken open after every healing.

Guilt. For what?

"For what?" she muttered and, even when she struggled, the words were louder than she meant them to be. She glanced around hurriedly to make sure they didn't hear. Her hands twisted in anguish.

They came back. She listened to the thud of their feet across the rug.

"I'll take you home," Gerald said quietly. She looked up at his impassive face. Mrs. Cruickshank touched his arm but he pulled away. Cathryn stood up nervously and took the arm he offered to her stiffly.

They started out of the room. She heard Mr. Cruickshank say something to his wife in an irritated voice. I don't ever want to come back here, Cathryn thought angrily. I hate the place. It's big and ugly and unfriendly. And what about the people who live in it? asked her mind. She ignored the question.

Gerald helped her on with her coat. She didn't look at him. She kissed Mrs. Cruickshank's cool cheek. She shook Mr. Cruiskshank's hand. I hate your house, she was thinking.

"Thank you for having me," she said. "It was lovely."

"We're so glad you could come," Gerald's mother said. Her husband nodded.

She and Gerald walked down the long path to his car. Once she looked back over her shoulder but the door had been closed.

They got into the car without a word. Inside, Gerald sat staring out through the windshield. She heard his heavy breathing in the darkness.

"Darling, what is it?" she asked.

He turned slowly and faced her. Suddenly he pulled her close to him and pressed his face against her soft hair.

She stroked his cheek. "Tell me," she asked.

"How...how can I ask you to marry me?" he said.

She swallowed, feeling herself grow cold.

"Don't you love me?" she asked in a thin frightened voice.

He kissed her and clung to her desperately.

"You know I love you," he said, "but you don't know what I'm asking you. What you'd be marrying into. The...the *evil*."

"Evil?" she repeated.

He pulled away from her. He looked out the windshield at the far-off sky.

"Yes," he said. "And I can't ask you to...live with it."

"You love me?"

"Yes. Of course I love you."

"Then nothing else matters."

"It *does*," he said, his voice angry. "You don't know what you're saying. Don't be silly and romantic. It does matter. My father may say it doesn't. My mother may say so. But it matters. It will always matter."

He reached over quickly and turned on the motor. He jerked down the gear shift and the car started around the wide elliptical drive. Gerald turned it sharply onto the road.

"I'm taking you home," he said harshly. "I'm not going to marry you."

She jolted on the seat and stared at him. She couldn't speak. Her body felt heavy and numb.

"What?" she murmured but she couldn't even hear it herself.

The dark woods flew by. She kept looking at his black outline, at the deep shadows of his face created by the minute glow from the dashboard. Her hands shook.

"Gerald," she said.

He didn't answer. She drew in a ragged breath and felt a tear run down her cheek.

"You...you have to t-tell me why," she said. "You..."

A sob caught her throat and she turned her head away.

"Listen, Cathryn," he said. His voice was hollow and he sounded lost. He sounded as if he were saying goodbye forever.

"Just listen to me. Love isn't enough. Believe me. My mother loved and still loves my father. But it isn't enough. You don't know what it is. You couldn't possibly. And I don't want you to know. I don't want you to ever have to know. To have to live with it, day after day, hour by hour, every minute without end. It's too terrible."

"But…"

"No. Listen to me, darling. My mother pretends it's in the past. She says it's over and done with. But I've heard her wake screaming in the night. God, how many times! And I've watched my father pretend that life was going on as usual and there was nothing wrong. And all the time it's killing him. He's pretending and living like a satisfied rich man and it's killing him."

"What? *What*, Gerald!"

He jammed his foot on the brake and the car jolted to a halt. She gasped and looked in fright at him. She caught her breath as his hand took hers, cold and shaking.

"All right," he said. "I'm going to show you. It will be fair that way. Then you'll know and you can decide. There'll be no secrets. Then you can see how you'd be trapped by marrying me."

"*Trapped*, Gerald?" she said miserably.

"Yes," he said, starting the car. He turned it and started back.

"It's our…money," he said.

"Your…"

"Our money. Oh, I know what you'll say. I've heard it so many times. It's not my father's responsibility, not mine, for what our ancestors did. The sins of the fathers and all that. Well, it's a lie. A lie."

He kept his eyes on the road, his foot pressing down on the accelerator.

"But darling, how can you…"

"Will you wait!" he almost cried. Then he forced calm into his voice.

"I'm sorry," he said. "Just wait. Please, Cathryn."

The car moved into the driveway and stopped silently before the house.

"Don't slam the door," Gerald said.

"Maybe I'd better not go in," she said.

She shivered as he pressed her hand in the darkness.

"Cathryn, it's this way or no way. If you don't come in now, there'll be no other time. I'll take you home and we'll never see each other again."

"All right," she said, "I'll go in."

She closed the door as quietly as she could. In the hallway of the house she stood timidly while Gerald relocked the front door.

He took her hand and led her quickly to the darkened library. Their footsteps rustled over the thick rug. From the fireplace a quivering golden layer extended over the floor. Cathryn's throat contracted. She could feel the hugeness and the hostility of the room about her.

They stood before the bookcase. She heard him pull open the door. Then the sound of books being withdrawn. She moved closer.

In the dim light from the fireplace she saw his white fingers moving on a safe dial.

She turned away. She heard the safe door open and the scrape of something being drawn out. She flinched as he took hold of her arm. She kept her eyes shut as he led her to the couch in front of the fireplace.

They sat down and he put the object in her lap.

"You mustn't show me," she said suddenly.

"Do you want to marry me?" he asked.

"Must I know?" He said nothing and she put her hands on the object. She looked at it. It was a dark, wood box.

She ran her hands numbly over its surface. The blood pounded through her as she reached over and unlocked it. She felt paralyzed.

"Open it," he said quietly, his voice trembling.

She lifted one shaking hand and opened the top. She took a deep breath and looked inside. She stared.

"This is where it came from." His voice was like a thought in her brain.

Her brow knitted. She reached into the box. By the flickering light she looked at what she held in her hand. She turned to him.

"But," she said, "this is only..."

"Silver," he said, his dark eyes wide and staring. "Count them. *There are thirty pieces.*"

"Interest" was first published in **Gamma**, *September 1965.*

"I think the story was rejected a number of times. Ultimately it was published in **Gamma**, *which was a magazine that Bill Nolan started. I always thought the idea was an interesting one: 'Whatever happened to those thirty pieces of silver?' I don't know why it was rejected so much, except maybe some editors thought it was somehow sacrilegious." —RM*

A DRINK OF
WATER
1967

THE MOVIE ENDED AT 1:12 A.M. When they left the theater the August heat pressed down on them.

"I'm thirsty," said George.

"Why didn't you get a drink before we left?" she asked.

"That stuff tastes like bath water," he said. "*Boy*, am I thirsty."

"What did you have to eat?" Eleanor asked.

"Buttered popcorn," he said.

"And—?"

"And I'm *dying*," he said.

"What else did you have besides the popcorn?"

"Some of those chocolate-covered ice cream things."

"What else?"

"A candy bar."

"I wonder why you're thirsty," she said.

He licked his lips. "Now I know how they feel in those desert pictures."

"We'll reach the oasis soon," said Eleanor.

The note was tacked to the apartment door. When Eleanor read it she laughed out loud.

"Well, you have to admit he warned us," she said. "We've been complaining about those pipes for a year."

"So he turns them off on a night like *this*?" Irritably, George unlocked the door and pushed it open. Walking into the kitchen, he switched on the light. She heard him turning faucets.

"Oh...Christ!" He came out of the kitchen, looking furious. He took the note from her. *"Turned back on tomorrow afternoon,"* he read. "Great!"

"There must be *something*," Eleanor said. She went into the kitchen and pulled open the refrigerator door. George followed her.

"Evaporated milk," she said.

"Come on."

"There's orange juice. Oh, no, we used that up at breakfast."

"Give me some ice cubes then."

She pulled out the tray, then looked at him guiltily. "I could have sworn—" she said.

"Any *fruit*?"

"I was going to shop tomorrow."

"That's great," he said. "That's just *great*."

She looked at him blankly. "Well," she said.

"Well, *what*?"

"I guess you'll have to go out and get a drink."

"*Where*?"

"A bar?"

"Oh, Christ." He sighed.

Let's see now, he thought, starting back toward the avenue, where were some bars? He remembered one and nodded to himself.

"Oh...*boy*," he muttered, walking faster. If this wasn't one for the books. Going out after one-thirty on a weekday morning to get a drink of water.

He exhaled heavily as he crossed a street. Strange, he thought, how all details of living could be overshadowed by the need for a drink of water. A person forgot how important water is. It took something like this to remind him.

He sighed, walking faster. It seemed as though his saliva had dried up. He licked his lips. *Man*, it was hot!

He reached the avenue. Now where was that bar? It was on this block, wasn't it? No, on the next; there was the neon sign. He hurried toward it. Boy, he thought, am I going to drink water.

He saw himself entering the bar, telling the bartender: man, what a stupid thing! Dying of thirst, I get home, and what has the janitor done? Had the pipes turned off! Yeah! On a night like this!

And all the time he talked, he'd be drinking glasses of water. Ice-cold water, clear as crystal, with those little ice cubes bobbing in it, the ones with little round holes in the middle. Six or seven of them clinking against the freezing sides of the glass as that cold, wet, delicious water trickled down his—

The bar was closed.

He stood looking at it dumbly. Closed? So *early*? What a stupid thing! He glared up at the neon sign. Why do they leave it on if the damn place is *closed*! He thought furiously.

Grunting, he turned and started down the avenue. *One* of these bars must be open. He started to run, then walked again. The fall of his shoes was the only sound he could hear.

A few blocks up there was another bar. Squinting, he could just make out the neon letters IRISH SHANTY. He'd been there years ago. He remembered the bartender drawing off a glass of ice-cold beer. He started to run again, the heat buffeting at his face like hot wings. Hey, bartender, a great big glass of water!

The Irish Shanty was closed. He stood outside it, panting, looking at a waterfall. It was a beer advertisement. *From the Land of Waterfalls*. An electrical gimmick made it seem as if there were a real waterfall in the window. Cold blue waters dashed down on rocks, casting up white spray.

He was startled at the faint sob in his throat.

He turned away. Let's not be ridiculous, he thought. You'll get a drink. Just don't stand there staring at a lousy, fake waterfall.

He looked up and down the avenue. In the distance, he could see a trolley car approaching. He thought of boarding it. Maybe someone on it would know where he could get a drink of water.

"*Oh…*" This was absurd. He was making a melodrama out of nothing. He couldn't be *that* thirsty. All he'd had was—

No, he didn't want to think about that. He tried to concentrate on finding a drink of water; but his torturing mind, released, began to cast off memories of how the popcorn had tasted, hot and slick with melted butter and very, very salty. He could taste the ice cream—cold, yes, but sweet and covered with sweeter, viscid chocolate that oozed slowly down his drying throat.

"Stop it," he mumbled.

And the candy bar—sweet and full of warm nuts and sticky caramel that stuck to the roof of his mouth and chocolate, thick, warm chocolate, melting in his mouth.

"*Stop it!*" His angry voice was drowned out by the clamor of the passing trolley car. He glared at the people sitting in it. What did they care that he was dying of thirst?

He shuddered, a flickering of raw emotion in him. Life is like that, he thought. All the ordinary details going on and on and underneath, the constant threat. All it took was the combining of a few effects like these—a sodden August night, popcorn and ice cream and candy and brackish-tasting water in the theater and the pipes turned off and nothing else to drink. No far-fetched happenings either. Small, possible, terribly logical happenings that—

He stopped with a gasp of excitement. Up the block, he saw a gas station. There must be a coke machine in front of it with an attached water fountain!

His rushing footfalls spattered on the sidewalk. His eyes held fixedly on the gas station as he came closer and closer. There *was* a coke machine! He began to sprint. It was almost over now. In a few seconds he'd have his drink and all this foolishness would be over. He rushed past the silent pumps and skidded to a halt in front of the coke machine. His fingers trembled as he pushed down the chrome button.

No water.

He stared at the fountain as if he were not seeing correctly. No, this was wrong. He depressed the button a second time. Nothing. And again. There was no water.

"No!" He shouted, his voice ringing out in the deserted station.

He slammed the side of a fist on the button, then jerked it back with a hiss of pain.

Suddenly, impossibly, he almost started crying. He caught himself. *Stop being such a fool*, he told himself. You'll get a drink soon enough.

He looked around. Down the avenue was the theater he and Eleanor had gone to. He stared at it with baleful animosity. Suddenly, he tensed. What if someone were still there, closing up—the cashier, the projectionist, the manager?

Excitedly, he ran across the avenue, leaped the curb, and raced beneath the marquee's overhang. Springing to the glass doors, he rushed from one to another pushing at them. They were all locked. He pounded on a door, but no one answered.

He stood staring in at the water fountain. He visualized himself bending over it and turning the knob, feeling a burst of water on his lips, inside his mouth. A terrible, malefic fury began to rise in him. The people who ran this lousy theater were at fault.

"Yes, *you*!" he yelled, his voice sounding shrill in the vaultlike outer lobby.

Suddenly, he kicked the door and cried out at the pain. Turning, he ran across the marble floor. I want a drink! He raged inside his mind. *I want a drink!*

Back on the sidewalk, breathing through clenched teeth, he looked up and down the silent avenue. *Now what*? He had to have a drink; he *had* to! But everything was closed, locked, barred. He looked around, head snapping from one direction to another, breath coming faster and faster. Here he was in a city that *swam* in water and he couldn't get a drink! *He simply could not get a drink!*

What if he went to someone's door, he calmed himself. Knocked or rang the bell, until they woke up and gave him a drink. Yes, that's what he'd do. That's what he'd have to do. He started limping down the avenue. It was so hot; so goddam *hot*! Thirst was searing through him, parching, baking.

Suddenly, a heart-deep burst of fear exploded in him. He started running mindlessly, without direction. Water. He had to get a drink of water before it was too late. Yes, it had come to that. *Before it was too late*. Water.

Water!

He left the avenue, a floundering rag doll of a man, eyes blank, mouth hanging wide, arms like twitching stalks. The heat was enveloping him now. It was going to dry him up, blotting all the juices in him, turning him into a crackling husk of dust-dry—!

He jarred to a halt, eyes unbelieving.

Up the block, someone had left a sprinkler on. In the light of a street lamp he could see the glistening mushroom of water falling to the lawn.

His legs began to move, slowly, first, then quickly. Now he was running, muttering to himself excited, lunatic sounds like the beginning laughter of a madman. He ran faster and faster. The world was gone; there was no world, no people, nothing in the whole wide universe except that sprinkler whirling, sending out its hissing spume of cool, cool—

He lurched into the spray, slipping on the wet grass. He did not try to rise. He crawled intently toward the sprinkler until the drops of water whipped across his face like storming rain and filled his yawning mouth and ran exquisitely down his throat.

He stumbled home, on his face the sated look of an animal that has fed. When he reached the apartment he shed his soaked clothes, put on pajamas, and climbed into bed.

At four-sixteen, he woke up, gasping, as a peal of thunder rocked across the sky. He looked around dazedly, mind insensible with sleep. Outside, it was pouring. He grunted and, pushing to his feet, stumbled to the window. The sill was covered with a film of drops. He lowered the window and staggered back to bed.

"Damn rain," he muttered.

"A Drink of Water" was first published in **Signature**, *April 1967.*

"The story actually happened to me. One night my mother and I went to the movies, and I went through almost everything that's described in the story. I think I actually did get a drink from a lawn sprinkler. The idea that in a modern, civilized setting a basic need such as thirst could go unanswered. Of course, at the end of the story, when it starts to rain and the windowsill gets wet he says 'Damn rain!' But that's the way people are. Still." —RM

THERESE
1967

April 23:

AT LONG LAST I HAVE found a way to kill Therese! *God*! I am so happy I could cry! To end that vile dominion after all these years! What is the phrase? *It is a consummation devoutly to the wished.* Well, I have wished it long enough. Now it is time to act. I will destroy Therese and regain my peace of mind. I *will*!

What distresses me is that the book has been there in our library all these years. Dear God! I could have done it ages ago, avoiding all the agonies and cruel humiliations I have borne! Still, I must not think like that. I must be grateful that I found it at all. *And* amused—how droll it really is!—that Therese was actually in the library with me when I came across the book.

She, of course, was poring avidly over one of the many volumes of pornography left by Father. I shall burn them all after I have killed Therese! Thank God our mother died before he started to collect them. Vile man that he was, Therese loved him to the end, of course.

She is just like him really—brutish, carnal and disgusting. I should not be at all surprised to learn that she shared his bed as well as his interests. Oh, God, I will sing a hymn of joy the day she dies!

Yes, there she was, below, darkly flushed with sensuality while I, attempting to avoid the sight of her, moved about on the balcony where the older volumes are kept. And there I found it on an upper shelf, a film of gray dust on its pages. *Voodoo: An Authentic Study*, by Dr. William Moriarity. It had been printed privately. God only knows where or when Father acquired it.

The astounding thing: I perused it, bored, then actually put it back in place! It was not until I had walked many yards from it and glanced through many other books that, suddenly, it came to me.

By use of voodoo, I could kill Therese!

April 25:

My hand is trembling as I write this. I have almost completed the doll which represents Therese. Yes! Almost completed it! I have made it from the cloth of her old dresses which I found in the attic. I have used two tiny jeweled buttons for its eyes. There is more to do, of course, but the project is, thank God, now under way.

I am amused to consider what Dr. Ramsay would say if he discovered my plans. Which would be his initial reaction? That I am foolish to believe in voodoo? Or that I must learn to live with Therese if not love her. Love that *pig*? Never! God, how I despise her! If I could—*believe me*—I would happily surrender my half of Father's inheritance if it would mean that I would never have to see her dissipated face again, never have to listen to her drunken swearing, to her tales of lewd adventuring!

But that is quite impossible. She will not leave me be. I have but one course therefore: to destroy her. And I shall. I *shall*.

Therese has one day left to live.

April 26:

I have it all now! *All!* Therese took a bath before she left tonight—to God knows what incontinent debaucheries. After the bath, she cut her nails. And now I have them; they are fastened to the doll with thread.

And I have made the doll a head of hair from the strands which I laboriously combed from Therese's brush. Now the doll truly *is* Therese. That is the beauty of voodoo. I hold Therese's life in my hands, free to choose, for myself, the moment of her destruction. I will wait and savor that delicious freedom.

What will Dr. Ramsay say when Therese is dead? What *can* he say? That I am mad to think that voodoo killed her? (Not that I will tell him.) But it will! I will not lay a hand on her—as much as I would like to do it personally, by hand, crushing the breath from her throat. But no, I will survive. That is the joy of it. To kill Therese willfully and yet to live! That is the utter ecstasy of it!

Tomorrow night. Let her enjoy her last adventure. No more will she stagger in, her breath a reeking fume of whiskey, to regale me, in lurid detail, with what foul obscenities she has committed and enjoyed. No more will she—Dear God, I cannot wait! I shall thrust a needle deep into the doll's heart! Rid myself of her forever! Damn Therese! *Damn* her! I shall kill her now!

From the notebook of John H. Ramsay, M.D.
April 27:

Poor Millicent is dead. Her housekeeper found her crumpled on the floor of her bedroom this morning, clutching at her heart, a look of shock and agony frozen on her face. A heart attack no doubt. No marks on her. Beside her, on the floor, was a tiny cloth doll with a needle piercing it. Poor Millicent. Had she some brain-sick notion of destroying me with voodoo? I had hoped she trusted me. Still, why should she have? I could never have helped her really. Hers was a hopeless situation. Millicent Therese Marlowe suffered from the most advanced case of multiple personality it has ever been my misfortune to observe...

"Therese" (as "Needle in the Heart") was first published in **Ellery Queen's Mystery Magazine**, *October 1969.*

"I just had this idea of a woman with a split personality who hated her alter ego, and was going to kill her alter ego with voodoo. And ended up of course killing herself. 'Needle in the Heart' was not my

title. I don't know what the editor thought it would mean. I'm still amazed that Bill Nolan got a half-hour segment out of it; the original story was something like a page and a half in length. Just a notion, really." —RM

It was later adapted by William F. Nolan as "Millicent and Therese," a segment of the classic **Trilogy of Terror** *(1975). The other two stories adapted were "The Likeness of Julie" and "Prey."*

PREY
1969

AMELIA ARRIVED AT HER apartment at six-fourteen. Hanging her coat in the hall closet, she carried the small package into the living room and sat on the sofa. She nudged off her shoes while she unwrapped the package on her lap. The wooden box resembled a casket. Amelia raised its lid and smiled. It was the ugliest doll she'd ever seen. Seven inches long and carved from wood, it had a skeletal body and an over-sized head. Its expression was maniacally fierce, its pointed teeth completely bared, its glaring eyes protuberant. It clutched an eight-inch spear in its right hand. A length of fine, gold chain was wrapped around its body from the shoulders to the knees. A tiny scroll was wedged between the doll and the inside wall of its box. Amelia picked it up and unrolled it. There was handwriting on it. *This is He Who Kills*, it began. *He is a deadly hunter*. Amelia smiled as she read the rest of the words. Arthur would be pleased.

The thought of Arthur made her turn to look at the telephone on the table beside her. After a while, she sighed and set the wooden box on the sofa. Lifting the telephone to her lap, she picked up the receiver and dialed a number.

Her mother answered.

"Hello, Mom," Amelia said.

"Haven't you left yet?" her mother asked.

Amelia steeled herself. "Mom, I know it's Friday night—" she started.

She couldn't finish. There was silence on the line. Amelia closed her eyes. Mom, please, she thought. She swallowed. "There's this man," she said. "His name is Arthur Breslow. He's a high-school teacher."

"You aren't coming," her mother said.

Amelia shivered. "It's his birthday," she said. She opened her eyes and looked at the doll. "I sort of promised him we'd...spend the evening together."

Her mother was silent. There aren't any good movies playing tonight, anyway, Amelia's mind continued. "We could go tomorrow night," she said.

Her mother was silent.

"Mom?"

"Now even Friday night's too much for you."

"Mom, I see you two, three nights a week."

"To *visit*," said her mother. "When you have your own room here."

"Mom, *let's not start on that again*," Amelia said. I'm not a child, she thought. Stop treating me as though I were a child!

"How long have you been seeing him?" her mother asked.

"A month or so."

"Without telling me," her mother said.

"I had every intention of telling you." Amelia's head was starting to throb. I will *not* get a headache, she told herself. She looked at the doll. It seemed to be glaring at her. "He's a nice man, Mom," she said.

Her mother didn't speak. Amelia felt her stomach muscles drawing taut. I won't be able to eat tonight, she thought.

She was conscious suddenly of huddling over the telephone. She forced herself to sit erect. *I'm thirty-three years old*, she thought. Reaching out, she lifted the doll from its box. "You should see what

I'm giving him for his birthday," she said. "I found it in a curio shop on Third Avenue. It's a genuine Zuni fetish doll, extremely rare. Arthur is a buff on anthropology. That's why I got it for him."

There was silence on the line. All right, *don't talk*, Amelia thought. "It's a hunting fetish," she continued, trying hard to sound untroubled. "It's supposed to have the spirit of a Zuni hunter trapped inside it. There's a golden chain around it to prevent the spirit from—" She couldn't think of the word; ran a shaking finger over the chain. "—escaping, I guess," she said. "His name is He Who Kills. You should see his face." She felt warm tears trickling down her cheeks.

"Have a good time," said her mother, hanging up.

Amelia stared at the receiver, listening to the dial tone. Why is it always like this? she thought. She dropped the receiver onto its cradle and set aside the telephone. The darkening room looked blurred to her. She stood the doll on the coffee-table edge and pushed to her feet. I'll take my bath now, she told herself. I'll meet him and we'll have a lovely time. She walked across the living room. A lovely time, her mind repeated emptily. She knew it wasn't possible. Oh, *Mom!* she thought. She clenched her fists in helpless fury as she went into the bedroom.

In the living room, the doll fell off the table edge. It landed head down and the spear point, sticking into the carpet, braced the doll's legs in the air.

The fine, gold chain began to slither downward.

It was almost dark when Amelia came back into the living room. She had taken off her clothes and was wearing her terrycloth robe. In the bathroom, water was running into the tub.

She sat on the sofa and placed the telephone on her lap. For several minutes, she stared at it. At last, with a heavy sigh, she lifted the receiver and dialed a number.

"Arthur?" she said when he answered.

"Yes?" Amelia knew the tone—pleasant but suspecting. She couldn't speak.

"Your mother," Arthur finally said.

That cold, heavy sinking in her stomach. "It's our night

together," she explained. "Every Friday—" She stopped and waited. Arthur didn't speak. "I've mentioned it before," she said.

"I know you've mentioned it," he said.

Amelia rubbed at her temple.

"She's still running your life, isn't she?" he said.

Amelia tensed. "I just don't want to hurt her feelings anymore," she said. "My moving out was hard enough on her."

"I don't want to hurt her feelings either," Arthur said. "But how many birthdays a year do I have? We *planned* on this."

"I know." She felt her stomach muscles tightening again.

"Are you really going to let her do this to you?" Arthur asked. "One Friday night out of the whole year?"

Amelia closed her eyes. Her lips moved soundlessly. I just can't hurt her feelings anymore, she thought. She swallowed. "She's my mother," she said.

"Very well," he said, "I'm sorry. I was looking forward to it, but—" He paused. "I'm sorry," he said. He hung up quietly.

Amelia sat in silence for a long time, listening to the dial tone. She started when the recorded voice said loudly, "Please hang up." Putting the receiver down, she replaced the telephone on its table. So much for my birthday present, she thought. It would be pointless to give it to Arthur now. She reached out, switching on the table lamp. She'd take the doll back tomorrow.

The doll was not on the coffee table. Looking down, Amelia saw the gold chain lying on the carpet. She eased off the sofa edge onto her knees and picked it up, dropping it into the wooden box. The doll was not beneath the coffee table. Bending over, Amelia felt around underneath the sofa.

She cried out, jerking back her hand. Straightening up, she turned to the lamp and looked at her hand. There was something wedged beneath the index fingernail. She shivered as she plucked it out. It was the head of a doll's spear. She dropped it into the box and put the finger in her mouth. Bending over again, she felt around more cautiously beneath the sofa.

She couldn't find the doll. Standing with a weary groan, she started pulling one end of the sofa from the wall. It was terribly heavy. She recalled the night that she and her mother had shopped for the furniture. She'd wanted to furnish the apartment in Danish modern. Mother had insisted on this heavy, maple sofa; it had been on sale. Amelia grunted as she dragged it from the wall. She was conscious of the water running in the bathroom. She'd better turn it off soon.

She looked at the section of carpet she'd cleared, catching sight of the spear shaft. The doll was not beside it. Amelia picked it up and set it on the coffee table. The doll was caught beneath the sofa, she decided; when she'd moved the sofa, she had moved the doll as well.

She thought she heard a sound behind her—fragile, skittering. Amelia turned. The sound had stopped. She felt a chill move up the backs of her legs. "It's He Who Kills," she said with a smile. "He's taken off his chain and gone—"

She broke off suddenly. There had definitely been a noise inside the kitchen, a metallic, rasping sound. Amelia swallowed nervously. What's going on? she thought. She walked across the living room and reached into the kitchen, switching on the light. She peered inside. Everything looked normal. Her gaze moved falteringly across the stove, the pan of water on it, the table and chair, the drawers and cabinet doors all shut, the electric clock, the small refrigerator with the cookbook lying on top of it, the picture on the wall, the knife rack fastened to the cabinet side—

—its small knife missing.

Amelia stared at the knife rack. Don't be silly, she told herself. She'd put the knife in the drawer, that's all. Stepping into the kitchen, she pulled out the silverware drawer. The knife was not inside it.

Another sound made her look down quickly at the floor. She gasped in shock. For several moments, she could not react; then, stepping to the doorway, she looked into the living room, her heartbeat thudding. Had it been imagination? She was sure she'd seen a movement.

"Oh, come on," she said. She made a disparaging sound. She hadn't seen a thing.

Across the room, the lamp went out.

Amelia jumped so startledly, she rammed her right elbow against the doorjamb. Crying out, she clutched the elbow with her left hand, eyes closed momentarily, her face a mask of pain.

She opened her eyes and looked into the darkened living room. "Come on," she told herself in aggravation. Three sounds plus a burned-out bulb did not add up to anything as idiotic as—

She willed away the thought. She had to turn the water off. Leaving the kitchen, she started for the hall. She rubbed her elbow, grimacing.

There was another sound. Amelia froze. Something was coming across the carpet toward her. She looked down dumbly. No, she thought.

She saw it then—a rapid movement near the floor. There was a glint of metal, instantly, a stabbing pain in her right calf. Amelia gasped. She kicked out blindly. Pain again. She felt warm blood running down her skin. She turned and lunged into the hall. The throw rug slipped beneath her and she fell against the wall, hot pain lancing through her right ankle. She clutched at the wall to keep from falling, then went sprawling on her side. She thrashed around with a sob of fear.

More movement, dark on dark. Pain in her left calf, then her right again. Amelia cried out. Something brushed along her thigh. She scrabbled back, then lurched up blindly, almost falling again. She fought for balance, reaching out convulsively. The heel of her left hand rammed against the wall, supporting her. She twisted around and rushed into the darkened bedroom. Slamming the door, she fell against it, panting. Something banged against it on the other side, something small and near the floor.

Amelia listened, trying not to breathe so loudly. She pulled carefully at the knob to make sure the latch had caught. When there were no further sounds outside the door, she backed toward the bed. She started as she bumped against the mattress edge. Slumping down, the grabbed at the extension phone and pulled it to her lap. Whom could she call? The police? They'd think her mad. Mother? She was too far off.

She was dialing Arthur's number by the light from the bathroom when the doorknob started turning. Suddenly, her fingers couldn't move. She stared across the darkened room. The door latch clicked. The telephone slipped off her lap. She heard it thudding onto the carpet as the door swung open. Something dropped from the outside knob.

Amelia jerked back, pulling up her legs. A shadowy form was scurrying across the carpet toward the bed. She gaped at it. It isn't true, she thought. She stiffened at the tugging on her bedspread. *It was climbing up to get her.* No, she thought; *it isn't true.* She couldn't move. She stared at the edge of the mattress.

Something that looked like a tiny head appeared. Amelia twisted around with a cry of shock, flung herself across the bed and jumped to the floor. Plunging into the bathroom, she spun around and slammed the door, gasping at the pain in her ankle. She had barely thumbed in the button on the doorknob when something banged against the bottom of the door. Amelia heard a noise like the scratching of a rat. Then it was still.

She turned and leaned across the tub. The level of the water was almost to the overflow drain. As she twisted shut the faucets, she saw drops of blood falling into the water. Straightening up, she turned to the medicine-cabinet mirror above the sink.

She caught her breath in horror as she saw the gash across her neck. She pressed a shaking hand against it. Abruptly, she became aware of pain in her legs and looked down. She'd been slashed along the calves of both legs. Blood was running down her ankles, dripping off the edges of her feet. Amelia started crying. Blood ran between the fingers of the hand against her neck. It trickled down her wrist. She looked at her reflection through a glaze of tears.

Something in her aroused her, a wretchedness, a look of terrified surrender. *No*, she thought. She reached out for the medicine-cabinet door. Opening it, she pulled out iodine, gauze and tape. She dropped the cover of the toilet seat and sank down gingerly. It was a struggle to remove the stopper of the iodine bottle. She had to rap it hard against the sink three times before it opened.

The burning of the antiseptic on her calves made her gasp. Amelia clenched her teeth as she wrapped gauze around her right leg.

A sound made her twist toward the door. She saw the knife blade being jabbed beneath it. *It's trying to stab my feet,* she thought; *it thinks I'm standing there.* She felt unreal to be considering its thoughts. *This is He Who Kills*; the scroll flashed suddenly across her mind. *He is a deadly hunter.* Amelia stared at the poking knife blade. *God,* she thought.

Hastily, she bandaged both her legs, then stood and, looking into the mirror, cleaned the blood from her neck with a washrag. She swabbed some iodine along the edges of the gash, hissing at the fiery pain.

She whirled at the new sound, heartbeat leaping. Stepping to the door, she leaned down, listening hard. There was a faint metallic noise inside the knob.

The doll was trying to unlock it.

Amelia backed off slowly, staring at the knob. She tried to visualize the doll. Was it hanging from the knob by one arm, using the other to probe inside the knob lock with the knife? The vision was insane. She felt an icy prickling on the back of her neck. *I mustn't let it in*, she thought.

A hoarse cry pulled her lips back as the doorknob button popped out. Reaching out impulsively, she dragged a bath towel off its rack. The doorknob turned, the latch clicked free. The door began to open.

Suddenly the doll came darting in. It moved so quickly that its figure blurred before Amelia's eyes. She swung the towel down hard, as though it were a huge bug rushing at her. The doll was knocked against the wall. Amelia heaved the towel on top of it and lurched across the floor, gasping at the pain in her ankle. Flinging open the door, she lunged into the bedroom.

She was almost to the hall door when her ankle gave. She pitched across the carpet with a cry of shock. There was a noise behind her. Twisting around, she saw the doll come through the bathroom doorway like a jumping spider. She saw the knife blade glinting in the light. Then the doll was in the shadows, coming at her fast. Amelia scrabbled back. She glanced over her shoulder, saw the closet and backed into its darkness, clawing for the doorknob.

Pain again, an icy slashing at her foot. Amelia screamed and heaved back. Reaching up, she yanked a topcoat down. It fell across the doll. She jerked down everything in reach. The doll was buried underneath a mound of blouses, skirts and dresses. Amelia pitched across the moving pile of clothes. She forced herself to stand and limped into the hall as quickly as she could. The sound of thrashing underneath the clothes faded from her hearing. She hobbled to the door. Unlocking it, she pulled the knob.

The door was held. Amelia reached up quickly to the bolt. It had been shot. She tried to pull it free. It wouldn't budge. She clawed at it with sudden terror. It was twisted out of shape. "No." she muttered. *She was trapped.* "Oh, God." She started pounding on the door. "Please help me! *Help me!*"

Sound in the bedroom. Amelia whirled and lurched across the living room. She dropped to her knees beside the sofa, feeling for the telephone, but her fingers trembled so much that she couldn't dial the numbers. She began to sob, then twisted around with a strangled cry. The doll was rushing at her from the hallway.

Amelia grabbed an ashtray from the coffee table and hurled it at the doll. She threw a vase, a wooden box, a figurine. She couldn't hit the doll. It reached her, started jabbing at her legs. Amelia reared up blindly and fell across the coffee table. Rolling to her knees, she stood again. She staggered toward the hall, shoving over furniture to stop the doll. She topped a chair, a table. Picking up a lamp, she hurled it at the floor. She backed into the hall and, spinning, rushed into the closet, slammed the door shut.

She held the knob with rigid fingers. Waves of hot breath pulsed against her face. She cried out as the knife was jabbed beneath the door, its sharp point sticking into one of her toes. She shuffled back, shifting her grip on the knob. Her robe hung open. She could feel a trickle of blood between her breasts. Her legs felt numb with pain. She closed her eyes. Please, someone help, she thought.

She stiffened as the doorknob started turning in her grasp. Her flesh went cold. It couldn't be stronger than she: It *couldn't* be. Amelia tightened her grip. *Please*, she thought. The side of her head bumped against the front edge of her suitcase on the shelf.

The thought exploded in her mind. Holding the knob with her right hand, she reached up, fumbling, with her left. The suitcase clasps were open. With a sudden wrench, she turned the doorknob, shoving at the door as hard as possible. It rushed away from her. She heard it bang against the wall. The doll thumped down.

Amelia reached up, hauling down her suitcase. Yanking open the lid, she fell to her knees in the closet doorway, holding the suitcase like an open book. She braced herself, eyes wide, teeth clinched together. She felt the doll's weight as it banged against the suitcase bottom. Instantly, she slammed the lid and threw the suitcase flat. Falling across it, she held it shut until her shaking hands could fasten the clasps. The sound of them clicking into place made her sob with relief. She shoved away the suitcase. It slid across the hall and bumped against the wall. Amelia struggled to her feet, trying not to listen to the frenzied kicking and scratching inside the suitcase.

She switched on the hall light and tried to open the bolt. It was hopelessly wedged. She turned and limped across the living room, glancing at her legs. The bandages were hanging loose. Both legs were streaked with caking blood, some of the gashes still bleeding. She felt at her throat. The cut was still wet. Amelia pressed her shaking lips together. She'd get to a doctor soon now.

Removing the ice pick from its kitchen drawer, she returned to the hall. A cutting sound made her look toward the suitcase. She caught her breath. The knife blade was protruding from the suitcase wall, moving up and down with a sawing motion. Amelia stared at it. She felt as though her body had been turned to stone.

She limped to the suitcase and knelt beside it, looking, with revulsion at the sawing blade. It was smeared with blood. She tried to pinch it with the fingers of her left hand, pull it out. The blade was twisted, jerked down, and she cried out, snatching back her hand. There was a deep slice in her thumb. Blood ran down across her palm. Amelia pressed the finger to her robe. She felt as though her mind was going blank.

Pushing to her feet, she limped back to the door and started prying at the bolt. She couldn't get it loose. Her thumb began to ache. She pushed the ice pick underneath the bolt socket and tried to force it off the wall. The ice pick point broke off. Amelia slipped and almost fell. She pushed up, whimpering. There was no time, no time. She looked around in desperation.

The window! She could throw the suitcase out! She visualized it tumbling through the darkness. Hastily, she dropped the ice pick, turning toward the suitcase.

She froze. The doll had forced its head and shoulders through the rent in the suitcase wall. Amelia watched it struggling to get out. She felt paralyzed. The twisting doll was staring at her. No, she thought, it isn't true. The doll jerked free its legs and jumped to the floor.

Amelia jerked around and ran into the living room. Her right foot landed on a shard of broken crockery. She felt it cutting deep into her heel and lost her balance. Landing on her side, she thrashed around. The doll came leaping at her. She could see the knife blade glint. She kicked out wildly, knocking back the doll. Lunging to her feet, she reeled into the kitchen, whirled, and started pushing shut the door.

Something kept it from closing. Amelia thought she heard a screaming in her mind. Looking down, she saw the knife and a tiny wooden hand. The doll's arm was wedged between the door and the jamb! Amelia shoved against the door with all her might, aghast as the strength with which the door was pushed the other way. There was a cracking noise. A fierce smile pulled her lips back and she pushed berserkly at the door. The screaming in her mind grew louder, drowning out the sound of splintering wood.

The knife blade sagged. Amelia dropped to her knees and tugged at it. She pulled the knife into the kitchen, seeing the wooden hand and wrist fall from the handle of the knife. With a gagging noise, she struggled to her feet and dropped the knife into the sink. The door slammed hard against her side; the doll rushed in.

Amelia jerked away from it. Picking up the chair, she slung it toward the doll. It jumped aside, then ran around the fallen chair. Amelia snatched the pan of water off the stove and hurled it down. The pan clanged loudly off the floor, spraying water on the doll.

She stared at the doll. It wasn't coming after her. It was trying to climb the sink, leaping up and clutching at the counter side with one hand. It wants the knife, she thought. It has to have its weapon.

She knew abruptly what to do. Stepping over to the stove, she pulled down the broiler door and twisted the knob on all the way. She heard the puffing detonation of the gas as she turned to grab the doll.

She cried out as the doll began to kick and twist, its maddened thrashing flinging her from one side of the kitchen to the other. The screaming filled her mind again and suddenly she knew it was the spirit in the doll that screamed. She slid and crashed against the table, wrenched herself around and, dropping to her knees before the stove, flung the doll inside. She slammed the door and fell against it.

The door was almost driven out. Amelia pressed her shoulder, then her back against it, turning to brace her legs against the wall. She tried to ignore the pounding scrabble of the doll inside the broiler. She watched the red blood pulsing from her heel. The smell of burning wood began to reach her and she closed her eyes. The door was getting hot. She shifted carefully. The kicking and pounding filled her ears. The screaming flooded through her mind. She knew her back would get burned, but she didn't dare to move. The smell of burning wood grew worse. Her foot ached terribly.

Amelia looked up at the electric clock on the wall. It was four minutes to seven. She watched the red second hand revolving slowly. A minute passed. The screaming in her mind was fading now. She shifted uncomfortably, gritting her teeth against the burning heat on her back.

Another minute passed. The kicking and the pounding stopped. The screaming faded more and more. The smell of burning wood had filled the kitchen. There was a pall of gray smoke in the air. That they'll see, Amelia thought. Now that it's over, they'll come and help. That's the way it always is.

She started to ease herself away from the broiler door, ready to throw her weight back against it if she had to. She turned around and got on her knees. The reek of charred wood made her nauseated. She had to know, though. Reaching out, she pulled down the door.

Something dark and stifling rushed across her and she heard the screaming in her mind once more as hotness flooded over her and into her. It was a scream of victory now.

Amelia stood and turned off the broiler. She took a pair of ice tongs from its drawer and lifted out the blackened twist of wood. She dropped it into the sink and ran water over it until the smoke had stopped. Then she went into the bedroom, picked up the telephone and depressed its cradle. After a moment, she released the cradle and dialed her mother's number.

"This is Amelia, Mom," she said. "I'm sorry I acted the way I did. I want us to spend the evening together. It's a little late, though. Can you come by my place and we'll go from here?" She listened. "Good," she said. "I'll wait for you."

Hanging up, she walked into the kitchen, where she slid the longest carving knife from its place in the rack. She went to the front door and pushed back its bolt, which now moved freely. She carried the knife into the living room, took off her bathrobe and danced a dance of hunting, of the joy of hunting, of the joy of the impending kill.

Then she sat down, cross-legged, in the corner. He Who Kills sat, cross-legged, in the corner, in the darkness, waiting for the prey to come.

*"Prey" was first published in **Playboy**, April 1969.*

*"I had originally submitted the story—or at least a similar premise—to **The Twilight Zone**. And they rejected it because they thought it was too grim. So I turned it around into a science fiction story—and it became 'The Invaders,' the episode that Agnes Moorehead was in. Because it's the same damn story—except here there's only one doll. Later on I wrote the premise as the short story called 'Prey' and **Playboy** bought it.*

"Then Dan Curtis bought it. Dan once showed me a slightly longer version of the television adaptation, and it was even more scary than what was broadcast. And this was before digital effects. Dan was able to get so much sense of total movement from that doll when that's all it was. The sound effects were fairly effective, but to me it sounded like Snoopy having a nervous breakdown. But I think I'm the only one who ever felt that way." —RM

*It was later adapted by the author under the title "Amelia" as part of **Trilogy of Terror** (1975). Director Dan Curtis and William F. Nolan brought back the Zuni doll in "He Who Kills," a segment they co-wrote—using RM's character—for **Trilogy of Terror II**, which was first broadcast on October 30, 1996.*

BUTTON, BUTTON
1970

THE PACKAGE WAS LYING by the front door—a cube-shaped carton sealed with tape, the name and address printed by hand: MR. AND MRS. ARTHUR LEWIS, 217 E. 37TH STREET, NEW YORK, NEW YORK 10016. Norma picked it up, unlocked the door, and went into the apartment. It was just getting dark.

After she put the lamb chops in the broiler, she made herself a drink and sat down to open the package.

Inside the carton was a push-button unit fastened to a small wooden box. A glass dome covered the button. Norma tried to lift it off, but it was locked in place. She turned the unit over and saw a folded piece of paper Scotch-taped to the bottom of the box. She pulled it off: "Mr. Steward will call on you at eight p.m."

Norma put the button unit beside her on the couch. She sipped the drink and reread the typed note, smiling.

A few moments later, she went back into the kitchen to make the salad.

The doorbell rang at eight o'clock. "I'll get it," Norma called from the kitchen. Arthur was in the living room, reading.

There was a small man in the hallway. He removed his hat as Norma opened the door. "Mrs. Lewis?" he inquired politely.

"Yes?"

"I'm Mr. Steward."

"Oh, yes." Norma repressed a smile. She was sure now it was a sales pitch.

"May I come in?" asked Mr. Steward.

"I'm rather busy," Norma said. "I'll get you your watchamacallit, though." She started to turn.

"Don't you want to know what it is?"

Norma turned back. Mr. Steward's tone had been offensive. "No, I don't think so," she said.

"It could prove very valuable," he told her.

"Monetarily?" she challenged.

Mr. Steward nodded. "Monetarily," he said.

Norma frowned. She didn't like his attitude. "What are you trying to sell?" she asked.

"I'm not selling anything," he answered.

Arthur came out of the living room. "Something wrong?"

Mr. Steward introduced himself.

"Oh, the…" Arthur pointed toward the living room and smiled. "What is that gadget, anyway?"

"It won't take long to explain," replied Mr. Steward. "May I come in?"

"If you're selling something…" Arthur said.

Mr. Steward shook his head. "I'm not."

Arthur looked at Norma. "Up to you," she said.

He hesitated. "Well, why not?" he said.

They went into the living room and Mr. Steward sat in Norma's chair. He reached into an inside coat pocket and withdrew a small sealed envelope. "Inside here is a key to the bell-unit dome," he said. He set the envelope on the chairside table. "The bell is connected to our office."

"What's it for?" asked Arthur.

"If you push the button," Mr. Steward told him, "somewhere in the world, someone you don't know will die. In return for which you will receive a payment of fifty thousand dollars."

Norma stared at the small man. He was smiling.

"What are you talking about?" Arthur asked him.

Mr. Steward looked surprised. "But I've just explained," he said.

"Is this a practical joke?" asked Arthur.

"Not at all. The offer is completely genuine."

"You aren't making sense," Arthur said. "You expect us to believe…"

"Whom do you represent?' demanded Norma.

Mr. Steward looked embarrassed. "I'm afraid I'm not at liberty to tell you that," he said. "However, I assure you the organization is of international scope."

"I think you'd better leave," Arthur said, standing.

Mr. Steward rose. "Of course."

"And take your button unit with you."

"Are you sure you wouldn't care to think about it for a day or so?"

Arthur picked up the button unit and the envelope and thrust them into Mr. Steward's hands. He walked into the hall and pulled open the door.

"I'll leave my card," said Mr. Steward. He placed it on the table by the door.

When he was gone, Arthur tore it in half and tossed the pieces onto the table. "God!" he said.

Norma was still sitting on the sofa. "What do you think it was?" she asked.

"I don't care to know," he answered.

She tried to smile but couldn't. "Aren't you curious at all?"

"No," he shook his head.

After Arthur returned to his book, Norma went back to the kitchen and finished washing the dishes.

"Why won't you talk about it?" Norma asked later.

Arthur's eyes shifted as he brushed his teeth. He looked at her reflection in the bathroom mirror.

"Doesn't it intrigue you?"

"It offends me," Arthur said.

"I know, but—" Norma rolled another curler in her hair "—doesn't it intrigue you, too?"

"You think it's a practical joke?" she asked as they went into the bedroom.

"If it is, it's a sick one."

Norma sat on the bed and took off her slippers.

"Maybe it's some kind of psychological research."

Arthur shrugged. "Could be."

"Maybe some eccentric millionaire is doing it."

"Maybe."

"Wouldn't you like to know?"

Arthur shook his head.

"Why?"

"Because it's immoral," he told her.

Norma slid beneath the covers. "Well, I think it's intriguing," she said.

Arthur turned off the lamp and leaned over to kiss her. "Good night," he said.

"Good night." She patted his back.

Norma closed her eyes. Fifty thousand dollars, she thought.

In the morning, as she left the apartment, Norma saw the card halves on the table. Impulsively, she dropped them into her purse. She locked the front door and joined Arthur in the elevator.

While she was on her coffee break, she took the card halves from her purse and held the torn edges together. Only Mr. Steward's name and telephone number were printed on the card.

After lunch, she took the card halves from her purse again and Scotch-taped the edges together. Why am I doing this? she thought.

Just before five, she dialed the number.

"Good afternoon," said Mr. Steward's voice.

Norma almost hung up but restrained herself. She cleared her throat. "This is Mrs. Lewis," she said.

"Yes, Mrs. Lewis." Mr. Steward sounded pleased.

"I'm curious."

"That's natural," Mr. Steward said.

"Not that I believe a word of what you told us."

"Oh, it's quite authentic," Mr. Steward answered.

"Well, whatever..." Norma swallowed. "When you said someone in the world would die, what did you mean?"

"Exactly that," he answered. "It could be anyone. All we guarantee is that you don't know them. And, of course, that you wouldn't have to watch them die."

"For fifty thousand dollars," Norma said.

"That is correct."

She made a scoffing sound. "That's crazy."

"Nonetheless, that is the proposition," Mr. Steward said. "Would you like me to return the button unit?"

Norma stiffened. "Certainly not." She hung up angrily.

The package was lying by the front door; Norma saw it as she left the elevator. Well, of all the nerve, she thought. She glared at the carton as she unlocked the door. I just won't take it in, she thought. She went inside and started dinner.

Later, she carried her drink to the front hall. Opening the door, she picked up the package and carried it into the kitchen, leaving it on the table.

She sat in the living room, sipping her drink and looking out the window. After awhile, she went back into the kitchen to turn the cutlets in the broiler. She put the package in a bottom cabinet. She'd throw it out in the morning.

"Maybe some eccentric millionaire is playing games with people," she said.

Arthur looked up from his dinner. "I don't understand you."

"What does that mean?"

"Let it go," he told her.

Norma ate in silence. Suddenly, she put her fork down. "Suppose it's a genuine offer," she said.

Arthur stared at her.

"Suppose it's a genuine offer."

"All right, suppose it is!" He looked incredulous. "What would you like to do? Get the button back and push it? Murder someone?"

Norma looked disgusted. "Murder."

"How would *you* define it?"

"If you don't even know the person?" Norma asked.

Arthur looked astounded. "Are you saying what I think you are?"

"If it's some old Chinese peasant ten thousand miles away? Some diseased native in the Congo?"

"How about some baby boy in Pennsylvania?" Arthur countered. "Some beautiful little girl on the next block?"

"Now you're loading things."

"The point is, Norma," he continued, "that *who* you kill makes no difference. It's still murder."

"The point is," Norma broke in, "if it's someone you've never seen in your life and never will see, someone whose death you don't even have to know about, you still wouldn't push the button?"

Arthur stared at her, appalled. "You mean you would?"

"Fifty thousand dollars, Arthur."

"What has the amount…"

"Fifty thousand dollars, Arthur," Norma interrupted. "A chance to take that trip to Europe we've always talked about."

"Norma, no."

"A chance to buy that cottage on the Island."

"Norma, no." His face was white. "For God's sake, no!"

She shuddered. "All right, take it easy," she said. "Why are you getting so upset? It's only talk."

After dinner, Arthur went into the living room. Before he left the table, he said, "I'd rather not discuss it anymore, if you don't mind."

Norma shrugged. "Fine with me."

She got up earlier than usual to make pancakes, eggs, and bacon for Arthur's breakfast.

"What's the occasion?" he asked with a smile.

"No occasion." Norma looked offended. "I wanted to do it, that's all."

"Good," he said. "I'm glad you did."

She refilled his cup. "Wanted to show you I'm not…" she shrugged.

"Not what?"

"Selfish."

"Did I say you were?"

"Well—" She gestured vaguely. "—last night…"

Arthur didn't speak.

"All that talk about the button," Norma said. "I think you— well, misunderstood me."

"In what way?" His voice was guarded.

"I think you felt—" She gestured again. "—that I was only thinking of myself."

"Oh."

"I wasn't."

"Norma."

"Well, I wasn't. When I talked about Europe, a cottage on the Island…"

"Norma, why are we getting so involved in this?"

"I'm not involved at all." She drew in a shaking breath. "I'm simply trying to indicate that…"

"What?"

"That I'd like for us to go to Europe. Like for us to have a nicer apartment, nicer furniture, nicer clothes. Like for us to finally have a baby, for that matter."

"Norma, we will," he said.

"When?"

He stared at her in dismay. "Norma…"

"When?"

"Are you—" He seemed to draw back slightly. "Are you really saying…?"

"I'm saying that they're probably doing it for some research project!" she cut him off. "That they want to know what average people would do under such a circumstance! That they're just saying someone would die, in order to study reactions, see if there'd be guilt, anxiety, whatever! You don't really think they'd kill somebody, do you?"

Arthur didn't answer. She saw his hands trembling. After awhile, he got up and left.

When he'd gone to work, Norma remained at the table, staring into her coffee. I'm going to be late, she thought. She shrugged. What difference did it make? She should be home anyways, not working in an office.

RICHARD MATHESON

While she was stacking the dishes, she turned abruptly, dried her hands, and took the package from the bottom cabinet. Opening it, she set the button unit on the table. She stared at it for a long time before taking the key from its envelope and removing the glass dome. She stared at the button. How ridiculous, she thought. All this over a meaningless button.

Reaching out, she pressed it down. For us, she thought angrily.

She shuddered. Was it happening? A chill of horror swept across her.

In a moment, it had passed. She made a contemptuous noise. Ridiculous, she thought. To get so worked up over nothing.

She had just turned the supper steaks and was making herself another drink when the telephone rang. She picked it up. "Hello?"

"Mrs. Lewis?"

"Yes?"

"This is the Lenox Hill Hospital."

She felt unreal as the voice informed her of the subway accident, the shoving crowd. Arthur pushed from the platform in front of the train. She was conscious of shaking her head but couldn't stop.

As she hung up, she remembered Arthur's life insurance policy for $25,000, with double indemnity for—

"No." She couldn't seem to breathe. She struggled to her feet and walked in the kitchen numbly. Something cold pressed at her skull as she removed the button unit from the wastebasket. There were no nails or screws visible. She couldn't see how it was put together.

Abruptly, she began to smash it on the sink edge, pounding it harder and harder, until the wood split. She pulled the sides apart, cutting her fingers without noticing. There were no transistors in the box, no wires or tubes. The box was empty.

She whirled with a gasp as the telephone rang. Stumbling into the living room, she picked up the receiver.

"Mrs. Lewis?" Mr. Steward asked.

It wasn't her voice shrieking so; it couldn't be. "You said I wouldn't know the one that died!"

"My dear lady," Mr. Steward said, "do you really think you knew your husband?"

*"Button, Button" was first published in **Playboy**, June 1970.*

*"**Playboy** did a nice job of presenting it; the illustration was very interesting, too: I think it was of the box itself. It was later adapted for the first reincarnation of **The Twilight Zone**. But they screwed it up terribly; they didn't even use my original ending! I thought my ending was a nice blow to the solar plexus. I wrote the script and they revised it. They just should have followed the story—I mean, I write visual stories. And if it was a good story to begin with, they should have just done it as written. Why some people are so compelled to add their own creative thrust to it...they ruined it. So it became one of Logan Swanson's credits. But luckily, in the majority of cases, I've managed to work with people who were very loyal to what I wrote."*
—RM

*Adapted by the author (as by "Logan Swanson") for an episode of the CBS **Twilight Zone** revival. First broadcast on March 7, 1986, it starred Mare Winningham and was directed by Peter Medak.*

FROM
DENNIS ETCHISON

THESE LINES ARE AS DIFFICULT for me as any in the last twenty years. This is because Matheson is a realized artist and does not need my remarks to draw attention to his accomplishment or to sell you on his work.

In contrast, it is easy to talk about secondary talents who have yet to fulfill their promise. In that case one offers encouragement and makes a statement of faith, singling out the more praiseworthy aspects and relying on misdirection to gloss over the shortfall. Or one takes advantage of the platform to address some private concern, tying it in loosely to the person who is supposed to be the subject while doing more to advertise oneself than anything else. Failing that, one covers pages with slyly exaggerated anecdotes in order to suggest an intimacy that is ultimately self-serving.

Nothing of the kind is called for here.

Matheson is and always has been a writer's writer. His influence, a singularly compelling voice that runs through the contemporary history of science fiction, terror and horror literature, is better left for assessment by scholars and critics. For now it is enough to say that his courage, his measured understatement and his refusal to court fashion by accommodating popular trends exemplify an integrity that is unsurpassed in the commercial arena. His novels are relentless in their intensity, written in the cold sweat of absolute conviction; his screenplays are models of structural economy, tightly suspenseful without sacrificing larger meanings; and his short stories are tours de force, demonstrating the strength of obsessive narrative freed from stylistic indulgence.

His work provides an ideal to which I have aspired since I discovered it in the Fifties, and I have not yet begun to approach its power. I have learned more from him about what is important on the printed page and what is not—how to eliminate unnecessary words in favor of white space, how to cut a story to the bone so that characters have room to breathe and take shape in a reader's imagination—than from any other living writer. He is the very best of the best, an archetype of what such a career is supposed to be all about.

—*Dennis Etchison*

BY APPOINTMENT ONLY

ONLY
1970

At 11:14 THAT MORNING, Mr. Pangborn came into the barbershop. Wiley looked up from his *Racing Form*. "Morning," he said. He glanced at his wrist watch and smiled. "You're right on time."

Mr. Pangborn did not return the smile. He removed his suitcoat wearily and hung it on the rack. He trudged across the clean-swept floor and sank down in the middle chair. Wiley put down his *Racing Form* and stood. He stretched and yawned. "You don't look so hot, Mr. Pangborn," he said.

"I don't feel so hot," Mr. Pangborn replied.

"Sorry to hear that," Wiley said. He cranked up the chair and locked it. "Usual?" he asked.

Mr. Pangborn nodded. "Okeydoke," said Wiley. He pulled a clean cloth from its shelf and shook it out. "Whatcha been doin' with yourself?" he asked.

Mr. Pangborn sighed. "Not much."

"Kind o' run down, are you?" Wiley asked, wrapping tissue around his customer's neck.

"That's the word," said Mr. Pangborn. "What've *you* been doing?"

"Not a hell of a lot," Wiley answered. He pinned the cloth in place. "Drove up to Vegas last week." He made a rueful sound. "Lost a pile."

"Too bad," said Mr. Pangborn.

"Oh, well," Wiley grinned. "Easy come, easy go." He picked up the electric clipper and switched it on. "Maria!" he called.

She made an inquiring noise in the back room.

"Mr. Pangborn's here."

"Be right out," she said.

Wiley started working on the back of Mr. Pangborn's neck. Mr. Pangborn closed his eyes. "That's it," Wiley told him. "Take it easy."

Mr. Pangborn shifted on the chair uncomfortably.

"You sure don't look so hot," said Wiley.

Mr. Pangborn sighed again. "I don't know," he said. "I just don't know."

"What's the problem?" Wiley asked.

"The leg," said Mr. Pangborn. "The back. My right arm, off and on. My stomach."

"*Jesus*," Wiley said, concerned. "You seen your doctor?"

"He doesn't know what it is," Mr. Pangborn answered scornfully. "I don't bother going to him anymore. All he ever does is send me to specialists."

Wiley clucked. "That's lousy, Mr. Pangborn."

Mr. Pangborn exhaled. "Dr. Rand's the only one who ever helps," he said.

"He *does*?" Wiley looked delighted. "Hey, I'm glad to hear that," he said. "I wasn't sure whether I should even mention him or not, him not being an MD and all. My brother swore up and down that he was something else, though."

"He is," said Mr. Pangborn. "If it weren't for him—"

"Hello, Mr. Pangborn," said Maria.

Mr. Pangborn glanced aside and managed a smile. "Maria," he said.

"How are you today?" she asked.

"Getting by," he said.

Maria set her manicuring table and chair beside the barber chair. As she sat down, her bust swelled out against the tightness of her sweater. "You look tired," she said.

Mr. Pangborn nodded. "I am," he said. "I don't sleep too well."

"That's a shame," she sympathized. She began to work on his nails.

"Well, I'm glad this Rand is working out," Wiley said. "I'll have to try him myself sometime."

"He's good," said Mr. Pangborn. "The only one who's given me relief."

"Good deal," said Wiley.

It was quiet for awhile, as Wiley cut Mr. Pangborn's hair and Maria did his nails. Then Mr. Pangborn asked, "Business slow today?"

"No," said Wiley. "I do it all by appointment now." He smiled. "It's the only way."

When Mr. Pangborn had gone, Maria carried his hair and nail clippings into the back room. Unlocking the cupboard, she took out the doll labeled PANGBORN. Wiley finished dialing the telephone and watched her as she replaced the doll's hair and nails with the fresh clippings.

"Rand?" he said when the receiver was lifted at the other end of the line. "Wiley. Pangborn was just in. When's he seeing you again?" he listened. "Okay," he said, "give him something for his back and we'll take that pin out for a couple o' weeks. All right?" He listened. "And, Rand," he said, "your check was late again this month. *Watch that.*"

He hung up and walked over to Maria. As she worked, he slid his hands up inside her sweater and cupped them over her breasts. Maria pressed back against him with a sigh, her face tightening. "When's the next appointment?" she asked.

Wiley grinned. "Not till one-thirty," he answered.

By the time he'd locked the door, hung up the OUT TO LUNCH sign and returned to the back room, Maria was waiting for him on the bed. Wiley took his clothes off, running his gaze over her brown body as it writhed on the mattress. "You little Haitian bitch," he muttered, grinning.

At twenty minutes after one, Mr. Walters came into the shop. Removing his coat, he hung it on the rack and sat down in the middle chair. Wiley put down his *Racing Form* and stood. He made a clucking sound. "Hey, you don't look so hot, Mr. Walters," he said.

"I don't feel so hot," Mr. Walters replied.

*"By Appointment Only" was first published in **Playboy**, April 1970.*

"That was published as a one-page story. And I remember getting a check for a thousand dollars. And I thought, 'My God—a thousand dollars for one page!'" —RM

THE
FINISHING TOUCHES
1970

HOLLISTER STOOD OUTSIDE the balcony window watching them make love. His breath smoked whitely in the darkness. At his sides, his gray-gloved hands kept flexing to retain their circulation. The night air seemed to penetrate his flesh and settle like a mist around his bones.

Inside the bedroom, Rex Chappel and his wife lay across the bed. Rex wore pajama bottoms, Amanda a black, transparent nightgown. Hollister's throat was clotted as he watched her body responding to her husband's touches. He clenched his teeth, his face pale beneath the shadow of his Homburg. Soon now, he told himself. His lips turned upward in a joyless smile.

Now Chappel was pulling off Amanda's gown. Languidly, she sat erect, arms raised, while he drew it up across the jutting thickness of her breasts, across her flushed and smiling face, across the golden tangle of her hair, her ivory arms, her long, red-nailed fingers.

The nightgown fluttered darkly to the floor. Amanda sank back, arms extended, fingers curved like beckoning talons. Chappel stood and jerked apart the drawstring bow of his pajama bottoms. They slithered down his muscular legs and he stepped out of them. Amanda moved back sinuously, propping herself against a bank of pillows. Hollister saw how fitfully her hardened breasts rose and fell. He saw Chappel start to lean himself across her waiting body, saw her arch up eagerly to meet him. *Now*, he thought. His face a twisted mask, he edged the balcony door ajar and slipped the pistol from his pocket.

There were tiny, popping sounds as the muzzle-silenced gun expelled six bullets into Chappel's lowering back.

Hollister drove slowly through the city streets. The pistol, amply weighted, rested on the bottom of the river. Nor had Amanda seen him. Caught beneath the lifeless burden of her husband, she had witnessed nothing of his flight. He was inviolate. Let them try to prove his guilt.

For instance, what motive had he? Chappel was his employee. He had nothing to offer a man of Hollister's position. Except Amanda, of course, and that would not be pertinent to the matter. They had rarely met, and when they did, he'd never shown by word or look that he wanted her. Hollister released a sigh of pleasure. It had been a perfect evening all in all. A perfect killing at the perfect moment resulting in a perfect satisfaction.

Now for the finishing touches. To return to Chappel's house just as the initial shock was passing from Amanda. To ring the doorbell and inquire if the extra work he'd given Chappel that afternoon was completed yet. The aghast demeanor, the shocked apologies. The clutch of savage exultation at the sight of Amanda's stricken face, for he despised her, too. It was a loveless, harsh desire he felt. When the time came, he would take her with the same contempt with which he'd taken her husband's life.

Hollister smiled. At long last he could think of Rex Chappel with composure. He'd hated Chappel almost from the day he'd come to work for *Hollister & Ware, Inc.*, hated him for possessing everything he lacked—youth, appearance, manner. The evening he had met Amanda at a company dinner had been the final blow; that a man possessing every other quality should have, as well, a beautiful and sensuous wife was just too much. He'd known that night that for his soul's sake, he must destroy them and their relationship.

But how? The feasibility of murder had not been at first apparent. Time, however, soon augmented its attractiveness with logic. He could not procure Amanda from her handsome, charming husband. Nor could he hope to shatter Chappel on the rack of business. At best, Chappel would retreat and seek employment elsewhere. At worst, his agile mind might overcome the tangling convolutions of his own. No, physical destruction was inevitable; for, dominating all else, was Chappel's virility. What better vengeance than to extinguish that virility in its most imperious moment?

Now it *was* extinguished and the rest was simple: Withdrawal at first. Then discreet attentiveness, occasional thoughtful presence— the available shoulder to lean on in times of stress. Gradual encroachment until eventually the day of subjugation came, and Amanda, falling, found no hand to help her rise again.

The dashboard clock read eleven-twenty as he braked in front of Chappel's house. Nearly two hours had elapsed since the murder. Enough time for the removal of worthless flesh and querying policemen. Hollister strolled around the car and crossed the sidewalk to the house. He pressed the button lightly and the doorbells chimed. Intriguing how detached he felt; due, of course, to Chappel's being dead. The passing of that damned Adonis was a weight lifted from his shoulders.

The door opened and Amanda stood before him in a scarlet robe, her features drawn and lifeless. *My dear, what's wrong?* The words began in Hollister's mind. He cut them off. It would be suspect for him to notice anything. He crimped politely at his hat brim.

"I apologize for disturbing you at such an hour," he said. "However, I'm afraid I must examine the papers I gave Mr. Chappel at the office today. They're for a most important client, you see, and—" As he rambled on, his dark eyes searched her face for sorrow.

"Come in," she said. She drew back with a crackling rustle of silk and Hollister entered, Homburg in hand.

"I'll take your things," Amanda said.

"Well, uh—" Hollister feigned uncertainty. "I really shouldn't—"

"Please," she said.

This was better than he'd hoped for. Hollister moved into the living room while Amanda hung his coat and hat and followed.

"A drink?" she asked.

He nodded once. "That's kind of you," he said. "A little Scotch with water." Again he searched her face, but it was almost blank. He'd hoped for sobbing, tears, hysteria.

Ah, well; mentally, he shrugged. This, too, was reaction—in a way, more total. The death of Chappel had shocked her into muteness. Quite satisfactory, decided Hollister. He settled on the sofa with a smile and crossed his impeccably trousered legs. "Where is Mr. Chappel?" he inquired off-handedly.

"Upstairs," she answered.

Her back was turned to him; he gaped at it. *Upstairs*? Hollister felt wintry fingers plucking at his heart. Then, suddenly, he understood, an extra rush of joy expanding his enjoyment. *She must not have told the police yet!* Hollister shuddered. Upstairs, the corpse. Downstairs, the murderer being served Scotch and water by the grieving widow. It was too good to be true, yet it was true! He had to close his eyes and fill his lungs before he could control the tremble of his body.

As he opened his eyes, Amanda was turning from the sideboard, silk robe flaring, open slightly. Hollister felt the muscles in his stomach tighten. He'd seen her thighs. Was it possible that she was nude beneath the robe? A shiver hunched his shoulders as she brought the drink. Handing it to him, she was compelled to lean forward, and Hollister's eyes could not avoid the weighty shifting of her breasts. His fingers twitched on contact with the glass and with Amanda's hand.

"He's, uh, finished with the papers?" he inquired.

"Yes," she answered. She stood in front of him as though in deep thought.

"Good." Hollister took a sip of the drink and coughed. Why didn't she tell him? There was a tightening in his chest and stomach as he wondered.

"I haven't told the police," she said.

The glass hitched in Hollister's grip and spouted liquid across his legs. "Oh, my," he heard himself declaring thinly. Setting down the glass, he pulled the handkerchief from his breast pocket and started dabbing at the wet spots.

Amanda sat abruptly, clutching at his hand. "I said—" she started.

"*Yes*. Yes, I heard," Hollister said in a tremulous voice. "Wh-why should you call the police, however?"

Her fingers tightened as she turned to face him, drawing in a shuddering breath that swelled her bust against the silk. Dear God, she *was* nude underneath. A hot-cold shiver ran up the backs of Hollister's legs. He couldn't take his eyes from her.

"*Don't mock me*," said Amanda.

"Mock—?" Hollister gaped at her.

A terrible sob convulsed Amanda's chest, and she fell against him. "Help me," she begged. "Please, help me."

Hollister's lips worked soundlessly. He tried to thrust away her body, but he couldn't. Nor could he keep his gaze from the parting folds of her robe.

"Mrs. Chappel—" he started in a choking voice.

"*Take me*," she whispered. "You killed him. Now *you* have to satisfy me." She tore apart the edges of her robe; her breasts fell white and heavy on his chest. "You *have* to!" Her eyes were feverish, her lips drawn back form clenching teeth. Hollister felt her steaming breath across his cheek. He trembled with a horror of revulsion. This was too soon, too soon! He'd planned—

Upstairs, someone staggered in the hallway, uttering muffled, frenzied sobs.

"No," Amanda said again.

Hollister felt her fingers drawing in across his back until the nails pressed painfully. "*What*?" he whimpered.

She sat transfixed beside him, looking toward the stairs. A low, demented moaning started in her throat.

"*What is it*?" he demanded.

Gasping suddenly, she pressed her face against his chest and clung to him. "Rex!" she cried.

A vise clamped shut on Hollister's heart. He shrank into the cushion, gagging, tried to speak but was unable to produce more than a blurred and imbecilic mumbling. Upstairs, the maddened floundering drew closer, started down the steps.

"Don't let him get me," whined Amanda. It seemed as though she grew into his flesh. Hollister kept trying, in vain, to push her off. His heartbeat crashed against his chest like hammer blows. He felt a spastic pulse of blood at both his temples. Footsteps banged and thudded on the stairs. A body crashed against the banisters; a maddened groan erupted in the air.

"*Don't let him get me!*" Amanda's voice was shrill, unbalanced. Hollister tried to answer her but only strangling gurgles passed his lips. He kept staring toward the hall, his eyes congealed. No, he thought. *Oh, God no!*

"*Don't let him get me!*" Screamed Amanda.

Just before the bloody figure lunged into the room, Hollister heard an incredible shrieking in his ears and, somehow, realized it was his own.

"He confessed?" she said.

The detective sergeant nodded slowly. He had not yet quite recovered from the sight of Mrs. Chappel, almost naked, clutching at the little screaming man as he had, per her instructions, reeled into the living room, arms reaching from the blood-soaked sheet.

"I still don't see how you knew it was him," he said.

Amanda Chappel's smile was bleak. "Call it intuition," she said.

Five minutes later, Sergeant Nielson was driving back to headquarters, thinking what remarkable instruments women were. There had been no indication, much less proof, that Hollister had been the murderer. Only Mrs. Chappel's insistence that he wait with her for Hollister's arrival had enabled them to establish any evidence; and only her weird assault on Hollister's nerves had made it possible to incriminate the man. True, most emotional murderers were ripe for confession, but by the time normal methods of investigation had reached him, Hollister would have steeled himself to all inquiry. Insane as it had seemed, Nielson was forced to admit that Mrs. Chappel's method was, perhaps, the only one that would have worked. He shook his head in baffled admiration. Actually, he thought, his part had almost been superfluous. Amanda Chappel had finished Hollister with her touches.

"The Finishing Touches" was first published in **Shock Waves** *(Dell, 1970) by Richard Matheson.*

"Editors were always genre happy—and this didn't fit as either a supernatural story or a straight crime story. So it kept getting reject-ed, which is why it ended up going directly into the collection. As you know, I never cared for genres. I simply wrote an idea the way it was called for, and let the chips fall where they may." —RM

TILL DEATH DO US PART

1970

SHE WAS ASLEEP NOW. Merle lay stiffly on his side. Her ragged snoring set his teeth on edge; he couldn't stand much more of it. Still, he'd had to wait.

Moving carefully he eased aside the bedclothes and stood up. His footsteps rustled on the carpeting. Entering the bathroom he switched on the light and opened the right sink drawer. He removed a pair of small scissors and returned to the bedroom.

He stood beside the bed for several minutes, gazing down at Flora with disgust. Good lord, she looked revolting. She may claim to be 52, but she was 60 if she was a day—gaunt, ugly, trying to fight the years with whiskey, makeup, red bleached hair, and long painted fingernails—and losing the battle hands down. One quality was all she had: money. He'd married her for that a month ago.

Now he meant to have it and be rid of her.

Leaning over the bed he carefully snipped away a lock of her hair and several fragments of nail. Flora stirred in her drunken sleep, making him flinch. Then she sighed, swallowed, and began to snore again. Pig, he thought, his youthful face curling with distaste.

Hastily he went back to the bathroom, put away the scissors, and switched off the light. He felt his way through the darkness to the hall door. Thank God that Flora had suggested separate rooms for sleeping. He would have gone demented otherwise. The thought of sleeping in the same bed with her, all night, every night, made him shudder.

He closed the door and hurried to his room. He simply had to shower, he felt so unclean. Dear God, how totally repulsive Flora was! How he'd managed to survive even a month with her he'd never know. Thank heavens he was not the violent type. If he were he might have strangled her a dozen times!

After he'd showered and donned his gold-colored pajamas, rubbed cologne on his face and throat and got into bed, he nudged a cigarette into his ivory holder, lit it, and began to work on the doll. It was almost finished—all he had to do was sew on Flora's hair and nails.

Done, he smiled and sighed. There, he thought. Freedom at last from that female ogre. Never again would he have to abide her cloying voice, her clumsy, dry-skinned touches, her whiskeyed breath, her barnyard grunts. Another month of all that and he'd positively be gibbering!

Smiling fiercely, Merle began to jab pins into the doll's abdomen, back, and chest. Die, you harridan, he thought elatedly. Die! Die!

Flora snorted in her sleep and woke up with a start. She looked around the darkness of her room with half-shut eyes. After several moments she reached out groggily and felt the other side of the bed.

She smiled. Oh, good, she thought, switching on her bedside lamp. Putting aside the bedclothes, she rose and weaved to the hall door, locked it clumsily, then staggered into the bathroom.

Standing in front of her dressing-table mirror she peeled off her eyelashes and removed her makeup. She smiled drunkenly at her reflection. Merle, oh, Merle, she thought. How she adored his attentions. Opening her mouth she tugged out her upper plate and dropped it in a glass of water. Merle was so romantic, so exciting. Flora reached up and skinned back her wig, pulling it off.

She pouted momentarily at the sight of her pale bald head, then shrugged, and giggling, turned out the light and stumbled back to bed. No matter. Merle would never know. She scratched her false nails on the bedsheet. How she loved to rake them down his back. Oh, Merle, she thought, and hiccupped loudly.

She just *knew* that it was going to last forever and ever!

"Till Death Do Us Part" was first published in **Ellery Queen's Mystery Magazine**, *September 1970.*

"I suppose it could have gone to **Playboy**, *except that they probably wouldn't have liked the idea of the fake body parts being so central; I guess it would have had to be a young woman, too. It was just a nice little sardonic tale with a surprise ending." —RM*

THE
NEAR DEPARTED
1987

THE SMALL MAN OPENED the door and stepped in out of the glaring sunlight. He was in his early fifties, a spindly, plain looking man with receding gray hair. He closed the door without a sound, then stood in the shadowy foyer, waiting for his eyes to adjust to the change in light. He was wearing a black suit, white shirt, and black tie. His face was pale and dry-skinned despite the heat of the day.

When his eyes had refocused themselves, he removed his Panama hat and moved along the hallway to the office, his black shoes soundless on the carpeting.

The mortician looked up from his desk. "Good afternoon," he said.

"Good afternoon." The small man's voice was soft.

"Can I help you?"

"Yes, you can," the small man said.

The mortician gestured to the arm chair on the other side of his desk. "Please."

The small man perched on the edge of the chair and set the Panama hat on his lap. He watched the mortician open a drawer and remove a printed form.

"Now," the mortician said. He withdrew a black pen from its onyx holder. "Who is deceased?" he asked gently.

"My wife," the small man said.

The mortician made a sympathetic noise. "I'm sorry," he said.

"Yes." The small man gazed at him blankly.

'What is her name?" the mortician asked.

"Marie," the small man answered quietly. "Arnold."

The mortician wrote the name. "Address?" he asked.

The small man told him.

"Is she there now?" the mortician asked.

"She's there," the small man said.

The mortician nodded.

"I want everything perfect," the small man said. "I want the best you have."

"Of course," the mortician said. "Of course."

"Cost is unimportant," said the small man. His throat moved as he swallowed dryly. "Everything is unimportant now. Except for this."

"I understand."

"She always had the best. I saw to it."

"Of course."

"There'll be many people," said the small man. "Everybody loved her. She's so beautiful. So young. She has to have the very best. You understand?"

"Absolutely," the mortician reassured him. "You'll be more than satisfied, I guarantee you."

"She's so beautiful," the small man said. "So young."

"I'm sure," the mortician said.

The small man sat without moving as the mortician asked him questions. His voice did not vary in tone as he spoke. His eyes blinked so infrequently the mortician never saw them doing it.

When the form was completed, the small man signed and stood. The mortician stood and walked around the desk. "I guarantee you you'll be satisfied," he said, his hand extended.

The small man took his hand and gripped it momentarily. His palm was dry and cool.

"We'll be over at your house within the hour," the mortician told him.

"Fine," the small man said.

The mortician walked beside him down the hallway.

"I want everything perfect for her," the small man said. "Nothing but the very best."

"Everything will be exactly as you wish."

"She deserves the best." The small man stared ahead. "She's so beautiful," he said. "Everybody loved her. Everybody. She's so young and beautiful."

"When did she die?' the mortician asked.

The small man didn't seem to hear. He opened the door and stepped into the sunlight, putting on his Panama hat. He was halfway to his car when he replied, a faint smile on his lips, "As soon as I get home."

"The Near Departed" was first published in **Masques II** *(Maclay & Associates, 1987), edited by J.N. Williamson.*

"The notion was just that this guy goes to a funeral parlor, and sets up an entire parlor, and gives a little hint that the person the funeral is for isn't dead, and that he's going to go home and kill them. The last group of stories I wrote in my career were more cross-genre than anything else, though they were usually disguised as horror stories. This story—and 'Buried Talents'—were actually written years before, even before 'Duel,' I think, and came out because the editor specifically asked me if I had any stories still unpublished at the time of his inquiry." —RM.

BURIED TALENTS
1987

A MAN IN A WRINKLED, black suit entered the fairgrounds. He was tall and lean, his skin the color of drying leather. He wore a faded sport shirt underneath his suit coat, white with yellow stripes. His hair was black and greasy, parted in the middle and brushed back flat on each side. His eyes were pale blue. There was no expression on his face. It was a hundred and two degrees in the sun but he was not perspiring.

He walked to one of the booths and stood there watching people try to toss ping-pong balls into dozens of little fish bowls on a table. A fat man wearing a straw hat and waving a bamboo cane in his right hand kept telling everyone how easy it was. "Try your luck!" he told them. "Win a prize! There's nothing to it!" He had an unlit, half-smoked cigar between his lips which he shifted from side to side as he spoke.

For awhile, the tall man in the wrinkled, black suit stood watching. Not one person managed a ping-pong ball into a fish bowl. Some of them tried to throw the balls in. Others tried to bounce them off the table. None of them had any luck.

At the end of seven minutes, the man in the black suit pushed between the people until he was standing by the booth. He took a quarter from his right hand trouser pocket and laid it on the counter. "Yes, sir!" said the fat man. "Try your luck!" He tossed the quarter into a metal box beneath the counter. Reaching down, he picked three grimy ping-pong balls from a basket. He clapped them on the counter and the tall man picked them up.

"Toss a ball in the fish bowl!" said the fat man. "Win a prize! There's nothing to it!" Sweat was trickling down his florid face. He took a quarter from a teenage boy and set three ping-pong balls in front of him.

The man in the black suit looked at the three ping-pong balls on his left palm. He hefted them, his face immobile. The man in the straw hat turned away. He tapped at the fish bowls with his cane. He shifted the stump of cigar in his mouth. "Toss a ball in the fish bowl!" he said. "A prize for everybody! Nothing to it!"

Behind him, a ping-pong ball clinked into one of the bowls. He turned and looked at the bowl. He looked at the man in the black suit. "There you are!" he said. "See that? Nothing to it! Easiest game on the fairgrounds!"

The tall man threw another ping-pong ball. It arced across the booth and landed in the same bowl. All the other people trying missed.

"Yes, sir!" the fat man said. "A prize for everybody! Nothing to it!" He picked up two quarters and set six ping-pong balls before a man and wife.

He turned and saw the third ping-pong ball dropping into the fish bowl. It didn't touch the neck of the bowl. It didn't bounce. It landed on the other two balls and lay there.

"See?" the man in the straw hat said. "A prize on his very first turn! Easiest game on the fairgrounds!" Reaching over to a set of wooden shelves, he picked up an ash tray and set it on the counter. "Yes, sir! Nothing to it!" he said. He took a quarter from a man in overalls and set three ping-pong balls in front of him.

The man in the black suit pushed away the ash tray. He laid another quarter on the counter. "Three more ping-pong balls," he said.

The fat man grinned. "Three more ping-pong balls it is!" he said. He reached below the counter, picked up three more balls and set them on the counter in front of the man. "Step right up!" he said. He caught a ping-pong ball which someone had bounced off the table. He kept an eye on the tall man while he stooped to retrieve some ping-pong balls on the ground.

The man in the black suit raised his right hand, holding one of the ping-pong balls. He threw it overhand, his face expressionless. The ball curved through the air and fell into the fish bowl with the other three balls. It didn't bounce.

The man in the straw hat stood with a grunt. He dumped a hand-ful of ping-pong balls into the basket underneath the counter. "Try your luck and win a prize!" he said. "Easy as pie!" He set three ping-pong balls in front of a boy and took his quarter. His eyes grew nar-row as he watched the tall man raise his hand to throw the second ball. "No leaning in," he told the man.

The man in the black suite glanced at him. "I'm not," he said.

The fat man nodded. "Go ahead," he said.

The tall man threw the second ping-pong ball. It seemed to float across the booth. It fell through the neck of the bowl and landed on top of the other four balls.

"Wait a second," said the fat man, holding up his hand.

The other people who were throwing stopped. The fat man leaned across the table. Sweat was running down beneath the collar of his long-sleeved shirt. He shifted the soggy cigar in his mouth as he scooped the five balls from the bowl. He straightened up and looked at them. He hooked the bamboo cane over his left forearm and rolled the balls between his palms.

"Okay, folks!" he said. He cleared his throat. "Keep throwing! Win a prize!" He dropped the balls into the basket underneath the counter. Taking another quarter from the man in overalls, he set three ping-pong balls in front of him.

The man in the black suit raised his hand and threw the sixth ball. The fat man watched it arc through the air. It fell into the bowl he'd emptied. It didn't roll around inside. It landed on the bottom, bounced once, straight up, then lay motionless.

The fat man grabbed the ash tray, stuck it on the shelf and picked up a fish bowl like the ones on the table. It was filled with pink colored water and had a goldfish fluttering around in it. "There you go!" he said. He turned away and tapped on the empty fish bowls with his cane. "Step right up!" he said. "Toss a ball in the fish bowl! Win a prize! There's nothing to it!"

Turning back, he saw the man in the wrinkled suit had pushed away the goldfish in the bowl and placed another quarter on the counter. "Three more ping-pong balls," he said.

The fat man looked at him. He shifted the damp cigar in his mouth.

"Three more ping-pong balls," the tall man said.

The man in the straw hat hesitated. Suddenly, he noticed people looking at him and, without a word, he took the quarter and set three ping-pong balls on the counter. He turned around and tapped the fish bowls with his cane. "Step right up and try your luck!" he said. "Easiest game on the fairgrounds!" He removed his straw hat and rubbed the left sleeve of his shirt across his forehead. He was almost bald. The small amount of hair on his head was plastered to his scalp by sweat. He put his straw hat back on and set three ping-pong balls in front of a boy. He put the quarter in the metal box underneath the counter.

A number of people were watching the tall man now. When he threw the first of the three ping-pong balls into the fish bowl some of them applauded and a small boy cheered. The fat man watched suspiciously. His small eyes shifted as the man in the black suit threw his second ping-pong ball into the fish bowl with the other two balls. He scowled and seemed about to speak. The scatter of applause appeared to irritate him.

The man in the wrinkled suit tossed the third ping-pong ball. It landed on top of the other three. Several people cheered and all of them clapped.

The fat man's cheeks were redder now. He put the fish bowl with the goldfish back on its shelf. He gestured toward a higher shelf. "What'll it be?" he asked.

The tall man put a quarter on the counter. "Three more ping-pong balls," he said in a brisk voice. He picked up three more ping-pong balls from the basket and rolled them between his palms.

"Don't give him the bad ones now," someone said in a mocking voice.

"No bad ones!" the fat man said. "They're all the same!" He set the balls on the counter and picked up the quarter. He tossed it into the metal box underneath the counter. The man in the black suit raised his hand.

"Wait a second," the fat man said. He turned and reached across the table. Picking up the fish bowl, he turned it over and dumped the four ping-pong balls into the basket. He seemed to hesitate before he put the empty fish bowl back in place.

Nobody else was throwing now. They watched the tall man curiously as he raised his hand and threw the first of his three ping-pong balls. It curved through the air and landed in the same fish bowl, dropping straight down through the neck. It bounced once, then was still. The people cheered and applauded. The fat man rubbed his left hand across his eyebrows and flicked the sweat from his fingertips with an angry gesture.

The man in the black suit threw his second ping-pong ball. It landed on the same fish bowl.

"*Hold* it," said the fat man.

The tall man looked at him.

"What are you doing?' the fat man asked.

"Throwing ping-pong balls," the tall man answered. Everybody laughed. The fat man's face got redder. "I know that!" he said.

"It's done with mirrors," someone said and everybody laughed again.

"*Funny*," said the fat man. He shifted the wet cigar in his mouth and gestured curtly. "Go on," he said.

The tall man in the black suit raised his hand and threw the third ping-pong ball. It arced across the booth as though it were being carried by an invisible hand. It landed in the fish bowl on top of the other two balls. Everybody cheered and clapped their hands.

The fat man in the straw hat grabbed a casserole dish and dumped it on the counter. The man in the black suit didn't look at it. He put another quarter down. "Three more ping-pong balls," he said.

The fat man turned away from him. "Step right up and win a prize!" he called. "Toss a ping-pong ball—!"

The noise of disapproval everybody made drowned him out. He turned back, bristling. "Four rounds to a customer!" he shouted.

"Where does it say that?" someone asked.

"That's the rule!" the fat man said. He turned his back on the man and tapped the fish bowls with his cane. "Step right up and win a prize!" he said.

"I came here yesterday and played *five* rounds!" a man said loudly.

"That's because you didn't win!" a teenage boy replied. Most of the people laughed and clapped but some of them booed. "Let him play!" a man's voice ordered. Everybody took it up immediately. "Let him play!" they demanded.

The man in the straw hat swallowed nervously. He looked around, a truculent expression on his face. Suddenly, he threw his hands up. "All right!" he said. "Don't get so excited!" He glared at the tall man as he picked up the quarter. Bending over, he grabbed three ping-pong balls and slammed them on the counter. He leaned in close to the man and muttered, "If you're pulling something fast, you'd better cut it out. This is an honest game."

The tall man stared at him. His face was blank. His eyes looked very pale in the leathery tan of his face. "What do you mean?" he asked.

"*No one can throw that many balls in succession into those bowls*," the fat man said.

The man in the black suit looked at him without expression. "*I* can," he said.

The fat man felt a coldness on his body. Stepping back, he watched the tall man throw the ping-pong balls. As each of them landed in the same fish bowl, the people cheered and clapped their hands.

The fat man took a set of steak knives from the top prize shelf and set it on the counter. He turned away quickly. "Step right up!" he said. "Toss a ball in the fish bowl! Win a prize!" His voice was trembling.

"He wants to play again," somebody said.

The man in the straw hat turned around. He saw the quarter on the counter in front of the tall man. "No more prizes," he said.

The man in the black suit pointed at the items on top of the wooden shelves—a four-slice electric toaster, a short wave radio, a drill set and a portable typewriter. "What about them?" he asked.

The fat man cleared his throat. "They're only for display," he said. He looked around for help.

"Where does it say *that?*" someone demanded.

"That's what they are, so just take my word for it!" the man in the straw hat said. His face was dripping with sweat.

"I'll play for them," the tall man said.

"Now *look!*" The fat man's face was very red. "They're only for display, I said! Now get the hell—!"

He broke off with a wheezing gasp and staggered back against the table, dropping his cane. The faces of the people swam before his eyes. He heard their angry voices as though from a distance. He saw the blurred figure of the man in the black suit turn away and push through the crowd. He straightened up and blinked his eyes. The steak knives were gone.

Almost everybody left the booth. A few of them remained. The fat man tried to ignore their threatening grumbles. He picked a quarter off the counter and set three ping-pong balls in front of a boy. "Try your luck," he said. His voice was faint. He tossed the quarter into the metal box underneath the counter. He leaned against a corner post and pressed both hands against his stomach. The cigar fell out of his mouth. "God," he said.

It felt as though he was bleeding inside.

*"Buried Talents" was first published in **Masques II** (Maclay & Associates, 1987), edited by J.N. Williamson.*

"I was never able to sell it. I remember trying to sell it to Harlan Ellison for one of his anthologies, but he didn't like it at all. I guess he didn't get the point of the story; the idea was that this guy had incredible powers—and all he used them for was to win prizes at a carnival. If parapsychologists could have taken him in and studied him, they would have found out a great deal about the unknown. As it was, he had this remarkable gift which he used for the most banal of purposes, and had no idea that his powers had any more significance than that. That was the point of the story, which may be why Harlan didn't dig it. The title is from the Bible of course—the tale of the man who had so many talents and he buried them and so lost those he already had." —RM

DUEL
1971

AT 11:32 A.M., Mann passed the truck.

He was heading west, en route to San Francisco. It was Thursday and unseasonably hot for April. He had his suitcoat off, his tie removed and shirt collar opened, his sleeve cuffs folded back. There was sunlight on his left arm and on part of his lap. He could feel the heat of it through his dark trousers as he drove along the two-lane highway. For the past twenty minutes, he had not seen another vehicle going in either direction.

Then he saw the truck ahead, moving up a curving grade between two high green hills. He heard the grinding strain of its motor and saw a double shadow on the road. The truck was pulling a trailer.

He paid no attention to the details of the truck. As he drew behind it on the grade, he edged his car toward the opposite lane. The road ahead had blind curves and he didn't try to pass until the truck had crossed the ridge. He waited until it started around a left curve on the downgrade, then, seeing that the way was clear, pressed down on the accelerator pedal and steered his car into the eastbound lane. He waited until he could see the truck front in his rearview mirror before he turned back into the proper lane.

Mann looked across the countryside ahead. There were ranges of mountains as far as he could see and, all around him, rolling green hills. He whistled softly as the car sped down the winding grade, its tires making crisp sounds on the pavement.

At the bottom of the hill, he crossed a concrete bridge and, glancing to the right, saw a dry stream bed strewn with rocks and gravel. As the car moved off the bridge, he saw a trailer park set back from the highway to his right. How can anyone live out here? he thought. His shifting gaze caught sight of a pet cemetery ahead and he smiled. Maybe those people in the trailers wanted to be close to the graves of their dogs and cats.

The highway ahead was straight now. Mann drifted into a reverie, the sunlight on his arm and lap. He wondered what Ruth was doing. The kids, of course, were in school and would be for hours yet. Maybe Ruth was shopping; Thursday was the day she usually went. Mann visualized her in the supermarket, putting various items into the basket cart. He wished he were with her instead of starting on another sales trip. Hours of driving yet before he'd reach San Francisco. Three days of hotel sleeping and restaurant eating, hoped-for contacts and likely disappointments. He sighed; then, reaching out impulsively, he switched on the radio. He revolved the tuning knob until he found a station playing soft, innocuous music. He hummed along with it, eyes almost out of focus on the road ahead.

He started as the truck roared past him on the left, causing his car to shudder slightly. He watched the truck and trailer cut in abruptly for the westbound lane and frowned as he had to brake to maintain a safe distance behind it. What's with you? he thought.

He eyed the truck with cursory disapproval. It was a huge gasoline tanker pulling a tank trailer, each of them having six pairs of wheels. He could see that it was not a new rig but was dented and in need of renovation, its tanks painted a cheap-looking silvery color. Mann wondered if the driver had done the painting himself. His gaze shifted from the word FLAMMABLE printed across the back of the trailer tank, red letters on a white background, to the parallel reflector lines painted in red across the bottom of the tank to the massive rubber flaps swaying behind the rear tires, then back up again. The reflector lines looked as though they'd been clumsily applied with a stencil. The driver must be an independent trucker, he decided, and not too affluent a one, from the looks of his outfit. He glanced at the trailer's license plate. It was a California issue.

Mann checked his speedometer. He was holding steady at 55 miles an hour, as he invariably did when he drove without thinking on the open highway. The truck driver must have done a good 70 to pass him so quickly. That seemed a little odd. Weren't truck drivers supposed to be a cautious lot?

He grimaced at the smell of the truck's exhaust and looked at the vertical pipe to the left of the cab. It was spewing smoke, which clouded darkly back across the trailer. Christ, he thought. With all the furor about air pollution, why do they keep allowing that sort of thing on the highways?

He scowled at the constant fumes. They'd make him nauseated in a little while, he knew. He couldn't lag back here like this. Either he slowed down or he passed the truck again. He didn't have the time to slow down. He'd gotten a late start. Keeping it at 55 all the way, he'd just about make his afternoon appointment. No, he'd have to pass.

Depressing the gas pedal, he eased his car toward the opposite lane. No sign of anything ahead. Traffic on this route seemed almost nonexistent today. He pushed down harder on the accelerator and steered all the way into the eastbound lane.

As he passed the truck, he glanced at it. The cab was too high for him to see into. All he caught sight of was the back of the truck driver's left hand on the steering wheel. It was darkly tanned and square-looking, with large veins knotted on its surface.

When Mann could see the truck reflected in the rearview mirror, he pulled back over to the proper lane and looked ahead again.

He glanced at the rearview mirror in surprise as the truck driver gave him an extended horn blast. What was that? he wondered; a greeting or a curse? He grunted with amusement, glancing at the mirror as he drove. The front fenders of the truck were a dingy purple color, the paint faded and chipped; another amateurish job. All he could see was the lower portion of the truck; the rest was cut off by the top of his rear window.

To Mann's right, now, was a slope of shalelike earth with patches of scrub grass growing on it. His gaze jumped to the clapboard house on top of the slope. The television aerial on its roof was sagging at an angle of less than 40 degrees. Must give great reception, he thought.

He looked to the front again, glancing aside abruptly at a sign printed in jagged block letters on a piece of plywood: NIGHT CRAWLERS—BAIT. What the hell is a night crawler? he wondered. It sounded like some monster in a low-grade Hollywood thriller.

The unexpected roar of the truck motor made his gaze jump to the rearview mirror. Instantly, his startled look jumped to the side mirror. By God, the guy was passing him *again.* Mann turned his head to scowl at the leviathan form as it drifted by. He tried to see into the cab but couldn't because of its height. What's with him, anyway? he wondered. What the hell are we having here, a contest? See which vehicle can stay ahead the longest?

He thought of speeding up to stay ahead but changed his mind. When the truck and trailer started back into the westbound lane, he let up on the pedal, voicing a newly incredulous sound as he saw that if he hadn't slowed down, he would have been prematurely cut off again. Jesus Christ, he thought. What's *with* this guy?

His scowl deepened as the odor of the truck's exhaust reached his nostrils again. Irritably, he cranked up the window on his left. Damn it, was he going to have to breathe that crap all the way to San Francisco? He couldn't afford to slow down. He had to meet Forbes at a quarter after three and that was that.

He looked ahead. At least there was no traffic complicating matters. Mann pressed down on the accelerator pedal, drawing close behind the truck. When the highway curved enough to the left to give him a completely open view of the route ahead, he jarred down on the pedal, steering out into the opposite lane.

The truck edged over, blocking his way.

For several moments, all Mann could do was stare at it in blank confusion. Then, with a startled noise, he braked, returning to the proper lane. The truck moved back in front of him.

Mann could not allow himself to accept what apparently had

taken place. It had to be a coincidence. The truck driver couldn't have blocked his way on purpose. He waited for more than a minute, then flicked down the turn-indicator lever to make his intentions perfectly clear and, depressing the accelerator pedal, steered again into the eastbound lane.

Immediately, the truck shifted, barring his way.

"Jesus Christ!" Mann was astounded. This was unbelievable. He'd never seen such a thing in twenty-six years of driving. He returned to the west-bound lane, shaking his head as the truck swung back in front of him.

He eased up on the gas pedal, falling back to avoid the truck's exhaust. Now what? he wondered. He still had to make San Francisco on schedule. Why in God's name hadn't he gone a little out of his way in the beginning, so he could have traveled by freeway? This damned highway was two lane all the way.

Impulsively, he sped into the eastbound lane again. To his surprise, the truck driver did not pull over. Instead, the driver stuck his left arm out and waved him on. Mann started pushing down on the accelerator. Suddenly, he let up on the pedal with a gasp and jerked the steering wheel around, raking back behind the truck so quickly that his car began to fishtail. He was fighting to control its zigzag whipping when a blue convertible shot by him in the opposite lane. Mann caught a momentary vision of the man inside it glaring at him.

The car came under his control again. Mann was sucking breath in through his mouth. His heart was pounding almost painfully. My God! he thought. *He wanted me to hit that car head on.* The realization stunned him. True, he should have seen to it himself that the road ahead was clear; that was his failure. But to wave him on…Mann felt appalled and sickened. Boy, oh, boy, oh, boy, he thought. This was really one for the books. That son of a bitch had meant for not only him to be killed but a totally uninvolved passer-by as well. The idea seemed beyond his comprehension. On a California highway on a Thursday morning? *Why?*

Mann tried to calm himself and rationalize the incident. Maybe it's the heat, he thought. Maybe the truck driver had a tension headache or an upset stomach; maybe both. Maybe he'd had a fight with his wife. Maybe she'd failed to put out last night. Mann tried in vain to smile. There could be any number of reasons. Reaching out, he twisted off the radio. The cheerful music irritated him.

He drove behind the truck for several minutes, his face a mask of animosity. As the exhaust fumes started putting his stomach on edge, he suddenly forced down the heel of his right hand on the horn bar and held it there. Seeing that the route ahead was clear, he pushed in the accelerator pedal all the way and steered into the opposite lane.

The movement of his car was paralleled immediately by the truck. Mann stayed in place, right hand jammed down on the horn bar. Get out of the way, you son of a bitch! he thought. He felt the muscles of his jaw hardening until they ached. There was a twisting in his stomach.

"Damn!" He pulled back quickly to the proper lane, shuddering with fury. "You miserable son of a bitch," he muttered, glaring at the truck as it was shifted back in front of him. What the hell is wrong with you? I pass your goddamn rig a couple of times and you go flying off the deep end? Are you nuts or something? Mann nodded tensely. Yes, he thought, he *is*. No other explanation.

He wondered what Ruth would think of all this, how she'd react. Probably, she'd start to honk the horn and would keep on honking it, assuming that, eventually, it would attract the attention of a policeman. He looked around with a scowl. Just where in hell *were* the policemen out here, anyway? He made a scoffing noise. What policemen? Here in the boondocks? They probably had a sheriff on horseback, for Christ's sake.

He wondered suddenly if he could fool the truck driver by passing on the right. Edging his car toward the shoulder, he peered ahead. No chance. There wasn't room enough. The truck driver could shove him through that wire fence if he wanted to, sure as hell, he thought.

Driving where he was, he grew conscious of the debris lying beside the highway: beer cans, candy wrappers, ice-cream containers, newspaper sections browned and rotted by the weather, a FOR SALE sign torn in half. Keep America beautiful, he thought sardonically. He passed a boulder with the name WILL JASPER painted on it in white. Who the hell is Will Jasper? he wondered. What would he think of this situation.

Unexpectedly, the car began to bounce. For several anxious moments, Mann thought that one of his tires had gone flat. Then he noticed that the paving along this section of highway consisted of pitted slabs with gaps between them. He saw the truck and trailer jolting up and down and thought: I hope it shakes your brains loose. As the truck veered into a sharp left curve, he caught a fleeting glimpse of the driver's face in the cab's side mirror. There was not enough time to establish his appearance.

"Ah," he said. A long, steep hill was looming up ahead. The truck would have to climb it slowly. There would doubtless be an opportunity to pass somewhere on the grade. Mann pressed down on the accelerator pedal, drawing as close behind the truck as safety would allow.

Halfway up the slope, Mann saw a turnout for the eastbound lane with no oncoming traffic anywhere in sight. Flooring the accelerator pedal, he shot into the opposite lane. The slow-moving truck began to angle out in front of him. Face stiffening, Mann steered his speeding car across the highway edge and curbed it sharply on the turnout. Clouds of dust went billowing up behind his car, making him lose sight of the truck. His tires buzzed and crackled on the dirt, then, suddenly, were humming on the pavement once again.

He glanced at the rearview mirror and a barking laugh erupted from his throat. He'd only meant to pass. The dust had been an unexpected bonus. Let the bastard get a sniff of something rotten smelling in *his* nose for a change! he thought. He honked the horn elatedly, a mocking rhythm of bleats. Screw you, Jack!

He swept across the summit of the hill. A striking vista lay ahead: sunlit hills and flatland, a corridor of dark trees, quadrangles of cleared-off acreage and bright-green vegetables patches; far off, in the distance, a mammoth water tower. Mann felt stirred by the panoramic sight. Lovely, he thought. Reaching out, he turned the radio back on and started humming cheerfully with the music.

Seven minutes later, he passed a billboard advertising CHUCK'S CAFÉ. No thanks, Chuck, he thought. He glanced at a gray house nestled in a hollow. Was that a cemetery in its front yard or a group of plaster statuary for sale?

Hearing the noise behind him, Mann looked at the rearview mirror and felt himself go cold with fear. The truck was hurtling down the hill, pursuing him.

His mouth fell open and he threw a glance at the speedometer.

He was doing more than 60! On a curving downgrade, that was not at all a safe speed to be driving. Yet the truck must be exceeding that by a considerable margin, it was closing the distance between them so rapidly. Mann swallowed, leaning to the right as he steered his car around a sharp curve. Is the man *insane*? he thought.

His gaze jumped forward searchingly. He saw a turnoff half a mile ahead and decided that he'd use it. In the rearview mirror, the huge square radiator grille was all he could see now. He stamped down on the gas pedal and his tires screeched unnervingly as he wheeled around another curve, thinking that, surely, the truck would have to slow down here.

He groaned as it rounded the curve with ease, only the sway of its tanks revealing the outward pressure of the turn. Mann bit trembling lips together as he whipped his car around another curve. A straight descent now. He depressed the pedal farther, glanced at the speedometer. Almost 70 miles an hour! He wasn't used to driving this fast!

In agony, he saw the turnoff shoot by on his right. He couldn't have left the highway at this speed, anyways; he'd have overturned. Goddamn it, what was wrong with that son of a bitch? Mann honked his horn in frightened rage. Cranking down the window suddenly, he shoved his left arm out to wave the truck back. "*Back*!" he yelled. He honked the horn again. "Get back, you crazy bastard!"

The truck was almost on him now. He's going to kill me! Mann thought, horrified. He honked the horn repeatedly, then had to use both hands to grip the steering wheel as he swept around another curve. He flashed a look at the rearview mirror. He could see only the bottom portion of the truck's radiator grille. He was going to lose control! He felt the rear wheels start to drift and let up on the pedal quickly. The tire treads bit in, the car leaped on, regaining its momentum.

Mann saw the bottom of the grade ahead, and in the distance there was a building with a sign that read CHUCK'S CAFÉ. The truck was gaining ground again. This is insane! he thought, enraged and terrified at once. The highway straightened out. He floored the pedal: 74 now—75. Mann braced himself, trying to ease the car as far to the right as possible.

Abruptly, he began to brake, then swerved to the right, raking his car into the open area in front of the café. He cried out as the car began to fishtail, then careened into a skid. *Steer with it*! Screamed a voice in his mind. The rear of the car was lashing from side to side, tires spewing dirt and raising clouds of dust. Mann pressed harder on the brake pedal, turning further into the skid. The car began to straighten out and he braked harder yet, conscious, on the sides of his vision, of the truck and trailer roaring by on the highway. He nearly sideswiped one of the cars parked in front of the café, bounced and skidded by it, going almost straight now. He jammed in the brake pedal as hard as he could. The rear end broke to the right and the car spun half around, sheering sideways to a neck-wrenching halt thirty yards beyond the café.

Mann sat in pulsing silence, eyes closed. His heartbeats felt like club blows in his chest. He couldn't seem to catch his breath. If he were ever going to have a heart attack, it would be now. After a while, he opened his eyes and pressed his right palm against his chest. His heart was still throbbing laboredly. No wonder, he thought. It isn't every day I'm almost murdered by a truck.

He raised the handle and pushed out the door, then started forward, grunting in surprise as the safety belt held him in place. Reaching down with shaking fingers, he depressed the release button and pulled the ends of the belt apart. He glanced at the cafe. What had its patrons thought of his breakneck appearance? he wondered.

He stumbled as he walked to the front door of the café. TRUCKERS WELCOME, read a sign in the window. It gave Mann a queasy feeling to see it. Shivering, he pulled open the door and went inside, avoiding the sight of its customers. He felt certain they were watching him, but he didn't have the strength to face their looks. Keeping his gaze fixed straight ahead, he moved to the rear of the café and opened the door marked GENTS.

Moving to the sink, he twisted the right-hand faucet and leaned over to cup cold water in his palms and splash it on his face. There was a fluttering of his stomach muscles he could not control.

Straightening up, he tugged down several towels from their dispenser and patted them against his face, grimacing at the smell of the paper. Dropping the soggy towels into a wastebasket beside the sink, he regarded himself in the wall mirror. Still with us, Mann, he thought. He nodded, swallowing. Drawing out his metal comb, he neatened his hair. You never know, he thought. You just never know.

You drift along, year after year, presuming certain values to be fixed; like being able to drive on a public thoroughfare without somebody trying to murder you. You come to depend on that sort of thing. Then something occurs and all bets are off. One shocking incident and all the years of logic and acceptance are displaced and, suddenly, the jungle is in front of you again. *Man, part animal, part angel.* Where had he come across that phrase? He shivered.

It was entirely an animal in that truck out there.

His breath was almost back to normal now. Mann forced a smile at his reflection. All right, boy, he told himself. It's over now. It as a goddamned nightmare, but it's over. You are on your way to San Francisco. You'll get yourself a nice hotel room, order a bottle of expensive Scotch, soak your body in a hot bath and forget. Damn right, he thought. He turned and walked out of the washroom.

He jolted to a halt, his breath cut off. Standing rooted, heartbeat hammering at his chest, he gaped through the front window of the café.

The truck and trailer were parked outside.

Mann stared at them in unbelieving shock. It wasn't possible. He'd seen them roaring by at top speed. The driver had won; he'd *won*! He'd had the whole damn highway to himself! *Why had he turned back?*

Mann looked around with sudden dread. There were five men eating, three along the counter, two in booths. He cursed himself for having failed to look at faces when he'd entered. Now there was no way of knowing who it was. Mann felt his legs begin to shake.

Abruptly, he walked to the nearest booth and slid in clumsily behind the table. Now wait, he told himself; just wait. Surely, he could tell which one it was. Masking his face with the menu, he glanced across its top. Was it that one in the khaki work shirt? Mann tried to see the man's hands but couldn't. His gaze flicked nervously across the room. Not that one in the suit, of course. Three remaining. That one in the front booth, square-faced, black-haired? If only he could see the man's hands, it might help. One of the two others at the counter? Mann studied them uneasily. Why hadn't he looked at faces when he'd come in?

Now *wait*, he thought. Goddamn it, *wait*! All right, the truck driver was in here. That didn't automatically signify that he meant to continue the insane duel. Chuck's Café might be the only place to eat for miles around. It *was* lunchtime, wasn't it? The truck driver had probably intended to eat here all the time. He'd just been moving too fast to pull into the parking lot before. So he'd slowed down, turned around and driven back, that was all. Mann forced himself to read the menu. Right, he thought. No point in getting so rattled. Perhaps a beer would help relax him.

The woman behind the counter came over and Mann ordered a ham sandwich on rye toast and a bottle of Coors. As the woman turned away, he wondered, with a sudden twinge of self-reproach, why he hadn't simply left the café, jumped into his car and sped away. He would have known immediately, then, if the truck driver was still out to get him. As it was, he'd have to suffer through an entire meal to find out. He almost groaned at his stupidity.

Still, what if the truck driver *had* followed him out and started after him again? He'd have been right back where he'd started. Even if he'd managed to get a good lead, the truck driver would have over-taken him eventually. It just wasn't in him to drive at 80 and 90 miles an hour in order to stay ahead. True, he might have been intercepted by a California Highway Patrol car. What if he weren't, though?

Mann repressed the plaguing thoughts. He tried to calm himself. He looked deliberately at the four men. Either of two seemed a likely possibility as the driver of the truck: the square-faced one in the front booth and the chunky one in the jumpsuit sitting at the counter. Mann had an impulse to walk over to them and ask which one it was, tell the man he was sorry he'd irritated him, tell him anything to calm him, since, obviously, he wasn't rational, was a manic-depressive, probably. Maybe buy the man a beer and sit with him awhile to try to settle things.

He couldn't move. What if the truck driver were letting the whole thing drop? Mightn't his approach rile the man all over again? Mann felt drained by indecision. He nodded weakly as the waitress set the sandwich and the bottle in front of him. He took a swallow of the beer, which made him cough. Was the truck driver amused by the sound? Mann felt a stirring of resentment deep inside himself. What right did that bastard have to impose this torment on another human being? It was a free country, wasn't it? Damn it, he had every right to pass the son of a bitch on a highway if he wanted to!

"Oh, hell," he mumbled. He tried to feel amused. He was making entirely too much of this. Wasn't he? He glanced at the pay telephone on the front wall. What was to prevent him from calling the local police and telling them the situation? But, then, he'd have to stay here, lose time, make Forbes angry, probably lose the sale. And what if the truck driver stayed to face them? Naturally, he'd deny the whole thing. What if the police believed him and didn't do anything about I? After they'd gone, the truck driver would undoubtedly take it out on him again, only worse. *God!* Mann thought in agony.

The sandwich tasted flat, the beer unpleasantly sour. Mann stared at the table as he ate. For God's sake, why was he just *sitting* here like this? He was a grown man, wasn't he? Why didn't he settle this damn thing once and for all?

His left hand twitched so unexpectedly, he spilled beer on his trousers. The man in the jump suit had risen from the counter and was strolling toward the front of the café. Mann felt his heartbeat thumping as the man gave money to the waitress, took his change and a toothpick from the dispenser and went outside. Mann watched in anxious silence.

The man did not get into the cab of the tanker truck.

It had to be the one in the front booth, then. His face took form in Mann's remembrance: square, with dark eyes, dark hair; the man who'd tried to kill him.

Mann stood abruptly, letting impulse conquer fear. Eyes fixed ahead, he started toward the entrance. Anything was preferable to sitting in that booth. He stopped by the cash register, conscious of the hitching of his chest as he gulped in air. Was the man observing him? he wondered. He swallowed, pulling out the clip of dollar bills in his right-hand trouser pocket. He glanced toward the waitress. Come *on*, he thought. He looked at his check and, seeing the amount, reached shakily into his trouser pocket for change. He heard a coin fall onto the floor and roll away. Ignoring it, he dropped a dollar, and a quarter onto the counter and thrust the clip of bills into his trouser pocket.

As he did, he heard the man in the front booth get up. An icy shudder spasmed up his back. Turning quickly to the door, he shoved it open, seeing, on the edges of his vision, the square-faced man approach the cash register. Lurching from the café, he started toward his car with long strides. His mouth was dry again. The pounding of his heart was painful in his chest.

Suddenly, he started running. He heard the café door bang shut and fought away the urge to look across his shoulder. Was that a sound of other running footsteps now? Reaching his car, Mann yanked open the door and jarred in awkwardly behind the steering wheel. He reached into his trouser pocket for the keys and snatched them out, almost dropping them. His hand was shaking so badly he couldn't get the ignition key into its slot. He whined with mounting dread. Come on! he thought.

The key slid in, he twisted it convulsively. The motor started and he raced it momentarily before jerking the transmission shift to drive. Depressing the accelerator pedal quickly, he raked the car around and steered it toward the highway. From the corners of his eyes, he saw the truck and trailer being backed away from the café.

Reaction burst inside him. "No!" he raged and slammed his foot down on the brake pedal. This was idiotic! Why the hell should he run away? His car slid sideways to a rocking halt and, shouldering out the door, he lurched to his feet and started toward the truck with angry strides. *All right, Jack*, he thought. He glared at the man inside the truck. You want to punch my nose, okay, but no more goddamn tournament on the highway.

The truck began to pick up speed. Mann raised his right arm. "Hey!" he yelled. He knew the driver saw him. "*Hey!*" He started running as the truck kept moving, engine grinding loudly. It was on the highway now. He sprinted toward it with a sense of martyred outrage. The driver shifted gears, the truck moved faster. "Stop!" Mann shouted. "Damn it, *stop!*"

He thudded to a panting halt, staring at the truck as it receded down the highway, moved around a hill and disappeared. "You son of a bitch," he muttered. "You goddamn, miserable son of a bitch."

He trudged back slowly to this car, trying to believe that the truck driver had fled the hazard of a fistfight. It was possible, of course, but, somehow, he could not believe it.

He got into his car and was about to drive onto the highway when he changed his mind and switched the motor off. That crazy bastard might just be tooling along at 15 miles an hour, waiting for him to catch up. Nuts to that, he thought. So he blew his schedule;

RICHARD MATHESON

screw it. Forbes would have to wait, that was all. And if Forbes did-n't care to wait, that was all right, too. He'd sit here for a while and let the nut get out of range, let him think he'd won the day. He grinned. You're the bloody Red Baron, Jack; you've shot me down. Now go to hell with my sincerest compliments. He shook his head. Beyond belief, he thought.

He really should have done this earlier, pulled over, waited. Then the truck driver would have had to let it pass. *Or picked on someone else,* the startling thought occurred to him. Jesus, maybe that was how the crazy bastard whiled away his work hours! Jesus Christ Almighty! Was it possible?

He looked at the dashboard clock. It was just past 12:30. Wow, he thought. All that in less than an hour. He shifted on the seat and stretched his legs out. Leaning back against the door, he closed his eyes and mentally perused the things he had to do tomorrow and the following day. Today was shot to hell, as far as he could see.

When he opened his eyes, afraid of drifting into sleep and los-ing too much time, almost eleven minutes had passed. The nut must be an ample distance off by now, he thought; at least 11 miles and likely more, the way he drove. Good enough. He wasn't going to try to make San Francisco on schedule now, anyways. He'd take it real easy.

Mann adjusted his safety belt, switched on the motor, tapped the transmission pointer into the drive position and pulled onto the highway, glancing back across his shoulder. Not a car in sight. Great day for driving. Everybody was staying at home. That nut must have a reputation around here. When Crazy jack is on the highway, lock your car in the garage. Mann chuckled at the notion as his car began to turn the curve ahead.

Mindless reflex drove his right foot down against the brake pedal. Suddenly, his car had skidded to a halt and he was staring down the highway. The truck and trailer were parked on the shoulder less than 90 yards away.

Mann couldn't seem to function. He knew his car was blocking the west-bound lane, knew that he should either make a U-turn or pull off the highway, but all he could do was gape at the truck.

He cried out, legs retracting, as a horn blast sounded behind him. Snapping up his head, he looked at the rearview mirror, gasping

334

as he saw a yellow station wagon bearing down on him at high speed. Suddenly, it veered off toward the eastbound lane, disappearing from the mirror. Mann jerked around and saw it hurtling past his car, its rear end snapping back and forth, its back tires screeching. He saw the twisted features of the man inside, saw his lips move rapidly with cursing.

Then the station wagon had swerved back into the westbound lane and was speeding off. It gave Mann an odd sensation to see it pass the truck. The man in that station wagon could drive on, unthreatened. Only he'd been singled out. What happened was demented. Yet it was happening.

He drove his car onto the highway shoulder and braked. Putting the transmission into neutral, he leaned back, staring at the truck. His head was aching again. There was a pulsing at his temples like the ticking of a muffled clock.

What was he to do? He knew very well that if he left his car to walk to the truck, the driver would pull away and repark farther down the highway. He may as well face the fact that he was dealing with a madman. He felt the tremor in his stomach muscles starting up again. His heartbeat thudded slowly, striking at his chest wall. Now what?

With a sudden, angry impulse, Mann snapped the transmission into gear and stepped down hard on the accelerator pedal. The tires of the car spun sizzlingly before they gripped; the car shot out onto the highway. Instantly, the truck began to move. He even had the motor on! Mann thought in raging fear. He floored the pedal, then, abruptly, realized he couldn't make it, that the truck would block his way and he'd collide with its trailer. A vision flashed across his mind, a fiery explosion and a sheet of flame incinerating him. He started braking fast, trying to decelerate evenly, so he wouldn't lose control.

When he'd slowed down enough to feel that it was safe, he steered the car onto the shoulder and stopped it again, throwing the transmission into neutral.

Approximately eighty yards ahead, the truck pulled off the highway and stopped.

Mann tapped his fingers on the steering wheel. *Now* what? He thought. Turn around and head east until he reached a cutoff that would take him to San Francisco by another route? How did he know the truck driver wouldn't follow him even then? His cheeks twisted

RICHARD MATHESON

as he bit his lips together angrily. No! He wasn't going to turn around!

His expression hardened suddenly. Well, he wasn't going to *sit* here all day, that was certain. Reaching out, he tapped the gearshift into drive and steered his car onto the highway once again. He saw the massive truck and trailer start to move but made no effort to speed up. He tapped at the brakes, taking a position about 30 yards behind the trailer. He glanced at his speedometer. Forty miles an hour. The truck driver had his left arm out of the cab window and was waving him on. What did that mean? Had he changed his mind? Decided, finally, that this thing had gone too far? Mann couldn't let himself believe it.

He looked ahead. Despite the mountain ranges all around, the highway was flat as far as he could see. He tapped a fingernail against the horn bar, trying to make up his mind. Presumably, he could continue all the way to San Francisco at this speed, hanging back just far enough to avoid the worst of the exhaust fumes. It didn't seem likely that the truck driver would stop directly on the highway to block his way. And if the truck driver pulled onto the shoulder to let him pass, he could pull off the highway, too. It would be a draining afternoon but a safe one.

On the other hand, outracing the truck might be worth just one more try. This was obviously what that son of a bitch wanted. Yet, surely, a vehicle of such size couldn't be driven with the same daring as, potentially, his own. The laws of mechanics were against it, if nothing else. Whatever advantage the truck had in mass, it had to lose in stability, particularly that of its trailer. If Mann were to drive at, say, 80 miles an hour and there were a few steep grades—as he felt sure there were—the truck would have to fall behind.

The question was, of course, whether he had the nerve to maintain such a speed over a long distance. He'd never done it before. Still, the more he thought about it, the more it appealed to him; far more than the alternative did.

Abruptly, he decided. *Right*, he thought. He checked ahead, then pressed down hard on the accelerator pedal and pulled into the eastbound lane. As he neared the truck, he tensed, anticipating that the driver might block his way. But the truck did not shift from the westbound lane. Mann's car moved along its mammoth side. He

336

glanced at the cab and saw the name KELLER printed on its door. For a shocking instant, he thought it read KILLER and started to slow down. Then, glancing at the name again, he saw what it really was and depressed the pedal sharply. When he saw the truck reflected in the rearview mirror, he steered his car into the westbound lane.

He shuddered, dread and satisfaction mixed together, as he saw that the truck driver was speeding up. It was strangely comforting to know the man's intentions definitely again. That plus the knowledge of his face and name seemed, somehow, to reduce his stature. Before, he had been faceless, nameless, an embodiment of unknown terror. Now, at least he was an individual. All right, Keller, said his mind, let's see you beat me with that purple-silver relic now. He pressed down harder on the pedal. *Here we go*, he thought.

He looked at the speedometer, scowling as he saw that he was doing only 74 miles an hour. Deliberately, he pressed down on the pedal, alternating his gaze between the highway ahead and the speedometer until the needle turned past 80. He felt a flickering of satisfaction with himself. All right, Keller, you son of a bitch, top that, he thought.

After several moments, he glanced into the rearview mirror again. Was the truck getting closer? Stunned, he checked the speedometer. Damn it! He was down to 76! He forced in the accelerator pedal angrily. *He mustn't go less than 80!* Mann's chest shuddered with convulsive breath.

He glanced aside as he hurtled past a beige sedan parked on the shoulder underneath a tree. A young couple sat inside it, talking. Already they were far behind, their world removed from his. Had they even glanced aside when he'd passed? He doubted it.

He started as the shadow of an overhead bridge whipped across the hood and windshield. Inhaling raggedly, he glanced at the speedometer again. He was holding at 81. He checked the rearview mirror. Was it his imagination that the truck was gaining ground? He looked forward with anxious eyes. There had to be some kind of town ahead. To hell with time; he'd stop at the police station and tell them what had happened. They'd have to believe him. Why would he stop to tell them such a story if it weren't true? For all he knew, Keller had a police record in these parts. *Oh, sure, we're on to him,* he heard a faceless officer remark. *That crazy bastard's asked for it before and now he's going to get it.*

Mann shook himself and looked at the mirror. The truck *was* getting closer. Wincing, he glared at the speedometer. Goddamn it, pay attention! Raged his mind. He was down to 74 again! Whining with frustration, he depressed the pedal. Eighty!—80! He demanded of himself. There was a murderer behind him!

His car began to pass a field of flowers; lilacs, Mann saw, white and purple stretching out in endless rows. There was a small shack near the highway, the words FIELD FRESH FLOWERS painted on it. A brown-cardboard square was propped against the shack, the word FUNERALS printed crudely on it. Mann saw himself, abruptly, lying in a casket, painted like some grotesque mannequin. The overpowering smell of flowers seemed to fill his nostrils. Ruth and the children sitting in the first row, heads bowed. All his relatives—

Suddenly, the pavement roughened and the car began to bounce and shudder, driving bolts of pain into his head. He felt the steering wheel resisting him and clamped his hands around it tightly, harsh vibrations running up his arms. He didn't dare look at the mirror now. He had to force himself to keep the speed unchanged. Keller wasn't going to slow down; he was sure of that. *What if he got a flat tire, though?* All control would vanish in an instant. He visualized the somersaulting of his car, its grinding, shrieking tumble, the explosion of its gas tank, his body crushed and burned and—

The broken span of pavement ended and his gaze jumped quickly to the rearview mirror. The truck was no closer, but it hadn't lost ground, either. Mann's eyes shifted. Up ahead were hills and mountains. He tried to reassure himself that upgrades were on his side, that he could climb them at the same speed he was going now. Yet all he could imagine were the downgrades, the immense truck close behind him, slamming violently into his car and knocking it across some cliff edge. He had a horrifying vision of dozens of broken, rusted cars lying unseen in the canyons ahead, corpses in every one of them, all flung to shattering deaths by Keller.

Mann's car went rocketing into a corridor of trees. On each side of the highway was a eucalyptus windbreak, each trunk three feet from the next. It was like speeding through a high-walled canyon. Mann gasped, twitching, as a large twig bearing dusty leaves dropped down across the windshield, then slid out of sight. Dear God! he thought. He was getting near the edge himself. If he should lose his nerve at this speed, it was over. Jesus! That would be ideal for Keller! He realized suddenly. He visualized the square-faced driver laughing as he passed the burning wreckage, knowing that he'd killed his prey without so much as touching him.

Mann started as his car shot out into the open. The route ahead was not straight now but winding up into the foothills. Mann willed himself to press down on the pedal even more. Eighty-three now, almost 84.

To his left was a broad terrain of green hills blending into mountains. He saw a black car on a dirt road, moving toward the highway. *Was its side painted white?* Mann's heartbeat lurched. Impulsively, he jammed the heel of his right hand down against the horn bar and held it there. The blast of horn was shrill and racking to his ears. His heart began to pound. Was it a police car? *Was it*?

He let the horn bar up abruptly. *No, it wasn't.* Damn! His mind raged. Keller must have been amused by his pathetic efforts. Doubtless, he was chuckling to himself right now. He heard the truck driver's voice in his mind, coarse and sly. *You think you gonna get a cop to save you, boy? Shee-it. You gonna die.* Mann's heart contorted with savage hatred. *You son of a bitch*! he thought. Jerking his right hand into a fist, he drove it down against the seat. Goddamn you, Keller! I'm going to kill you, if it's the last thing I do!

The hills were closer now. There would be slopes directly, long steep grades. Mann felt a burst of hope within himself. He was sure to gain a lot of distance on the truck. No matter how he tried, that bastard Keller couldn't manage 80 miles an hour on a hill. But *I* can! Cried his mind with fierce elation. He worked up saliva in his mouth and swallowed it. The back of his shirt was drenched. He could feel sweat trickling down his sides. A bath and a drink, first order of the day on reaching San Francisco. A long, hot bath, a long, cold drink. Cutty Sark. He'd splurge, by Christ. He rated it.

The car swept up a shallow rise. Not steep enough, goddamn it! The truck's momentum would prevent its losing speed. Mann felt mindless hatred for the landscape. Already, he had topped the rise and tilted over to a shallow downgrade. He looked at the rearview mirror. *Square*, he thought, everything about the truck was square:

the radiator grille, the fender shapes, the bumper ends, the outline of the cab, even the shape of Keller's hands and face. He visualized the truck as some great entity pursuing him, insentient, brutish, chasing him with instinct only.

Mann cried out, horror-stricken, as he saw the ROAD REPAIRS sign up ahead. His frantic gaze leaped down the highway. Both lanes blocked, a huge black arrow pointing toward the alternate route! He groaned in anguish, seeing it was dirt. His foot jumped automatically to the brake pedal and started pumping it. He threw a dazed look at the rearview mirror. The truck was moving as fast as ever! It *couldn't,* though! Mann's expression froze in terror as he started turning to the right.

He stiffened as the front wheels hit the dirt road. For an instant, he was certain that the back part of the car was going to spin; he felt it breaking to the left. "No, don't!" he cried. Abruptly, he was jarring down the dirt road, elbows braced against his sides, trying to keep from losing control. His tires battered at the ruts, almost tearing the wheel from his grip. The windows rattled noisily. His neck snapped back and forth with painful jerks. His jolting body surged against the binding of the safety belt and slammed down violently on the seat. He felt the bouncing of the car drive up his spine. His clenching teeth slipped and he cried out hoarsely as his upper teeth gouged deep into his lip.

He gasped as the rear end of the car began surging to the right. He started to jerk the steering wheel to the left, then, hissing, wrenched it in the opposite direction, crying out as the right rear fender cracked a fence pole, knocking it down. He started pumping at the brakes, struggling to regain control. The car rear yawed sharply to the left, tires shooting out a spray of dirt. Mann felt a scream tear upward in his throat. He twisted wildly at the steering wheel. The car began careening to the right. He hitched the wheel around until the car was on course again. His head was pounding like his heart now, with gigantic, throbbing spasms. He started coughing as he gagged on dripping blood.

The dirt road ended suddenly, the car regained momentum on the pavement and he dared to look at the rearview mirror. The truck was slowed down but was still behind him, rocking like a freighter on a storm-tossed sea, its huge tires scouring up a pall of dust. Mann shoved in the accelerator pedal and his car surged forward. A good, steep grade lay just ahead; he'd gain that distance now. He swallowed blood, grimacing at the taste, then fumbled in his trouser pocket and tugged out his handkerchief. He pressed it to his bleeding lip, eyes fixed on the slope ahead. Another fifty yards or so. He writhed his back. His undershirt was soaking wet, adhering to his skin. He glanced at the rearview mirror. The truck had just regained the highway. *Tough!* he thought with venom. Didn't get me, did you, Keller?

His car was on the first yards of the upgrade when steam began to issue from beneath its hood. Mann stiffened suddenly, eyes widening with shock. The steam increased, became a smoking mist. Mann's gaze jumped down. The red light hadn't flashed on yet but had to in a moment. How could this be happening? Just as he was set to get away! The slope ahead was long and gradual, with many curves. He knew he couldn't stop. Could he U-turn unexpectedly and go back down? the sudden thought occurred. He looked ahead. The highway was too narrow, bound by hills on both sides. There wasn't room enough to make an uninterrupted turn and there wasn't time enough to ease around. If he tried that, Keller would shift direction and hit him head on. "Oh, my God!" Mann murmured suddenly.

He was going to die.

He stared ahead with stricken eyes, his view increasingly obscured by steam. Abruptly, he recalled the afternoon he'd had the engine steam-cleaned at the local car wash. The man who'd done it had suggested he replace the water hoses, because steam-cleaning had a tendency to make them crack. He'd nodded, thinking that he'd do it when he had more time. *More time!* The phrase was like a dagger in his mind. He'd failed to change the hoses and, for that failure, he was now about to die.

He sobbed in terror as the dashboard light flashed on. He glanced at it involuntarily and read the word HOT, black on red. With a breathless gasp, he jerked the transmission into low. Why hadn't he done that right away! He looked ahead. The slope seemed endless. Already, he could hear a boiling throb inside the radiator. How much coolant was there left? Steam was clouding faster, hazing up the windshield. Reaching out, he twisted at a dashboard knob. The wipers started flicking back and forth in fan-shaped sweeps. There had to be enough coolant in the radiator to get him to the top. *Then* what? cried his mind. He couldn't drive without coolant, even downhill. He glanced at the rearview mirror. The truck was falling behind. Mann snarled with maddened fury. *If it weren't for that goddamned hose he'd be escaping now!*

The sudden lurching of the car snatched him back to terror. If he braked now, he could jump out, run and scrabble up that slope. Later, he might not have the time. He couldn't make himself stop the car, though. As long as it kept on running, he felt bound to it, less vulnerable. God knows what would happen if he left it.

Mann started up the slope with haunted eyes, trying not to see the red light on the edges of his vision. Yard by yard, his car was slowing down. Make it, make it, pleaded his mind, even though he thought that it was futile. The car was running more and more unevenly. The thumping percolation of its radiator filled his ears. Any moment now, the motor would be choked off and the car would shudder to a stop, leaving him a sitting target. *No*, he thought. He tried to blank his mind.

He was almost to the top, but in the mirror he could see the truck drawing up on him. He jammed down on the pedal and the motor made a grinding noise. He groaned. It had to make the top! Please, God, help me! screamed his mind. The ridge was just ahead. Closer. Closer. Make it. "Make it." The car was shuddering and clanking, slowing down—oil, smoke and steam gushing from beneath the hood. The windshield wipers swept from side to side. Mann's head throbbed. Both his hands felt numb. His heartbeat pounded as he stared ahead. Make it, please, God, make it. Make it. *Make* it!

Over! Mann's lips opened in a cry of triumph as the car began descending and shaking uncontrollably, he shoved the transmission into neutral and let the car go into a glide. The triumph strangled in his throat as he saw that there was nothing in sight but hills and more hills. Never mind! He was on a downgrade now, a long one. He passed a sign that read, TRUCKS USE LOW GEARS NEXT 12 MILES. Twelve miles! Something would come up. It had to.

The car began to pick up speed. Mann glanced at the speedometer. Forty-seven miles an hour. The red light still burned. He'd save the motor for a long time, too, though; let it cool for twelve miles, if the truck was far enough behind.

His speed increased. Fifty...51. Mann watched the needle turning slowly toward the right. He glanced at the rearview mirror. The truck had not appeared yet. With a little luck, he might still get a good lead. Not as good as he might have if the motor hadn't overheated but enough to work with. There had to be some place along the way to stop. The needle edged past 55 and started toward the 60 mark.

Again, he looked at the rearview mirror, jolting as he saw that the truck had topped the ridge and was on its way down. He felt his lips begin to shake and crimped them together. His gaze jumped fitfully between the steam-obscured highway and the mirror. The truck was accelerating rapidly. Keller doubtless had the gas pedal floored. It wouldn't be long before the truck caught up to him. Mann's right hand twitched unconsciously toward the gearshift. Noticing, he jerked it back, grimacing, glanced at the speedometer. The car's velocity had just passed 60. Not enough! He had to use the motor now! He reached out desperately.

His right hand froze in mid-air as the motor stalled; then, shooting out the hand, he twisted the ignition key. The motor made a grinding noise but wouldn't start. Mann glanced up, saw that he was almost on the shoulder, jerked the steering wheel around. Again, he turned the key, but there was no response. He looked up at the rearview mirror. The truck was gaining on him swiftly. He glanced at the speedometer. The car's speed was fixed at 62. Mann felt himself crushed in a vise of panic. He stared ahead with haunted eyes.

Then he saw it, several hundred yards ahead: an escape route for trucks with burned-out brakes. There was no alternative now. Either he took the turnout or his car would be rammed from behind. The truck was frighteningly close. He heard the high-pitched wailing of its motor. Unconsciously, he started easing to the right, then jerked the wheel back suddenly. He mustn't give the move away! He had to wait until the last possible moment.Otherwise, Keller would follow him in.

Just before he reached the escape route, Mann wrenched the steering wheel around. The car rear started breaking to the left, tires shrieking on the pavement. Mann steered with the skid, braking just enough to keep from losing all control. The rear tires grabbed and, at 60 miles an hour, the car shot up the dirt trail, tires slinging up a cloud of dust. Mann began to hit the brakes. The rear wheels sideslipped and the car slammed hard against the dirt bank to the right. Mann gasped as the car bounced off and started to fishtail with violent whipping motions, angling toward the trail edge. He drove his foot down on the brake pedal with all his might. The car rear skidded to the right and slammed against the bank again. Mann heard a grinding rend of metal and felt himself heaved downward suddenly, his neck snapped, as the car plowed to a violent halt.

As in a dream, Mann turned to see the truck and trailer swerving off the highway. Paralyzed, he watched the massive vehicle hurtle toward him, staring at it with a blank detachment, knowing he was going to die but so stupefied by the sight of the looming truck that he couldn't react. The gargantuan shape roared closer, blotting out the sky. Mann felt a strange sensation in his throat, unaware that he was screaming.

Suddenly, the truck began to tilt. Mann stared at it in choked-off silence as it started tipping over like some ponderous beast toppling in slow motion. Before it reached his car, it vanished from his rear window.

Hands palsied, Mann undid the safety belt and opened the door. Struggling from the car, he stumbled to the trail edge, staring downward. He was just in time to see the truck capsize like a foundering ship. The tanker followed, huge wheels spinning as it overturned.

The storage tank on the truck exploded first, the violence of its detonation causing Mann to stagger back and sit down clumsily on the dirt. A second explosion roared below, its shock wave buffeting across him hotly, making his ears hurt. His glazed eyes saw a fiery column shoot up toward the sky in front of him, then another.

Mann crawled slowly to the trail edge and peered down at the canyon. Enormous gouts of flame were towering upward, topped by thick, black, oily smoke. He couldn't see the truck or trailer, only flames. He gaped at them in shock, all feeling drained from him.

Then, unexpectedly, emotion came. Not dread, at first, and not regret; not the nausea that followed soon. It was a primeval tumult in his mind: the cry of some ancestral beast above the body of its vanquished foe.

"Duel" was first published in **Playboy**, *April 1971.*

"The idea came to me on the day that President Kennedy was assassinated. Writer Jerry Sohl and I were playing golf, and when we came in for lunch, everyone was talking about the news reports that Kennedy had been shot. And we were so depressed by that, we just put our golf bags in the car and started home. And as we were going through this mountain pass, this huge truck began tailgating us—in exactly the way it's described in the story. It kept coming closer and closer and closer... Until Jerry finally had to pull onto a dirt siding, and his car was skidding around, with dust flying everywhere, and the driver then went zooming by. And we were screaming out the window at him in an absolute rage. And I grabbed an envelope out of Jerry's glove box because, like most writers, the idea came to me after things settled down, 'Hey this would make a good story...!'

"That was 1963, but I didn't write the story until 1970. And the way I got the descriptions of the road trip was because I drove from my house in the west part of the San Fernando Valley, up to Ventura and back. And I just described into a tape recorder everything I saw. Then I wrote the story. And it sold to **Playboy**. *Then when I was told that Universal wanted to buy it for a* **Movie of the Week**, *my immediate reaction was 'My God, it's not long enough for an hour and a half movie.' Then of course Steven Spielberg came in, and added his brilliant vision to it."* —RM

"Duel" was later adapted by the author into an **ABC Movie of the Week**, *and was first telecast on November 13, 1971. It was directed by a then-unknown Steven Spielberg and starred Dennis Weaver. A slightly longer version was released theatrically overseas in 1973 and domestically in 1983.*

345

FROM
RICHARD CHRISTIAN
MATHESON

Do you remember the one?
The one who opened the door, turned on the light and showed
you the secrets?
The really great secrets?
Why dogs seem to be smiling. How to tie a tie.
How to figure out what people are actually saying when they
say stuff.
Taught you how to be silly. How to be serious.
How to dream.

Everyone in this collection who has shared feelings about my father has already told you what a brilliant presence he is in American literature.

It would be hard not to. Who could deny a sky so perfectly blue?

I'd rather tell you other things. Things more personal.

I'd rather tell you about how he was always there for me, and still is, no matter what. How his guidance and discipline were endlessly thoughtful, endlessly loving. I'd rather tell you about the way he always treated me as an equal. Treated me like my ideas, views and feelings mattered. I'd rather tell you how he tried like no one I've ever met to be involved with his son.

When I was a kid, it was my dad who enthusiastically suggested we do things together. Dinner and a movie once a week. A chance to be alone and talk about anything; no locks, no curfews. School. Our family. Things that scared me, worried me.

But mostly, my *dreams*. Small, medium or large. They mattered to him and he always took them seriously.

I learned how to from him.

Do you remember who it was?
The one who taught you how to mix ideas like they were col-
ors? Stood behind you and held your hands while you learned
to pan for gold? The gold that was everywhere.
In people's faces. A random thought. In insignificant frag-
ments of behavior and occurrence that gather like forgotten
mail if you don't bother to hold them to the light. The one who
showed you sorcerer methods for capturing perceptions so
abstract they melt if you look at them from the wrong angle.

I'd rather tell you about one summer when I was about ten and my dad suggested we build a soapbox racer together. We designed it from scratch. Intensely negotiated points of structure and esthetic. Made passionate revisions. Carefully reviewed color options. We built a rolling marvel, right on schedule and it's rumored the entire staff of Ferrari wept in admiration.

It was our first collaboration and as I got older, my dad and I never stopped inventing stuff, one way or the other. Stories. Gags. Theories. Whenever we hung around and talked, in no time flat, we basically had it all figured-out.

We did all kinds of things.

We did archery. Ping-pong. We played golf, real and miniature. On the big guy courses we could be seen from far; a bearded writing legend and son, riding the fairway like magic scape, laughing and talking any absurdity that struck us, any philosophy we felt applied.

I'd rather tell you about how he bought me my first set of drums and handed me the sticks; keys to a rhythmic kingdom where the solo to *Inna-Gadda-Da-Vida* ruled. Or about how he always came to see me with my mom whenever my rock bands played gigs. He even danced and had a blast; an understated Jagger.

I'd rather tell you how he tried to teach me to write stories that could mean something; be tools not simply for external explanation but internal journey. How, as a mentor, his support and belief orbited my spirit like a guardian satellite. How he would always read whatever I wrote, no matter how awkward or misshapen by early talent. And always he was kind. And always, he lent me his personal rocket so I could get up higher and see what I'd done from a bigger point of view.

The lap I'd sat on when I was a child and the laughing, helium imagination that had held me, never stopped holding me. Or caring.

Or helping me to dream.

Try to see the expression.
Remember the one who gave you yourself free of charge. The one who never asked you for anything except to follow your own heart. The one you'll never be able to pay back, even if you live forever.

Lastly, I'd rather tell you that for every drop of delicate, luminous heart my dad put into these stories, I promise you he put as much into being a father.

A sky so perfectly blue. So filled with dreams.

I guess we all got very, very lucky.

—*Richard Christian Matheson*